NICK AUCLAIR

STEEL'S GOLD

Steel's Gold
Copyright © 2016 by Nick Auclair. All rights reserved.
First Print Edition: Febuary 2017

Cover and Formatting: Streetlight Graphics

ISBN: 978-0-9986707-0-6 (print)
ISBN: 978-0-9986707-1-3 (ebook)

steelstreasure@gmail.com
http://www.steelstreasure.blogspot.com

This is a work of fiction. Names, characters, places, and incidents either are the product of the author's imagination or are used fictitiously, and any resemblance to locales, events, business establishments, or actual persons—living or dead—is entirely coincidental.

To Katherine Sullivan Sparks, for your love, support, and brilliant literary insight reshaping my painful prose. To Fredda Sparks, for your surgical edits. To John Dufresne, for your review and pithy comments. And finally, to Henry, for being Cat-Cat's biggest fan.

1

**Philippines Zambales Mountains—
West of Clark Air Base
Friday, 25 October 1985**

A STACCATO BURST OF MACHINE GUN fire shattered the quiet jungle. Bullets ripped through the thick air, ricocheted off tree limbs, and shredded foliage around USAF Captain William Armand Steel. Startled parrots beat their wings, a spider monkey screeched, and Steel belly-flopped onto the jungle floor. He jammed his face into soft rich humus that muffled his screamed "Fuuuuck." Two more bursts of rounds zapped by like pissed-off comets.

After what felt like forever, Steel raised his head, blew out a mouthful of dirt, and scanned the bush ahead. A cascade of branches, leaves, and jungle debris dropped from the trees above. Silence fell as quickly as the gunfire had erupted.

"Jesus Maria Joseph," a muted voice to Steel's right called out. "Who the hell's firing at us?"

Steel looked over to see his pal Maximo "Jo Jo" Bato—Steel's Filipino aide-de-camp, martial arts instructor, and best friend—facedown in the dirt.

"Fuck if I know. Sounded like an AK-47. Maybe NPA." Steel bobbed his head, waiting for more fire.

"Maybe NPA guerrillas, but not an AK-47," said Jo Jo. "I

saw a shadow of a man with a Japanese type-96 light machine gun. The type with a long clip holding a maximum of thirty 6.5 mm rounds."

"No shit. How did you know that it was a type-96?"

"I saw a picture in the book of Japanese WWII weapons you keep in the basket in the comfort room at the house."

"No shit," said Steel again, trying to erase the visual of Jo Jo sitting on the toilet, reading.

"So what do we do now?" Jo Jo crawled over to Steel.

"Let's try slithering back the way we came in. I hope Tony and boys heard the shots and are getting the bastard. Thank God the shooter fired into the trees," Steel said.

"Yeah, he could have shot at us instead of killing birds," said Jo Jo.

"Damn. Hell of a welcome."

A crash of brush announced Tony's arrival. He emerged covered in scraps of vegetation. He glared down at Jo Jo and Steel and smiled. He sheathed his long, sharp bolo in a crudely-stitched leather case that hung on a hemp belt around his reed-thin waist.

Standing there, dark-skinned, bare-chested, and dressed in a red loincloth, Tony looked the archetype of the Negrito, primitive mountain pygmy tribesmen whose ancestors were thought to be the original inhabitants of the Philippines. A thick, brightly-beaded headband pushed his kinky black hair into a mound and added six inches of false stature to his four-foot ten-inch height.

"Tony, some crazy bastard is shooting at us," Steel said in Aeta, as he motioned for Tony to get down. Though Tony could speak English, Steel preferred to use Tony's native language in situations in which clarity was of utmost importance.

Tony shrugged. "He is gone now. He fled into the jungle.

Pongpet said the man disappeared like a Negrito but smelled like a foreigner. Pongpet was confused."

Steel stood, eyeballed the terrain in front of them, and switched to English. "Who the fuck was he? What's his beef with us?"

Tony shrugged his shoulders again.

"Was he NPA?" said Jo Jo.

"Not a lowlander but some other human. Smelled like him." Tony gestured with his chin towards Steel.

Steel stared at Tony then sniffed the air. Other than sweat, dirt, and fear, Steel had no words to describe his odor. "So what now, Tony?"

"We're not far from the cave. Maybe a couple more hours, and we'll camp for the night and hit the cave early in the morning."

"Okay. As long as you keep watch for this guy. And maybe alert us when you smell him this time? Before he starts shooting?" said Steel.

Tony shot Steel a dirty look, muttered something unintelligible, and disappeared into the bush.

"Well, let's get out of here. I'll try and keep up with the Negritos." Steel gritted his teeth and limped forward. Despite being shot at, nauseated, and winded, his morale was excellent. Treasure fever will do that.

Steel stopped and leaned his tall frame on two bamboo walking sticks. It was taking much longer than the promised two hours to get to the campsite. Tony had assigned a pair of Negritos to bring up the rear and keep watch on Steel. They seemed bored. Even Jo Jo had walked ahead.

Steel dropped one stick, reached into the large pocket of his camouflaged military-issue pants, and retrieved a small soggy towel. He wiped the torrent of dirt and sweat from his eyes. He had deliberately chosen a mismatch of military and civilian clothing. The rip-stop material and plethora of pockets of the jungle fatigues were practical and essential. The red bandanna and lime-green Izod shirt gave anyone with an aimed weapon a visual clue that his target was a civilian, not a military combatant. The Phil government was at war with the Communist NPA, and Steel didn't want to look allied with either side.

He crammed the towel back into a pocket while he watched Norgot fidget with an arrow fletched with white and black jungle cock feathers, the arrow itself nocked on a four-foot-tall black longbow. The other escort, Ganchee, was nowhere to be seen. A crashing in the brush drew Norgot's attention from the arrow. Steel resisted the urge to hit the deck again and crouched instead. Was the machine gunner back?

Norgot drew back the bowstring and fired into a clump of bamboo. He disappeared in the dense vegetation and reappeared seconds later dragging a three-foot-long lizard by its thick scaly tail. Steel watched the reptile struggle and slash at the air with a mouthful of serrated white teeth. Norgot took one hand off the tail and removed a well-worn steel bolo from a sheath tied to his back. He wacked the lizard's head with the dull side of the blade, and the beast stiffened and fell. It was just dinner for the Negritos.

It only took a few minutes for Norgot and Ganchee to tie the lizard to a bamboo pole and set off again along the trail. Steel again lagged behind, following the fresh blood drizzling on the dirt path. From the high ridgeline they walked, Steel could see the full sweep of the rugged Zambales Mountains. They were less than a day's hike from the perimeter fence of the U.S. Air Force's massive Clark Air Base. The Zambales were treacherous, unforgiving. Parts were covered in deep jungle, classic triple canopy, dense groves of bamboo, and wild banana plants; other areas were rough scrub hills with seas of eight-foot-tall elephant grass. Sources of fresh water were scarce. The crevices and shadows held poisonous snakes, leeches, and unexploded WWII munitions. The only inhabitants were small bands of nomadic Negritos and a few Communist guerrillas. It was raw, primitive, and Steel liked it that way.

For the last four years Steel, along with Jo Jo and a band of Negritos, had dug out and crawled through scores of caves and tunnels in the Zambales in a quest for WWII Japanese treasure—treasure entombed by General Tomoyuki Yamashita, the infamous Tiger of Malaya. The Tiger's men had looted billions of dollars of gold and precious gems from temples, businesses, and the capital cities of Southeast Asia and stashed the king's ransom in secure vaults scattered around the Philippine islands.

Steel had tasted the Tiger's treasure, but his memories of it were bitter. Four months earlier, with the help of a Filipino professor of history and Imperial Japanese Army war documents, Steel and Jo Jo discovered a secret Japanese WWII command post a day's walk from the spot where he now stood. There, he had dug out decayed wooden boxes laden with pillaged gold bars, coins, and religious icons, only to lose it all. Recalling the treachery that led to the loss filled Steel with rage.

He took a deep breath to clear his head. He peered into a ravine lined with thorny scrub trees and watched a flock of intensely green hanging parrots in noisy flight. In spite of the machine gun ambush, he had a good feeling this time. In the small canvas pack on his back was a worn leather-bound diary that Steel had found on a previous expedition. It had been a Japanese soldier's wartime journal, and Steel had had it translated. They were headed to the tunnel where the author, Sergeant Toshito Mitofumi, had penned his dying words to his wife and alluded to hidden riches. Mitofumi's poignant prose reverberated in Steel's brain: "I will give you, Miko, a life of a princess. I will build a big house and a temple and pray daily for the souls of my dead comrades and for the people I have killed, for the faces of the dead that visit me at night. I raise my head now and look up at the wall. My gift for Miko is safely hidden there."

"Yep," Steel mumbled to himself. Something had been safely hidden there. But the million-dollar question was, was it still there? Steel snatched up his walking stick, fumbled for a moment, and wrinkled his face. His ass throbbed. The gunshot wound he had sustained nearly four months ago was healing slowly. He should have put the expedition off, but he had a deadline to meet. Four days from now, Cham would be at Clark Air Base for an overnight exchange visit.

Royal Thailand Air Force Flight Lt. Chamlong Srimuang, or "Cham" as his American friends called him, was an intelligence officer whom Steel considered a close friend. Cham had trained as a mining engineer and participated in the family gem business. He had fenced some minor finds of gold jewelry and coins for Steel. If Steel found treasure on this trip, Cham would transport it back to Bangkok in his classified diplomatic courier attaché case, out of sight of police and customs officers. Steel and Cham made a great team. Steel enjoyed the harsh jungle treks and had a knack for finding looted treasure; Cham understood the mysterious and treacherous world of the Asian black market in gold and gems.

Steel heard Jo Jo backtracking down the trail, muttering about his stubborn and slow butt-shot Americano friend. A casual observer would think them an odd pair. Steel was a head taller than Jo Jo and lanky with side-parted brown hair that pushed against military regulations. His skin was fair with uneven farmer-tan lines. Jo Jo was dark, even by Philippine standards, and his hair was crew-cut and black peppered with gray. A scraggy mustache and goatee added menace to his appearance. Jo Jo had a third-degree black belt in kuntaw, an indigenous Philippine martial art.

Steel and Jo Jo met first as kuntaw student and teacher, but Jo Jo soon added language lessons in Tagalog and guide services for Steel during his forays into the countryside. As their friendship and partnership deepened over the years, Jo Jo reduced his number of students to just Steel, who provided Jo Jo a large monthly stipend.

"You okay, William-san?" Jo Jo wheezed, his voice. "That's a huge lizard." He pointed to the reptile lashed to the pole.

"Yeah, sort of the Negrito version of Hemingway's *Moveable Feast*," Steel chuckled to himself.

"Hemingway?" Jo Jo seemed not to be able to take his eyes off the bloodied creature.

"Never mind. I'm doing okay." Steel was lying. He was sucking hind tit, punished for months of neglected physical training. Amazing how the body goes flabby without a consistent workout schedule, Steel thought, and blamed the gunshot wound for his exhaustion. Normally, he prided himself on at least sometimes being able to keep up with the Negritos, who can walk with heavy packs along grueling trails for miles, seemingly without effort.

Steel thought Jo Jo also looked bushed. He hadn't been training either. He'd been depressed ever since his wife, Baby, had returned home after four years of working in Toronto and stayed in Angeles only long enough to get their two daughters' travel papers in order. The trio's departure hit him hard.

Jo Jo stood and adjusted his pack straps. "Boss-san, you'll be pleased to know that the cave is just over there." He pointed with his chin. Steel checked his watch and looked up. It was five p.m., and the blazing sun was, thankfully, settling down below the ridgeline. He had been scorched enough.

Ignoring Jo Jo's annoying new habit of using the Japanese language honorific, Steel answered, "Excellent."

"Hai, Steel-san. Tony said he wanted to have time before dark to hunt for wild chickens."

"Roasted manok would be a nice addition to the evening meal," Steel said, as he and Jo Jo slogged on after the Negritos.

By early the next morning, Steel was in the cave and headed toward the spot he had found the diary. He inched forward, crawling on his hands and knees, fighting claustrophobia. The air was filled with dust. That, and lust for treasure, blinded him to the dangers that lay around every tight corner.

The passage was as tight as a birth canal. Steel pushed his stuttering flashlight forward with one arm and inched ahead on his belly. He fought the urge to go back. He guessed he had had slithered several hundred yards. A spasm erupted from his throat and echoed off the stone walls. One-million-year-old cave grime, fermenting bat guano, and mold filled his lungs.

Using his crappy flashlight in this inky black was like using a plastic knife to carve chocolate pudding. He cursed Jo Jo for forgetting new batteries, wasn't like him. Well, not like the old Jo Jo anyway.

The cave opened into a large room with high ceilings. Steel jammed his arms into the air, thrilled to be able to stand. A minute later, Jo Jo emerged, banging dust from his pants.

"Ah good, that the bats are asleep, eh, William-san." Jo Jo said.

Steel ignored Jo Jo. The bat attack had been on a previous hike, but late in the day. The bats wouldn't leave their roosts until this evening.

"If I remember from last time, we're in a more developed part of the complex," Steel choked.

"Yes, I think you are right," Jo Jo said and studied his fingernails.

He was bored, and Steel wasn't surprised. He hadn't told Jo Jo the specifics of the Japanese soldier's diary. Steel didn't want to set expectations too high.

"Tayo na, let's go." Jo Jo marched into the darkness.

Steel let Jo Jo get ahead. Pieces of WWII junk littered the floor: broken green sake bottles, chunks of rusted unidentifiable metal, and twisted Osaka rifle parts lay scattered where they were dropped forty years ago. Steel scanned the walls with his dimming flashlight, but he held off using his emergency light. A shadow fell over his shoulder, and he heard the sound of shallow human breaths. He swung around, and his fist slammed into a mortal form.

"Jesus Christ, Tony, I thought you were a damn ghost. How the hell can you get around in here without a light?"

"No, Captain Steel, it is Tony, not a ghost," Tony called out in English, giggling. "You know the forest spirits guide good Negritos. We have no need of light."

Steel shone a beam in Tony's face. He recoiled, hands up, preparing to deflect further blows. Behind him, Pongpet and Ganchee blinked rapidly. God, Steel hated it when they crept up on him, but he was impressed too. They definitely had some sort of sixth sense.

He redirected the light to their bare feet. "You're damn lucky I didn't have a bolo in my hand or I'd have chopped you down to two-feet tall. Why don't you join Jo Jo up ahead? You can help him."

Tony shrugged, and the trio evaporated into the abyss. Steel figured there was no point in warning Jo Jo. He should have heard the commotion.

Steel continued his way down the tunnel muttering about crazy little bastards navigating without light. Periodically, he flipped around and scanned the tunnel behind him. He was not going to be surprised by any other stragglers.

Tony waited until Steel's light had disappeared, then reached into the cloth sack dangling at his side and removed a newly purchased flashlight. He flicked it on and smiled. He didn't want Steel to stop believing in the forest spirit powers the Negritos possessed.

It only took a few minutes more before Steel found the hidden entrance to Mitofumi's crypt. Steel stared at the ragged Imperial Japanese Army soldier's uniform, loosely housing the white bones of the man who had penned so many soulful words in his diary. The last time he had seen the skeleton, he thought it macabre in its Halloween pose. Now, because of the diary, the scene felt intimate. Steel had found many remains of Japanese soldiers, half-buried in caves and strewn on overgrown jungle battlefields, but he had desensitized to it. The Japanese government had no interest in the bodies, so Steel mostly left them where they fell.

A couple of years ago, Steel had found the bones of an American soldier and gave them to officials at Clark. There had been personal effects but no dog tag. He knew that without tags, the chances of matching the bones with a name were nil. Steel hoped his own father's body, resting in some remote Laotian jungle, would be discovered, with tags.

Steel shook his head, dropped to his knees, and removed his pack. He fumbled through and found the typed translation folded neatly into the ratty leather-bound pages of the diary. He read one marked page aloud: "I raise my head now and look up at the wall." Steel illuminated Mitofumi's white skull, its mouth gaping open to expose a four-inch-long centipede scurrying amongst the white teeth like legged dental floss. Steel scanned the wall trying to see what he had overlooked.

"What wall were you looking at?" he said aloud, and the flashlight died.

Where was the backup light? The black void was disorienting. He wobbled off-balance, steadying himself with one hand on the cool jagged surface of the rock wall and furiously searching his pants' pockets with the other.

Disheartened, he sank down on all fours and poked at the darkness for his backpack. But unlike the sightless cave insects that darted from his hands, he did not possess evolved sensor appendages. His crude human arms were dumb and blind. His breathing became labored, and his heart pounded loudly. He'd always had a fear of the dark. Steel glanced to where he thought Mitofumi lay. Was he laughing at Steel's panicked performance?

"Ah, but you can give me a hand," Steel whispered, remembering he had Mitofumi's lighter, a good-luck keepsake that Steel always carried.

He flipped open the lighter's lid, heard the familiar mechanical popping, rolled the wheel with his thumb, and watched the spark ignite the fuel soaked cotton wick. Suddenly the crypt was awash in light. Glorious light. He touched the engraved inscription on the side of the silver lighter: "Keep safe—come home to me, my darling Edward. Love, Beth." Steel guessed Mitofumi had salvaged the memento on the battlefield. Still, Steel hoped Edward had made it home.

In the light of the flame, he located the backpack and the pocket holding the spare flashlight. He aimed it at the wall, looking for Mitofumi's hiding place. His heart leapt as he noticed a dark cavity, but he did not, as he wanted to, plunge his hand right in. Cobras. He whipped out a K-bar combat knife from a sheath strapped to the side of his boot and probed the crevice. Nothing rose to the occasion. Satisfied, he reached in, felt cloth, and pulled out a bag.

"Well, well, my friend—what the hell have you been hiding all these years?" Steel sat down on the floor, wedged the flashlight under his chin, pulled open the sack's drawstring, and removed a small statue of a sitting Buddha. The eight-inch-tall, six-inch-wide religious icon was delicately shaped with a dull gold sheen. Three large, rough-cut stones, possibly rubies, were embedded in the base. It had to be gold and the rough-cut red stones must be worth something. He pocketed the small treasure, grabbed a plastic rice sack from his pack, and placed Mitofumi's bones in it. Steel couldn't bear to leave him here again.

He wandered back into the main tunnel, trying to decide if he should press on after Jo Jo and Tony or head back outside. Dancing light interrupted his thought, and a rush of crashing bodies knocked him to the cave floor. He managed to hang on to his light. In its beam, he made out Tony and Pongpet on top of him and Ganchee staring at them wide-eyed. Before Steel could speak, Jo Jo blasted out of the darkness.

"Jesus Christ, Jo Jo. Get off of me, you crazy bastards," Steel said.

As quickly as they had come, the three Negritos scrambled up and fled. Jo Jo looked ready to do the same.

Steel latched onto Jo Jo's arm, "Bats again?"

Jo Jo's scream reverberated off the rock walls.

A hideous half-man, half-beast emerged from the darkness—the kind of creature that inhabited Steel's dreams. It had a dragon face, and its body was covered with long, shaggy, fibrous hair.

Steel's grip on Jo Jo's arm tightened as a screech, like a raccoon in heat, erupted from the ghoul. It rushed them, waving a flaming torch in one hand and a sword in the other. Steel, frozen with fear, recognized the sword: a Japanese samurai sword.

As the beast approached close enough for Steel to smell burning rags, Jo Jo jerked forward. They ran down the tunnel, Steel pausing only a second to take one last look at what he would later learn the Negritos called Banchee Tarachita: the Evil Moon-Chaser Who Steals Souls.

Sixty-two-year-old Japanese Imperial Army Lt. Nagano Nada watched the group flee and lowered his mahogany kabuki mask, a fire red face with hand-painted arched eyebrows and white jagged fangs. Nada laughed with his comrade Sergeant Kami, something they had not done in a long time. Nada recalled the terror in the eyes of the annoying small black men and the white American GI. Nada had grown weary of the intrusions of the small black men into the forest sanctuary where he and Kami had lived for four decades.

He thrust the tip of his sword into the soft dirt of the floor. He was angry at the American who persisted despite the machine gun warning. Once Nada discovered that the band had camped near the cave, he planned an ambush that would use the darkness of this underground tunnel to his advantage. Nada knew of other secret entrances. He and Kami had long ago visited this cave, removed the corpses of fellow countrymen, and buried them in the jungle. Even though he had not commanded these men—his own specialized unit had been miles away in Manila—he still tended their graves and someday hoped to return their bones to Japan for a glorious ceremony honoring their sacrifice.

Nada's superiors had deployed him here in 1943, when it became clear the Yankees would invade Manila. He was to use his experience as a seasoned intelligence operative to organize

Japanese stragglers and form a guerrilla force to harass the Americans. As the years went by, Nada assumed the American invasion of the Philippines had been successful. He vowed to fight to the death or until he heard word from the emperor that the war was over. Neither event happened, so he fought on.

In addition to himself and Kami, there had originally been four other soldiers in his squad of holdouts. He wished he had been able to assemble a larger fighting force. In 1947, Filipino soldiers killed two of his men—part of the government's efforts to hunt Japanese army guerrillas. Nada, Kami, and his two remaining companions deployed deeper into the mountains and lessened their contact with Filipinos. For Nada, time was seasonal, fuzzy, and hard to quantify. He wasn't quite sure how many years went by before Private Kotoyot went mad and died of natural causes. Soon after, Corporal Kosuma fled into the night to surrender and brought shame to himself and his family.

Nada struggled on. Sometimes he wrestled with hellish dreams, and only Kami's words could calm him. More times than he could count, he wished death would take him. Dishonorable thoughts often hijacked his mind, thoughts of surrendering and going home to Japan. Would his friends and family remember him? Would they even be alive? These impure deliberations confused him. Maybe he was mad, mad like his Corporal Kotoyot-san.

"Kami-san, am I mad? Are you ashamed of me?"

"No, Nada-san, you are a loyal samurai warrior who has honorably fought a long, valiant war."

"There are too many days and nights when I wonder what we are," said Nada.

These days, he only left the mountains to raid remote farms for salt, sugar, and whatever else he could steal. He occasionally killed a farmer's carabao, butchered it, and hauled huge chunks of meat back to his cave where he dried and preserved them.

Doing so was risky. Killing the beasts drew the ire of villagers who called in police and troops.

"Look, Kami, at my costume. Is it not hideous? If you did not know I was mortal flesh, would you not be afraid?" Nada smiled at Kami.

Nada liked that the Negritos seemed to fear him as a ghost. He certainly looked like one. He had worked for weeks on the outfit. Initially, he was unsure if he was going to model himself after a Jinki supernatural being or a Kijin demon. In the end, he opted for a combination of both. He carved the mask carefully and attached tuffs of scraggly wild pig hair for a beard. He wove the cape, which covered him from shoulder to toe, out of dried palm fronds.

His boyhood friend, Nakamura Taranosuke would have been proud. Long ago, Nada had worked as a costume designer and stagehand for Taranosuke's kabuki troupe. During summer breaks from university, Nada would visit Nakamura and travel with the company from village to village. Ah, the great times they had. To be young and on the road, late nights drinking sake with the lusty young country women. But the war had changed everything.

"Kami, why has the world gone mad?"

"The world is mad, but the war made madmen of innocents," Kami answered.

"Yes. The war did this to us. We didn't change because we have bad demons inside."

"No, Nada-san, before the war, we were good men," said Kami.

Nada stared into the black tunnel. A single tear formed and dropped onto the blade of his sword lying in the dust. Their country was now these tunnels and the forest. Was he really a warrior of the emperor, or just a clown in a costume? It had to be the former. He couldn't believe so many comrades had died for nothing. No, he was determined to wait until his commanding officer terminated the mission. The loyal Kami would wait with him. It was their sworn duty. He took off the cloak, tucked it under his arm, mindful of the torch flame, and picked up his sword. The appearance of the Yankee devil made it clear they were still looking for him. With his samurai warrior spirit, he would fight on.

2

Angeles
Monday, 28 October 1985

STEEL SAUNTERED OUT OF HIS bedroom toward the kitchen and scanned his realm. He was pleased with the airy three-bedroom home situated on an expansive double lot on New York Avenue, a bustling mixed neighborhood of Filipino and American servicemen and their families. His home was his sanctuary from work and the outside world. The house was surrounded by an eight-foot concrete block wall topped with barbed wire and embedded with shards of glass. The only access was a forbidding heavy metal gate across the driveway.

The house was a ten-minute walk in one direction to the red light district with its seedy bars and beautiful bargirls. A short drive in the opposite direction was Friendship Gate, one of the main entrances to Clark Air Base. With his captain's salary, overseas allowance, and housing supplement, Steel lived well, very well, though many of his fellow servicemen wouldn't agree. Most lived on base, where they could patronize movie theaters, pizza parlors, and bowling alleys. Not for me, thought Steel, standing in his living room under the large metal ceiling fan and enjoying the cool morning air.

He adjusted the collar on his blue Class B Air Force

uniform shirt and examined the knife-like creases that his housekeeper Rosa pressed into his pants. He felt clean and unusually professional. He didn't want to give management at the 13th Air Force's Intelligence Division any more reasons to scrutinize him.

This was his first day back in the office after a month's convalescence leave to recover from a bullet to the ass. Though the operation in which he had sustained the wound had worked out for the Command in the end, it hadn't exactly been by the book and had drawn the ire of his immediate chain of command and outright anger from the U.S. Embassy spooks. With everything that had happened over the last few months, he was never sure where he stood with his boss, his co-workers, or, for that matter, any of the officers of the 13th Air Force headquarters.

"Good morning, William," Rosa greeted him as he walked in the kitchen. "It is a wonderful day today. Do you want some eggs?"

"Good morning, Rosa. Sure," Steel said and kissed her on the cheek.

"Oh, it is good to finally see a friendly face here in the morning," she said, glaring at Jo Jo, who was seated at the table, reading the paper with his usual frown. Rosa strode over to the stove and lit a burner. Dressed in her neat white maid's attire, she was queen of her kitchen. Steel sat and tried not to stare. Jo Jo was dressed in a bright blue yukata, a Japanese bathrobe.

"Ohayou gozaimasu," Jo Jo said.

Steel knew how to reply back correctly but was distracted by Jo Jo's attire. "Ohio- something . . . something . . . Oh fuck it. Nice robe." Steel had been the one to tell Jo Jo to find a hobby, get his mind off his girls. Steel had only himself to blame for Jo Jo's Japanization.

"Oh-ay-ou go-zai-masu, Steel-san," he said slowly, rolling his eyes.

Jo Jo had become a permanent houseguest, moving into Steel's spare bedroom the week his wife and kids moved to Toronto. Steel didn't mind putting up Jo Jo while he worked his way through this funk. He was like a brother, having saved Steel's hide more than once.

"So, I had this bizarre dream last night about that crazy ghost thing we saw in the cave," Steel said.

Jo Jo scratched his head with a fork. "I guess too many soldiers died in those caves. Their spirits can't find peace."

Steel played with his new Seiko dive watch. "Do you think we should go back and look again? The bullets ripping through the jungle above us were real, not ghosts. Something was warning us off."

"Hard to believe that we consider gunfire routine now," said Jo Jo.

"Yeah, some of us dodge better than others." Steel rubbed his ass.

"So nothing in today's paper from Ms. Abucayan?" Rosa called out. "I haven't seen her articles for days now." She hovered over Steel until he moved the paper so she could place down a plate with eggs, pandesal, bread, and sliced mango. "Will she be visiting us this week, William? I don't think she has called in a while."

"She's been busy." Steel said.

"Well, she hasn't written many articles for the paper. She must be too busy with other important things to call or visit. You would think she could find time to call you. You insist she is your girlfriend. So why wouldn't your girlfriend call you? Maybe this was the reason her relationship to Lieutenant Colonel Devincia failed," Rosa said.

"Steel-san, can you believe this story?" Jo Jo pointed at an article in the paper spread in front of him. "They're putting to death two Filipinos in Saudi Arabia, one is a woman— supposedly for robbery. This is what happens to my countrymen when they are forced to work abroad."

Steel was all too familiar with Jo Jo's thoughts on Filipinos abroad. He was saddened by how many of his countrymen had been lured to foreign lands by jobs in sweatshops or domestic work for slave-labor wages. Steel didn't completely agree. Many Filipinos, like Jo Jo's wife, did find happiness overseas. But Steel kept quiet.

He could see the anguish on Jo Jo's face. Baby had presented an ultimatum: if Jo Jo didn't accompany her and their daughters back to Toronto, the marriage was over. Jo Jo loved his family, but he loved the Philippines too.

"I tell you, Steel-san, anytime a boat sinks, a building collapses, or any other goddamn—"

"Jo Jo, language please," Rosa said. "Bakit ba ang mukhang biyernes sabado, why do you have your Good Friday face on? It is too early in the morning. Let William eat his breakfast in peace." She poured Jo Jo some more coffee and continued, "It is God's will that foreigners want to hire talented Filipinos. Aren't you proud of that?"

Jo Jo ignored her. "Steel-san, any chance I can have an advance on my salary? This story makes me realize I have to do something. I need to organize a plan. We have to find some more gold."

Steel was surprised. Jo Jo rarely asked for money. "Any specific problems?"

"No. But I found a girl in my neighboring barrio who worked as an entertainer in Japan for a couple of years. She speaks Haponese. She is going to give me language lessons. I need more motivation than I'm getting from textbooks."

"What did you do, boy, get yourself one of those long-haired sleeping dictionaries?" Steel said, attempting a Southern accent, borrowing the question from an old, crusty USAF F-105 pilot, who had once asked it of Steel.

"We're not sleeping together, yet. She is maganda, beautiful," Jo Jo said, smiling. His despair seemed to be dissipating.

Rosa called out from the sink, "Maganda, maganda, is that all you want in a woman? How about good and smart and loyal? A virtuous woman. That is what you should want."

"Good points, Rosa." Steel smirked at Rosa's back, mimed holding up two big tits, and winked at Jo Jo, forcing another smile out of him. Steel pulled out his wallet and removed a twenty-dollar bill. "I'll stop by the club later and cash a check to give you the rest. I'm all in favor of you learning to speak Japanese." Anything to keep his mind off his freaking problems. "It'll come in handy for treasure hunting. And besides, there is no better way to learn the language than from a pret—I mean intelligent woman."

Steel had decided to wait to tell Jo Jo about the Buddha until Cham appraised it. No point in getting him spun up. If there were money to be had, he'd get his cut.

Steel finished breakfast and packed his gear for work. He wrapped the Buddha in a towel and stashed it in his gym bag. He had a lunch date with Cham at the officer's club.

Steel slid out the front door and walked over to a wall of orchids. He had found them on his jungle trips and attached them to the cement fence of his compound. It must have been the perfect spot, with just enough shade and moisture, because the plants thrived. He had some rare ones—flowers that collectors would pay a fortune for. But he preferred to keep them here.

Over the years, Steel had transformed the wasteland that had been his yard— wilted vegetation, chucks of concrete, and trash—into a verdant oasis of plants and water gardens. He enjoyed working on the big projects himself, but his yard boy, Joseph, took care of the weekly maintenance. Steel walked over to where Joseph was bent, raking some dead leaves from around a massive, tangled mango tree. The short, skinny nineteen-year-old—shirtless, shoeless, and in ripped gym shorts—was a gifted gardener and tireless and loyal worker. He was part of Steel's family.

"Good morning, Captain Steel," Joseph dropped his broom and snapped to attention. Steel had given up trying to get Joseph to use "Will."

"Morning, Joseph, how's the chore list going?"

"Excellent, Captain Steel. The cement pad for the water tower is dry now. The bolts we sunk into the concrete are strong." The pad was to support a tank to provide water to his Japanese bathhouse.

The bathhouse was conceived and partially constructed while Steel was convalescing. He wanted a teak and bamboo structure and a large tub, its water heated with a wood-burning fire. He had bought materials and hired a local welder named Junior. He owned Junior's Welding, a ramshackle business located outside the main gate of Clark Air Base that specialized in building outdoor barbeque grills.

Steel checked his watch. "All right, Joseph, I'd better get going. Get the gate for me, will you?" They walked together to the carport.

"Captain Steel, will you be going to the mountains soon to look for treasure?"

"Definitely. You're still planning on joining us, right?"

"Yes, sir."

"Great," Steel nodded. Joseph had never been before. Jo Jo wasn't keen on the idea, but Steel figured, why not? Joseph was smart. Being a partner in Steel Enterprises could make him and his family rich.

As they passed Steel's bedroom windows, Joseph glanced at the pea-gravel walkway and made the sign of the cross, as he seemed to always do at that spot.

"Joseph, how come you do that Jesus thing here?"

Joseph marched toward the tall metal front gates as if he hadn't heard.

Steel shrugged. He followed Joseph to the driveway and climbed into his beloved 1981 blue Datsun 4x4 king-cab truck with off-road tires and a custom-made roll bar. He had had designed a canvas roof for the back bed—a modern version of the Old West Conestoga wagon cover. He started the engine and adjusted the air-conditioning. Joseph opened the gate and scanned the area. Steel waited for the all-clear sign. The NPA, the armed wing of the Communist Party of the Philippines, was at war with the Philippine government and had been killing Americans—five so far. No point in making it too easy for an NPA hit team to assassinate him. An Air Force intelligence officer would be a nice coup for their propaganda machine.

Steel watched Joseph wave on a group of emaciated Filipino children pushing a rickety wooden cart. It was garbage day, and they were scavenging before the city trash truck arrived. The kids, reed-thin limbs poking from scraps of filthy rags, struggled with their heavy haul. There was a time when the sight would have bothered Steel. But he had lived side-by-side with poverty for so long, he was numb to it. He waved at Joseph and headed down New York Street toward the base.

After the Datsun disappeared into the traffic and haze, Joseph almost skipped back to the garden. He was excited by the prospect of finally getting to accompany Captain Steel and Jo Jo to the mountains. If only they could find gold. He could buy his mother and father and brothers and sisters so many things. He walked back past Captain Steel's bedroom and crossed himself again at the spot where, just two months ago, a huge pool of blood and gore had congealed to black and buzzed with flies. When Joseph told Rosa, she ordered him to clean the mess and not tell anyone, including Captain Steel. She had said he didn't need any more problems. Joseph obeyed. He hosed and raked out the guts and smoothed the trail where it looked as though a body had been dragged. No one mentioned it after, but Joseph never failed to cross himself when he passed.

Steel barreled into the parking lot behind the four buildings comprising the 13th Air Force headquarters. His cassette player was blasting Foreigner's new album, *Can't Slow Down*. The band sang about wanting to know what love is. Steel was certain he knew. But the real question was: Where the hell was his love? He had no idea. He hadn't heard from his girlfriend, Vida Abucayan, star reporter for the *Malaya*, for weeks. As he exited the truck, his pounding heart replaced the rock and roll beat. The gym bag with the Buddha inside bounced off his hip as he walked.

Steel checked his watch and girded himself to enter the building. He felt as anxious as he might infiltrating an NPA camp. The only superior he trusted was General Smith, the commander whom he considered a friend and protector. Steel was sure his immediate boss, Lt. Col. Kuncker, would not have minded had the Air Force medically discharged or transferred Steel stateside. But Steel had been adamant about remaining at Clark, and the general agreed to keep Steel under his command.

He had been to the office numerous times over the last three weeks but only after duty hours and on weekends. He didn't want to run into anyone. His mission for the last two weeks had been putting together a classified briefing on the

Spratly Islands. It was part of the pretext for Cham's visit. Cham's boss and several other Thai senior officers were at Clark as an advance team for Thai Air Force training at the Crow Valley Range.

Steel slunk into the building and popped into the bathroom. As he passed by the sinks, he saw himself in the mirror and hoped his crisp uniform would ease his transition back with the management.

"Not that simple," Steel muttered as he unzipped his fly. The bathroom door opened and Staff Sergeant Curtis Washington entered. Curtis was one of five enlisted guys assigned to the intelligence division. He was also a confirmed Steel ally.

"Cap S, my man, good to see you," Curtis said.

"Curtis Washington, you're a sight for sore eyes."

"Got some great news, Cap, you're looking at the next NCO of the quarter."

Steel zipped his pants and offered a hand to Curtis. Curtis looked down and said, "Cap, I can only imagine where that dick has been." Steel washed at the sink and offered a clean hand.

"I knew you were a shoo-in," Steel said. "I can see your ride parked in that reserved spot at the NCO club." Steel was pleased he had gone to the general about Curtis's nomination. Kuncker had never been pleased that Steel had befriended Curtis and had quietly nixed Curtis's award. The general overrode Kuncker. Good to be king, Steel thought, or in this case, on good terms with the king.

Curtis, who always clothed his short stocky frame in perfectly pressed Class Bs, reached over and brushed a piece of fuzz off Steel's shoulder. He looked at Steel for a moment then bent down and peered under the stalls.

"You won't believe this, but Major Thimble has been assigned to 13th as the assistant intel chief, and since he made major, he's been in everyone's shit."

"No way," Steel said.

"He's got this tiny, half-assed moustache. Looks like Hitler." Curtis laughed. "Why the fuck white guys have those moustaches? It kills me. The Air Force don't let you have a full one. Why even bother? And get this. His wife bought him a huge eel skin briefcase. He clicks it open—plop... plop. I looked in it the other morning. He got nothing there but his cigarettes and a big hunting knife."

"Really," said Steel. "I had no idea he was transferred here, or that he made major. I don't know him that well, but I thought he seemed like a good guy."

And Cap," Curtis said and moved closer to Steel. "Colston overheard Thimble and Kuncker talking. Neither one of them is a big fan of yours. I'd watch your back."

With Curtis a step behind, Steel entered the secure vault where the intelligence division was housed and walked over to his desk—or where his desk used to be. A bigger desk now sat there, and on it, an eel skin attaché case.

"Sorry Cap, I didn't mention the desk. Someone rearranged things over the weekend," Curtis whispered. He pointed over to the wall of document safes where Steel's old metal desk was shoved into the corner.

Steel went over and pushed a pile of folders to one side to clear a spot for his hat. He looked at the bare wall behind where his desk used to be. Where were his fucking maps of the Philippines and all the plastic colored pins marking NPA attacks and sightings? He'd worked years on those. Steel clenched and unclenched his fist.

"Curtis, what the fuck?" He pointed to the wall.

Curtis shrugged, closed his eyes, and shook his head.

Steel heard laughter, and Thimble and Kuncker appeared

in the doorway. Kuncker looked straight past Steel, giggled at something Thimble said, and exited the room.

"Well, there he is. The phantom of the office, Captain Steel," Thimble said, walked to his desk and sat. Curtis buried his head in a file.

Steel strode over to Thimble, prepared to raise holy hell over the map, but before he spoke, paused. "Pick your battles, Steel," he muttered under his breath. He extended a hand. "Congratulations on your promotion, John. Major rank looks good on you,"

"Thanks." Thimble shook Steel's hand firmly then dropped it and pulled away, as if shocked. He looked around the room. "Sergeant Washington, would you mind leaving us alone, so Captain Steel and I can get reacquainted?"

Curtis waited until Thimble turned his head, popped Steel a thumbs-up, and exited.

"Have a seat, Captain Steel." Thimble pointed the chair next to his desk. "I'm afraid I'll have to ask you to call me Major Thimble, or sir. It's not good for my position as assistant division chief to have informality shown by subordinates."

Steel focused first on the gold oak leaf clusters on Thimble's collar and then on the moustache. Curtis was right: pure Third Reich.

"Now that you've finished your medical leave, it will be good to have the unit at strength. The Colonel and I have been discussing some organizational changes. We're refocusing our analytical efforts. Lieutenant O'Brien from the Intelligence Watch has been assigned to us. He and I are going to be the briefing team for the general."

Thimble continued to drone on about effective analysis and a new professionalism and respect for hierarchy. This is all about me, Steel thought as he waited for his turn to respond. It took a good thirty minutes for Thimble to shut up.

"You have quite an agenda for us," Steel said. "So in addition to O'Brien, myself, and you, any more bodies?"

"No. Not for now. We're just going to work harder, that's all. I like to think of myself as the 'sunrise-to-sundown kid.' It's a nickname they gave me at the wing."

Steel checked his watch. He had had enough for this morning. "Sir, can we continue this valuable conversation later in the afternoon? I'm sure you recall we have some Thai officers coming this morning for a briefing, and I'd like to run over my slides."

Thimble cocked his head and smiled. "Well, that was my next point. There has been a change of plans concerning the Thai brief. The Colonel and I feel that I should handle our relationships with our allies. I took the liberty of rewriting the briefing and will be presenting it to them personally." Thimble leaned back in his chair and took a gulp of coffee.

"Really. I hadn't been informed of the changes," Steel said slowly.

"Oh, it's not a direct criticism of you. It's just we need a new set of eyes on this. After the brief, the Colonel and I are taking them to the club for lunch. The Colonel and I have some other projects for you while we're gone," Thimble said.

One more "Colonel and I" and Steel would shove the attaché case up Thimble's ass. Fortunately for the major's anus, Washington and Colston reentered the room right then. Thimble frowned and curtly waved the enlisted troops in. Steel stood up. He got the point. He wasn't invited. He marched back to his desk.

He flipped through papers without looking at them, slammed them down, and glared at Thimble, who was rearranging his desktop. It was all Steel could do not to walk over there and bitch-slap the smug look off his face. Thimble clicked open the latches of the attaché case, and a mechanical "flop-flop" echoed around the room. He snatched out a pack of cigarettes, slowly removed one, and lit it with a cheap plastic lighter. Steel could hear his own teeth grinding as he watched Thimble inhale the smoke, savoring it – and, no doubt, his emasculation of the so-called Hero Steel.

Steel and Cham burst out of the main doors of the O'Club and ran down the stairs, the two of them laughing like schoolboys heading out for recess. They only had a few minutes to get to Steel's truck in the parking lot across the street and transfer the Buddha before Cham had to head to the airport for the long RTAF C-130 flight back home. Steel had ended up joining the Thai officers, Thimble, and Kuncker for lunch at the club at the request of the Thai general leading the delegation. Thimble had barely managed to hide his anger.

"My God, William, that Thimble is one pompous prick," said Cham as he wrestled his bulky leather briefcase into the 4x4 king-cab.

"I wish I could have seen his face when General Shinawathra wondered where I was."

"I told him he was not getting the best possible briefing since you were kept away by office politics. Shinawathra said to the 13th Vice-Commander that he would consider it a favor to him if you were present."

"That's so fucking funny. I owe you big time for that."

"My general was most pleased with the presentation. He said he felt like he received the real story. I don't think I'll have any problems tagging along to Clark for future trips."

"Great, Jo Jo and Rosa were sad that they didn't have a chance to see you."

"Yes, and I haven't had the opportunity to meet this woman you've supposedly fallen in love with—Vida, right?" Cham poked him in the ribs. "Maybe she's already been pushed aside, another of your conquests?"

"Nope, she's still around and excited to meet you," Steel lied. Maybe something happened to her. He hadn't called her mother yet to check. Her parents weren't exactly fans of his. "It would have been fun to hit the clubs and shoot some pool," Steel said, to steer the conversation away from Vida.

"Yes, it would have been very pleasurable to have kicked your ass again."

"Wait a minute; I was set for a comeback if that fight hadn't broken out," Steel said.

"I told my uncle about that. He pretended to be shocked, but I think he was most pleased."

"Good for you." Cham's family had a history of mocking their effeminate son.

"So, William, what great treasure have you found for me to examine? We'd better have a look." Cham glanced toward the entrance to the club.

Steel reached behind his seat for the Buddha.

"Now that looks promising," Cham said, "May I hold it?"

He grasped the Buddha gently in one hand while he fished in the pocket of his pants and pulled out a jeweler's loupe. He sucked his teeth as he examined each of the large, rough-cut red stones, the back, and the flat bottom of the base.

"Well?"

"I'd say it is very old—possibly 4th or 5th century. A classic design, nearly pure gold," Cham said, angling the statue.

"Gold? That's great—and those stones?"

"Uncut rubies of excellent quality," Cham nodded. "They will fetch a nice price."

"So it's worth something?"

"Of course. Probably worth quite a bit sold as antique and left intact. I won't know until I get a friend of mine to look at it. If it is worth more for its gold and rubies, then it would be better to have it melted down." Cham paused, shaking the Buddha, slowly at first, then vigorously.

"Listen," he said.

Steel heard nothing but the rush of air blasting out of the air conditioning vents. Cham flipped the Buddha upside down, peered under its chin, then twisted its head.

"Hold out your hand, my naive friend," Cham said.

Steel did, and Cham poured a rainbow of uncut stones into Steel's palm. Steel blinked at the flashes of blue, green, and amber.

Cham gave a low whistle, squealed out something in Thai, and continued in English. "Those, my friend, are emeralds, sapphires, rubies, and topaz, all rough, very precious gems." He carefully poured out a few more of the stones, the size of fingernails, into Steel's open palm. He rolled the gems around like he was panning for them.

"All right now, be careful, William. We don't want to lose even one of those little darlings," Cham picked the stones up one by one, oohing and aahing as he slid them back into the Buddha.

"How'd you know?" Steel said.

"It was commonplace to hide gems inside of statues made of non-precious metals. Since this is made of gold with ruby decorations, I was confused at first."

"How much do you think its worth—a ballpark figure?"

"I couldn't even say. Each gem will have to be examined."

"A million dollars?" Steel asked.

"Be realistic, William." Cham shook his head. "Whatever it is, it will be significant—minus my twenty percent, of course." He smiled.

Steel looked at the Buddha, then at Cham. "Make it forty

percent. I would never have known about the gems without you. Besides, I have no idea how to fence those stones."

"Forty percent? You are nuts, William, I could not take that much from you."

"We're partners, Cham. It is going to be a lot of work to sell the stuff, and you're taking risks moving it back home." Steel heard the rumble of engines behind him and in his rearview mirror watched a blue Air Force staff car and two vans arrive. "Shit, looks like your ride is here."

Cham swiveled his head, "Yes, we'd better get going." He wrapped the Buddha back in the towel. "Are you sure you want me to take it? I won't be offended if you say no."

"Just make us some money."

"William, can I ask you something personal?"

"Sure."

"Why are you risking your career to do this? Your Air Force is not as . . . as forgiving on the subject of corruption in its officer ranks as mine is. You could face serious punishment if we're caught, maybe even go to prison."

Steel drummed on the steering wheel. "For the money, adventure, and beautiful girls?"

"You're not in it just for the money. I know you."

Steel stopped drumming and turned to face him. "Sort of for the money. I need cash, lots of it, to find out if my Dad's still alive." He turned his head and stared blankly at the windshield. "The fucking U.S. doesn't care. I need a shitload of money to finance my own search. In Laos." He turned to face Cham. "Since I was a little kid, I've always had this hope, this dream, that one day he'd just show up. I know it's crazy, but I'm going to find gold and go to Laos. Truth is, though, that's as far as I've gotten on a plan. Pretty pathetic rescue mission, right?"

"I'm sorry," Cham said, and they sat in silence for a moment.

Steel watched Shinawathra and the rest of the Thai leadership party exit the O Club. "You better go," he said.

Cham nodded and stowed the Buddha in his attaché case, which he secured with a small padlock. The Royal Thai Air Force C-130 that would carry Cham home would fly directly into the RTAF's base at Korat, bypassing Bangkok's International Airport's customs and police. They exited the truck, and Steel reached for Cham's arm. "Hey, old buddy, I'll say goodbye here. I'm not looking forward to being with Thimble."

Cham smiled. "Ignore the man. He is nothing. Just concentrate on spending the money we'll get from this." He held up the briefcase. "I'll be in touch. As you Americans say, 'keep your fingers crossed.'"

Cham got into a van with two other Thai officers and watched Steel's truck depart the parking lot. Cham wished they could have spent more time together. He wondered if he had so much faith in anyone that he would blindly give him a fortune of gems to sell. He'd make sure they got their money's worth out of the stones. In Steel, Cham had found someone he could trust, a rare thing in this world.

The vehicles sped off to the airport.

3

Manila
Monday, 28 October 1985

L t. Col. Antonio Devincia hung up the phone and picked up a china cup. Cold, he thought. Damn. He put it back down, arched his back, and stretched his arms. His uniform strained against hard muscles, honed by years of combat in the field, and maybe a little fat, put on recently—too many hours sitting in headquarters. He rubbed his hands through thick black hair then smoothed his bushy mustache. He looked and acted the role of renegade officer. Even when he was alone. With cold coffee.

His throat was sore from all the talking he had been doing that morning. He scanned the list of missed calls and noted he owed one to his on-again, off-again, now-back-on-again fiancée, Vida. She had phoned an hour or so ago from Mindanao, where she was working on a story—probably her usual human-interest bullshit.

His last call had been from his boss, the Secretary of the Department of National Defense, Juan Ponce Enrile. Devincia had worked as Enrile's chief of security for many years. Now, they worked together to overthrow the Marcos regime. Devincia was the head of a cabal of young military officers, members of groups with names like "Reform the Armed Forces," or "RAM," and the "Young Officer's Union." Enrile provided support from the establishment. In fact, he was currently meeting with two army commanders in Leyte—meetings Devincia had set up. He hoped the defense secretary could convince the commanders to join anti-Marcos operations.

Devincia had been spending most of his time away from the official Secretary of the Department of National Defense's office complex in Camp Aquinaldo. Instead he worked out of this converted home in one of Manila's most exclusive residential neighborhoods, not far from the defense secretary's home. Devincia and his small staff had set up a de facto operations center. Hard to make coup plans in a government building.

It was difficult for Devincia to believe, sometimes, how far his boss and mentor, Enrile, had strayed. Back in the 1970's, Enrile had stood beside Marcos when he declared martial law. But Enrile had been horrified by the assassination of opposition leader Senator Benigno "Ninoy" Aquino, Jr. in 1983. After that, Enrile had aligned himself with dissident elements in the army.

Devincia's administrative assistant, Hermie Catipunan, a hard-faced army sergeant, entered the office and handed his boss a fresh cup of coffee. Devincia nodded politely. They went back a long way. Early in their careers, they had fought fanatical Muslim separatists in Southern Mindanao and later, NPA guerrillas. Mindanao had been particularly bloody, rife with atrocities against civilians, assassinations, and torture. The experience had shaped both of their perspectives on the military. Devincia had also learned that Catipunan was the sort of man he wanted around in a firefight and, since Mindanao, had surrounded himself with similar sharp and loyal combat veterans.

Devincia rounded out his corps with both enlisted men and junior officers. Many of the officers came from the Philippine Military Academy, where Devincia was considered a living legend. Idealistic PMA graduates with key army positions around the country had pledged to follow Devincia, seduced by his charisma and his reputation for being a soldier's soldier, a rare attribute among the senior members of the army's inept and crooked officer corps. Too many army officers led from behind the lines. Philippine soldiers routinely went into battle poorly equipped. Army officials sold the troops' ammunition and weapons on the black market. Devincia and the RAM railed against such practices and pushed for drastic change.

Catipunan handed Devincia a brown folder. "Sir, I know it's been a long morning, but you have one more call to make before we are scheduled for lunch with Colonel Panglio."

"That snake in the grass makes me sick," Devincia sighed. "But like they say, keep your friends close and your enemies closer."

Catipunan laughed and nodded. "Sir, the call is to ..." He peered over Devincia's shoulder. "Captain Reyes. He is PMA class of '79. He has reportedly organized a group of young officers in his battalion and has put out feelers. It looks like he wants to be part of RAM."

Devincia flipped through the folder. "A strong record, highly decorated, well placed in the battalion. Has he been vetted?"

"Yes sir."

"Am I calling him at work?"

"No sir, he has given us his home number and will be there today, waiting."

Devincia picked up the phone and dialed. "His first name is Reynaldo?"

"Yes sir, but he goes by 'Boy,'" Catipunan said.

"Ah, is this Boy? Good, this is Colonel Devincia." Devincia closed his eyes leaned back in his chair. "No, Boy, the pleasure is all mine. I'm so pleased you reached out to us. And thank you for your brave service to our country and the people."

4

Angeles
Monday, 4 November 1985

S TEEL BEEPED HIS TRUCK HORN a second time. The big gate shook, one side opened, and Joseph waved Steel in. A pile of grocery bags spilled from the passenger seat onto the truck's floor. Steel had left work early to go to the commissary. His domestic entourage required ample provisioning. He pulled under the carport and exited the truck.

"Ms. Abucayan is calling for you," Rosa waved with both hands from the front doorway. "It is a very bad connection."

Steel navigated past her to the phone. At first all he could hear was static — and Jo Jo and Rosa's loud complaints about having to lug the water jugs in. Vida was over a thousand miles away, in Marawi City, Mindanao, following a news story. When it finally came through, her muted voice claimed to miss him and to long to spend Thanksgiving together.

"Long distance romance sucks," he muttered to a dial tone after she hung up. But what was he going to do? She had a job that required traveling. She was successful, a professional woman. He was hopelessly in love and screwed. "Yep, screwed," he said. "Or not screwed . . . Not screwed enough." The left side of his brain argued for love, family, and commitment. The cum-infused right side countered that short-term flings with bar girls were drama free and sexually satisfying. And to further make its point, the right side projected a porn film on Steel's cerebellum, sweaty and naked hard-assed Filipinas with full—

"William, are you eating an early dinner tonight?" Rosa's voice killed carnal fast. He walked into the kitchen, thinking, round one—victory for left brain. Rosa's glare stopped him short. "So, Ms. Abucayan sounds well. She said she is coming to our Thanks-to-giving feast. What is this event?"

"Oh yeah, I've been waiting to tell you. We're going to do Thanksgiving here this year. I thought you'd enjoy cooking it." Steel looked around the kitchen. "Did you bring in the bag with the book in it?"

Jo Jo pointed to the kitchen table.

"Oh good, I bought this present for you." Steel handed her a copy of *Betty Crocker*'s *Cookbook New and Revised Edition*.

She flipped the pages. "I have heard of this Thanks-to-giving feast, but you have always gone to your friends for it."

Steel ignored her sarcastic tone. He was tired of being a bit player in other families' holidays. This year, he would assemble his own family and start a new Steel tradition.

"Steel-san, is that a massive frozen chicken you brought home for the feast?" Jo Jo pointed to the plastic-wrapped Butterball turkey sitting on the countertop.

"That's a twenty-five pound turkey, not a chicken."

"What do they feed such a huge chicken? Jo Jo said.

"Oh, William, this book is such a good present. I will be most happy to cook this big manok, chicken. It has been my dream to plan the feast of the Thanks-to-giving," she said, clutching her book. "Tell me William, what is your tradition to this American holiday."

"Well, the first white people to come to America were called Pilgrims. They had a hard time living the first year, but they had some help from the natives, whom they called Indians. So at the end of the first year, they had a party— I mean feast—to celebrate their good fortune. They invited the Indians."

"I still can't imagine how big that manok was with its feathers on," Jo Jo said, staring at the bird.

"Oh Indians," said Rosa. "Of course. My sister in Manila took me to an Indian restaurant once, and their food was very good. I like the spice called curry powder."

Before Steel had time to ponder how to tackle the distinction between the South Asian Indian and the American Indian, the phone rang. He raced to it, hoping it was Vida again.

Steel dropped the phone receiver. He was breathing hard. He had promised to fly to Bangkok. Cham had news on the Buddha statue. "Incredibly good news." Good enough that Steel needed to open a secret bank account, something you apparently can't do over the phone. Monday was Veterans Day, so he wouldn't have to try and wheedle a day of leave off Thimble, thank God. "Incredibly good news." Steel whistled as he walked back to the kitchen.

"Hey, Jo Jo, I mean Jo Jo-san, I need a workout. We've got to get back on a regular schedule. My ass was dragging on our last hike."

"Good idea. Did you remember to cash a check for my salary?"

Steel opened his wallet and counted out the bills. He would have to pay for the Bangkok trip too. November was going to be an expensive month.

5

Angeles
Wednesday, 6 November 1985

STEEL MARCHED INTO THE KITCHEN, gave Rosa a kiss on the cheek, which she ignored, and sat at the breakfast table across from Jo Jo. Routine calmed Steel. He slid the *Malaya* over from a stack and quickly scanned the headlines. Rosa placed a coffee mug next to him, shrugged her shoulders, and returned to the sink.

Jo Jo tapped the paper with his index finger. "William-san, did you book your plane trip to Thailand? If you didn't then I'm hopeful we can take a trip to the mountains. I have some interesting news."

Steel peered at Jo Jo, confused by his uncharacteristically chipper tone. "What news?"

"Tony stopped by yesterday and said a Negrito found a big metal box loaded with papers."

"What kind of papers?"

"You know Tony—not the most descriptive guy. He did say the writing wasn't English or Tagalog."

"Wow, maybe Japanese?"

"That's what I was thinking, and that's why we should plan a trip soon."

"We'll organize something when I get back. I'm gone for the weekend. Monday is a holiday for us."

"Tony also had some ink pens and a sword he wants to sell you."

"A samurai sword?"

"No, boss-san, just the rusty handle and damaged blade. Not a good sword. He's going to bring it back again."

"What about the pens?" Steel collected fountain pens, brands like Parkers with gold nibs that were worth some money.

Jo Jo shrugged his shoulders. "Just maybe three pens. He said he's saving them for you."

"Okay, but you know he plays off sales between us and that other Americano," said Steel, gesturing with a thumb towards New York Avenue.

"Yeah, yeah, the mystery retired Americano." Jo Jo rolled his eyes.

Rosa placed a plate beside Steel with an omelet, toast, and fruit. "You want some more coffee, William?"

"Please. By the way, Rosa, I'm not going to be around this weekend starting Saturday if you want to go to Manila and visit your sister."

"Maybe we can go shopping at Shoemart," Rosa said. "I need a dress for the Thanks-to-giving feast."

"Buy yourself some nice clothes." He dug into his wallet and pulled out some cash and gave it to her.

"You don't have to do that, but thank you, William. I will find a nice dress for the feast."

He nodded and chuckled. He had no idea what feast dress Rosa had in mind. He imagined her in a 1950's long dress, hat, and white gloves. He tucked the wallet back into his Air Force blue pants. The cash made him think of Cham's mystery news about the Buddha. He hoped to God it was worth a wad of cash and lamented to himself how much the last minute plane ticket was costing.

Jo Jo shuffled a newspaper. "Maybe that metal box has maps in it with treasure locations. If we find some, I'm booking my flight to Canada. With money in the bank, I can bring my girls home." He slapped the table with both hands and grinned.

"Amen to that." Steel raised his coffee cup, and they clinked porcelain.

"Oh, I almost forgot." Jo Jo clanked his mug down hard on the table. "It turns out that Tony's Uncle June said the ghost creature is a man, and, from his uncle's description, I think the man is a Japanese straggler, a soldier from WWII."

"You're kidding," said Steel.

"I heard stories from the old people of my barrio about soldiers still in the mountains hiding out," said Jo Jo, scratching his head with a spoon.

"That would be crazy. A Japanese WWII army soldier holdout was found in the Philippines in 1974 and a couple more on Guam in the early 1970's. Hard to believe another decade could have passed without someone finding this guy. He'd have to be ancient, in his sixties or seventies. Seems farfetched, but it would explain a lot."

"I think we should stop by that cave again. I'm going to put some Japanese things there for him and maybe some newspapers and a letter. I would love to discover him. Maybe the Japanese government would offer a reward if we found him. Or maybe the newspapers would pay big pesos for the story. I'm going to talk to Josie. She has newspapers and magazines from Japan, and, of course, she can get me some Japanese canned foods."

"Sure, and with your Japanese, you can communicate with him. We're headed that way anyway," Steel said.

"I'll arrange it with Tony." Jo Jo returned to his paper. "Can you believe this news?"

"What news?" Rosa called out from the sink.

"Marcos has called for a snap election." Jo Jo spit out the words as though they tasted bitter.

Again the voice from the sink. "The Marcos's are under the spell of bad elements of government. Imelda is such a beautiful classical Filipina. How could she not see her husband is being corrupted?" Rosa placed one hand on her chest.

"Maybe, Rosa, but I wouldn't underestimate just how cunning your beautiful classical Filipina is," Jo Jo said.

Rosa slammed a pot in the sink, and Jo Jo grimaced.

"What are you f-ing nuts, besmirching Queen Imelda?" said Steel in a hushed grunt. "What does the article say?"

"Marcos suddenly announced that a presidential election would take place next year, one year ahead of the regular schedule." Jo Jo mumbled a summary of the rest of the piece, peppering it with expletives, until Rosa interrupted.

"Zeus na lang, is that language necessary this early in the morning?" She scowled at Jo Jo, refilled the mug of coffee beside Steel, and went back to her dishwashing, all the while muttering about Marcos and railing about the mayor of Manila's scandalous involvement with a movie starlet. Replies to or acknowledgements of her soliloquies were not expected.

Steel picked up the *Malaya* again, hoping he would find an article by his girlfriend Vida. Finding nothing, he flipped to the front page and scanned through the piece on the snap election. At work, he had been reading classified U.S. Embassy Manila reports describing how the U.S. had been pressuring the Marcos government to hold elections to quell national unrest. People were angry about Marcos's sham criminal investigations of the assassination of a popular opposition senator.

In 1983, Senator Benigno Aquino, on his return from exile in the U.S., had been publicly and brutally murdered on the tarmac of the international airport in Manila. The event shook the Philippines at its political core. Aquino had been a vocal anti-Marcos politician and would have been a potent political challenger to Marcos in any presidential election. By 1984, Filipinos had had it with a foot-dragging and farcical government investigation of the assassination. Marcos attempted to bring legitimacy to it by trying to recruit the popular Catholic Cardinal Jaime Sin, the Archbishop of Manila, for a presidential commission. Sin not only declined the offer but also took to his pulpit many times to castigate the government over the whole affair.

Taking advantage of the popular unrest, some elements of the opposition hoped Aquino's widow, Corazon, would run for president. They were optimistic about the chances of winning a fair election. For the most part, people were dissatisfied with Marcos's tenure in office, one that had been marred by charges of corruption, cronyism, and the destruction of a once vibrant Philippine economy. Steel also recalled classified U.S. cables that reported Marcos's ill health. They suggested that elements of the Marcos family and senior military officials had been making poor political decisions for an incapacitated president.

Steel's friends in Philippine military intelligence described a meeting that occurred the night after the Aquino's assassination at which a furious Marcos threw an ashtray at his wife Imelda, nearly hitting her. Rumor had it she had been the one to give orders to assassinate Aquino. Steel thought it might be true. Marcos, forever the sly tactician, wasn't dumb enough to have undertaken such a blatantly public operation, but Imelda was.

Steel stopped reading and sipped some more of Rosa's strong coffee. It's just like Marcos to throw the opposition off balance by holding elections more than a year ahead of schedule. It gives him a better chance of winning a strong popular mandate, which would placate his American benefactors. It wouldn't be an easy task to get a dark horse like Cory Aquino, or even a mainstream opposition candidate, to ready their campaign organization in less than three months. Yeah, Steel was going to have a busy week preparing briefings and background papers for his chain of command.

6

Manila
Mandarin Oriental Hotel
Wednesday, 6 November 1985

"ROOM ATTEN-HUT," A BARITONE VOICE barreled out.

Four men snapped to attention. General John K. Singlaub nodded at them. "As you were gentlemen. Make us proud."

"Aye aye, sir," one barked.

All eyes followed Singlaub, the sixty-four-year-old former U.S. Army general, as he exited the room. Dressed in an ill-fitting blue sports coat, the typical garb of an ex-military man accustomed to letting Uncle Sam pick out his clothes, and sporting a grey crew-cut, which left bare his large ears, he hardly looked the part of a high-level, clandestine, special operations icon. But when he spoke, he commanded respect, and his eyes pierced with a fanatical intensity. It was no stretch to call him America's premier anti-Communist warrior. Everyone in the room was familiar with his legendary bio. He had been commissioned as a lieutenant in the U.S. Army in 1943 and shortly thereafter parachuted into Nazi-occupied France to organize pre-D-Day invasion plans. For the next thirty-four years, Singlaub was at the center of almost every controversial U.S. military action. After retiring from the

Army, Singlaub founded the United States Council for World Freedom, the U.S. chapter of the World Anti-Communist League. His organization served as the bagman for President Reagan's Iran–Contra dealings, soliciting funds from rich U.S. conservative groups to buy arms for the Nicaraguan rebels. The World Anti-Communist League worked closely with Taipei to help them stave off the People's Republic of China, aka "the red horde."

Singlaub had stopped over in Manila after spending three days in the Republic of China visiting with government officials. The general's current mission was only nominally related to supporting the Marcos government's democratic struggle against Communism. Fighting worldwide Communism was expensive, and the general had latched onto rumors of lost Japanese treasure in the mountains of the Philippines —billions worth of gold for the taking. He had agreed to finance an exploratory operation, staffed by a group of Vietnam Special Forces veterans working out of a Philippine shell company. This first visit to them had been low key. Singlaub knew Marcos wouldn't take kindly to anyone interfering with what he saw as his absolute monopoly on stealing gold.

After Singlaub left the room, his new employees milled about the luxury suite of the swank Mandarin Oriental Hotel, excited, in awe, and intensely curious about why they were all in Manila with such a legendary anti-Communist warrior. Their nervous chatter silenced when Benjamin Harkins, a retired U.S. Army Special Forces colonel, entered. He was tall and lean with corded muscles showing through his tight fitting polo shirt, his faced tanned and lined from years overseas. He, too, commanded respect.

He marched over to the men, who stood in a loose at-ease, and called out in a Southern twang. "Gentleman, have a seat." He sat down hard in big easy chair, relieved the general was headed back to his room. Harkins pulled a rumpled pack of Marlboro cigarettes from inside his sock and lit one with a well-worn Zippo. He stared at the lighter's engraving of airborne jump wings and the words, "de oppresso liber," to free from oppression, and formulated his thoughts. "Gentlemen, the general was most pleased by what he heard and saw today. We are fully onboard with getting this treasure-hunting organization up and running."

"Treasure hunting?" one voice called out.

"You heard it right, Captain, we're not here to train Filipinos to fight godless Commies. We're here to find gold. Lost Japanese dubya dubya II treasure."

"Sir, are we going to get rich doing it?"

"In your dreams men. But you will be well paid and will receive my love and respect." The colonel hacked out a smoker's laugh as he picked up a brown file sitting on the floor. "We are going to spend a couple of weeks setting up an office in a hotel, but not this luxury place. Something you're more familiar with."

"You mean a whorehouse—sir?" called out an exceedingly white man, his large form filling a chair.

Harkins smirked. "No, Whale, it will be at least one step above your usual quarters."

Ralph "Whale" White laughed loudly. He was a highly decorated former U.S. Navy SEAL with three tours in Vietnam. Despite his outward appearance, a colossal frame covered in what looked like layers of soft baby fat, he was unusually strong and fit. In SEAL lore, Whale was known for his exfiltration from a reconnaissance mission that went awry in North Vietnam's Haiphong Harbor. With only dive mask and fins, he swam twenty miles to a rendezvous point and treaded water for eight hours waiting for his ride on the amphibious transport submarine, the USS Grayback.

Harkins continued, "Gentlemen, once we have set up shop and have oriented ourselves, we've a shitload of potential operations available to us. We will be recruiting additional personnel, but for now, our first mission is to surveil a U.S. military officer, Air Force type, who has connections in the treasure world and with Phil military and Phil intelligence." Harkins pointed a finger. "You, Captain Hobbs, will be the officer-in-charge for the shop."

Whale elbowed the former Special Forces U.S. Army captain in the ribs. The chiseled black man was nicknamed "Hollywood Hobbs." He earned the moniker when he served as Francis Ford Coppola's military advisor on the set of *Apocalypse Now*. Hobbs, like Whale, had multiple tours in Vietnam and ample chest candy to testify to his valor. The captain and colonel went way back in the murky world of Special Ops. They were part of the tightknit ex-military vet-for-hire community in Bangkok, where both lived between jobs.

"Reliable sources indicate that Air Force Captain William Steel has sponsorship high up in the AFP command structure," Harkins said, "possibly with anti-Marcos groups involved. Now get this." He paused and scratched his head. "He has an indigenous hill tribe force of Ne-gree-toes, and I sheet thee not, they're pygmies, the little guys." He held his hand three feet from the floor.

"Sir, you mean insurgent midgets?" a wiry man called out to a chorus of laughs.

Hobbs elbowed Whale and whispered, "I met those badass little black dudes in the P.I. when I was shooting *Apocalypse*. They're #1 GI."

"At ease, men. They're supposedly top rate troops who excelled in WWII. This Captain Steel uses them for force protection and recon on treasure ops. We are planning to surveil him 24 -7, with phone taps. All pretty standard stuff. We have some good intel support in country from unnamed sources and a satisfactory budget to buy equipment and . . ."

7

Bangkok, Thailand
Saturday, 9 November 1985

THEY SLID OUT THE BISTRO's private door and directly into a bustling Bangkok nighttime market. Steel's senses whirled at the dazzling lights, exotic smells, and staccato screams of merchants hawking wares, but Cham seemed in his element. He and Romy, his longtime partner, a well-known Bangkok artist, had hosted Steel at a trendy restaurant in the Soi Cowboy red-light district. The pair had held court for a parade of officious managers, while throngs of beautiful waitresses dressed in traditional chang kben and sabai costumes served a five-course meal. Cham had ensured Steel's favorite dish, twelve-inch-long black tiger prawns sautéed in butter and coconut milk, were featured.

Cham took Steel's arm as they followed Romy, who negotiated the tangled market crowd. Romy had high cheekbones and a strong jawline with perfect teeth. His hair was long and tied back in a neat ponytail. He was dressed in a Parisian black suit. He had just finished a successful tour in Europe, where his paintings had sold well.

Steel staggered from the Singha beers and Mekhong whisky cocktails, which came in tall glasses, garnished with tiny umbrellas and skewers of exotic fruits. Mekhong, the Thai national drink, was called a whisky, but was closer to rum and made from sugar cane and a blend of secret herbs and spices. Steel had definitely begun to feel its storied potency.

From the market, the trio navigated the crowded street that angled into the heart of Soi Cowboy. The neighborhood attracted packs of foreign tourists, who flowed between zipping tuk tuks, sprawling food stands, and boisterous street vendors. Pulsing neon lights and a barrage of music emanated from scores of nightclubs. In front of some, semi-naked women yelled, cajoled, and promised passersby that indescribable pleasures awaited them inside.

Steel focused on one woman, who gyrated in narcotic rhythm beneath a flashing blue-green sign reading "Midnight Bar." She had a beautiful face and long hair that hung below her ass. She was tall and thin and dressed in a short skirt and tube top. Steel thought she seemed oblivious to the world around her. Her arms and hands moved and floated as if they were woven into the music coming from behind her, the Door's "Light My Fire." When she finally noticed him, she smiled and motioned him to join her. Her gyrations captured him, hypnotized. She slipped down her top offered him bare breasts. Steel leaned forward, hungry.

A tug, then a stiff jerk, jolted him out of his trance. Cham pulled Steel after Romy, who was headed towards a narrow, dark alley, muddy and littered with trash, smelling of garbage and human feces. In the flash of passing vehicle headlights, Steel saw two rats scurry into rubble.

Off-duty Royal Thai Police Sergeants Jomdet Trimek and Sriwarah Rangsipramkul, dressed in slacks and loose shirts that concealed holstered handguns, stood in the shadows and monitored the drunken trio. The pair had been hired by Hobbs to keep Steel under surveillance. Trimek mused to himself how the alley would have been the perfect spot to waylay the naïve American had their mission been otherwise. He watched Steel and his compatriots slog towards a popular high-end nightclub. Not a place he frequented, but he would enjoy lording his badge over the armed doormen.

Steel shuffled and followed Romy's bobbing ponytail another twenty or so yards to a blinking orange sign advertising the Fish Bowl Club. They entered the metal door single file. The nightclub's two bouncers ushered them inside.

It took a moment for Steel's eyes to adjust enough to see the bar, teakwood stained dark and adorned with carved dragons and demons. A line of heavy stools sat parallel to it, on which sat an assortment of Japanese, Chinese, and Caucasian men. Yamaha stereo speakers oozed subtle, smooth jazz, setting a tone more sophisticated than the carnal atmospherics in the neighboring clubs.

Steel followed Romy and Cham past the bar into an adjacent room, where a twenty–foot-long, eight-foot-tall smoky glass window separated them from three dozen beautiful Thai women of various shapes and sizes. Steel halted and his mouth gaped open like a baby bird awaiting a grub. Behind the glass, the women perched on bar stools. They were dressed in high heels and layers of gold jewelry and black dresses that exposed mounds of cleavage and supple flesh. To each was pinned a white card with a black number, the only thing that marked them as for sale, as opposed to just out for a night on the town. Steel focused on the women's head movements and their hand gestures. Several waved to him.

Cham motioned at the window with a hand. "I thought you'd enjoy this. The glass wall reminds me of an aquarium with all the beautiful women floating behind it like exotic tropical fish," Cham paused staring at the women, his faced screwed up into a display of mild fascination. "I think this place is very . . . Steel."

"I'm told there are several famous movie starlets and models." Romy peered at the women.

Steel focused on number 22. She could have been one of those models. When their eyes met, Steel smiled at her until Cham shoved him forward. "Ah, but before I lose you, we have that meeting with the business associate I told you about."

"Madam Chong?" Steel whispered.

"Yes. But keep that name to yourself," Cham said. He asked Romy to wait for them at a nearly table and hustled Steel across the room. They halted at a heavy wooden door guarded by an enormous Thai man whose sweaty bald head glistened even in the dim lighting. Steel thought he resembled the Thai version of Mr. Clean. The big man frisked Steel, banging hands hard enough to rattle ribs, then held the door open, and Cham and Steel moved inside.

The Mekhong was making Steel's head spin, and it took a few seconds for his mind to clear. The compact office was a jumble of Chinese porcelain, jade, wood antiques, and heavy furniture. A blue cigarette haze swirled in the air. The source of the smoke sat behind an ornately carved desk. Madam Chong, Steel presumed. She was probably in her sixties. Her hair was grey and tightly pulled back in a bun. She had tiny frameless reading glasses perched on the end of her pug nose and wore a conservative black business suit, the severe look punctuated with a plethora of shiny jewelry. Entwined among the small delicate fingers of her right hand was a long, shiny black lacquered cigarette holder. Steel watched her move it to her lips and take a puff. She studied him intently. Another security guard, wearing dark shades, leaned against a bookshelf behind her.

Cham bowed slightly and raised his head slowly, a show of

respect. She spoke to him in Thai, a soft raspy smoker's voice, and motioned for them to sit in two stiff wooden chairs in front of her desk. Cham had explained earlier that she was a key figure in Bangkok's criminal underworld, a specialist in illicit banking and fraudulent documents, and, more importantly, a distant relative on his mother's side. While they spoke Steel tried to absorb their conversation, observing body gestures and listening for tone.

"Captain Steel, my cousin Cham speaks highly of you." Her switch to English startled Steel. "I normally don't get involved with foreigners directly, but I'm intrigued with your WWII treasure." She paused and took another hit from her cigarette. "I have thought that such legends were just that . . . but with the gems you found, that's rather convincing. We have the potential to make substantial money. My organization is prepared to take you on as a client—but we expect exclusivity."

Steel nodded in affirmation, then spoke, "Sure. Whatever Cham thinks best, he—" Steel felt Cham's fingernails dig through the thin fabric of his pants. He took it as a signal to keep his mouth shut. She shifted in the chair and switched back to Thai and Cham.

After five minutes of back and forth, she slid over a large Manila envelope, its bulging contents hidden. Cham pulled the folder to him and stood. Steel recognized the Thai words for "thank you" and "long life." He stood too, and Cham whispered in English at Steel, "Nod and say thank you." Steel did.

As they headed to the door, the man behind Madam came around the desk and leaned into Steel. He could feel the guard's hot breath on his neck as he said, in English, "My aunt is a polite lady. But let me be clear. You're dealing with us solely now. We have a long reach, even in the Philippines, and we will watch you, the Filipino Jo Jo, and your household staff. Betrayal will be dealt with severely." The man, obviously more than a guard, gave Cham and Steel a hard glare then slammed the door behind them.

Cham waited until they were out of earshot, reached into the envelope, and handed Steel small blue object, a Canadian passport. "Here you are. You are now a citizen of Canada."

"Jesus, Madam Ch- I mean X. She's intense."

"Yes. Their organization is not be trifled with."

Steel peered at the passport. "Mr. Smith . . . how original. Thanks, eh?" Steel smirked, but the joke was lost on Cham.

"William, concentrate. I wanted you to meet them so you could see the price we have to pay to be able to move large amounts of gold and jewels. Now this little paper book will definitely interest you." Cham held it in an outstretched hand. The Bangkok Bank's logo was visible on the front cover. Steel fumbled it open to the first page and was mesmerized by all the tiny penned in numbers. "Damn . . . Very nice. Baht, pesos, or dollars?"

"Baht for now, but we can get you dollars if necessary."

Steel pulled the booklet up to his lips and kissed it.

"Ah there's Romy. Let's play a little pool and discuss our great fortune and plans for the future." He waved and headed over to his lover, who appeared with a drink in hand.

Steel's eyes flipped around the club. Adjacent to the glass partition shielding the women, sat four full-size pool tables, each illuminated by a bright center-mounted light, which accentuated the deep green felt. Two pool tables were occupied with white-haired white men. Steel could hear their singsong Australian lilt, as their laughter pierced the air. Cham and Romy moved to an empty table. Steel nodded to two clean cut Thai men sitting on stools against the wall—they had a military or police vibe to them, he thought. A bevy of waitresses and table attendants fluttered around the pool tables. Cham ordered drinks, and balls were racked. At Cham's urging, Steel broke first. After several more drinks, he lost the game, quicker than he would have liked. He recovered, fell into a groove, and won the second.

"So we're fucking rich," Steel slurred his words as he tried to focus enough to make a bank shot on what seemed like a sea of green felt.

"S'hhh. Not so loud." Cham glanced around the room. Cham chalked his cue and spoke in a low tone. "We are indeed fortunate. The lord God Buddha has smiled upon us, but we must not stop here. No, no, no." He wagged his finger at Steel. "There is so much out there for us to take."

"Oh yeah, this is just the start." Steel grabbed at the large front pocket on his shirt and whipped out the bankbook, simultaneously shooting the passport onto the green felt of the empty table next to them. One of the Thai military types slid off his stool and grabbed it, perused it, and handed it back to Steel.

Police sergeant Trimek returned to his stool and elbowed Rangsipramkul. "Looks like our Steel is now a Smith. From Canada." Rangsipramkul nodded without turning his head.

Steel shoved both the passport and the bankbook back in his pocket. Cham slid up next to him and whispered, "William quit flashing that around. This is serious business. I'm risking Romy's and my life dealing with the Madam."

Steel winked and patted the pocket.

They played more pool and drank more.

"Yep . . . now I'm in a groove." Steel attempted a wink at number 22 and missed his next shot.

Cham walked over to Steel and poked a cue into his chest. "You must develop a plan to find more treasure. You are a brilliant analyst and need to organize a strategy. You can't just expect to operate blindly." He poked Steel again.

"Ouch. Why don't you develop a plan to find more mangoes?" Steel snickered and rubbed his chest.

"You said you wanted to search for your father. That will take lots of money."

"I know," Steel winced, expecting another cue poke.

"We'll need police and military contacts on the Laos border, but it won't be cheap."

"I know." Steel's chin bounced onto his chest.

"What have you done to further your dream except to complain and read newspaper articles?"

"I . . . sometimes I'm overwhelmed by the enormity of it," Steel said, spinning his cue in his hands until it burned.

Cham put a hand on Steel's shoulder. "Our new business partners," Cham tilted his chin towards the Madam's office, "as you were told have a web of shipping contacts in Manila that can handle the product." Cham said.

"I know I need to get a plan. A fucking plan." His mind wandered.

"Good," Cham said.

"I was this . . . this close, to having the mother lode of barrels full of . . . figs." Steel measured with outstretched arms and nearly toppled over but caught himself with the butt of the cue. He sank two more balls then missed an easy one. He stared at number 22. She'd bewitched him, that's what was going on.

Cham sidled next to Steel and gently tapped him on the cheek several times. "Yes, number 22, she is indeed gorgeous, if you go for that type of incredible beauty."

"You mean in a woman?"

"This place seems overwhelming for William," Romy called out.

Steel looked at number 22, who was chatting to 17 seated next to her. Both so beautiful and so available. Tight, ripe bodies. Steel squirmed.

"No. William must learn how to deal with life's distractions. Less chasing trollops," Cham said.

Steel watched the two models chatting and laughing. They were exotically beautiful, but maybe Cham was right. Getting involved with Chong's enterprise took his little treasure hobby to a whole new level. He had to focus. But goddamn. Number 22.

From behind the glass, Apichaya Nitibhon, or "Oom" as her friends called her, could see the foreigners milling about. The glass kept her safe and removed from the farang, Caucasians. It was only her second week working at the Fish Bowl Club. She had started here because she had tired of sleazy so-called agents, fake modeling jobs, and being poor. Her application for a stewardess position with Thai Airlines had gone nowhere; there were too many unemployed beautiful women to competing for the legit work.

Her friend Anoma had convinced her to take a job here. Anoma had worked at the Bowl for two months and made thousands of baht a week by going home with farangs. Despite the promise of money, Apichaya hadn't yet been able to bring herself to leave with one of the customers. The warnings from her co-workers, seated around her, echoed in her head. "They smell bad. They are ugly, fat, and old and slobber and spit all over you. They have diseases."

Still, for the last two weeks, she came back, night after night, collecting a small salary for showing up. The big money was available, but only if you went home with one of the slobberers. She needed cash for food and rent but also to pay for her business degree. Tuition was due in a month. Apichaya glanced around the room, hoping one of the foreigners might appeal to her. They were all so old. Anoma nudged her again in the ribs and laughed. "Oom, why don't you wave to the young white man who keeps smiling at you? At least he is young and handsome."

"Yes, he is handsome and young, but is he rich? The young ones are never rich, right?"

"That is true. The old ones are rich, and appreciative," Anoma acknowledged.

Saiporn, who sat near them, leaned in. "The old ones are much better. They only cum once then want to sleep. The young men want to fuck all night. Too much work." She covered her mouth with a hand and laughed.

"Princess, Princess," a short woman, busting out of her low cut black dress, called out to Oom. "Are you too much a Princess? What are you waiting for? Someone said you've never left with a man."

"What is your pussy made of? Gold?" another yelled, and more laughter erupted.

"Its gold compared to that filthy thing you sell," Anoma said and slapped Oom a high-five.

"Oh no, here come the two old men," someone called out. "I bet they are from Australia. Their clothes are terrible. So many colors in their shirts and short pants."

Two white-haired, overweight men in loud Hawaiian shirts, shorts, and leather sandals with socks stood in front of the glass and leered. The women watched the men as they pointed and gestured. One pointed to Anoma and Oom, then spoke to a manager who was nearby. The manager nodded and waved with his fingers down, the Thai gesture for "come here." Oom and Anoma had been chosen. Oom took a deep breath. The club gave the girls the option of saying no. She clung to the barstool. Her moral sensibility was at war with her common sense and will to survive. Why couldn't it at least have been the young white man instead of these old lechers? Her stomach growled, loudly. Nerves and no food since breakfast argued for the ugly Australians. Anoma gently pulled Oom toward the door, and she hoped she wouldn't cry.

8

Manila
Friday, 15 November 1985

Fifty-seven-year-old Cardinal Jaime Sin sat behind an expansive 17ᵗʰ century wood desk brought over from Spain by one of his predecessors. He stared out the window of his comfortable study in the Catholic Church's official residence in Villa San Miguel in Mandaluyong, the approximate geographical center of Manila. He was short, overweight, and wore reading glasses with black frames. He did not look the role of a radical theologian and political kingmaker. He had trained as a priest, excelling in theology and church politics, and had risen to the position of Archbishop of Manila. Despite his powerful role, he never forgot growing up in rural poverty, or the injustices and hardships inflicted on his family and friends by the Ilustrados, the landed gentry class.

Sin dropped his pencil. His eyes were aching. For the last two hours, as the sun climbed up the eastern sky, he had scribbled letters, notes for sermons, and script ideas for the *Veritas* show, the church's electronic voice in the Philippines. The document in front of him was the fourth rewrite of correspondence to concerned high-level officials in the Vatican. He couldn't decide whether to explain his vocal criticisms of the snap election or to knuckle under to Vatican pressure and tone down his rhetoric.

He believed steadfastly that his primary religious obligation was to the quality of life of his flock, but that necessitated getting involve in national policy—his flock constituted a broad majority of the Philippine people. Of the eighty-five million Filipinos who inhabited the seven thousand plus islands of the Republic of the Philippines, eighty-five percent were believers, making him the shepherd of the third largest Catholic country in the world. That gave him some leeway in dealings with the Vatican. Nonetheless, they tracked his growing radicalism carefully.

Sin checked his watch: 11:30 a.m. He had a 12:30 lunch engagement with the prominent businessman and political activist Chino Roces. Sin figured Roces was coming to seek help rallying anti-Marcos political forces. Roces's group had gathered over one million signatures nationwide to draft Cory Aquino, the fifty-two-year-old widow of Senator Aquino, to run against Marcos. But the United Nationalist Democratic Organization, the country's oldest and largest opposition party, and Senator Salvador Laurel of Batangas, its standard bearer, were against opening up the race. Sin picked up his pencil again and fiddled with it, wondering whether Roces was right and the UNDO wrong. Maybe some new blood was needed. She had the Aquino name, after all.

Theodore Pineta, Sin's dutiful and efficient aid, scurried in and shut the door behind him. "Your Eminence, we have a problem. A Mr. David from Vice President Tolentino's office is outside, and he's brought security." Theodore whispered with an uncharacteristic fluster to his voice. "He is not on the schedule and is most insistent you meet with him."

Sin leaned back in his chair. "Well, now they are showing up without appointments. Bold, but not entirely unexpected."

"Should I ask them to make an appointment and come back?"

"With the announcement of the snap election, I'm sure Malacanang Palace is sweating out rumors of Aquino's potential run for the presidency. Marcos's spies likely know about Roces's meeting with me today. Marcos is shrewd and knows Laurel isn't really a threat. Cory, on the other hand, she just might be." Sin bit into his pencil's eraser and spit a pink fleck out. Marcos was scared of the little widow. Well, well. "Roces might just be right," he muttered to his blotter.

"Excuse me, your Eminence. Who is right?"

"Nothing. I think I just made a decision concerning my luncheon engagement; maybe the pious widow is the answer."

"So, your Eminence, should you want to exit out your private entrance, I'll dissuade the waiting goons from bothering you," Theodore said.

Sin laughed. "Teddy, let the goons in. They're still God's children, albeit badly behaved children. I'm curious what could be so urgent. I have the feeling it's the election. I'll meet with them for a few minutes before lunch. Bring me some tea and offer them some as well."

Teddy nodded and exited. Sin rose from his desk, adjusted his white zucchetto skullcap and strode to the door, throwing it open with a wide grin. He greeted the group with his trademark salutation:

"Gentlemen, welcome to the House of Sin."

9

Angeles
Friday, 15 November 1985

STEEL WATCHED THE TRAFFIC AHEAD of him slow before the base's main gate. His Datsun 4x4 inched to a stop fifty feet from the security police checkpoint, but his mind was miles away. Number 22 was naked, sliding on top of him, slippery with a lather of soapy water. Steel lay on a king's-sized inflatable air mattress and grasped at slick limbs. Strong legs coiled around him—smothering, exhilarating, and intoxicating. He shook his head like a dog drying off, slinging off the imaginary tryst. He needed to focus. Like the song "One night in Bangkok," his Thailand excursion was a blur. He faulted the Mekhong whiskey. But Cham had been right. The gems were exceptional, the gold pure, and the payout staggering. The exact figure, minus Cham's forty-percent cut, was close to $170,000—eight times his annual captain's salary. Jesus. He could actually see himself getting enough cash to find his Dad. But he had to stop letting pussy get in his way. "Yep," he mused aloud. "Get thy shit together William Steel . . . get thy shit-" A blast from a car horn dragged Steel back to the present. He stepped on the gas, and the truck rolled forward.

He'd been back from Thailand a week and the time had flown by—his mind preoccupied with thoughts of new treasure and secret bank accounts. At work, Thimble had been frosty. Steel was sure the OSI had been informed of his foreign travel. He just took everyone's shit and went about Thimble's interpretation of Air Force intelligence business.

Steel finally passed through the gate and raced towards Marcos Highway. He was on his way to see his boys, Renaldo and Manuel, two street kids he had adopted unofficially. For now, they were staying at Mabuhay House, a home for some one hundred orphans run by a renegade Catholic priest. USAF Major Gary O'Dell, a Falstaffian Irish Catholic helicopter pilot who had been transferred stateside three years previous, had bamboozled Steel into taking on the role of Mabuhay House's Americano patron.

O'Dell sent monthly checks for the house's operations and unexpected crises. But the day-to-day money worries fell on Steel's shoulders. O'Dell had promised to return as retired Major O'Dell and resume his post as full-time Mabuhay House saint but not for several more years. For now, that fell to Steel, a job that most of the time induced ulcers. But today, with a large check in his wallet from the Bangkok Bank, he whistled while he drove, knowing that the boys at Mabuhay House would stay housed and fed for at least a few more weeks.

The Marcos Highway originated in Manila, bottlenecked in Angeles, then continued through dozens of towns before it ended in the mountains to the north. The Angeles portion of the highway was always congested with horse-drawn carts, brightly painted trikes, motorcycles with sidecars, and private autos. The loudest and most numerous vehicles on the road were commercial jeepneys, emblazoned with names like "Playboy Bong" and "Lover Boy." Their paint schemes would make a peacock envious.

Along both sides of the Angeles portion of the highway were scores of sari-sari, grocery and hardware stores and building supply companies with a mishmash of rough-cut lumber, concrete blocks, and bamboo. Nestled alongside the stores were low-end bars and nightclubs with names like "Doll House" and "Fire Empire." Steel had patronized these dives when he first got to Clark and thought they were pinnacles of exotic entertainment. Today, in harsh daylight, he recoiled at the disheveled, half-dressed entertainers loitering outside the ramshackle places.

Five minutes out of town, the scene along the highway drifted into rickety residential housing, big shady trees, and clumps of bamboo. Chickens, dogs, and people wandered on the dusty berms. Steel's vehicle turned into a gravel side street and into Mabuhay House's compound. A throng of boys swarmed his truck. Father Rudy, dressed in a brown robe cinched with a rope belt, a large wooden cross banging on his narrow chest, pulled Steel out of his truck and into the rectory. They sat on rattan chairs set between side tables covered in a jumble of books, papers, and empty tea cups.

"William, so what brings you here on this glorious day? Had you come this morning, you could have joined us in worship service." He nudged Steel in the shoulder. "Heaping some coals off your head, eh?"

Steel smiled. Father Rudy said the same thing every visit.

"So it's not bad news I hope?" He placed his hand on Steel's shoulder.

"Not at all." Steel handed Father Rudy the check.

He pulled out a pair of reading glasses from a pocket of his robe. The black metal frames slid down his nose, and he examined the numbers on the green slip in the bright sunlight pouring in in the screened window. "Good lord, this amount can't be right. What's this for?"

"For the bank, Father R. We'll use some of it for programmed projects and the rest for day-to-day expenses. Don't you need to buy a new wooden cross or something?" Steel pointed to Rudy's crucifix. "Hell, maybe we could upgrade you to brass."

"Can I ask who this generous 'William Smith' is and how we can ever thank him?"

"Oh, he's just a kind old Canadian I met when I was visiting my friend Cham in Thailand. I told him all about your work here, and he insisted on sending a check."

"Well Mr. William Smith, Canadian, will receive extra thanks in our prayers, as will you, William Steel." Father Rudy put the check into the pocket of his robe. "I will use it well. Sister Josephine was just saying she needed some medical supplies for our clinic, and it will go a long way with the food bills for the next several months."

"Perfect." Steel stood. "Are Reynaldo and Bong Bong around? I only have a few minutes, but I wanted to say hi."

"No, they're out on a shopping trip with the sisters."

"Okay, I'll catch them later."

As Father Rudy ushered Steel out to his car, he remembered to invite the Father, his assistant, and Renaldo and Bong Bong to the house for Thanksgiving. Father Rudy readily accepted, and Steel figured Rosa had already issued the invitation

As Steel drove out of the compound, he peered at USAF Lt. Col. Snowden's memorial basketball hoop and wooden plaque and recalled the moving ceremony the base had had for the fallen hero. Steel had pushed to have Snowden remembered, not only for his last brave deeds but also for his generous support of the orphanage.

Steel bumped down the dirt road back towards the Marcos Highway. He went over the list of Thanksgiving invitees in his head. The event was coming quick. Jo Jo was heading over to Tony's today to ask him and his family. With Joseph and Curtis as definite yeses, Steel figured there would be fifteen or so guests, including Vida, the star attraction as far as he was concerned.

10

Zambales Mountains
Friday, 22 November 1985

THE SHOCKWAVES FROM THE EXPLOSION hit them with a tsunami of supersonic tropical air propelling debris hundreds of yards and pummeling the assembled observers. Steel raised his head, scanning the terrain, got up all fours, and, like a dog, shook off leaves and twigs.

"Christ, how much fucking explosives did that crazy bastard set off?" said Steel, shouting over the ringing in his ears.

The ground moved, and Jo Jo emerged from terra firma like a groundhog from his den, his eyes wide and bits of vegetation stuck in his close-cropped hair.

Steel pointed a finger at Jo Jo. "Don't say a fucking word." Steel knew he was anxious to get to the cave where they thought they had seen the Japanese straggler. He had begged Steel to make quick work of the stopover at Nanpo's camp to investigate a metal box the Negrito had found and said was filled with Japanese documents. They found Nanpo and his family —cousins, uncles, aunts, parents, three wives, and a platoon of children—in an assemblage of temporary grass and bark huts. They had come down from their mountain village to sell explosives to lowlanders. Nanpo salvaged the material from unexploded WWII U.S. and Japanese aerial bombs, artillery shells, mortar rounds, grenades, and other small arms. Tony had said Nanpo learned the art of WWII ordinance disposal from his father and grandfather, both of whom had guided American forces. It was dangerous work. Tony could recite a list of friends and family who'd been blown apart trying to salvage munitions. Steel surmised the process was Darwinian: the familial lines of those with shaky hands or little technical expertise died off. Jo Jo had to understand, theirs was an operation that needed a top-notch explosive expert once in a while. It just made sense to let Nanpo show them his stuff.

Steel glanced at Jo Jo, trying to gauge his level of anger. Beside him, Tony and Nanpo peered over the rotting log, which they had sheltered behind. "Jesus, Tony, that was one hell of an explosion," Steel called out.

"He could have killed us," said Jo Jo, still brushing dirt from his shirt.

Steel watched Joseph lift his head. His eyes were pinned open wide and his jaw slack. Blood trickled down the side of the yard boy's face and neck.

Steel rolled several times then popped up in a squat next to Joseph. Steel removed a bandanna from his pocket and pressed it against the boy's head wound. "You've been hit. I told you to keep your head down."

Pushing aside the bunched bandanna clutched in Steel's hand, Jo Jo leaned in to examine the wound. "It's a nasty gash."

"Captain Steel. It's okay. I'm fine. Something hit my head. I lifted it to see the big explosion. It was like a monster," Joseph said.

Jo Jo glanced Steel's way and muttered, "I warned you about bringing him." He used his head to point at Joseph who was blinking spastically.

Steel went for the first aid kit. Jo Jo applied antiseptic

cream and a butterfly bandage to the gash. In a few minutes, the bleeding had slowed.

"We'll have to keep an eye on him," said Jo Jo.

"Yes, Doc," said Steel.

Jo Jo laid a hand on Joseph's shoulder. "The next time we tell you something. Like to keep your head down. You do it. You hear me?"

Joseph nodded, still eyeing the pile of rubble.

Tony joined them. He stared at Steel and then at the crater the blast had blown.

"I think Nanpo was excited by your visit and maybe he wanted to impress you too much with his knowledge of the things exploding," Tony said.

Nanpo stood a few feet away, a goofy grin on his face, clearly pleased with the demonstration. Besides his obvious glee, made more childlike by his height of 4'8", his countenance was nothing if not regal. A man's shirt hung open, like a cape, over his woven loincloth, and his tanned skin glinted like bronze. A thick ponytail of kinky gray hair flowed down his back, complementing the beige, amber, and white of his many necklaces and bracelets, each composed of a unique assortment of shells, beads, and the flattened brass of spent cartridge shells. Steel marveled at the centerpiece of one necklace, an eight-inch tusk from a wild pig; from the tooth's size, the beast must have been a Godzilla porker.

"Why was he trying to impress us?" Steel asked.

"Maybe I told to him that you were . . . er . . . the king of the white men," said Tony.

"More like an idiot jester of the white men," said Jo Jo, looking again at Joseph's wound. He took the boy's arm and led him to a shady spot to rest.

Steel readjusted his headband and followed Tony and Nanpo over to the crater, the size of a mini-bus, which the bomb had blown out in a grove of bamboo. The air smelled like a jungle Fourth of July, a fog of burnt sulfur fumes and steamed vegetation. Steel peered into the pit and shot a thumb up at Nanpo.

"How big's a bomb have to be to make a hole like that?" Steel asked.

Nanpo thought for a second, measured out a four-foot length with his hands, and explained that he had used the lightning black powder from more than twenty Japanese metal bombs.

"Lightning powder," Steel muttered. That was a unique name for TNT, RDX, and ammonium nitrate.

Jo Jo appeared at Steel's side and stared into the pit.

"The boy okay?" Steel said.

"I'm worried he may have a concussion. Had to make him rest."

"Okay," Steel said.

Jo Jo peered into the crater. "I've read that Haponese explosives can be unreliable. Trinitroaniline was used by the Japanese in naval shells. It's like TNT. The Haponese also used picric acid, a mixture of TNT and powdered aluminum, in light antiaircraft shells. There's another explosive similar to TNT, which the Japanese refer to as Type 91 explosive."

Everyone stared at Jo Jo.

"Bathroom reading again?" said Steel.

"I'd prefer to use a public library—if Angeles had one," Jo Jo replied.

"Nanpo and his clan have spent six months gathering metal weapons and taking them apart to sell. He would like to show you some," Tony said.

"Sure." Steel said.

Jo Jo shot a look at his bulging backpack. Steel knew he was thinking of the supplies he had in there for the straggler:

Japanese magazines, newspapers, tins of buckwheat noodles and dried squid, and even a battery-powered bullhorn.

"C'mon Jo Jo, it will just take a second," Steel said.

They followed Nanpo to a clearing a hundred yards away where he removed a woven vine and palm frond screen, which had been camouflaging the entrance to a compact cave. Wood crates full of mortar, artillery, grenade and small arms rounds, and scrap metal lined the narrow space.

Steel eyes were drawn to two long rows of white plastic jugs. "What are these?"

Nanpo explained that the jugs held lightning powder from rifle and machine gun cartridges.

"He must have a good supply of weapons to extract so many explosives. Maybe he knows caves to explore," Steel whispered.

"Maybe," said Jo Jo. He was still mad, Steel thought.

Tony explained that Nanpo traded plastic bottles full of explosives for cooking pots, knives, and other essentials. Steel figured the jugs would wind up on the black market, selling for hundreds of pesos each to buyers from the NPA to mining companies to fishermen, who used homemade explosives to dynamite reefs.

"Say boss, why don't we leave this place now. It's making me nervous with all this lightning powder," said Jo Jo.

"Good point," Steel said and took one last look at the arms dealer's sari-sari store.

"And maybe now we can finally see the mysterious box we allegedly stopped for?" Jo Jo continued.

"Also a good point," said Steel. He glanced around and spotted Tony sitting with Pongpet and Joseph in the shade. "Tony, the steel box?"

Tony nodded and called out that Captain Steel wanted to see the box. A murmur rippled through the crowd of Nanpos' family and hangers on. A few minutes passed, and four Negritoes shuffled like pallbearers through the crowd, carrying the three-foot-by-three-foot metal box. The scene was Hollywood. The only thing it lacked was a big orchestra playing exotic Eastern music. Steel scanned the rust-orange container and was pleased to see it seemed to be a security box with a locking hasp, though minus a lock.

"Steel-san, the box could be full of secret documents," said Jo Jo and bent forward, apparently forgetting his eagerness to get to the straggler's cave.

The four Negritos struggled to set the box on the ground. Nanpo announced that he wanted to present it to Steel as a gift to the white king. Steel thanked Nanpo with a little bow then peered into the box.

It was empty. He fought back the urge to yell out an obscenity. He didn't want to insult his host, especially one as heavily armed as this one. Instead, he turned and glared at Tony. Tony slinked forward. Jo Jo blurted out, "Wala na, nothing."

"What happened to the papers?" Tony asked Nanpo.

Nanpo waved his hand. "They worked well as fire starters and for wrapping food. We are happy to clean out the box as our gift to the white king."

Steel rubbed his forehead and shook his head. The papers could have held treasure maps. Bahala na, whatever. He gushed thanks for the present and Nanpo's hospitality and reached into the compact canvas pack at his feet and pulled out two Zippo lighters and a can of fluid. He lit one then closed it and gave it Nanpo, taking a few minutes to show how to light and refill it. Jo Jo stomped around muttering for Tony to organize and head out.

Twenty minutes later Steel and company were out of the village and slogging down a trail heading westward. Jo Jo insisted the wobbly-legged Joseph remain behind in the village under the care of Nanpo's family. The boy was crushed, but obeyed Jo Jo's directive. The expedition waved good-bye to the last of Nanpo's children and pushed through six-foot-tall elephant grass and scrub bushes. After just a few minutes, the only sounds carried on the arid breeze were the slap of bare feet and the crackle of the dry grass.

Jo Jo huffed and grunted, and Steel limped. His gluteus maximus, medius, and minimus muscles seized up one at a time and in pairs and triplets, a symphony of butt cramps. It took four hours and thirty-seven minutes to arrive at a campsite. He was glad they had decided to leave Joseph with Nanpo's family, the three wives vying to see who got to nurse the handsome boy. This hike was kicking Steel's aching ass, and he hadn't recently sustained a head wound.

Their camp was in a shady clearing in a massive grove of twenty-foot bamboo with a stream of cool water for bathing. Steel and Jo Jo's fluorescent orange tent, the only unnaturally colored object in the scene, was pitched on a flat spot, cushioned by a several inch layer of fresh banana leaves, which the Negritos had cut and stacked. The Negritos, for their camp, had strewn woven reed mats on the ground, preferring to sleep in the open air. They lit an enormous fire of thick tree limbs, mounds of dry palm fronds, and dead bamboo to develop a layer of hot coals to cook their sweet potatoes and rice. Then they set out to hunt for their dinner.

An hour later, the men reemerged from the bush and paraded into camp with bloodied animal carcasses dangling from bamboo poles. They had killed two wild chickens, a two-foot-long lizard, and several brown rodents that looked like rats but without the scaly tail. Thankfully, Steel thought, no monkeys. Skinned out, they resembled human babies. Steel and Jo Jo took only a chicken from the Negrito's bounty, and Jo Jo cleaned and roasted it.

After dinner, Steel washed up in the stream. He stood for a moment and enjoyed the nighttime breeze as it drove the stagnant air and buzzing mosquitos out of the campsite. The wind swayed the tall bamboo, which groaned and creaked, the sound blending with the raucous chorus of tree frogs and insects. He could see the red glow of the lantern against the fabric side of their tent and a silhouette of Jo Jo, with his head stuck in a book.

Steel wished the glowing form was Vida. He hadn't seen her in weeks. The charged political atmosphere in the Philippines kept her away on business and away from his bed. Damn, he was horny. He'd badger her to visit him when he finished this treasure hunting.

Before he popped into the tent, Steel took one last look at the campfire. The Negritos, bathed in flickering light, were in various states of repose. All were shirtless, dressed in traditional loincloths. From Steel's line of sight, there wasn't anything that placed the scene in this century, or for that matter, in the last five hundred years.

Steel focused on one form: Tony, who stood while others sat or lounged on the ground. He and Steel had come a long way in their relationship, from mutual annoyance and suspicion to mutual respect and friendship. He watched Tony gesture to his comrades and imagined he was retelling centuries-old fables of forest spirits and wild pig hunts. Tony unswervingly believed in the forest spirits and claimed to interact with them regularly. Steel would have scoffed at the claims, but Tony's otherworld communications had saved Steel's life on more than one occasion. Spooky stuff, he thought, and wished he heard the voices too.

Tony pushed another log into the fire sending a huge plume of sparks surging into the sky, then leaned over, picked up a plastic jug, and took a long drink of tuba, a home brew of fermented palm wine.

"I can't believe my wife wanted me to buy her a telebision," Tony said using the American word, or his best approximation. "But what was I to do? They are expensive, but I wanted her to be happy and keep peace in my home."

The other Negritos nodded. Tony was rich with lowlander things thanks to his relationship with the white Americano Steel.

Ganchee pulled at Tony's loincloth and demanded his turn with the jug. "I have seen one of those tellbision in your village before," he said, to appear worldly to his pals. "They are like this." He made the sign of a square with his hands. "And they are black, with the shiny eye of the python, sitting quietly waiting for its prey." He smiled at his description, thought it was pretty good. It was what he imagined, since he had never actually seen one switched on.

"A tel-lee-e-bision—what is that word?" Dungee scrunched his face.

Tony hesitated. His brain was clouded by excessive tuba. He did not know where to begin to explain the concept of a TV to his country cousin Dungee. Tony had only bought the machine to impress people in Sampung Bato, his village near Clark Air Base. He rarely watched it. His wife and kids enjoyed it though. Sometimes he wished he hadn't married a lowlander woman and instead lived simply in the mountains with a Negrita.

"The tellbision is used to watch lowlanders talking to each other," Pongpet said as he reached up and grabbed the jug from Tony. "Tony's wife can use it to talk to the people who she works for on the Americano Clark base."

Piepet poked around the fire and repositioned a stick with an impaled and skinless rodent on it then spoke. "I was in the white man's Clark when I was a small boy. I saw healers there who helped me with medicine for my sick leg. They were scary white spirit people, but my leg was fixed."

A couple of Negritos nodded. They also knew people who had received medical care on Clark. For their service to American GI's during WWII, Negritos, unlike lowlanders, were authorized to use the hospital at the base.

Tony squatted down next to the fire and dug around in the coals with a stick, looking for his sweet potato. It should be done by now. He had given up trying to explain what the telebision was. He stared into the fire, pleased. He loved being out in the great mountains, sitting with his friends, drinking tuba, hunting, hiking, and fighting like young boys again. Back with their families, there was too much responsibility. No drinking, just keeping up appearances for your village.

"Tony, so how many mountain wives do you have now? You have enough money to buy many. You must be tired now from all the screwing." Ganchee nudged Tony with his elbow and laughed.

"No. The more wives . . . " Tony motioned wildly with his hands. "The more wives, the more headaches you have. I'm not getting any more wives, only women who want to screw and not get married."

"Those kind of women are hard to find," Pongpet said.

"Is Steel married?" Ganchee asked.

"I thought Jo Jo was his woman," Piepet said, flat on his back, his eyes closed, nearly asleep. "Jo Jo cooks for him and they share that cloth hut together." He smiled.

Several laughed loudly, while those who knew Jo Jo well glanced at the tent hoping that the lowlander who could fight like a demon with his hands and feet had not overheard.

Tony spoke in a low voice. "No, Steel has a woman. He is in love with her like only a young man can be. Once I met her at Steel's house. She is a very beautiful lowlander, like a queen of a huge magical tribe and so . . . so smart for a women. She writes the stories in the paper that the lowlanders read. She works in the far south, in a place where so many lowlanders live. Yes, soooo many." Tony paused and shook his head in disbelief. "Yes, they are all smashed together so that no one can count them all. More than many, many, many Sampang Bato's together. More than all the stars in the sky." Tony raised his arms and examined the sky, and the group responded by peering up into the heavens too.

"Look, a star has a fire tail." Ganchee followed the shooting star with his stick.

"I saw it too. Someone will be lucky tomorrow. The spirits always pick one to receive the falling star's luck," Tony said, pleased it had appeared during his oration.

"Ah, I'm sure Captain Steel will find more trash tomorrow—lots of things he values. The most fortunate always get the extra blessings from the spirits, always," one-eyed Tikpit said, and he spit on the ground. No one begrudged him his bitterness. He had had a long history of bad luck—the loss of an eye and several fingers, not to mention rumors that his wife had a secret lover.

Dungee sat up, still pondering Tony's description of so many people in one village. His thoughts were jumbled by the tuba. He was shocked that the world beyond the valley where he lived, a three-day walk from here, was so different and difficult to understand. "I wouldn't like living in place with so many people," he said. "No place to shit in peace. You'd be stepping in it all the time."

More laughter.

After their meal, the men curled up on the ground atop piles of woven mats and underneath cloth covers. A slight chill tinted the night air. As they dropped off to sleep, one by one, the creatures of the dark went about their business, some silent predators, some scrabbling prey, and many calling out to each other in in wails of longing and lust.

Thanks to Jo Jo, they had gotten up early. Steel appreciated the coffee, the tocino, sweet ham, eggs, and bread that Jo Jo had prepared. No way could Steel stomach a Negrito breakfast of canned sardines, left-over rice, and cold roasted rodent. Steel looked over at the pile Jo Jo had stacked up near the cave entrance and then glanced around the jungle, wondering if the straggler was aware of their presence. Steel took another swig of coffee from his metal mess kit cup and watched Jo Jo fumbling with his gear.

From his hillside lair adjacent to the cave command post, Nada watched his prey through the side-mounted 2.5 power telescopic sight of the type 97, sniper rifle. Killing would be easy, but evading the little men after the shot could be problematic. Nada was sweating under his palm-frond cloak. Beads of salty water cascaded through the black charcoal smeared on his face. Both the suit and paint were necessary camouflage to fool the little black men who possessed extraordinary senses. He and Kami had also gone to great lengths to clean themselves this morning, taking a brisk bath without soap, only coarse stream sand. They dried off and rubbed jungle dirt and rot all over their bodies. Human scents had to be masked.

Deep down, Nada knew they were at a safe distance and well hidden. They had easy avenues of retreat. Yet, here they lay, frozen with indecision and debating the white interloper's fate. It wasn't that he was afraid of killing. He had killed many men during his military career, dozens in Korea and many here in the Philippines. But Kami-san was right when he reminded Nada that he hadn't killed in many decades. They argued day and night about the American's death. It was their sworn duty to fight the Americans, and, though much time had passed, they had received no counter commands. Kami-san contended that maybe commands had been issued but had been lost; or maybe couriers couldn't find their secret jungle hideouts.

Nada again put the fine crosshairs of the scope on the American's head. The red bandana made homing in on the target easy. All Nada had to do was use his thumb and slide the safety off, A round was already in the chamber. Kami whispered for Nada to control his breathing and praised his excellent rifle skills and noting that the 6.5x50 mm was a mild cartridge giving off little flash or smoke, which made countersniper activity difficult. Kami's whispered babble was disrupting Nada's concentration, yet Kami continued.

"The lack of flash and smoke comes from the length of the barrel; a 31.4-inch-long barrel allows cartridge propellant to burn fully and attain the optimum combination of accuracy and bullet velocity." Nada rolled his eyes. He could tell Kami was nervous about the killing. "The scope is uniquely offset left of the bolt to allow clip loading like other Mauser pattern rifles; it has a five-round box magazine. And of course, it can be loaded with either a five round stripper clip or single rounds."

Nada would have insisted Sergeant Kami take the shot, but the man was ill and his hand unsteady, and Nada did not want Kami to lose face because of a missed shot. So Nada held the rifle. For more than a decade Kami had cared for the rifle like his baby. He was a superb sniper, a killing machine in wartime and decorated marksman in peacetime.

Nada glared at Kami-san, and he stopped his history lesson. Nada moved the rifle inches to his left and put the crosshairs on the head of the Yankee's Filipino companion.

"No, Nada-san not the Filipino. If you have to kill, eliminate their officer, the American G.I.," Kami whispered.

"You are always by the book." Nada put the crosshairs back on the American and tensed his trigger finger.

"Kon'nichiwa watashi no yūjin, hello my friend," a bellowing voice shattered Nada's concentration and he froze. He blinked his eyes, trying to focus. Again the mechanical voice screamed at him in Japanese. "We are friends and we mean you no harm." Nada dropped the rifle and crammed his face into the dirt and covered his ears. Other than Kami, and his voice when he spoke aloud, Nada had not heard Japanese for decades: only Filipinos whispering in their huts or shouting at him when he made nighttime forays into their villages.

Stunned, Nada, kept his face in the dirt for several minutes before lifting it up just enough to cough sand out of his nose. He removed his hands from his ears and listened to the shrill, badly-accented Japanese, which called to him and offered gifts. "The war is over; Japan has surrendered," the voice screamed.

"Look, Nada-san, look," Kami whispered.

Nada hesitated and then forced himself to look. He watched the people around the entrance of the cave. They looked so small and insignificant.

"Use the scope again and watch and listen," Kami pleaded.

Nada did. The Yankee's Filipino man was using a loud speaker and calling out to them "to be friends."

"They are saying the war is over," Kami said.

"It is a trick," Nada said, pushing his face back into the dust. "Remember when the Yankee planes would fly over the jungle and scream to us on loudspeakers that the war was over and drop papers with messages. It was lies."

"Nada-san, that was so long ago."

"No, it . . ." Nada's voice trailed off and confusion swirled. Time was blurred.

"No, Nada-san, maybe it is the truth. Maybe the war is over."

"It is a lie," Nada said.

"Why don't you believe these men? Who would you believe? Are you so naïve that you think the Emperor himself is going to notify you?"

Nada jerked at Kami's insubordinate tone and hissed, "You are of out of line, Sergeant Kami-san. I only need confirmation from our commanding officer." Nada immediately regretted his tone.

"Please forgive me, Lieutenant Nada." Kami collapsed.

Nada dropped his head, listening to Kami's whimpers, and sighed, "All is forgiven, Kami. Let us retreat from here and discuss this some more."

"Hai, Nada-san, hai. Let us discuss this." They gathered gear and low-crawled away.

Twenty-four hours passed, and Nada, tired of Kami's barrage of questions and late night discussions about the Japanese voice, agreed to return and see if the interlopers were still there. Nada and Kami hiked three hours to the command post and took up their earlier positions, this time with a pair of binoculars instead of the rifle. Nada was surprised to see that the group had left a small pile of equipment at the cave's entrance. He suspected a booby trap.

Curiosity got the best of Kami and Nada, and they went to investigate. Nada crept slowly up to up to the cardboard box and woven basket, scanning the terrain with the barrel of his Type 96 machine gun. Satisfied they were alone, he knelt down and considered how to proceed. The containers were sealed in see-through fabric bags, the type of material he had encountered on raiding missions in the Filipino villages. These bags were better than gold because they would keep possessions dry in the wet season. Nada slowly and carefully untied them and probed the contents. The first item was a letter written in Japanese, which he scanned briefly and put aside.

The next items were Japanese newspapers and flimsy books with strange photos that shimmered in the harsh morning sunlight. He squatted on his haunches and examined the front page of the paper. It was a Tokyo daily and dated January 15, 1985. 1985? 1985. The date slammed him hard, and his brain raced. His knees buckled, and he ended up flat on his back. How could he have missed so many years? He was an officer in the Japanese Army. He sat back up and read for an hour, then two. He and Kami read and stared at the photos of people, sleek cars, and consumer goods, all from an alien world. Kami said he hoped he would recognize a photograph of a face or a place.

Nada laughed. "These are certainly elaborate fabrications. The American has gone to great lengths to create these papers." He jabbed at the newspaper with his index finger, hard enough to puncture it.

"I must politely offer a different opinion, Nada-san. These are genuine. Why would they go to so much trouble for old soldiers like us?"

Nada huffed and stared into the jungle.

"Nada-san, look at the cans of food. Japanese noodles and fish and even a bottle of sake. At least we must celebrate our good fortune and toast the Emperor," Kami said in his soft voice.

Nada turned his head away from the spoils.

"Nada-san, I beg you to look."

He swiveled back slowly and stared at the cans of food and wine until the squawking of a bird drove Nada to his feet. He grabbed the Type 96, aiming it at the noise.

"Relax, Nada-san, it is only a bird laughing at us," Kami said.

"I can't relax. We are exposed here. My brain hurts from looking at all this." He rubbed his eyes and then his shaved head.

Kami laughed. "Both our brains hurt. You're right we should take the things and leave this place. But maybe you should leave a letter. You read their letter. Didn't they ask you to leave a letter? They want to know how they can convince you that the war is over."

"More tricks."

"Not tricks. There's no harm in leaving a letter for them. At least thank them for the food," Kami said

"I want to think about it." Nada started packing up the food. He folded the plastic garbage bags and put them in the basket.

"It would only take a minute to write the note." Kami pressed.

Nada dropped the box of cans and screamed, "What is a minute? Do you know what you are saying?"

Nada looked on it horror as Kami dropped to the ground, cowering and covering his head with his hands. Nada dropped too and placed a hand on his Kami's shoulder and in whisper said, "Kami . . . Kami . . . dear friend how can you possibly know what a minute is? We have no minutes, hours, days, months, or years—only the night and the day and the rain and the dry. The papers, if they are real, say it is 1985. How is that possible? How is that possible?" He fought back tears.

Kami raised his head and wiped his cheeks with the sleeve of his soiled and frayed fatigue shirt. "Let's go. We can discuss this at home over dinner and sake."

"Hai. Let us leave this place."

Nada fashioned a pack and hoisted it onto his back and struggled under the weight of printed word, tinned food, and the realization he had lost decades of time. He carried his heavy load into the jungle.

11

Angeles
Thursday, 28 November 1985
U.S. Thanksgiving

S TEEL SLAMMED OPEN THE METAL gate to his house, and he and Jo Jo marched in. They had taken advantage of the cool, early morning air to hike ten miles around Angeles. Each carried an army-issue rucksack loaded with thirty pounds of dead weight. They were back on a regular schedule of training for mountain hikes. Jo Jo, flush with cash, was a cheerful training buddy, rehashing plans for treasure excursions and his future trip to Canada to bring his girls home.

It was Thanksgiving, and Steel was on a four-day break from work; the Commander had declared tomorrow, Friday, a down day. Steel felt strange not treasure hunting on these free days but giddy about the prospect of having Vida for the weekend. He was like a schoolboy on his first date. Naked alone-time with Vida was long overdue. He had forced Rosa to plan a visit to her sister after Thursday's festivities. Jo Jo was also under orders to vacate Steel's Love Shack for the holiday weekend.

He unslung his pack and kicked off his boots, on the polished parquet wood floor of his living room. Even from there, he could hear the activity in the kitchen. He checked his watch: 0800. Rosa was up and at it, continuing the frenzy she had been in the last few days, preparing for the feast.

He looked over at Jo Jo and pointed at the kitchen. "I ain't going in there. Enter at your own risk. I'll be at the bathhouse. I lit the wood before we left."

"I'd better have a look and see what I can do to help," Jo Jo said, easing toward the kitchen.

"You're a better man than I am, Gunga Din." Steel slipped to his room to get a bathrobe.

After a long soak, Steel wandered whistling into the kitchen for coffee. Tinny Filipino pop tunes blared from Rosa's ancient transistor radio. Rosa herself was at the stove, sweating, stirring a huge pot. Two women worked beside her, surrounded by scattered pans and dishes. One was thirty-something with mannish hair and a squat build. The other was bone-thin with thick black glasses. Without missing a stir, Rosa explained they were both nieces, there to help with the festivities. Steel nodded a greeting, wondering if they had all bunked in Rosa's room last night or arrived early this morning.

Cooking smells stacked in the air, and half-filled sagging burlap sacks littered the floor: carrots, broccoli, cabbage, mangoes, pineapples, and bananas.

A sandbag-sized sack of rice stood between Steel and Rosa. "Rosa, I," Steel stopped as he caught sight of a bright yellow-green Dorado fish, its head and tailfin overflowing the kitchen sink by a foot. "You know there are at most fifteen guests," he continued.

"William, that number might be low. You said I could invite some of my family. So I did."

"Oh, okay," His gaze fixed on the twenty-five pound turkey minus plastic wrap, thawed and sprawled out on the kitchen counter. He was thankful he had gone with the biggest size.

"Let's do a headcount of invited guests and estimate who is really going to show up. For example, I—"

"Jo Jo said you were worried about Ms. Abucayan," Rosa interrupted. "I know you are worried that she might not come. I hope and pray she wouldn't do such a thing for so important a celebration as the Feast of the Thanks-to-giving." She placed the back of her hand to her forehead. Her nieces echoed Rosa's tone in their screwed-up facial expressions and vigorous nods.

"She'll come," said Steel.

Rosa stirred the pot with increased intensity, "I tried to call Miss Abucayan last night, to ask her a food question, but a man answered her phone, and when I said who I was, he hung up. Most strange. But maybe there was a bad line, or I misdialed. When I tried again, no one answered the phone. Very strange."

"Very strange," Rosa's Greek chorus of nieces echoed.

"You called Vida?" asked Steel.

"Yes, I wanted to include her in the food discussions. She is your . . . your . . . woman. It would be rude to not check with her. But . . . Wala na, nothing. I tried." She rolled her eyes.

Steel glared at her. "You can say girlfriend. Vida is my girlfriend. You're right. You did a good thing trying to check with her. I spoke to her briefly a couple of weeks ago. The connection was very bad. She was still in Mindanao and was coming back to Manila in time to come to our party. We're staying the weekend together."

"So I have heard."

Steel poured some coffee, and Rosa handed him a tray with buttered pandesal bread, guava jelly, and a bowl of fruit. He took a slurp of coffee. A cardboard box hit the floor beside him. He saw Joseph bent over pulling large sweet potatoes out and placing them on the kitchen counter. His was soaked with sweat and streaked with dirt, as if he'd picked the potatoes himself.

"Thank you Joseph. Joseph has been such a big help carrying all the heavy boxes of food for us," Rosa said.

"Good morning, Captain Steel. My family is very excited about coming to your feast today."

Steel tilted his head and checked out the side of Joseph's head. It had healed nicely.

Steel nodded, smiled, and patted Joseph's shoulder. "I'll check back with you all later to see if you need any help. Nice to meet you ladies," he said, glancing at his watch. He still had plenty of time before the four o'clock start of the party. Most guests, true to Filipino tradition, would arrive late. In the meantime, he'd do some reading and take notes on a book on Vietcong counterinsurgency tactics for school. He had only four more classes to take before he finished his master's degree from the University of the Philippines.

A knock on his bedroom room door disturbed Steel's thoughts. Was it Vida? He glanced at his clock radio. Noon.

Jo Jo peeked in and announced, "Steel-san the first guests are here."

"Vida?"

"No," Jo Jo called out as he went to let them in.

They were introduced as Rosa's family and guests. Steel had recognized only Rosa's sister. He counted seventeen others, men, women, and children. They straggled in carrying two folding tables, armloads of bags and dishes, and a three-foot-long puffy paper piñata. They were all in a festive mood, laughing and calling out to Steel and Rosa. Rosa's nieces draped silver gold and purple streamers around the living room in between a rainbow assortment of balloons. He'd never considered decorations and especially not this color scheme.

He had a suspicion that Rosa's guest list and his weren't going to jibe.

At two o'clock Steel heard the front gate clanking open, and Jo Jo rattling off Japanese. Steel slammed down his book and got dressed. He couldn't continue ignoring the early arrivals. He wandered down to the living room, now filled with more strangers and more crappy pop music, pretty much indistinguishable from an Angeles disco. Jo Jo held court in the center of the room, resplendent in a powder blue Barong Tagalog, a traditional male Filipino shirt, and shiny black pants. Steel stared down at Jo Jo's small feet, swimming in the size ten Air Force ultra-gloss Corfram shoes he had borrowed from Steel.

Jo Jo introduced his Japanese language instructor, Josie, and her equally attractive cousin, Jacki. No wonder Jo Jo's Japanese was improving. Steel tried not to stare at Josie's low-cut dress and ample cleavage. After a few moments of pleasantries, Jo Jo escorted his ladies to the kitchen, chatting in what seemed like passable Japanese. "How the fuck are all those people fitting into the kitchen?" Steel muttered and followed them.

He waded through a clan of women cooking, gossiping, and laughing. Other guests had overflowed out the backdoor of the steaming kitchen into a back courtyard, which was shaded by a huge avocado tree. Some sat and chatted, others drank beer, while children played with a jump rope. Nervous about running out of drinks, he had Jo Jo and Joseph make a run to the corner sari sari store for more ice, San Miguel beer, and sodas.

At 2:30, Steel excused himself from Father Rudy and walked out the front door and into rows of tables and chairs under his carport, spilling out towards his bathhouse. Where was his truck? Guests were milling about; some were seated at the tables. Children played tag and threw a ball. Renaldo, Bong Bong, and Joseph had set up Steel's dart board and were chucking darts and laughing.

Curtis Washington, his girlfriend, and her two sisters dodged a stray dart and greeted Steel. Curtis was decked out in a long-sleeved, white shirt with a Nehru collar and a black vest. His pants were shiny blue and his black shoes highly polished. His three female companions were rocking floral sundresses and high heels.

At 3:30 p.m. Jo Jo pushed his way into the living room and grabbed Steel's arm, pulling him from a conversation with Curtis. "Boss-san, you'd better brace yourself," Jo Jo said, as he dragged Steel through the crowd and into the street.

"What the hell Jo Jo?" Steel jabbed his hands at two jeepneys unloading a tribe of Negritos.

"I just invited Tony and his family." Jo Jo squeezed his forehead with his hand. "I think Tony's definition of family is different than mine."

It took ten minutes for the Negritos, fifteen adults and five children, to unload bags and a thirty-pound fully roasted pig impaled on a wooden spit.

Tony walked over to Steel with an extended hand. Steel burst out laughing. He had no idea Tony owned a white shirt, especially one with sequined pockets, which nicely set off his black pants and dress shoes. Steel ignored Tony's outstretched hand, instead giving him a hug that lifted him off his feet.

"Captain Steel, I want you to meet my family," Tony grunted and straightened his shirt.

Jo Jo and Steel ushered them in. The women carried their pots and pans on their heads; others held crying children.

"Well William-san, at least they are a tiny people. Maybe they only take half the space of regular Filipinos," said Jo Jo.

At 4:19 p.m. a metallic clanking rose over the caterwaul of the party. Rosa, in her best drum majorette form, marched into the living room, banging a soup pot with a metal spoon. She was followed in close order by her two nieces, who solemnly held between them a three-foot-long wooden platter with a turkey roasted to *Betty Crocker's Cookbook New and Revised Edition* specifications and garnished with fruit and orchid flowers.

Rosa, still clanging the pot, led the Thanksgiving procession outside and directed the nieces to place the turkey on the banquet table overflowing with food. Steel checked his watch. He couldn't believe Vida was F-ing late.

Calls for silence, in three languages, rippled through the air. Steel blinked at the eerie calm that descended over the masses. Children stopped playing and people stood. Father Rudy rose and said a prayer thanking God for his glory and the opportunity for such a diverse group to assemble and celebrate the Feast of the Thanks-to-giving. He waved his hands and blessed the thirty-foot-long spread. The guests who had been fanning the food with long feathery wands to keep the flies at bay resumed their labors. Father Rudy thanked Steel and Rosa for putting on such a beautiful feast. Tony stood, teetering on a chair, and roughly translated Father's Rudy's words into Aeta, and then Rudy called for Steel to say something.

Steel, head bowed, paused for a few seconds as all eyes focused on him. The only sounds were a car driving by and a small Negrito baby babbling. He glanced up at the eclectic assortment of souls gathered. He rambled on about how the group was his family. He was perplexed by how inarticulate he suddenly found himself. As a USAF intelligence officer, public speaking was normally second nature. He choked out a thank you to Rosa and his kuya, brother, Jo Jo, and everyone who brought food and supplies. He raised his beer and toasted the turkey and the pig in turn.

At six p.m. and five beers later, Steel ducked back inside and called Vida's house, but no one answered. He was having such a great time. He wasn't going to let her absence get to him. Nope, he thought. But maybe she was in a car crash and lying in a ditch. Oh fuck, he returned to the party.

At seven p.m. Joseph's father, who resembled an older version of Joseph, cornered Steel. He spoke at length in a composed voice about how he had worked hard as a carpenter for his family, and how they had saved money so that Joseph could go to a good high school and, they hoped, to college. But they were concerned about Joseph's going into the mountains where bandits and NPA roamed. He implored Steel not to take Joseph on any more trips. The head wound had been a sign from God. Steel promised that there'd be no more hiking for Joseph. He'd let Jo Jo, who was of a similar opinion, break the news to the boy

At midnight, beer in hand, Steel staggered out his front door and into his garden. All the guests had gone, and Rosa and her crew had cleaned up. The crowd had embraced Steel's idea of Thanksgiving and enriched it with their mix of Catholic and Negrito rites. He was also pleased that his truck had made it back to its proper parking spot. He opened the Datsun's door, poured himself in, and fiddled with his key ring, looking for the one that would start the vehicle.

Steel startled at the creak of the passenger door, as Jo Jo jumped in. "Where we going Steel-san?" he asked, sleepily and yawned.

"You and I aren't going anywhere. I'm going to see what the fuck happened to Vida."

"Don't you think it is better to wait until morning," said Jo Jo.

"No, I'm worried. She didn't call."

"Okay, we'll go then."

"I don't need an escort." Steel fumbled with his set of keys. "Where the fuck is my key?" He looked over at Jo Jo.

"I have it."

"I want it."

"Unless I'm driving, no one is going anywhere." Jo Jo crossed his arms and closed his eyes.

Steel gritted his teeth. "Fine." He opened the door, kicked it with his foot, and stood too quickly, His head spun from the San Miguel. He clung to the side of the truck, worked himself around to the passenger side, and took Jo Jo's seat.

Steel spent the hour-and-fifteen-minute drive half passed out. From Angeles to Vida's luxury apartment building on the edge of Manila's Makati business district, he slumped against the passenger door, periodically jolting awake, expecting to see her crashed car burning on the side of the road.

Jo Jo parked the Datsun under a huge awning in front of Vida's building. A uniformed security guard emerged from the shadows, a 12-gauge pump shotgun with a pistol-grip stock slung across his chest, and scrutinized the vehicle. Jo Jo leaned out the window and told him they were visiting a resident. Steel got out of the truck, stretched, and tried to shake off his grogginess. He walked up to the lobby entrance, rattled the locked doors, and banged on the glass. A sleepy night clerk peered at them from behind a tall counter. He recognized Steel and buzzed them in.

"We're heading up to see Vida Abucayan."

"I'm sorry, but Ms. Abucayan is not at home."

"I was supposed to meet her in Angeles City, but she

never arrived. I tried calling, but she never answered. So I'm a little worried."

The clerk hesitated, considering Steel over the top of his thick glasses. "She was here earlier but left around six p.m."

"Did she say where she was going?"

"No."

"She took her car?"

He hesitated again. "No, she got into Colonel Devincia's car."

"Devincia?" Gut-punched. Steel leaned over the clerk's desk.

The clerk took two steps backwards. "Yes, her fiancée, Colonel Devincia."

"Fuck," Steel slammed his hand on the counter, and the clerk backed against the mail cubbies.

Jo Jo grabbed Steel's arm. "Come on, William, let's go. It is no good. Rosa said a man answered the phone at Vida's. It must have been Devincia."

"Fucking bastard!" Steel growled. He pulled away from Jo Jo's grasp and stormed out of the lobby.

12

Manila
Miramar Hotel
Saturday, 30 November 1985

HOBBS AND WHALE SAT ACROSS from each other at a folding banquet table covered with a stained white cloth and littered with maps, papers, food containers, cups, glass bottles, and plates of half-eaten food. Singlaub's treasure operation was now headquartered in the storied Miramar Hotel on Roxas Boulevard, just blocks away from the U.S. Embassy.

Hobbs' mind was racing. He scanned the notes he had put together to brief the colonel when he arrived for the 0900 morning meeting. Hobbs lifted his eyes from the file and glanced at Whale, who was smoking a cigarette and drinking Thai-style milky coffee from a big glass, oblivious to the brown liquid dripping down his chin and onto his T-shirt. He was deep into a folder full of newspaper and magazine articles that Hobbs had handed him to read. Next to Whale, three black telephones competed for space with piles of paper. The extra phone lines, which the hotel manager had said would be impossible to acquire, had miraculously appeared, but only after Sergeant Travis "Gunny" Dixon, United States Marine

Corp, retired, the group's logistics chief, had threatened to drop the manager off the room's fifth-floor balcony.

In the background, the ancient air conditioner, set to its lowest setting, clanked and blasted cold air, which slowly circulated through the thick clouds of cigarette smoke. Dozens of guide and phone books lay on the floor. On one wall, the team had tacked a collage of maps, photos, several pairs of women's underpants, and a black bra.

Next to the board sat a Filipino-American ex-U.S. Navy Criminal Investigative Service enlisted technician, with a shoulder holster, reviewing recordings of Steel's home telephone conversations through round black headphones. The sailor moaned and muttered aloud about being bored out of his mind listening to Steel's housekeeper droning on in Tagalog to her sister in Manila.

Hobbs checked his watch then stared at Whale reading documents in a file folder splayed out on the table. A lady pal of Hobbs had assembled the file the navy man was immersed in. She worked in the National Library of Thailand, and he had used her on previous jobs. She was a thorough researcher and fucked like a rabbit—both worthy attributes. The file overflowed with information on the Japanese WWII treasure reportedly hidden in the Philippines, the sort of information Singlaub liked to keep from grunts like him and Whale. No one had told them there could be billions of dollars worth of treasure in those caves. Vaults and vaults of the stuff.

Hobbs stared at Steel's photo on the wall. Police sources in Bangkok had reported that Steel and the Thai officer Cham had met with a major player in Thailand's black-market underworld. They were probably trying to arrange fencing the loot. Hobbs chewed on his pencil and obsessed on the amount of money at stake. Enough so that Steel needed a false passport. He should have realized how big this fish was, with a powerbroker like Singlaub holding the rod. Hobbs was mad. Mad at the pittance he and Whale were getting paid . . . peanuts . . . chump change.

Whale leaned across the table, his belly smashing the file lying in front of him, and whispered, "Damn, this ain't what I imagined when the big hoss boss said treasure."

"Damn straight," said Hobbs.

"Colonel Harkins in line for the big bucks?" said Whale his mouth opened wide, eyes even wider.

"Naah, he's a foot soldier like us. The big money's going higher."

"Singlaub?" asked Whale.

"I bet even higher."

"Shit." Whale whistled low.

"We don't have to worry about all those zeros . . . Just one-tenth of one-tenth," Hobbs nodded.

Whale pushed in close to Hobbs. "We just want the leftovers running down the ass crack, divide that by two."

Hobbs pushed his chair backwards trying not to ponder Whale's math too long. "That would certainly be enough to set us up for life and not have to do this shit work anymore."

"One briefcase of gold could get me my White Whale."

"Say what?" said Hobbs.

"The name of the bar I'm gonna open. The White Whale."

"I like it."

Whale nodded and kept on shuffling the pages in the thick folder.

Harkins entered the room.

"Morning, gentlemen." Harkins glanced at Whale. "Whale, I see you failed to bring any clean laundry with you from that whorehouse you live in in Bangkok."

"Sir, I'm hurt. I picked out this new outfit especially for you," said Whale.

Harkins smirked, sat down next to Hobbs, grabbed a pack of cigarettes, and lit one. "Saw the note you slipped under my door. You find something?"

"Yes, sir." Hobbs pulled a stapled set of papers from his bag. Whale caught Hobbs' eye and nudged a phone book on top of Hobbs' folder full of independent research.

"Colonel, as you can see from our report, we had Steel tailed in Bangkok, where he stayed for two days," said Hobbs. "My sources report he and his Thai associate had a meeting with a prominent female Thai national in the underworld black market . . . They might have been discussing fencing options for treasure Steel found."

Hobbs paused and let Harkins flip through the report.

Hobbs continued. "Steel visited with a Thai military acquaintance of his, a military intelligence officer, Royal Thailand Air Force Flight Lieutenant. Chamlong Srimuang." Hobbs pronounced the Thai names precisely. "Steel has met the lieutenant on numerous occasions at Clark, both professional and personal occasions."

"Queer," said Whale, the word masked with a cough.

Harkins shot Whale a look. "You say something?"

Hobbs exhaled and said. "Yes, sir. Whale is noting that Lieutenant Chamlong Srimuang is a homosexual, who lives with his boyfriend."

"You think Steel's queer?" Harkins held out his hand and waggled it back and forth.

"Negative. I think he's straight. But nothing about the captain would surprise me. My sources tell me the Thai lieutenant is well connected in the military, and his family is in the gem business big time, boo-coup money there. Maybe this Srimuang guy is Steel's contact with the underworld."

"Damn good find. The boss will be pleased we're getting something out of the expenses you boys are running up." He took a long drag of his cigarette and a swig of coffee. "I had word from him. In addition to Steel, we're going to get involved with an operation near Manila. We have an area where target treasure objects might be located, and we're going to organize a local national civilian engineering outfit to do some digging in the dirt. If the Phil government gets wind of it, we get shutdown. We're mostly excavating in the evening, supposedly building a new house for an expat American. Whale, you're that expat. Hobbs, you'll be running the show from here."

"Sir, we're thin now on manning," said Hobbs.

"I know. We're in the process of rectifying that—have more bodies in the pipeline—especially some linguist types with operational experience for the overall mission. But the boss wants all hands on this one for a couple of weeks. Then back to Steel."

"Yeah, I want to follow him if he goes on another mission in the mountains. He might lead us to an active site. He's not putting his Air Force paycheck in that Bangkok bank," said Hobbs.

"Roger that. Whale just needs to make an appearance as the expat once in a while to tamp down suspicions with the locals," said Harkins. "Once Singlaub leaves town this week, we'll pull his security team and augment with a couple of Major Ross's guys. If we find anything big, we'll need trucks and armed men to get the extracted objects onto the private aircraft we have stationed at the Manila International Airport. And I know. We're headed to an over-extended cluster-fuck logistics nightmare. I'll keep on the boss to not put so many irons in the fire."

"Okay, sir," said Whale, taking a gulp of Thai coffee and resuming reading the treasure file and planning out the décor of his bar.

13

STEEL SLAMMED THE DATSUN INTO third gear. Tears for Fears blasted from the truck's new high-dollar Alpine speakers, purchased with Buddha cash. He had finally heard from her, two days after the party, but the tiny voice on the phone crushed him. Vida's remembered words pounded with the same intensity as the music, and he snarled and rehashed, regurgitated and relived the call. *William, I thought I could love two men—but it is impossible to have two lives. It's not fair to you, or to Antonio. I can't disappoint my family. Antonio is a good man.*

"Fuck Antonio. What about what we have?" Steel said aloud and banged the steering wheel. He veered around a slow-moving jeepney swollen with passengers. *There is so much political change coming to the Philippines, and Antonio is going to be a big part of it. He needs me . . .* "What about my needs?" Steel blurted out. "Blah, blah and fucking blah. Well at least I didn't beg." He nodded, self-satisfied.

He shifted hard into fourth gear, and the Datsun stalled and heaved until he downshifted. It was eight p.m., and he was racing towards the Sampung Bato River Bridge. He had fled the house shortly after the call. He was glad Jo Jo had left earlier to see his honey, Josie the Japanese teacher. Steel didn't want company.

He didn't even know where he was going. He scanned the road ahead. It was a moonless and clear night with a smattering of stars. Except for what his headlights illuminated, the terrain was pitch-black. Steel glanced at the speedometer needle as it danced at 70 mph, and he shifted into fifth gear. A cat-sized rat ran in front of him and into a ditch that paralleled the road.

Steel's attention was drawn to shadows and shapes on the outer reaches of the high beams. Figures emerged: silhouettes of men in the middle of the road, others clumped around a military jeep. In front of it, long, bamboo poles, a crude roadblock. Steel braked and downshifted several times and the truck slowed to a roll. He switched off the radio His eyes flicked from side to side, straining, collecting, and assessing. He flipped off his headlights, and an eerie green illumination from his dashboard lit the cab.

Some of the men ahead were dressed in military or Philippine Constabulary uniforms, others in white T-shirts, camouflaged pants, and baseball caps. They were all armed. Steel flashed to intel reports of NPA cadre pretending to be government forces manning roadblocks or corrupt PC staging checkpoints to shakedown motorists.

Neither scenario was appealing. Steel thought about fleeing. He imagined the sounds of weapons discharging. The machine gun ambush in the jungle a month ago was still fresh in his mind.

Headlights flared in his rearview mirror, and honking shattered the silence as vehicle tires squealed behind him. Steel jerked his head left and watched a jeepney's bouncing lights pass him—the same jeepney he had whipped by moments before. The driver lay on the horn and dazed passengers pushed their faces out of the open sides of the back compartment, gawking. Steel watched the driver brake hard at the bamboo roadblock.

Armed men enveloped the jeepney, like a pack of hungry hyenas. Anger superseded Steel's anxiety and fear. He wasn't paying bribes to scumbag cops or dying at the hands of a Communist hit squad. Not tonight. He stomped the gas pedal and shifted quickly into first gear, jerking the steering wheel right. He aimed for the grass berm on the side of the road, hoping he didn't hit a ditch. The truck bounced over a foot-deep depression, and he jolted hard into a three-sixty turn which jumped him back onto the road. He flipped on the headlights and checked six. The side and rearview mirrors reflected popping flashes of light, and the distinctive crack of rifle fire rose above the whine of the Datsun engine. Rounds burned by him at the speed of sound; one pinged off metal.

Steel hunkered down in the seat and watched the muzzle flashes in his rearview mirror. Were they PC or NPA shooters? He had no idea.

Forty-four-year-old NPA Commander Abraham Rojas stood and watched the small truck skid down the road. Rojas grinned. It was funny that its occupant, likely an Americano, had a dedicated NPA team to thank for saving his sorry Imperialist life. Rojas wasn't concerned about the vehicle. He and his squad's target were the five corrupt PC cops manning the roadblock. And they'd nailed all five as they were distracted firing at the vehicle.

Rojas was older, by more than twenty years, than all the members of his sixteen-man squad. He was short and thin and full of revolutionary fervor. Dressed in camouflaged pants and shirt and a green Mao hat emblazoned with a red star, he carried, like a bible, the Chairman's Little Red Book.

Rojas scanned the road in both directions: still no headlights.

He called for everyone to advance. The jeepney that the cops had stopped had fled as the first shots were fired, just like that little truck—which he presumed was filled with Americanos. There were some in the party who wanted to kill every Yankee Imperialist who frequented this busy road leading to and from the base. Rojas argued that killing Americanos in a town that depended upon U.S. dollars was counterproductive. How stupid the Party was. They collected revolutionary taxes from local businesses, and those businesses were fat with American dollars. But when NPA killed Americans, they shut their bases. Local businesses suffered, and the Party leaders complained that their tax revenue vanished. He shook his head.

Rojas walked over and, with the barrel of his M1 Garand, prodded the dead cop spread-eagle on the concrete, a baseball cap tipped jauntily on his head. His smashed glasses hung cockeyed across a face frozen in a grimace. Rojas smiled when he saw the large bullet hole in the center of the man's chest. He had fired the shot with the M1 his father had used against Japanese soldiers in WWII. The Garand wasn't sexy or stylish, like an M16, but he liked the M1's accuracy and powerful .30-06 round. It could shoot through clumps of trees or a concrete block wall.

Rojas reached down, and removed the cop's .45-caliber pistol, cleared it, and Rojas shoved it into his waistband. He twisted his head and watched Comrade Lim strip another dead cop of his web belt and pistol holster. That cop had half his face blown off. His fatigue jacket was ripped open and his tight white T-shirt bunched, exposing his fat stomach.

Rojas's hatred towards the Philippine police and military burned in him, but it hadn't always been so. The hardened commander had once taught high school in the mountains north of Angeles in a small village east of Baguio City. It was a simple and satisfying life. He and his wife and son had lived with his parents in his boyhood home. He had tended a large garden and raised some pigs.

The problems had begun when a foreign national company had, with the help of corrupt local politicians, the military, and police goons, acquired mining rights on some small farms. The landholders protested, and the Communists joined with them, rushing in armed NPA cadre. It wasn't long before there were violent confrontations, culminating in an NPA ambush on a military convoy. Ten soldiers were killed, and twelve were wounded.

Rojas had remained on the sidelines, thankful his family property was outside the areas in dispute. Then one day Philippine Constabulary troops entered his school and forcibly removed four students, among them his boy, Arvin. A week later, the village priest had informed Rojas that the body of his son and the other boys were at the funeral home. They had been shot trying to escape. Arvin's corpse had shown signs of torture. Something in Rojas had died that day. He joined the guerrillas and quickly impressed them with his methodical planning and killing prowess.

Flickering shadows in the dim-light beams of the PC jeep drew Rojas' attention back to the present. His men were ransacking the bodies of the dead cops. With additional weapons, he could add more cadres to his squad. His men were professional. They wore matching uniforms and were respectful of the people. As Chairman Mao says: "The guerrilla must move amongst the people as a fish swims in the sea." Rojas was proud of them. Some, like him, were motivated by justice. Others, mostly young men, were bored or without jobs. He didn't question their reasons for joining the fight. He worked them hard. The greedy, drunken cops were no match.

Rojas saw headlights approaching in the distance and called out, "Comrades, tayo na, tayo na, let's go." He surveyed the carnage one more time, motioned to his men, and together they disappeared in the night.

Steel downshifted, slowed, and chunked into a rut large enough to envelop a small car. Perimeter Road was always a congested, gravel-covered mess. Fortunately, it was the dry season. When it rained, it was even worse. Steel drove past the Flying Machine. He hadn't been to the bar in months, though it had once been a favorite haunt. He was tempted to pull in, but didn't. He knew too many folks who were likely to be there. Tonight he wanted anonymity. A smaller place, dark with a decent pool table and plenty of cold San Miguel.

Traffic crawled, and Steel had time to scan the jumble of stores across the road from the concrete and chain-link fence that protected Clark from gritty Angeles. Their wares spilled onto the sidewalk, souvenirs for TDY servicemen for the most part: salad bowls, cups, plates, statues of rice gods, carabao, water-buffalo, and three-foot nude women carved out of dark, rich monkey pod wood. Shiny capiz shells adorned lamps, vases, and jewelry boxes. A line of three-foot-long capiz mobiles fluttered in the slight breeze. Clusters of rickety stalls displayed flimsy clothes and T-shirts. Some sported slogans, like "I love the P.I." Others bore perverted images, like Lucy giving Charlie Brown a blow job. Art studio windows showed off idyllic landscapes and oil portraits of U.S. servicemen and their families.

Duran Duran's "A View to a Kill," the theme song for latest Bond movie, kept Steel company as he bumped and banged his way past the base's gate into a part of town crammed with bars: places with names like Vampire, Superhead, and Little Brown Fucking Machine. He turned onto a dark side street in the hope of cutting over to Macarthur Avenue. He turned again into a dimly lit, and seemingly vacant, cul-de-sac. An orange neon sign blinked the name Phantom's. Steel downshifted and stopped the Datsun. Phantom's . . . Phantom's. He cracked a smile as he recalled how he knew it. His pal Rand, a USAF HUMINT guy and font of all information bar-related, had given him the lowdown on the place.

As Rand had described it, Phantom's suited Steel's mood: dark. Statues of Greek gods loomed over a well-manicured courtyard in front of the parking lot. Steel switched off the truck and hopped out. An ancient private security guard greeted him.

"Evening." Steel checked the truck door to make sure it was locked. "Which way, Pops?"

The guard turned and marched towards the building. He rang a door buzzer mounted on a carved door and, after a minute of uncomfortable silence, ushered Steel in.

Purple lighting shot through clouds of white smoke, and the theme from *The Exorcist* rumbled from hidden speakers. A herd of lingerie-clad women in theatrical white paint death masks surrounded Steel and hustled him to an alcove with small tables. They pawed and manhandled him into one of the plush chairs, and all but one of the girls left. She asked him for his drink order.

"A cold beer," Steel said. He reached into his jean's pocket for his cigarettes. He hadn't smoked in a long time, but he had brought them tonight. He pulled out his lighter and examined the inscription: *Keep safe and come home to me my darling Edward. Love Beth.* He clicked the top open, spun the wheel with his thumb, and watched the flame. He lit the cigarette and inhaled. Fuck you, Vida.

Steel downed the first four beers rapidly, and then moved to rum shots. Dozens of other Americans and some Filipinos arrived and were accosted and seated by the ghouls. He chatted with a steady rotation of vampire girls, each of whom would sit with him until she saw he wasn't interested in going to a pleasure room.

Steel downed another rum shot and watched the latest vampire girl sashay off toward what looked like a couple of military guys. Maybe they were unlucky in love too. He thought about buying them a beer, when he felt a hand on his shoulder. He turned his head into a black satin bustier barely harnessing the largest rack of Filipina tits he'd ever seen. She introduced herself as Snooky. Steel agreed to buy her a drink and, in a rookie move explained only by all the rum he had consumed, pulled out a wad of cash, fumbled through it, and handed the waitress a 100 pesos bill. Snooky and he conversed in Tagalog, and he bought her several more drinks before excusing himself to hit the comfort room. When he returned, he found two enormous rums sitting on the tabled: a gift from her. Pleased, he buried one, and she, the other.

Snooky took his hand and guided him to an area partitioned off from the main bar by Japanese screens. She removed his shoes, socks, and shirt and settled him into a rattan chair facing the center of the room. Still standing, she stripped off her bustier and pushed her breasts into his face. With one hand, she unzipped his fly, reached inside, and stroked him. He inhaled her musk and pulled her into him. When she backed up, he was elated to see two more naked women had joined the party. They squirted each other with baby oil, and Snooky pulled her panties off and dove into what turned into a sort of rugby scrum of kissing, fondling, and moaning. It was the sexiest thing Steel had ever seen. He struggled to remove his own pants.

Snooky peeked her head out from the flesh pile and snuck a glance at Steel, gauging his mental state. This guy was stronger than most of the rubes. The ground animal tranquilizer she used should have kicked in by now. She visualized the mark's wad of cash and speculated how much money he had and was considering halting the show for a minute to get him another doctored drink, when a dazed bouncer crashed through the thin rice-paper wall and hit the floor feet from Steel. She gasped and the other girls screamed and grabbed for their clothes, slipping and sliding as they tried to gain traction on the well-oiled mat. The world around her flicked by in slow motion and she wondered if she had inadvertently drank the drug laced drink. She watched Steel stand, his naked body glistening with baby oil, and with his pants around his ankles, he staggered after the slippery bar girls. She clutched her bare breasts between crossed arms and joined the fleeing herd.

Some say the beer Red Horse is a hallucinogenic, though it is more likely that the intense buzz it offers is the product of its high alcohol content and an arm's-length list of probably-toxic chemical additives. Whatever the precise medical explanation, it was certainly the gallon or so of Red Horse he had consumed that led Mongo, a normally gentle giant of a man, a senior airman TDY from his civil engineering squadron on Osan Air Base, to believe that the Filipina hostesses were demons trying to steal his soul. And it was certainly that belief that led to the melee that ended with Mongo pitching the bar's bouncer into Steel's private peep show.

From her perch behind the bar, Gabby, its fifty-nine-year-old Filipina manager, looked on in horror as the gargantuan Mongo fought her staff. Gabby, while a brilliant accountant, normally let the owner deal with a crisis like this one, but he was back home in Melbourne. When she saw Ricardo, her most dependable bouncer, break a pool cue over the head of the Americano Goliath, and the Goliath chuck Ricardo through the sliding door, she knew it was time for reinforcements. She picked up the phone and called for the Americano cops.

USAF security policeman and Senior Airman Stephen "Stevie" Wonder, five foot six -and barely one-hundred twenty pounds, a streetwise, fast-talking brother from New York City, picked up the call. He relayed the directions to Phantom's to his partner and driver of their camouflaged Humvee, Rondell Jackson, six foot six and two hundred eighty-nine pounds, a farm boy from Sweetwater, Georgia. His family had farmed their land for generations, first as slaves and then as proud stakeholders.

The two SPs were greeted at the club by a disheveled and hysterical old security guard. Wonder gripped his baby M16 and kicked open his vehicle door, leading the way with the barrel of his weapon. He glanced around at the dark shrubbery and shadows. Rondell extracted himself from his side of the Humvee. The M16 looked like a toy in his hands. He wasn't nervous as much as he was bored. There was no sport in confronting rowdy GI's. Most folded without a fight when confronted by him. He was proud of his size and strength, but ferrying drunk airmen to jail wasn't a satisfying use of his assets.

Rondell had to reassess when they entered the bar and saw the massive man backed up against the wall, swatting with a broken pool cue at four relatively diminutive locals, who in turn were poking at him with broom handles. Reminded Rondell of a black-and-white Frankenstein movie he had seen as a kid.

Wonder, his weapon at port arms, leaned toward Rondell and said, "Thank Jesus you're the black Incredible Hulk."

Rondell smiled, handed his helmet and his rifle to Wonder, and unsheathed his nightstick. Finally, a worthy opponent.

"What the hell you doing?" Wonder yelled, struggling with the extra equipment.

Rondell ignored Wonder and surged forward, imagining a rhino-skin shield in his empty hand.

"Shit, he's gone Zulu again," muttered Wonder.

After an epic struggle, Rondell's nightstick landed a solid hit right between Mongo's spinning eyes, and the giant crumpled, out cold. Rondell put a size 14 black boot firmly on the beast's back.

"People, some room please," Wonder said into the crowd of staff and patrons who had gathered for the fight. "Damn Rondell, well played. That cracker—I mean suspect—was crazy."

Rondell cuffed Mongo and sent Wonder to the bar for a glass of water to splash on the guy. They weren't going to be able to move him if they couldn't wake him up.

"Rondell, over here. We got another one."

Rondell walked over to a huddle of waitresses and Americans near the bar. In the center, Wonder crouched next to a half-naked patron, another TDY airman by the looks of it, splayed on the floor.

"I've met him at Curtis Washington's parties," said Wonder. "He's an officer in Curtis's unit."

"You should call Curtis and see if he wants to pick him up," said Rondell. Those parties were nice. Maybe they'd get a few more invites if they saved Curtis's sorry-assed buddy. He was one lucky drunk. Most cops Rondell knew would have loved to haul in an officer.

"Cap. Cap Steel! Wake up." Curtis softly slapped Steel's face. "Don't be passing out on me again. I ain't lugging your ass inside your gate." Steel's eyes fluttered and he acknowledged Curtis's presence with a blink and a smile, then leaned out the cab of the trike taxi and puked. Much later, he had a vague memory of Curtis, Jo Jo, and Rosa maneuvering him into his house.

Steel opened his eyes, then blinked like a spastic. Bright light flooded his optical nerves. The ceiling fan rotated above, and his head spun throbbing in time. After a few seconds, he figured out he was in his bed. He shifted his focus right, and forms appeared. One was Rosa, arms folded across her chest, dressed in her starched white maid's smock. Like an angel of No-Mercy—Whatsoever. Then Jo Jo's compact frame. The third had a wooden cross hanging from its neck. This one gently laid a hand on Steel's arm. Steel knew he was in trouble: either it was Jesus, or Father Rudy had been called in.

Steel sat propped in bed. The clock radio read two p.m. Most of the dizziness had subsided, but the three-inch gash on the side of his head throbbed as did the swollen middle finger on his right hand.

"Quite a night you had." Jo Jo lifted the ice bag off Steel's hand. "Father Rudy thinks the laceration to your head isn't too serious, but the finger is broken. He said we should take you in and have it looked at." He shoved the pack back in place.

"Ow. Shit. Watch the finger. And yeah, it was quite a night," said Steel. "It's Sunday right? I was drunk—but it wasn't like I had a million beers or anything. I might have had some rum?"

"You had rum all right. A special rum. Or so the cops who found you thought. They're Curtis's friends. They said there have been reports of GI.'s being drugged and robbed there."

"Drugged. Wow, that makes total sense," said Steel, leaning forward. "I felt like I was on LSD. Shit. There was this chick. She had the biggest tits I've ever seen. She—"

"You were totally out of your mind last night when Curtis brought you home," Jo Jo said.

"I owe him big time. Fuck, where's the truck?" Steel jerked his head and tried to look out his bedroom window.

"I went to Phantom's this morning and got it."

"I owe you too."

"You don't owe me anything. But you owe it to yourself to quit this destructive behavior."

"Destructive behavior? What are you talking about? I was just upset about the Vida crap and needed to get drunk."

"Did you know there are bullet holes in the truck? A round hit the tailgate and ricocheted through the side of the bed near the gas tank. It looks like someone took a shot at you. Another two feet and the round would have penetrated the cab."

"I forgot about that. There was this roadblock. Someone shot at me."

"Roadblock?"

"PC roadblock. Or NPA." Steel scratched his head.

"How about both. The paper this morning said there was a NPA hit on a PC roadblock near Carmenville. Five cops were killed."

"Holy fuck!"

"Language please," said Rosa, entering the room with Father Rudy in tow.

"William, can we talk?" Father Rudy sat edge of the bed. "In private," Rosa and Jo Jo nodded at the priest and exited. "I think some thanks to God's good grace are in order."

Steel sighed and slumped back in bed.

14

STEEL LET HIS METAL GATE clunk shut behind him. His tennis shoes scuffed in the street dust. It was hot. Stifling. A whiff of burning garbage lingered in the air. A busy Friday night. New York Avenue was alive with vehicles and people. Eight p.m. Steel headed to the Red Baron, two blocks away.

It was one week ago he had been shot at and drugged. Steel wrote it off as a mere distraction from his problems with Vida. Jo Jo, however, wouldn't let it go. He had left in a huff to stay at his girlfriend's house. Good Riddance. All he did was lecture. *William-san you need to get yourself together* . . . bitch . . . bitch.

At work Steel had at first tried to hide his injuries, and when that didn't work, he had told folks it was from a gardening accident. He didn't mention the NPA attack. Curtis had covered for him, but like Jo Jo, the sergeant felt the need to counsel. Even the general had cornered Steel after a security brief to lay on the fatherly concern. Steel had given him the same story, but he squirmed at lying to his mentor.

Steel headed down a dinky, dark alley sandwiched between two houses, the short cut to the club. He was looking forward to numbing himself with beer and a few mindless games of pool. Rosa was off for two days, so no morning stink eye should he decide to bring home a hot dancer. He really needed to get laid. Fuck Vida. His new mantra.

Two headlights lit up the alley, and a car pulled up tight behind him. The engine rumbled low and tires crunched gravel. There was barely room for foot traffic in the alley, let alone a vehicle. Steel glanced over his shoulder. Two guys in the front seat. He picked up his pace. The car continued to roll behind, right on his ass. He kept his cool. Only thirty feet of alley left before the front door. A metal door chunked opened. Before Steel could turn his head, a hand grabbed his shoulder. "Captain Steel, we don't want to create a scene. Just stop walking. We are government soldiers. My boss—"

Steel bolted forward. Never get in the vehicle, the odds are stacked against you if you get in the vehicle. He made it four steps before two bodies piled onto his back. He landed hard on his good hand and shielded his crushed finger on the other side. He tasted blood and felt the metal barrel of a pistol press to the back of his head.

"Don't be stupid asshole, and you won't get hurt," the man spit out the words in Filipino-accented English.

Steel could smell garlic and coffee on the man's breath. A set of strong arms propelled Steel into the backseat of the Honda. Two dense bodies sandwiched him in. Tight civilian clothes and shaved heads. They looked rough, but military. Not NPA. Which was a relief.

"What the fuck's this about?" Steel thrashed his arms until the man on his right grabbed the bandaged finger. Lightning pain stopped Steel cold. The thug put a cloth bag on Steel's head. He tried to figure out where they were headed, but couldn't reason past the pain in his finger. The vehicle stopped, and the engine switched off. Unseen hands guided Steel inside something air-conditioned.

Someone tugged off his hood, and Steel gulped in a lung full of air, cool but tasting of mold and rot. His eyes adjusted. Crimson wallpaper, Spanish bullfighter paintings, and dirty green carpet. A typical Angeles hotel. He'd probably been here with some bargirl. Across from him on a faux leather couch sat a man he definitely recognized: Lt. Col. Antonio Devincia. Steel's gut tightened, and his teeth automatically clenched. They had history. "Fucking prick," Steel snarled.

"Good to see you too." Devincia smiled and stood. His eyes darted to Steel's bandaged hand, then to his face. "So I see you have been in some kind of accident. I hope nothing too serious. I'm so glad you could join us." He opened his hand to the smelly men who had dragged Steel in, now standing at parade rest to Devincia's left.

"What the fuck's this about, Colonel?"

"Captain Steel, may I call you William?" Devincia said, "I'll get right to the point. You know that Vida and I have worked out the problems between us. I assure you, I am a changed man. I realize I pushed her away. Quite frankly, I was an asshole. I blame my combat years. Long years. It makes one crazy. My men will tell you." He waved a hand towards the thugs. "Sergeant Mendoza, am I not doing better?"

Mendoza was short with arms as long and heavy as a gorilla's. His face was pockmarked, like he'd been hit by grenade fragments, which he probably had. He gazed at Devincia like a loyal hound. "Yes, sir, we have all suffered from too many years fighting."

Devincia closed the gap between himself and Steel. Steel braced for a blow. Devincia whispered, "So you see I am trying to change. And I forgive you for your indiscretion with my woman."

Steel recoiled from the hissing in his ear.

Devincia continued. "I promised her this as part of our reconciliation. You have nothing to fear from me. I would hope we can work together again, find some more treasure." He put a hand on Steel's shoulder and squeezed. Steel considered punching him in the throat. "We'll find a new map. This time I will not be outwitted by those Marcos dogs, but of course . . .

Steel leapt at Devincia. No practiced kuntaw stances or concern for his bandaged finger. He just wanted to choke the life out of the bastard.

It took less than ten minutes for Devincia's henchmen to beat the crap out of Steel and drag him back to the Honda. They drove him to his house and dropped him off. He staggered inside, showered, and collapsed into bed, sure he had a broken nose and fractured ribs. They hadn't touched his ass, which had begun to heal nicely from the wound he sustained in the jungle. That was a benison. He supposed he ought to say a prayer of thanks. Father Rudy would be pleased.

15

Clark Air Base
Sunday, 8 December 1985

STEEL RANG THE DOORBELL AT the sprawling pre-WWII tropical colonial that served as the home of the 13th Air Force commander, trying not to look as damaged as he was. It had been three days since Devincia's men had jumped him, leaving him with two black-eyes, bruises, cuts, and a cracked rib on the left side of his chest—and that was on top of the injuries he had sustained at Phantoms the week before. He had mixed emotions about the visit here tonight. He'd been to the general's for dinner several times since their adventure in the jungle, and he enjoyed meals with the general's wife Becky and their two sons. The home cooking was outstanding, and the whole experience was usually a welcome peek at a domestic life he had never experienced. But tonight he was embarrassed to show his beaten face. And there was no getting out of it. The general's exec, who issued the invite, informed Steel that acceptance was mandatory—a direct order.

The front door opened and a bulky plainclothes USAF security policeman filled the doorway. He had a radio in one hand, and his pistol bulged under his tactical vest. Ronnie and Johnny, the general's twin ten-year-old boys, ran up behind the sergeant, calling Steel's name in unison.

"Boys, let Sergeant Gibson do his job," boomed the general from deep within the house.

Johnny pointed at Steel and laughed. "What happened to your face? You look like a raccoon. What's in the bag?"

The general stood behind his boys, shaking his head.

Steel handed the bag to Johnny as the sergeant stepped back to his post by the door. "There's a Japanese helmet for each of you and a wooden chess set. Your father can show you how to play. Mine showed me how to play."

Johnny put on a rusted helmet. "Is this from the World War, like the other stuff you gave us?"

"Yep. You'll have a big collection by the time you leave the P.I."

"Did you thank Will?" the general said.

"Thank you," they howled and scurried off.

"They are such great kids. I think I was about their age when I learned chess." Steel tried to picture his father's face.

"You've taken another beating since I saw you a week ago," said the general. "We're gonna talk about that after supper."

"Yes, sir," Steel sighed and saluted with his bandaged right hand.

After dinner and the boys' exit for bed, Steel stood with the general on the porch and girded himself for a dressing down. Or maybe he could stall until it was time to leave.

"Wonderful meal, sir. Fried chicken is my favorite. And I can't believe I've never played Uno before," Steel offered.

"Those crazy boys will wear you out. Great idea on the chess set, it'll give me some quiet time with them."

"Yeah I have fond memories playing with my dad."

"Sounds like good memories."

"I find myself trying to keep those alive."

"Steamy tonight." The general grabbed the front of his

loose-fitting shirt with two hands and fanned it, then bent over and pulled out a rumpled pack of cigarettes from his sock. "Becky lets me smoke one after dinner. You want one? If I recall, that was how we first met. Me sneaking off to have a smoke and catching you in the bushes with old Joe, playing cards." He laughed. "I should have marched your ass to jail."

"I remember being locked at attention with a cigarette dangling from my lip. I was scared shitless."

"You shoulda been."

"Wait, sir, I have a present for you—for us." Steel reached into the back pocket of his baggy khaki pants, pulled out a skinny wood box, and opened it. He picked the general out a fat cigar and took one for himself. "A pal of mine, a Phil intel guy, got these Cubans from the Soviet Embassy."

"Real Cubans?" He held his under his nose and smelled it.

"Yes, sir." Steel pulled out a lighter and held out a flame. The general leaned over to accept the light and puffed. "Oh now that's a good smoke—damn Commies make a great cigar."

Steel lit his own cigar, and they smoked in silence for a few moments before the general spoke. "I got word from Sergeant—." The general stopped short of saying Curtis's name. "Anyway, he's worried about you, and judging from your face, I'd say there's good reason."

Fucking Curtis ratted me out, Steel thought. "Yes, sir. It's been a crazy week, first the gardening accident, then I took a beating in a martial arts tournament and—"

The general jammed a finger into Steel's chest, "Enough bullshit, Captain!"

"Yes, sir, I . . . " Steel's voice trailed off, and he stared at his shoes.

"It's time to grow up and be a man. Knock off the booze. You just can't handle it." The general got up in Steel's face. "Look, son, I'm not going to be around here long. I heard there are transfer orders coming my way. Plain and simple, there are folks here at 13th Air Force with sharp knives waiting to gut you." He placed a hand on Steel's shoulder and ushered him to two fat papasan chairs. "Have a seat."

They faced each other. "Let's be honest," the general went on. "You took a big risk when you told me the truth about the treasure a couple of months ago. You know you can be honest with me."

"I know that. You've been there for me, and I've tried to be there for you."

"Damn straight. I owe you my life, and Becky and I are forever grateful. I feel . . . I feel protective of you, for many reasons. I think what my boys' lives would have been had I died out there. They'd have had it like you . . . they could have turned out . . ."

"Fucked up?"

"Well, I wouldn't say that. More like lost souls."

"That's me," Steel said. "Dad MIA."

"I think of my academy roomie Robbie all the time. December, 1968, his F-4 disappeared somewhere near the Cambodian border. His body and his back-seater have never been found, not even a hint of a crash site. The thought of him rotting in a remote patch of jungle kills me. Must be even worse for you, it being your dad and all." The general took a drag on the cigar and blew out a plume.

"Yeah," said Steel.

"So, what's the real story with the ass-whipping you got?

Steel told him about Vida, Phantom's, and Devincia.

The general listened, nodding and occasionally asking questions, for thirty minutes.

"You're not crazy," he said when Steel finished, "You just need to cut out the booze and make a course correction."

"I hope so," Steel said.

"Alcohol was taking over my life at one time too. My mentor ordered me to get counseling. I was drinking to forget Robbie."

"Oh, Jesus."

They spoke for another ten minutes, then the general checked his watch and said, "I have an early start in the morning, but just a couple more things. First off, I got wind from a friend at the Military Personnel Center that my new assignment has been decided: it's the Pentagon. I'll stay here only as long as it takes to finish up business and help my replacement take over."

"Oh no." Steel stood.

"I'll probably retire after my next assignment. I'm ready for something different. But I promise you, I'll keep poking around looking at the POW/MIA files and listening for whispers and rumors about your dad and my roomie. I got a letter from my friend Eugene Tighe. He said he's still rattling cages in DC, trying to keep the POW/MIA issue on the front burner."

Steel nodded. He had read a lot about Lt. Gen Eugene Tighe, the former director of DIA, a fighter on POW/MIA issues. He was quoted in the *Washington Times* in June testifying that Hanoi was still holding fifty to sixty American POWs.

"I met Gene in 1972 when he was director for intelligence, U.S. Pacific Command. I was at Hickam for a couple of years."

"If anyone knows the real truth behind the POW issue, it's him," Steel said.

"We've kept in touch over the years. At Hickam I badgered him to let me look at aerial photos and satellite imagery of possible crash sites for Robbie's F-4. I was relentless then."

"You find anything?"

"Nothing definitive. Just too much jungle, and by 1972, four years' worth of vegetation had regenerated. I needed ground truth, spooks on site."

"The U.S. government has no interest in finding a POW alive nearly two decades after the fact," Steel said. "Shit, if they did, heads would roll, at DOD and all the way up to the White House."

"I'd lead the charge myself, with pitchfork in hand, if they'd been lying to us all these years," the general said. "So that's what I'm doing with my future. What about you? You gonna stay in?"

"For now. The Air Force has been good to me, and I have a home here at Clark."

"I had my aide do some research on the Air Force Reserves. You might want to consider folding the active Air Force and go part-time reserves. I'll have him call you with what he found out."

"Okay."

"One final thing: the Company's new station chief in Manila paid me a courtesy call and asked too many questions about you. I got the feeling that the CIA was not happy with your last encounter."

Several months ago, in front of a meeting packed with PACOM brass, Steel had made some controversial assessments regarding the NPA, which CIA analysts publically ridiculed. When his assessments proved true, the CIA looked none too good.

The general continued, "This new CIA chief reeks of ambition, a real Machiavellian."

Steel stared out the porch screen at the dark shadows of jungle foliage and nodded.

"William, look at me. His type don't mess around."

They talked for ten more minutes before Steel left. He walked back to his truck and tried to check his anger. Everyone was abandoning him. The general. Vida. Jo Jo had even moved out. Who's next, Rosa? Why was it that whenever he got close to the family he always wanted, the main players went MIA. Steel's face throbbed, his ribs ached. The general was right about one thing. Something had to change. Of that Steel was certain.

16

Angeles
Tuesday, 10 December 1985

S TEEL PULLED INTO THE FLYING Machine's parking lot. It was early, and there were plenty of choice spots. He cut the engine and the stereo hissed off in turn. Steel listened to the music rumbling from inside the club, but he couldn't make out the song.

It had been two days since dinner at the general's, but their talk was still on Steel's mind. He was ready to change. He sighed and gritted his teeth. He was willing to change. He closed his eyes tightly and slammed his hands on the steering wheel. But tonight, he needed to get laid.

A blue-uniformed security guard, no doubt paid by the bar, loitered outside the Datsun's dark-tinted driver's side window. The man had a battered Remington shotgun slung over his shoulder; Steel knew the guy wanted a tip for watching Steel's vehicle. Steel kicked open the door, twisted, and winced at the stab of pain in his ribs. He scowled at the guard, an obese, fleshy man in a tight uniform stained with his dinner— probably related to the bar owner somehow. No military bearing, definitely not a vet. Steel locked the truck and ignored the guard's singsong greeting. Steel looked around hoping the place's other security guard, a one-eyed sleazebucket with whom Steel had had run-ins in the past, wasn't around. If one-eye suddenly appeared, Steel wondered how he'd deal with it. The new Steel that is. It would be test of his ability to control his crazy temper—especially since Jo Jo wasn't there. He had become a voice of reason on whom Steel relied. Or should rely. That was part of the plan.

Steel climbed the stairs to the club and slid in. The interior was sporadically lit, but he left his sunglasses on—they nicely hid his black eyes. He paused in the doorway to let his vision adjust.

ZZ Top attacked him from towering speakers stacked next to a wall-sized projection TV screen. There, a long-legged woman strutted while the bearded boys from Texas wailed on shiny guitars. On a small stage next to the bar, two bikini-clad Filipinas, both short with big asses and tiny tits, struggled to move to the hard-driving riffs. The real dancers, the smoking hot sevens, eights, and maybe a nine, would take the stage for a later shift.

Less than a dozen GIs milled about. Steel had his choice of chairs. He decided on a stool at the end of the bar. A waitress snuggled up beside him and jumped up in his lap. Her pixie haircut framed a pretty face and her jeans shorts and a white tank top, emblazoned with the bar's logo, hung loosely on her boyish figure.

"William, long times no see." She pulled off his sunglasses. "What happened to your face?" She touched his cheek and nose and kissed him on the lips. He had known her for years.

"Yeah, Tessie, been a while. But goddamn, I missed the place." He pulled her close, slid his hands down her back, and grabbed her ass.

"So what happened to your face? Walang pogi na, without handsome now. And where you been? You have a steady girlfriend?"

"Not anymore."

"So you want a beer?" Tessie pushed herself off and waggled her eyebrows.

"Naah." *Stop the booze.* The general's words echoed in his head. Steel exhaled. "A Coke in the bottle. A real cold one. No glass."

She shrugged and walked off.

Steel reached into his jeans pocket and snaked out a crumpled pack of local cigarettes, pulled one out, and lit it. He leaned back and took a long drag.

After a long session of smoking, chatting with the girls, and slugging back Cokes, Steel checked his watch, 9:45 p.m. He'd been there two hours. The place was packed with GIs of every race and description. Ten new girls had taken to the main stage and the two side stages. The drill was, each would gyrate to three songs and then troll the crowd, looking for customers to buy them drinks and, they hoped, pay the 150 pesos, $35 dollar, bar-fine, the price to take them home.

Steel watched the new dancers climb up on the raised stage near him. He locked on the tallest of the girls, the one with the one-piece black swimsuit cut past her navel and short spiky hair, thick eyeliner, and black lipstick. Her well-developed leg muscles accented her high-heeled black boots. Steel thought she owned the Joan Jett, rough punk rock look—definitely different from the usual flouncy bargirl attire–and very sexy. She threw herself into her dance moves with an obvious badass attitude. Steel banged his hands on the bar to the beat. For a few dollars, she could be his for the night, even the weekend. What was he thinking, falling for Vida? He shook his head. This was his world, here inside the Flying Machine. No complications. No emotions. Safe. He watched punk girl dance two more songs, after which she hopped down from the stage and left without a single smile or moment of eye contact. Oh well, her loss, Steel thought.

Tessie plucked at his sleeve and pouted. "So, aren't you going to pay a bar-fine tonight?"

He shrugged.

"What? Too many beautiful women to choose from?" She hopped into his lap again.

Steel slid her tight into his crotch. "What about you?" Steel whispered. "How about it? Take a walk on the wild side?" He already knew the answer, but kissed her ear anyway.

She turned her chocolate eyes to him. "If you only had a pussy." She purred then flicked her tongue and left his lap.

"You cock tease," he whispered. She was specialist who only accepted bar fines from a select group of female GI's and a few dependent wives. She kissed the air and made to leave.

Steel called out, "Hey, you seen Gemma lately?" He had taken Gemma out a few times just prior to meeting Vida.

"No. You know you broke her heart. She waited for you." Her eyes narrowed. "She has a steady bar-fine now, a regular boyfriend. He's a pilot. She doesn't come in during business hours too much. Just now and then to say 'hi.'"

"A fucking pilot," Steel grunted. "He's probably an asshole, but . . . good for her." He gulped at the Coke then slammed it down. "What about that hot chick with the black boots. What's her name?"

Tessie shook her head. "Of course you're attracted to Tetchi. Join the crowd. She is the flavor of the week with your fellow GIs," she gestured around her. "She's only been here a month."

"Put in a good word for me with her. Is she still here?"

"In the dressing room. I doubt she'll talk to you. She's picky."

"Thanks," Steel said. "Have you had her?"

"No. Not that I haven't tried." The eyebrows waggle again. "I'd pay money to see that."

Steel checked his watch. 11:30 p.m. Tetchi had danced again but hadn't stopped by to see him. And none of the other dances took his fancy. He took a swig of Coke and contemplated heading to another bar, one with a pool table. But he'd have to drive across town to a find one that wasn't loaded with novices.

Steel felt a tug at his shirt sleeve and turned, expecting Tessie, but saw Tetchi instead. He grinned like a lottery winner.

"Tessie said you wanted to talk to me. I figured if I waited long enough, you'd leave," she said. She held a black and white batik wrap tight around her shoulders. "So you're buying me a drink?"

"If it isn't wicked Tetchi, the picky, dark, and sexy dancer." He was still grinning. Underneath the extreme eye makeup and spiked hair, there was a pretty woman.

She glared at him.

"I'm Will," he said.

"Is that short for Willy?" She hacked her laugh, the way pack-a-day smokers do.

"William Armand Steel."

She didn't comment on his injuries, which pleased him.

"So William, Buy me a drink, or I'm leaving."

Steel grabbed her arm. It felt taut, "That's the price for your company. Order away."

Like a powerful python, she slid up on the bar, her stomach down, her ass pushing the batik wrap up into a hard mound. She hissed out an order for a Mango daiquiri from the heavy-set and loose-jowled mamasan and bartender.

"Mango daiquiri? I figured you more of a rum woman," said Steel as Tetchi slithered back onto the stool beside him.

"I had figured you for more of a beer kind of man." She frowned at his Coke. "Tessie said you spoke Tagalog. How's that work? Is it a party trick?" She took the orange-colored drink that the mamasan placed on the bar and took a sip.

Steel struggled to make simple chit chat, but there was a hard-edged touch of anger in her. Steel watched her drink disappear quickly.

"You want another one?" Steel asked.

"Sure, but management says I have to tell you they are twenty pesos each, so you aren't shocked when you get the bill."

"No problem."

"Must be nice, no problem. Money's never a problem with you Americanos, is it?" She swiveled away from him.

"You are one angry chick," Steel muttered louder than he meant to.

She twirled back. Her brown eyes smoldered red, and one of her hands twitched. Steel braced for a slap.

"Working here, you're bound to have a bad day."

"Fair enough," Steel said.

"My bad day was not as bad as the one you had," she said. "Who beat you?"

"Touché," Steel said.

Tetchi tapped her glass lightly on the wood bar to the beat of the blaring music. "You go to university? You are obviously more educated than most of the— what's the English word . . . yotals?"

"Yokels."

"Right. Yokels," she said it as if she logged it in.

"Ohio State. BA in English, and I'm going to UP now working on my master's degree. Where'd you go to school?"

"Why? You hiring?"

"Maybe."

"I graduated from UP in dance," she said. "There aren't many legitimate jobs for a trained dancer. I've been trying to get work overseas. Working in Madrid has always been a dream."

Steel stared at her face. Great, the disgruntled yet highly

intelligent dancer trying to eke out a living here as a bargirl. Just my luck. I'm always attracted to the good-looking smart ones. He had just wanted to get laid.

"So you're trying to get a job overseas," he said and shut his eyes. This wasn't the first time he'd heard a bargirl fantasy.

"There's plenty of work shaking my naked ass here, and overseas. I'm just not going to travel a thousand miles to some foreign country to get exploited, enslaved . . . maybe raped. I'll sell my soul here for a while and wait for the right job."

Steel slowly shook his head, "Jesus Christ, you gotta meet Jo Jo."

"Who?"

"A pal."

She picked up her drink and finished the last gulp, "Let me have a cigarette."

"How do you know I smoke?"

"I saw you smoking earlier."

"So you were checking me out."

"Don't flatter yourself. You're not that handsome. I watch people while I'm dancing," she said in Tagalog.

"I'm aware I'm not that handsome. You still want another drink? And yes, I'm aware of management policies on bar drinks." He pulled out his cigarettes, fished one out and placed it in her black-painted lips. Just the briefest touch of her mouth made him hard.

"So you can speak Tagalog more than a trained monkey."

"I feel like a monkey some days."

She laughed.

"Tetchi," the mamasan called out. "You're up next."

"Time flies when you're having fun. If you're still around when I'm done, I'll take that drink." She dragged on the cigarette, gently stubbed it out, and placed it in the top of her boot.

Steel liked that she saved the smoke. He pulled another one out and lit it. He wasn't going anywhere.

The strobes that illuminated Tetchi made her athletic twists and turns even more sexy, so much so that Steel almost didn't notice the other thing they illuminated: Jo Jo, sitting on the stool next to Steel.

"Brother, good to see you," Steel rested his bandaged hand on Jo Jo's shoulder.

"You doing okay, William-san? When I got home Rosa said you had gone out. I figured I'd find you here."

"No worries, mate," Steel said in a bad Australian accent and took a swig of his drink.

"Coke?" said Jo Jo.

"Yep."

"That's a good thing. Hopefully the beatings did you some good."

"Tessie, a drink for my wise and ancient father." Steel grabbed Tessie's arm as she cruised by.

"Jo Jo, long time, no see." She got up on her toes and kissed Jo Jo on the cheek.

"Coke," Jo Jo said and reached over, grabbed Steel's cigarette pack, and banged out a stick. "We can't stop all our vices cold, diba?"

"Amen to that brother." Steel raised his smoke.

They watched Tetchi in silence until she finished her set. She climbed down from the stage and came straight to Steel. Jo Jo raised his left eyebrow.

"Tetchi, this is my good friend Jo Jo."

Jo Jo jumped off the barstool. He was a head shorter than her. "Nice to meet you." He offered his seat to her. "Maganda, beautiful." Jo Jo lifted her hand and kissed it and turned to walk off.

"Don't leave without me," Steel called after Jo Jo. "I'm not staying out late."

"Good. I have a big workout planned for us tomorrow afternoon," he answered.

"I can't. I'm convalescing," Steel said.

"Nice try. I'll modify it some." Jo Jo turned and headed into the milling crowd of GIs.

"You ready for that drink?" Steel said to Tetchi, who was wiping sweat from between her breasts with a sodden cocktail napkin.

"Yeah," she said.

They chatted until it was her turn to dance again.

Steel stood first, "Can I see you again?"

She slid off the stool. "Unless I get a contract in Madrid, you'll know where you can find me. Dancing and getting rich Americanos to buy me drinks."

"No bar-fines?"

"I didn't say that."

"Tessie said you were picky."

"I'm talking to you?"

"It's been nice," Steel said, "talking."

She walked away and, without looking back, raised her hand. "I'll see you soon."

It was a safe bet. He watched her batik wrap ebb and flow against her hard body until she was enveloped by the sea of GIs. Steel exhaled and pushed through the crowd to find Jo Jo.

17

J O JO DROPPED STEEL OFF in front of the U.S. Embassy's main gate and drove the truck over to the shady flame trees across the street to wait. The intense morning sun amplified the trees' orange flowers. Steel's gut churned with anxiety over the terse summons from the new CIA station chief. Steel had not forgotten Gen. Smith's warnings concerning the new guy.

Steel's boss, Lt. Col. Kuncker, had tried to protect Steel from this meeting. Not because Kuncker was a Steel fan, but because Major Thimble thought he and Kuncker should be going, not Steel. He heard that Thimble's expletives echoed off the walls of the Intelligence Division. Curtis told Steel that Thimble yelled about how it was a violation of chain of command. And according to the admin sergeant, Kuncker had complained to the 13th Air Force vice-commander, who spoke to the general, who countered with the letter from the CIA chief spook, who had, in bold courier font, requested Steel and Steel alone. The general had scrawled on the bottom of the missive: "Tell Thimble, the station chief outranks me. Captain Steel goes. End of subject."

Yeah, the CIA spooks in Manila loved to play that power trump card, Steel mused. In his long tour at Clark he'd had little interaction with the CIA toads. In fact, relations between the 13th Intelligence Division and the CIA primadonnas had been nonexistent. They had a reputation for being arrogant and aloof—recruiting predominately Ivy League graduates. How these white, male, case officers were supposed to blend in and operate in Third World countries baffled Steel. He imagined the senior case officer in Manila was named Sean O'Leary and had white skin and red hair. Steel's face scrunched into a smirk. Stupid asses believe that O'Leary wouldn't stand out in a Manila bar meeting a clandestine source.

Outside the air-conditioned sanctuary of the truck, the steam of a Manila morning assaulted Steel. A wall of hot exhaust fumes and the foul smell of carbon monoxide belched out from throngs of vehicles, most without catalytic converters. He was glad he wasn't in uniform. Despite the formal call to the meeting, the new station chief had authorized civilian dress. He wondered if he could get away with leaving his sunglasses on. His bandaged nose and blackened eyes made him look like a victim of botched plastic surgery. He tucked his splintered middle finger into his pants pocket.

He marched with stoic determination through the embassy's front gate. He was expecting the worst; pretty sure he wasn't being called in for "attaboys." The CIA was none too happy with the way he had embarrassed them. Ahead of him swung a thick mane of shoulder-length red hair pulled back into a ponytail. The white woman stood out in the sea of Filipinos. Her hair mesmerized him, a game fish watching a flashy lure. Must be Sean O'Leary, he laughed to himself.

Steel quickened his pace, closed in, and sniffed jasmine. It reminded him of the vine, ripe with flowers, growing outside his bedroom window; its fragrance called to mind sleep and sensual pleasures. She wore a conservative dress, loose and comfortable for the tropics, but despite its drape, Steel could tell she was toned, bordering on muscled. The skin on the back of her legs was milky with a smattering of brown freckles. No hint of overexposure to the harsh Philippine sun. She probably hadn't been in country long.

Steel followed her into the embassy and watched her slide some paperwork to a Marine guard standing behind a bulletproof glass window, working the non-visa business line. Steel moved close enough to see her profile. She had delicate Irish features, sharp cheekbones and green eyes hidden behind large black glasses. Those, in combination with the plain dress and neat ponytail, gave her an air of the sexy librarian just waiting to pull out her hair pins and unzip her twin. The Marine shuffled through the documents and examined her blue U.S. passport; she wasn't embassy staff. Business concluded, she marched forward through a security gate and towards the elevators. Steel slid his military I.D. to the guard and wondered who she was.

He walked into the reception area of the station chief's office precisely at 10:00 a.m. A buttoned-up admin type openly stared at Steel's face, smirked, then said, "Captain Steel, I presume."

No, its Dr. fucking Livingston, thought Steel, and nodded once.

The man checked his watch, "Good, right on time. Mr. Diamond is expecting you." He ushered Steel into another office and closed the door behind him. Diamond sat behind a huge mahogany desk flipping through a document. Steel stood at attention—the man's position in the embassy warranted it—and listened to the whisper of the paper as Diamond turned pages.

He put the document down and walked around the desk. He was short and wore round gold-framed glasses. His sandy hair was thinning and his beard was neat, the sort that hid a weak chin. Steel's blood pressure dropped twenty points. The man looked like a chubbier version of Radar O'Reilly, the M.A.S.H admin clerk, not the thug Steel had imagined.

"Captain Steel, thanks for coming on short notice. I'm Jason Diamond." He offered Steel a hand and a limp shake. Diamond's voice twanged with a nasal accent that matched his stature. Jason Diamond had to be his cover. He looked more like a Grover or a Eugene.

Diamond paused for a moment, examining Steel, and had a hard time believing what he'd been told. Supposedly this dork had supposedly outwitted the company's best analytical minds. And what was with the battered face? Without comment, Diamond motioned for Steel to an overstuffed brown leather couch, headed back around his big desk, and had a seat.

Steel noted Diamond's penny loafers, khaki pants, and tucked-in white dress shirt with the sleeves rolled up. Not a typical outfit for a senior embassy person. They usually wore the Filipino Barang Tagalog, a baggy dress shirt, hem out. It probably meant he hadn't been in country long. He resumed reading the file, and Steel thought the chief spook looked taller sitting behind the desk. Maybe he was sitting on phone books.

Diamond peered at Steel over the top of his glasses. "So, Captain Steel, thank you for traveling to Manila to see us."

"No problem, sir." As if I have a fucking choice, Steel thought.

"We have read reports of your recent activity here in the Philippines. We were surprised to see that, despite your unfortunate exploits and the wound you sustained, you are still stationed here. Considering the political repercussions, the fallout from the General Smith flap, we would have thought you would have been assigned elsewhere."

Steel nodded in the affirmative, figuring it best if he kept his yap shut.

"You have maintained the confidence of your command. Congratulations. But you should be aware; things have changed here at the embassy. We are taking quite a different approach with the Philippine government. Without besmirching the CIA leadership you worked with on your last, shall we say, adventure, let's just say we'll be taking a firmer lead collecting intelligence in country. I am, as you know, the eyes and ears of the Director of the Central Intelligence Agency here in the Philippines. I take that role very seriously." He placed his hands into a prayer position and stared at the ceiling.

Steel looked up. He couldn't make out any divine presence.

Diamond resumed his lecture. "Unauthorized gallivanting around the Philippines and-or unsanctioned liaisons with officials of the Philippine government and military will not be tolerated. Not even from you, Captain Steel. The ambassador and I are on the same sheet." He looked back at the file and stroked his beard. "Where did you get your fluency in the local language?"

"Books and some private instruction."

"You're also fluent in Negro-toe, mountain tribesman dialect." He didn't sound impressed.

"Yes sir. Negritos have their own language. I speak the Aeta dialect."

"I see here in addition to your duties as an Air Force officer, you have been out searching for Japanese World War II treasure." Diamond continued as if Steel had not spoken. "And you've had the help of Filipino nationals and AFP personnel. Is this sanctioned by your command?"

Steel winced, "No, sir. They don't mind me pursuing my hobby, provided it's my free time, but in no way is it sanctioned."

"Have you found any treasure?" Diamond asked. "I heard

rumor that substantial amounts could have been hidden here in the Philippines by the Japanese Imperial Army and that the source of Marcos's wealth was from the gold."

Steel answered without hesitation, "No, sir, no treasure. Just loads of war souvenirs and such. I found a couple of great Parker pens the other day." He was speaking too quickly. Had the general or Col. Morgan, the base OSI chief, told Diamond that Steel had found a cache? Steel never heard if the OSI had published an official debrief of his report to Gen. Smith.

Diamond marveled at Steel's poker face. Diamond had Morgan's classified report outlining how Steel had found gold. What had been left out of the report was exactly how much gold. Diamond was suspicious of the wording: "Small amounts of gold were found."

Diamond continued, "It does seem this Yamashita treasure legend is more fable than fact." He could lie too. "But then again, maybe some of Marcos's vast wealth could be from Japanese looted treasure. I haven't been here long enough to ascertain the truth. I'm just keeping my mind open to all potential explanations."

"Yes, sir, I'm keeping my mind open too," Steel nodded.

"Well, I've kept you long enough." Diamond pressed a buzzer. The admin clerk reappeared and guided Steel to the door.

"Thanks for coming," Diamond called out. "Morris here will take you to our small operations center. One of my officers wants to sit down with you and pick your brain."

"No problem, sir, nice to have met you," Steel said and thought, later motherfucker.

On the way out, Steel snuck a look at his profile in a large mirror hanging on the wall. He winked at himself—pleased that the dressing-down had been relatively mild and his injuries hadn't been discussed.

Diamond closed the file and walked over to the mirror. He shot an admiring look at his reflection then motioned to the observers behind to join him. In a few minutes, Hennings, Diamond's senior case officer, entered followed by a red-headed looker. Hennings stopped in front of a tall bookcase, his hands folded neatly over his crotch.

Diamond strode past Hennings and held out a hand to the woman. "Nice to meet you Miss Benton. May I call you Anne?"

An electric charge pulsed through her when Diamond addressed her by her cover name. "Anne Benton," she took his outstretched hand. It was limp and sweaty. Yuck. She was glad when he finally let go.

"So sorry for all the mystery surrounding your temporary transfer to us. Hennings will read you into the program and answer some questions after our little chat. Please have a seat." Diamond motioned for her to join him on the small couch.

She sat and he sat close, practically thigh-to-thigh. She tried to scoot over.

"You come highly recommended for our operation." Anne didn't like the leer with which he delivered the line. "The mirror gave you an unfiltered look at Captain Steel. What was your first impression?"

"Not exactly what I would call a polished military officer. I wouldn't have suspected he was military at all. What branch is he?"

"He's an Air Force intelligence officer assigned to the 13th Air Force at Clark Air Base. He is basically an analyst, but, interestingly, possesses freak language skills." He shrugged his shoulders. "William Steel has quite a history here in the

Philippines, not what one would expect out of such a bumpkin. Mr. Hennings will take you back into the skiff and brief you." Diamond waved a hand at Hennings who nodded with the demeanor of a funeral director. Diamond continued, "I just wanted to introduce myself and explain the importance I've placed on your mission here. Mr. Hennings has high hopes for you and your career at the agency. He's told me you are passionate about being a case officer. If your participation in the Steel case works out, I'm sure we can provide an outstanding recommendation for you to attend The Farm." Diamond placed a hand on Benton's leg. She tried not to gag. "I think it's time more women were trained for the world of spy craft. The agency should avail itself of the femme fatale in its work force."

Benton resisted the urge to smash the hand. "Thank you, sir. I won't let you down."

Two hours later, with butterflies churning in her stomach, Benton walked out into the main lobby and waited for Steel. There hadn't been near enough time to familiarize herself with his file and formulate a plan. She was still confused why she had been brought in instead of using a seasoned case officer already at the embassy. She had been with The Company for seven years working as a communications specialist. Two weeks ago, she had been pulled from a desk job at Langley and given a cover name with a corresponding civilian passport and told she was to report to an overseas station for special duties. Even her immediate chain of command at Langley hadn't known what was up. Hennings had met her at the airport in Manila a week ago, put her up in a nice hotel, and told her to lie low and acclimate. Hennings had prepared her a cover as an aid specialist with a nonprofit, fine by her. More than fine—a dream come true. It was strange, but nothing to do with The

Company's operations surprised her anymore. And maybe this was finally her chance for a shot at case officer school.

She glanced around the embassy's large waiting area. Two dozen or so dazed and nervous locals and Americans loitered, waiting to be admitted for official business. Where should she stand? Should she sit and wait? She pulled at the wood barrette in her hair and straightened her dress. Hennings's plan to force a casual encounter with Steel seemed contrived, but he was the boss. And she was eager to please.

She wondered why Diamond had chosen her—creepy letch. It would be a while before she forgot his hand rubbing her thigh. She had heard from a friend at the Manila station that Diamond was a rising star in the agency and a political player with clout, go figure. A slot in the CIA's training facility in Virginia could be hers if she survived his amorous management style.

She took a deep breath and tried to relax. She decided to stand in the open and then switched to leaning against a white wooden post. She wished she had a book to read or maybe a newspaper with a peephole in it. God, what was this—really bad James Bond shit. She stared into space, keeping one eye out for the target.

She'd watched the Air Force captain face Diamond in the office interview. This Steel didn't seem capable of the heroism he had been credited with. And what was with the bandages and black eyes? She couldn't believe Diamond hadn't said a word about it. But his file had a picture of him dressed in jungle fatigues pants and a tight green military issue T-shirt. That guy might have been capable of heroics. He might even be kind of sexy, if you like that type—which she did not. To be honest, there was something intelligent in his eyes she did like. Not in a bedroom sort of way, though. She wasn't sure if she had noticed this before she had read his file jacket. There were his language skills and the treasure hunting. She sighed, without a better plan, and there wasn't time for that, she'd have to revert to flirting to catch his attention. Flirty was not who she was, but she knew she could pull it off.

The elevators opened, and Steel popped out. He popped his sunglass back on and checked his watch—Christ it was half-past noon. Jo Jo had been waiting way too long. He'd take him out for a good lunch. Time with the case officer, Jones, had flown by. He was a decent sort. They had talked about the Communist party, the NPA, and Philippine politics. It was the most facetime he'd had with agency folks since he got in country. They even had him review a couple of unpublished intel cables that were about to be sent out. Maybe everyone had Diamond wrong. Maybe he was open to more cross-pollination between 13th Air Force intel and the embassy. And if that was the case, Steel thought, maybe he could mend bridges with Thimble by getting him and the CIA talking. He had kept mentioning Thimble's name so Jones would remember it, though Jones seemed indifferent. Steel thought he'd wait a few days then contact Jones and see if he'd be willing to host Kuncker and Thimble for a roundtable meeting.

Steel felt a tug on his shirt and turned his head. A pleasant surprise. The redheaded chick from this morning.

"Excuse me. You look like a friendly face. I saw you coming into the embassy this morning."

He looked down, self-conscious about his bandages. "Oh, hi, I remember you."

"Yeah, I'm trying to get a paperwork snafu taken care of. You wouldn't know any of the consular folks would you, or you wouldn't just happen to be one yourself?"

"Nah, sorry, I'm here on business myself. I'm stationed at Clark Air Base."

"Oh, military?"

"Yeah, you?

She laughed. "I'm not the military type."

She had a great laugh and beautiful teeth. "What type are you?"

"Probably the opposite of you. I'm a refugee specialist with a nonprofit. We're working with the Vietnamese camps here in the Philippines."

"Cool. I'm sure that's rewarding."

"I think so. By the way my name is Anne Benton." She extended a hand, and he took it without thinking and jumped when she squeezed the splint.

"Oh sorry, forgot about the finger." He offered her his left hand. "I'm Will Steel."

"You have a good strong name."

"I should have written romance novels. You know with titles like *Five Nights of Passion*, by Will Steel." He used his TV announcer voice.

"I've probably read it. Wow, so what happened, if you don't mind asking?" She glanced at his injuries.

My ex-girlfriend's off-and-on psycho boyfriend, who is a colonel in the AFP and likely a leader in future coups, has these bodyguards who beat the shit out of me. Oh sorry, that was after I was drugged by a big-titted dancer and was whacked with a pool cue. Probably too much detail. "I was in motorcycle accident," he said.

"That'll do it. Those things are always trouble."

"People who haven't red hair don't know what trouble is." Steel said in his official briefing voice.

"Excuse me?" she asked.

"So says Anne of Green Gables. My English advisor, Dr. Burke, had red hair and was fond of quoting *Anne of Green Gables*."

Anne peered intently into his eyes. Steel felt like she was examining his brain.

"You'll find it easier to be bad than good if you have red hair," Steel smiled.

"I'll have to read *Anne of Green Gables*."

"Yeah, you do that. Well, Anne of non-profits, nice meeting you. I've gotta run. My pal has been waiting for me for ages."

"Oh, you live on base?" she said.

"No, off base, in Angeles City," he said, turning to leave.

"I have to travel to Angeles on business sometime. Can I give you call and you can show me around? I'm pretty new in town."

Steel stared at her, taking in the whole package. A beautiful damsel in distress, and he was backing out the door. "Damn." he thought. Vida was still fucking with him. "Sure." He recovered. "Let me give you one of my cards. I'd be honored to show you around my hometown." Steel reached into his pants, fumbling for his wallet with his left hand.

She examined the card. "Captain William A. Steel, 13th Air Force Intelligence Division. Are you a spy?"

"Yeah something like that." He laughed. "More like a glorified research librarian and newscaster."

She gave him a confused look.

"I'll tell you more when we meet up next," he said. "And good luck with the paperwork."

"Thanks. I have a feeling I'm going to need a lot of luck."

Steel nodded, and headed out. He pushed through the people milling around the security checkpoint and walked into the street, ignoring the platoon of vendors who approached, hawking everything from soft drinks and ice cream to newspapers. He scanned the trees and saw Jo Jo sitting on a bench, reading a newspaper. Steel's mind was reeling. He was pleased by the lack of pyrotechnics during his meeting with Diamond; he'd endured far worse at 13th. It was a treat shooting the shit with Bob Jones. And there was Anne Benton. That was probably nothing. He was glad he had played it cool. She probably already trashed his card. He waited for a small gap in the line of cars and buses, sprinted across the boulevard and over to Jo Jo. "Sorry pare, for the long wait. Let's get some lunch, my treat."

Jo Jo stood and stretched. "I'll think of someplace expensive." He made a show of scrutinizing Steel's face and body. "I see no new injuries—how was your morning?" he asked.

"Not as bad as I feared." Steel followed Jo Jo to the truck

18

Angeles
Saturday, 14 December 1985

"THOSE FUCKING BLACK BOOTS," STEEL muttered.

Last night, she had been naked except for the boots when she strode out of his bathroom, her black mask of makeup intact. She had flung herself onto his bed, rolling on top of him, pinning his hands to the sheets. He would have liked to think he lasted a while but knew he hadn't. Steel tapped on the Datsun's steering wheel in tune with Duran Duran. "Damn that's a good song and damn that was wild sex," he said aloud.

Steel had met Tetchi on Tuesday but it took until Friday, last night, for him to get up the nerve to pay her bar-fine. The sex last night was life changing. This morning had been good, too. Afterwards, they had read the paper and drunk several cups of coffee in bed, but she declined breakfast, showered and gathered her things. He had offered to drive her home. She had insisted a taxi would do, took the wad of cash he proffered, stashed it in her purse without counting. Ain't love grand?

He bounced along Perimeter Road, the windows down. The warm air blew in, heavy with the scent of burning garbage, soapy water, feces, and steamed vegetation, but no dry, choking dust. A brief rain shower had weighted it down like a moist blanket. Steel took a deep breath and thought how the smells, when he first arrived in country, had seemed horrid and gut churning. But as time wore on, they had become familiar and reassuring.

A traffic jam of jeepneys hung behind a horse-drawn kalesa teetering with market wares, slowing down traffic to a 19th century village pace. In the distance, Mt. Pinatubo loomed. The rain had rinsed the sky clear of clouds. It was a semi-dormant volcano; it hadn't erupted since 1500 A.D. He finally got around the traffic jam and resumed speed. He lifted open his arm rest, keeping his eyes on the helter-skelter road activity, and fumbled with his bad hand until he felt the smooth plastic of a cassette tape box. He hit the eject button on the unmarked black radio cover, which camouflaged the expensive Alpine system from would-be thieves, and Duran Duran popped out and hung in the air like a black tongue. He slid in a new tape and keyed up U2's, "Bad." A buddy in Japan had sent a bootleg copy of the band's recent appearance at the Live Aid Concert in London.

He was glad he had taken the weekend off from hiking to think. He knew Jo Jo was miffed. He had wanted them to go to the mountains and check on the note he had left for the straggler. Steel told him to give Tony some bucks and have him go look. He'd be there and back in half the time.

Bono's voice filled the cab, and Steel wound his way through the maze of streets to Curtis's place. Steel was going to surprise his friend with two cassette tapes: Herbie Hancock's, "Village Life" and the Manhattan Transfer's, "Vocalese." Steel wasn't a fan, but Curtis was. They were gifts to say thanks for a long week working together on two tasking's, Air Force-speak for projects from on high.

It had been a few days since the meeting with the Manila CIA station chief, Diamond. Steel was surprised when Benton, the redhead he ran into at the embassy, called—in fact they had chatted for hours. She said she was going to be in town and wanted to get together for lunch. Steel had suggested Wednesday noon at the Chili-Pot restaurant. She accepted— good news there; he pictured her ass.

He pulled onto North Dakota Avenue and trailed behind a trike. It sped down the residential street, taking advantage of light Sunday traffic. The driver had "Live and Let Die" painted on his side-cab and a bouncy black mud flap with the Playboy bunny silhouette. Always good to see America's cultural legacy, thought Steel. The trike soon whipped out of sight, its Kawasaki Z 250 engine winding madly, choking out black smoke.

Steel slowed the truck, turned off U2, and perused metal gates looking for Curtis's place, the one with the hand painted sign that said "Washington Slept Here." He found it, flipped off the engine, and jumped out, grabbing the BX bag with the tapes. His ribs and ass still ached, but he was doing better. Felt better. He was putting a plan together to move treasure to Cham in Thailand should they find more. He was getting his life in control — thanks to family, friends, and the general, and possibly Tetchi. Definitely Tetchi. And Benton.

Curtis Washington had lived in his compact two-bedroom house, half of a residential duplex, for two years, and would happily make it three or four if Military Personnel Command approve his extension. Steel peered over the gate to the little house—then to a carport that was hidden by a rolled-down opaque bamboo screen. Behind it was Curtis's baby, a pristine 1980 Chevy Monte Carlo. Buffed dark burgundy exterior, a shiny soft top, windows blacked out, chrome Cragar rims, and a beast of a modified 454-cubic-inch V 8 engine. Steel had been to many parties here, but never during the day. He admired the Chevy for a second, before he fiddled with the gate latch, opened it, and yelled hello. Only the labored rattle and hum of several wall mounted air-conditioners answered. Curtis was not an open window or ceiling fan kind of guy. Curtis's ratty guard dog, Spud, was also nowhere to be seen—a major break in security.

Steel walked around the carport, and Spud started barking inside. Steel called out again, opened the unlocked door on the screened-in lanai, and went in. He knocked on the inner door, which only increased Spud's fury. Steel stared at the door carved with a scene of a man and women dressed in native garb and dancing.

The door cracked open and two Filipina eyes measured Steel. A little wider and he made out the face of Lettie, Curtis's longtime girlfriend. She threw the door open. She was wearing one of Curtis's white tank-tops and not much else. She was a tall, beautiful Visayan girl from Tacloban, Leyte.

"Honey, your friend William is here," she said, wrestling back Spud, a medium-sized, sleek-coated, black mongrel who growled and lunged at Steel.

Curtis appeared in baggy shorts, struggling to put on a blue tank-top T-shirt. "Whoa—Cap S—baby, get Spud outta the way—put him out."

Curtis put a heavy hand on Steel's back and ushered him into a wall of air-conditioning.

"So, Cap, what the hell brings you by this early on Jesus's day?"

"Shouldn't you be in church or something," said Steel.

"I ain't worried. He knows I believe. He's got my back. You want some coffee?"

"Coffee would be great."

Curtis yelled an order for two coffees to Lettie in the kitchen, then said to Steel, "So what brings you here?"

Steel handed him the bag.

"What's this?" He peered inside and pulled out the tapes. He shot Steel a look. "Ain't my birthday."

"Nope just saying thanks for all the help last week. It seems like Thimble was happy with the work."

"Thanks. You didn't have to do that. Let me put Herbie on." He walked over to an expansive rattan entertainment cabinet holding a new 27" Sony Trinitron TV and next to it, stereo components. Curtis flipped on the thick Pioneer receiver then pushed a button on the tape deck. Both units came to life: green lights blinked, glowed, and illuminated better than some aircraft cockpit displays. Curtis jabbed another button and various balance control indicators rose and fell in a pyramid of dashed illuminations. The door eased open, and Curtis exchanged the ejected cassette for the one Steel brought. A few seconds later, smooth jazz flowed from Bose 901 speakers sitting on metal stands in the corners of the living room.

Curtis joined Steel at the round dinette table topped with smoky black glass. "So what else is on your mind?"

"Do I need a reason to visit with you? I do owe you my life and career."

Curtis gave him a sideways look. "But, Cap, to be honest, you seem to attract trouble like flies to shit. And more often than not, you want me in that shit with you."

"We're friends, right? Close friends? So when we're out and about just call me Will, damn it."

"It's too easy to slip up at work, and fucking Thimble would be in my face, like that." Curtis snapped his fingers. "So what's the real reason behind the visit? I remember when you showed up at my home bar out of the blue? What? Four months ago? You said you were going off-reservation." He laughed. "Shit, it wasn't but a week later I'm on a video telecom system getting jacked up by a two-star admiral backed by a full house of cracker-ass officers, no offense."

"None taken."

"So what's up?"

Steel was about to answer when a shriveled old lady glided in, her mummified frame lost in a white blouse and long skirt, and her hands locked behind a hunched back. She was barefoot and skated on coconut husks tied to her feet, humming a happy tune. Steel had routinely seen one of Rosa's nieces performing this type of floor cleaning. The dried fibrous coconut husks produced a high-gloss on wood parquet floors.

Curtis called into the kitchen, "Baby, does Auntie have to do this now?"

Lettie came in with the coffee. "Sorry, honey," she said in English then switched to her native Visayan. "Auntie, wait until our guests have gone to do your work."

The old lady shrugged and glided out.

"There is some milk for your coffee, baby." Lettie put the tray down on the table and left.

Curtis shrugged, "Family."

"Yeah, family."

"I hope I'm skating on coconuts when I'm seventy-five," Curtis said.

"Damn, me too." Steel picked a mug up and poured in a dollop of sweetened condensed milk. "So I have a couple of projects I'm working."

"What kind of projects?" said Curtis.

"Nothing illegal. I need your help putting together a heavy transport vehicle."

"Depends what you're transporting in it whether it makes it illegal or not," said Curtis.

"Putting together a vehicle isn't illegal."

"Your definition of illegal and the man's definition don't square most of the time."

"You won't get in trouble, I promise." Steel placed his hand on his heart.

"I heard that before. I'm still in the dog house with Kuncker."

"Hell, you got a medal and NCO of the quarter. Anyways, it's not illegal, and you can pick up some extra cash. Take Lettie on a vacation somewhere nice. Go to her hometown, Tacloban. It's a wonderful place with great beaches. She'd love that."

"The last time someone offered me money for getting them a car, I almost found myself driving four dudes from a bank heist."

Look, Curtis, you're a car man. Your dad has a garage. I need to build a monster off-road vehicle, and I need you to supervise. You can rebuild an engine, right?"

"Nah, I only ever helped Dad out. He said he didn't want his son getting greased up and messing with vehicles, wanted me to get the education he never had. But I did hang at the garage. I know my way around a vehicle.

"Yeah, your ride is a beast."

"Beast? That lady is as smooth as velvet." He leveled the air with his hand. "You know, when he found out I was talking to those trash brothers who heisted the bank. I thought for sure he was going to take those big hands of his and wring my neck. Instead, he threw me in his '51 Ford and drove me down to the recruiting station. He knew the Air Force recruiter, a customer of his. I had good grades, but I was only seventeen. He signed the papers and the next thing you know I was waving to him from the bus to Lackland AFB."

"He probably saved your life."

"Yeah, the Air Force has done right by me. I made rank fast, finished my high school, and you know I'm finishing my degree. The last time I was home, he had my diploma hung in the garage. Hell, he'll probably build a shrine outta car parts for my college diploma."

"I never knew that. Sounds like he loves you. Family's a good thing," Steel said.

"You don't talk much about your people."

"Yeah, long story." Steel changed the subject. "So what I need is a souped-up off-road vehicle."

"What are you using it for?" said Curtis.

"That's need to know, and you don't. But it's got to be able to haul a heavy load. I already got a mechanic lined up."

"Junior?"

"You know him?"

"It's a small office. I can hear your calls."

"Junior's creative, and he has brothers who are excellent car guys."

"He got a good engine man?" asked Curtis.

Steel nodded. "Here's a list of what I want. See what you can find. Some GI farm boy on base has to have brought over his pickup. We can convert it. We'll make him an offer he can't refuse," Steel said, making a poor attempt at Brando's Don Corleone voice. "If that doesn't pan out we'll have to try the black market or a commercial lot in Manila."

Curtis pointed at the list and whistled. "Off-road tires, heavy-duty suspension lifts, springs, double fuel tanks, and a six-ton load capacity. Six-ton ain't possible," he grimaced and shook his head. "Three at best."

"Cool," Steel said and silently reviewed his calculations. A standard gold bar is seven-by-three inches wide and about an inch thick. A full-size pick-up truck bed will hold a sheet of four-by-eight plywood. He could stack sixteen bars side-by-side, then thirty-two the length of the truck bed or five hundred bars in a layer on the bed. The weight of a standard gold bar is around 400 ounces or 27.5 pounds. A thousand bars would weigh 2,700 pounds, or so. Could he get three or four layers and still have room for equipment and people. He wondered how much an oil drum full of gold or silver coins weighed?

"No way we could we do four or five tons of payload in a pickup?" Steel asked.

"I suppose, if we found a dually—you know, a truck with four tires in the back end we might do four but that would be a stretch—but that would still give you some major capacity."

"I need four-wheel drive for sure," said Steel.

"You gotta lot of needs. For the stash you left in the mountains?"

"I'm not confirming or denying."

"This is going to cost some serious cash."

"I got it."

"I just might know where to find the truck," Curtis said. "Those flight-line maintenance boys from down south or Texas are our best bet."

"Just add your mark-up. I want to pay for your time."

"I ain't cheap." Curtis rubbed his thumb and forefinger together. Steel didn't care. He wanted to give Curtis a share of the cash he got from the Buddha anyway. He'd earned it.

"Lettie, baby, bring me another cup of coffee." Curtis said. "So will you need a hard-shell for the truck bed or just a cover?" Curtis ran his finger down the list.

Steel smiled. The car man was hooked.

19

WITHOUT PAUSING TO CHANGE OUT of his work clothes, Steel marched through his living room and into his study. He flipped on the light and pulled the cord on the ceiling fan. The blades whirled, and the maps and papers he had thumbtacked in a crazy collage on the white walls danced in the breeze. Last week, he and Jo Jo had removed most of the study furniture and cleared the walls of decorations to create a treasure-hunting operations center. Like Cham had said: Put your skills to work. Steel was a methodical intelligence analyst, now he was going be a methodical treasure analyst. On the drive home from work, he thought about how the Japanese had moved the Tiger's treasure, considered routes from Angeles and Clark into the mountains. He figured the heavy crates of gold and gems were moved to Clark by Japanese aircraft, and maybe truck, then driven up primitive roads or dry season riverbeds into the mountains. Steel walked over to his cluttered desk and fished around until he found his magnifying glass. He perused a sprawling plat he had pieced together from four 1:50,000 scale maps of the Zambales. The detail was great, contrasting terrain, minutiae like rivers and streams. He pushed the glass up close to the map and followed the Bam Bam River as it snaked its way to where it split off into smaller tributaries, and then disappeared. He scrawled down some notes on a pad of paper, tore off the page, and thumbtacked it to the map. He'd get Tony to explore the smaller tributaries, anyplace a truck could have driven, and look for caves.

Jo Jo walked in dressed in his kuntaw kit. "William-san you haven't forgotten about the workout we scheduled?"

"Oh shit, that's right. I'll get a move on. I just wanted to write down some ideas I had. Oh yeah, I almost forgot to tell you, Curtis found a truck. It's a huge 1981 Ford pickup, a dually with four-wheel drive and a crew cab. Curtis said he walked into the hangar and found the owner, an airman in the F-4 unit, and asked him if he'd be interested in selling the truck. Curtis figured the guy would never sell. The truck was clearly well-maintained. Curtis tells the story better than me. He said the white dude, looking every bit like a southern bubba, said she weren't for sale. But Curtis is a car dealer at heart, like his poppa, and he dickered for a while. The redneck threw out a figure, and Curtis called his bluff, wrote him a check right on the spot. I had given him a signed blank one. Turns out, the guy needed it for a divorce back in the U.S., so we get the truck this weekend, and I'll take it straight to Junior's for modifications. This vehicle is going to be a beast."

Jo Jo peered at Steel's thumbtacked notes on the possible Japanese mountain routes. "Now that is using your brain, William-san."

"Oh yeah, I'm having lunch with the beautiful, smart woman I met at the embassy. We've been talking on the phone."

"So this is an Americana woman?"

"Yeah."

"I don't think you've had an Americana since I've known you."

"Nope."

"Maybe you don't know how to date them."

"I've dated white women before." Steel tried to recall when that had been.

"I don't think that's a good idea to get serious with a woman. Remember Vida."

"Me and Anne are just having lunch at the Chili Pot. She's interesting. I forgot how aggressive American women can be. She really has the hots for me. Sounds like she wants to hike in the mountains too."

"A woman in the mountains with us. That is not a good idea."

"I can handle her. I'm not going to rush into anything serious."

"I'm not talking about you fucking her. I'm talking about you taking her with us on a hike."

"She's in better shape than both of us."

"What is this bastos about an Americana woman?" said Rosa, who had popped into the doorway, her face set in a scowl.

"Nothing," said Steel.

"William-san wants to date a white woman he met at the U.S. Embassy."

"I haven't even had lunch with her yet."

"You shouldn't give up on finding a good Filipina woman because of Ms. Abucayan," said Rosa. "She is not an example of a virtuous Filipina. Those women you find in the bars are not good too. I will help you find a wonderful woman. My sister in Manila knows many women in business like lawyers, accountants, and sales women in department stores. They are smart and good women. I will call her today."

Steel exhaled, mimed a pistol with his index finger and thumb, and shot himself in the temple.

"Don't forget beautiful. William-san here is not going to be happy with a pangit woman," said Jo Jo.

"Beautiful. Bah, beautiful is not the only thing you want in a woman. She will have a beautiful soul."

"Not too old and not too fat too," Jo Jo added.

Rosa gave a wave of her hand, muttered something in Tagalog, turned, and left.

"I'm going to go and get dressed while you two figure out my life," said Steel.

"I'm just saying that an Americana on a hike sounds like trouble."

Steel ignored Jo Jo and headed up to his room. Those two weren't going to sour his day. He had a truck and Tetchi and now Anne.

20

Baguio
John Hay Air Station
Friday, 20 December 1985

STEEL STOPPED SHORT OF THE building entry and took a deep breath of cool mountain air. He smelled burning pine logs and it reminded him of his grandfather's cabin. But this was Baguio City, the summer capital of the Philippines, not Athens, Ohio. He was presenting a briefing at John Hay Air Station, or Camp John Hay, a rest and recreation facility for U.S. personnel. The camp sat at 5,000 feet, where the air was crisp and clean. Christmas was less than a week away, not his favorite time of the year, too much family, or in his case, lack thereof. But the cool temperatures and the spiced wood smoke went well with the Christmas trees and decorations he had seen around the base.

He and Jo Jo had driven the four hours from Angeles City, and they were billeted in a small cabin near the golf course clubhouse. It was good duty. Jo Jo was in a great mood. He was still bubbling about a note Tony had found inside an empty plastic bag at the ghost cave. Someone had taken the Japanese papers and food and scrawled thank you in Japanese. Steel was intrigued. Maybe it was a straggler. He promised Jo Jo they'd head back to the cave again soon.

Steel had toyed with the idea of bringing Tetchi along to Baguio. He'd also considered bringing Anne, instead of Tetchi, not with her, though there was an idea. Nah, neither seemed the type. He and Anne spoke regularly on the phone, but they had only had the one face-to-face at the Chili Pot. She was pushing for another. The idea of dating a woman rather than procuring one intrigued Steel, but he wasn't sure he was ready for the complications of a serious relationship so soon after Vida. Anne did have an incredible ass and a great rack. Bringing Anne to Baguio had been tempting, but the general's rules rattled in Steel's brain: Number one, get thy shit together. Besides, he wanted Jo Jo in Baguio for treasure hunting business, specifically for a meeting with Edgar Roxas, the brother of Rogelio Roxas, a local treasure hunter now in hiding, who reportedly had found an enormous gold Buddha, only to have it stolen by agents of the Philippine government. Some vehicle movement in the parking lot caught Steel's eye, and several staff cars pulled up. An entourage of U.S. and Filipino senior officers and their staffs piled out. Steel sighed. It was time to go in and perform.

Steel fidgeted with his notes on the shelf behind a chest-high wood podium while he kept an eye on Gen. Smith, twenty feet away, who was making opening remarks. Steel was waiting for the high sign to begin his 35mm slide brief on Soviet military activity in the region.

They were in one of the base library's large rooms. It sat thirty personnel, and the place was packed. The atmosphere was relaxed; the group knew each other well. They met a couple of times a year. Smith was sitting directly in front of Steel and behind a heavy dark wood table. Sitting next to Smith was Gen. Fidel "Eddie" Ramos, the co-chair of U.S./Phil Intelligence Exchange Conference.

Steel glanced at Ramos, trying not to stare. It was his first face-to-face encounter with the legendary Philippine general. He was dressed in olive-green fatigues and on his chest were pinned master jump wings. Four small black stars graced each collar. The uniform fit well. Ramos had a runner's build and looked younger than his fifty-seven years. Large and battered metal-rimmed glasses sat on an aquiline nose, and a fat unlit cigar bobbed between his lips. Ramos's cardboard name plate read "AFP Vice-Chief of Staff," not, as it might have, "Commander of the Armed Forces of the Philippines." Ramos was a West Point graduate and had led Filipino troops during the Vietnam War. His coziness with the U.S. military had finally caught up with him though. Only a few months ago, Marcos had passed Ramos over for the top army position. Gen. Fabian Ver, a Marcos crony, got the job instead.

Smith turned, faced the podium, and introduced Steel to the group. Ramos nodded at Steel then pulled the cigar from his mouth. Steel pressed the button on the projector remote, the black round carrousel clicked forward, and a slide popped in. It was a satellite photo that showed tiny Soviet aircraft lined up on the tarmac of a Vietnamese airfield. "The Soviet Union has increased its naval and air presence at its huge military facilities at Cam Ranh Bay, Vietnam, adding several new deployments of long range Bear and Badger bombers, which have the range to reach targets in the Philippines and Japan, and . . ."

The conference finished Friday leaving Steel and Jo Jo with the weekend to screw around in Baguio. They woke up early Saturday morning and wandered around the downtown, where shiny tinsel decorations and an outdoor nativity scene created a holiday atmosphere. There was an outdoor market with stalls full of local produce, meats, and crafts. Hill tribesmen and farmers from the mountains surrounding Baguio were famous for their vegetables, and their strawberries—on full display that morning—rivaled those grown in California.

They lingered over their late breakfast of eggs, rice and pork, and pandesal bread with hand-churned butter and honey and ordered refills of their strong coffee while reading the local papers. It was pleasant sitting at a rickety wooden table in the rustic courtyard surrounded by a five-foot centuries-old stone wall. Lush orchids cascaded from wooden trellises, and a manicured lemon tree cast dappled shadows on the uneven tile. The temperature was in the 70's without a hint of the thick humidity found in the lowlands. Why the Americans hadn't built Clark Air Base up here baffled Steel.

At noon, they folded up their newspapers and headed out for a rendezvous with Edgar Roxas. Arranging the meeting had been a monumental task. Jo Jo had made dozens of phone calls before finally making contact with a neighbor, who relayed messages to Edgar, who said he'd meet them at 12:30 p.m. He had said he didn't know where his brother was, and in any case, if he did, Rogelio wouldn't meet with strangers. Steel wasn't surprised. He had obtained microfiche copies of the Manila newspapers from May, 1971, that reported how Rogelio had found a tunnel complex built by the Japanese during World War II. It had been filled with wooden crates of gold bars and the famous golden Buddha statue. Rogelio and some friends removed the statue, which he estimated to weigh two-thousand pounds, along with a few gold bars, and took them home. Once there, Rogelio had discovered that the Buddha's head detached to reveal a small cavity filled with uncut precious stones. Steel had burst out laughing when he read that. It would have been nice to know prior to his own find.

The newspaper stories also reported that it had been Rogelio's plan to sell the Buddha, gems, and gold bars and use the money to buy trucks and construction equipment to re-dig the tunnel. Unfortunately, the man Rogelio approached to broker the deal told Marcos. Weeks later, agents of the Marcos government raided Rogelio's home, arrested him, and confiscated the treasure. He was tortured and his family threatened. He told them the location of the tunnel. Marcos's military men dug up it up and took the remaining gold bars.

Later newspaper articles reported that Rogelio appealed to left-leaning politicians for help after his release. Congressional hearings were convened. Under pressure, the government admitted only to what had already been reported: that they had arrested Rogelio for tax evasion and confiscated his Buddha but had determined it was made of lead and worthless. Rogelio was rearrested for fraud and forced to testify that the lead Buddha was the artifact he had found. Yep, Steel had thought then and still thought now, Rogelio was probably smart to hide out. The government would no doubt hound him to give up more cave sites. Marcos's ruthlessness was worth fearing. Steel needed to keep that in mind. He put his bags in the back seat of his king cab truck and jumped into the passenger seat. Jo Jo started the engine, and they headed out to meet Edgar.

It was less than twenty minutes through hilly back streets from Baguio's central market to the front porch of Edgar's modest wood house in Barangay Magsaysay. They had had to stop several times to ask strangers for directions. Jo Jo knocked on a worn and heavy plank board door, and they waited. It opened slowly to reveal a man and a boy. The older one was emaciated, with thinning hair and a dirty white T-shirt, black slacks, and flip-flops. Steel guessed he was in his mid-forties. Standing alongside him was a boy approximately twelve years old, dressed in ratty shorts and no shirt. The man stepped forward, craned his neck, and darted his eyes, scanning the area. He's checking to see if we were being followed, Steel thought. The man ushered them inside and shut the door. He stared at the floor and mumbled that he was Edgar Roxas and that the boy was his son. He asked for ID in a hushed tone. Steel fumbled for his wallet and removed his military credentials. Jo Jo showed his driver's license.

"Please, have a seat." Roxas passed them back the ID's and motioned toward some wood benches. "Can I offer you coffee? I'm afraid we don't have any milk for it. I do have some sugar."

"No, we're fine, thanks."

The house was small and dimly lit. Several large windows were shuttered tight and only a framed rim of sunlight entered the room. A Merry Xmas tinsel banner hung crooked on a wall, and a dusty wooden nativity scene sat on the mantle of the fireplace. The air was thick with smoke, body odor, and fear.

Edgar sat down across from them, carefully picked up a small china cup and plate, took a sip, then spoke, "So, Captain Steel and Maximo, what can I do for you? You were most insistent that you wanted to talk about my brother and the gold Buddha."

"Call me Will, and this is Jo Jo," said Steel. "First off, thanks for seeing us. I'm sure you're tired of talking about it. I just wanted to ask a few questions. Jo Jo and I are amateur treasure hunters ourselves."

"Ah, I thought so. Have you found any treasure?" asked Edgar.

Steel thought hard about how to answer. Edgar seemed to be trying to gauge with whom he was dealing. "Well to be honest, we did. And like your brother, we were cheated out of it by Marcos's cronies," Steel finally said.

Edgar's eyes widened. "So you have experienced similar treachery."

"But nothing like the torture and imprisonment your brother Roger endured," Steel said.

The half-naked boy reappeared and whispered something in Edgar's ear. "Just a minute. I have to attend to my daughter in the other room. She's very sick. She's been fighting sickness for some time now."

"I'm sorry to hear that," Steel said.

Edgar stood up and left them staring uncomfortably at the walls and the pathetic, droopy Christmas banner. Steel strained his ears and heard coughing.

Edgar returned a few minutes later, again offering apologies. His face was etched with deep worry lines

"We won't take much more of your time," Steel said. "I've read loads of newspaper accounts and interviews with your brother. I'm familiar with the story of his Buddha, but I don't know how he found the tunnel. Were you involved in it?"

Edgar stared into Steel's face and Steel could almost see the man decide to trust. "Yes and no. I was involved toward the end. I saw the Buddha and I helped Rogelio to unscrew the head and discover the precious gems inside. I know it was genuine treasure, but I was never inside the tunnel. I saw the outside after the Marcos goons had looted and resealed it."

Jo Jo leaned forward. "If I might say so, your English is very good. What is your profession?"

Edgar smiled. "Thank you. No one has paid me a compliment for a long time. I was a schoolteacher, but after all the notoriety around the discovery of the Buddha, no one will hire me. Quite frankly, I'm afraid to go out."

"What a nightmare," said Steel.

Edgar nodded, "Yes, but not as much as it is for Rogelio. His life is ruined."

"Sounds like it. How did Rogelio find the tunnel? Did he have a map?" said Steel.

Edgar took a sip of coffee. "My brother had a good friend. They were childhood pals. His name was Albert Fujigami. Albert's father was a Japanese soldier who married a Filipina after the war. There was a stigma to having a Japanese father. Most everyone shunned Albert except for Rogelio. Albert' father told of being a soldier and seeing a tunnel filled with gold; Albert told Rogelio. The father had been a sergeant and stationed in Baguio. He had shown Albert an old map that marked the location of the tunnel."

"So Albert had the map?"

"Albert's father died in car accident only weeks after he had shown Albert the map."

"Oh, no," said Jo Jo.

Edgar continued. "Albert recreated the map from memory, and he and Rogelio spent years trying to locate the tunnel."

"And finally they found it," Steel said.

"So there was only one tunnel?" asked Jo Jo.

"I'm afraid so," said Edgar.

"Is Albert still alive?" Steel asked.

"Yes. He lives in the mountains," said Edgar. "He is hiding with his mother's family."

"Did Marcos torture him as well?" said Jo Jo.

"No, Rogelio never let on that Albert was his partner."

"Loyalty like that is hard to find," said Steel. "I trust very few people in this life. This old dude is one of those." Steel laid a hand on Jo Jo's knee.

"So what other questions can I answer for you?"

Steel asked him about other potential treasure sites he might know of and whether or not Rogelio would consider meeting with them. After twenty minutes, a tiny girl dressed in a long, stained man's T-shirt floated in. She was thin, and her brown skin was washed out to a chalky white as if she had been powdered.

She asked for some water and grimaced into spasms of coughs. Edgar leapt up and helped her into the back room. He reemerged a few minutes later.

"Sorry. Josie's sickness is so hard. But her strong spirit keeps us going."

"Any idea what's wrong with her?" Steel asked.

"The doctor we have used isn't sure. He said more tests are needed. She has been sick now for more than six months."

"How do you survive financially without a teaching job?" Jo Jo asked.

"My wife works at the market, and I tutor. Also we get handouts from relatives and the church."

Steel stood. "So tell me, why did you agree to speak to us?"

Edgar paused for a moment. "I figured it wouldn't hurt to have an officer in the U.S. military as an ally." He smiled. "Maybe we could work with you on finding some . . . some more treasure someday. Now that I have met you, I would say I made a good decision. You have seen treasure and know how it feels to have it stolen."

"Does your brother have any ideas on where to look?" Jo Jo asked.

Edgar continued as if he hadn't heard. "Finding the treasure has only brought our family heartbreak. But if we had some extra money for Josie, I would say it was worth it."

"You have my phone number. Don't hesitate to call and let me know how you're doing. And if Rogelio has any ideas how to screw Marcos out of some fresh gold, let me know that too."

Edgar laughed. "I will do that." He held up Steel's card.

Jo Jo and I have put together a treasure hunting team with good equipment and people. We won't screw Rogelio out of his share. That we promise."

Jo Jo stepped forward and shook Edgar's hand. "Thanks for seeing us. We'll stay in touch." He glanced at the back bedroom.

As Edgar ushered them to the front door, Jo Jo whispered to Steel, "Brother, how much cash you have on you?"

"Why?" Steel asked.

"I can't stand the thought of that sick little girl. She reminds me of my Alma when she was that age," Jo Jo whispered.

Steel nodded, pulled out his wallet, and dug around for his emergency stash. He handed Jo Jo five thinly folded fifty dollar bills and five hundred in pesos. Jo Jo turned and handed the money to Edgar, who had joined them at the door.

"Edgar, please take this money and have Josie examined by a better doctor. Take her to the hospital in Baguio," Jo Jo said.

"Yeah, let us know, and I'll send more cash if you need it," Steel added.

Edgar looked at the cash. "But . . . but, this is too much."

"Don't worry. Just promise us you'll use it to get her seen too," Steel said.

"Yes, Will and Jo Jo, I promise. Bless you."

"Okay then, we'll be in touch. Tell Rogelio I said hello."

Edgar waved once and closed the door. Steel and Jo Jo headed back to the truck. Steel checked his watch. "Let's head to the base, and I'll cash a check so we have some money for the trip back to Clark. I want to have Sunday back home to get some stuff done."

"Okay. I'm glad we helped Josie out."
"Yeah, me too."

"You think we'll ever hear from Rogelio?" Jo Jo asked jumping in the driver's seat.

"Be nice to have a lead. But I'm afraid they've been too traumatized. Can't blame them." Steel swiveled his head looking for vehicles and prying eyes. Edgar's paranoia was both warranted and contagious.

Cashiered Philippine Army Scout Ranger Sgt. Romeo

Magos squirmed on a wooden bench strategically positioned on an acquaintance's front porch, catty-corner from Edgar Roxas's place. He scratched his ratty goatee as he watched Steel and Jo Jo exit the house. He saw a flicker of Edgar cowering behind the door. What the hell were they doing there, at the house of the brother of a famous treasure hunter? Magos had been following the two-faced bastard Steel and his bitch Jo Jo since he happened on them at the outdoor café. Lucky Magos chose this weekend to visit his family here in the mountains. Lucky he hadn't been spotted by Steel or Jo Jo. Magos glared at the traitors as they jumped into their truck. He had tried to apologize for the snafu during the expedition he had led Steel on a few months ago. He was just trying to make it easier for Steel to hike by flaming some undergrowth when the jungle started burning. It wasn't Magos's fault that Steel and his band of monkey men ran like women—afraid of a little fire. Magos slapped the empty seat beside him with the palm of his hand hard enough to make a nearby chicken squawk and fly off. And now the arrogant Americano was spreading lies about Magos, telling people that he had tried to kill Steel, that he was an inept guide. Inept! Magos, the great Scout Ranger and treasure hunter! He watched Steel's truck drive off. He would regret losing Magos's mountain treasure hunter skills. Yes, he would regret making an enemy of Scout Ranger Magos. For now, however, he needed to know why Steel was talking to Roxas. He must be comparing notes on treasure he is going to find, or has already found. Yes, that had to be it. Steel had found treasure. Treasure he didn't deserve. Well what has been found can surely be lost again. Magos would keep following Steel. He would take his revenge. And then we'll see who is the best at finding, and hanging onto, treasure.

21

Angeles
Saturday, 28 December 1985

EIGHT A.M. SATURDAY MORNING. STEEL heard banging on his front gate. Right on time. He jetted outside. He was glad Joseph was off today. Steel felt bad he'd gotten him fired up about treasure hunting. Jo Jo had broken the news to Joseph that he'd been cut from the trips. Steel hadn't asked what excuse Jo Jo used and blamed Jo Jo when Joseph had appealed the decision.

Steel hurried to the gate. He wanted to greet his guest before Rosa or Jo Jo. Anne stood on the curb and smiled at him. She gave a quick wave and then another at a small Toyota sedan that sat idling. As the car sped off, Steel noted the driver was Caucasian.

Anne seemed to pick up on Steel's scrutiny. "That's Robert, a colleague of mine. He lent me this." She pointed to a sturdy green backpack, fat and stuffed with equipment and what looked like a sleeping bag. A ground pad was rolled and tied beneath the pack. Before he could offer to grab the kit, she bent over and hoisted it to her shoulder.

Steel watched Anne's eyes flick from his boots to his jungle fatigue pants and lucky lime green Izod T-shirt then to a Tour-de-France bicycle cap perched backward on his head. She smirked and jabbed the tiny alligator on his chest, "Very stylish."

Steel dropped his gaze down to her white tank top and the firm round cleavage that heaved against the fabric, her white skin speckled with hundreds of tiny freckles. She had told him she had been a forward on her college field hockey team. She still kept buff. She looked sexy enough to bulldoze any apprehensions he had about letting her tag along. There were several long steamy jungle nights ahead of them, and it looked like she had her own tent. Maybe he wouldn't have to bunk with Jo Jo the entire time. He just might get laid. That would be a first for him in the Zambales Mountains.

"You have a shirt to wear on the top of this? "He fingered the strap of her top.

She flicked his hand away. "Got a lightweight long sleeved shirt and lots of bug spray. Don't worry about me, Jungle Jim. I've camped my whole life." She popped him a salute.

He looked at her red hair tied tightly in a braid hanging down her back. "You have a hat?"

She screwed up her face and pulled out a worn and faded Georgetown Hoyas cap she had tucked into the back of her pants. "This do?"

He remembered she mentioned at lunch she was an alumna. "Sure. Just don't want the white flesh to burn." He touched her nose, and she tried to bite his finger.

"Hey, it's Robin the Boy Wonder." She directed her comment at Jo Jo who stood with hands on hips, glaring.

"Robin?" Steel queried.

"You said he was aide-de-camp. Isn't that another name for a sidekick? Every superhero needs a sidekick. You know, Batman and Robin.

"I see myself as more of the Green Hornet type, if you need an analogy."

She extended her hand, and Jo Jo shook it gingerly, as if were dirty. "Cato it is then," she said.

Steel herded them back inside the gate. "So let's get loaded up and hit the road."

Steel helped her off with the pack and handed it to Jo Jo, who snatched and heaved it into the back of the truck, where it landed with a crack. Steel sighed. It was going to be a long weekend.

It was it was only a fifteen-minute drive to Barangay Sampung Bato, Tony's village on the outskirts of Angeles. His wife met the truck and reported Tony had departed that morning. He had left word that Steel should head to their base camp at June's village. She shrugged her shoulders saying there were problems.

Another thirty minutes of bone-jarring driving and they reached a large dusty clearing in the middle of a dense grove of bamboo and banana trees. Steel could see a cluster of native huts, several smoky campfires, and a smattering of Negritos, small skinny dogs, and chickens. After rendezvousing with Tony, they would head out on foot. Steel bounded out of the truck to help Anne, who had to be stiff after sitting in a cramped jump seat without padding. She squinted at the harsh morning sunlight, slid her sunglasses down from the perch on her head, then stretched while Steel bent down to check the driver's side tires and shocks. They had made some troubling noises on the trip. He wished his new super truck were ready. He turned his attention back to Anne, who looked to be struggling to take in the scene unfolding around her. She focused on a Negrito family dismounting from the truck bed; hitchhikers Steel had picked up a few miles down the road. He extended a hand to a small Negrito child, who recoiled and dove away. He must look like a huge white devil to the kid. He switched to helping Jo Jo unload the equipment.

It only took a few minutes before a crowd of two dozen Negritos, mostly children, had gathered around the vehicle. Steel recognized a few who knew he sometimes handed out candy. He pulled out a plastic bag of lollypops and threw handfuls into the air. The kids scrambled, yelling and laughing.

"Where's Tony? Steel called out in Aeta to one of the Negritos, probably a teenager, but not too old to be scrabbling in the dirt for treats.

"Over there," the boy said, pointing.

Tony walked towards the chaos. He was in dirty shorts and no shirt and had a M1 Garand rifle slung on his shoulder. The long, heavy weapon looked enormous against his diminutive frame. Pippip and Pongpet followed behind, their M1's pointing skyward like swollen radio antennae.

Steel called out, "Tony, why the fuck is everyone armed?"

"Yeah, why the guns?" Jo Jo asked.

Tony and his mini-platoon halted in front of Steel. The Negritos shot glances at Anne, then averted their eyes. Tony's hands were balled up into tight fists and his face scrunched into a scowl. Without any greeting he announced that two distant cousins of his had been shot dead. He suspected bandits, some army deserters and thieves who had been hiding in the mountains. Rumor was they had robbed some lowlander banks. That was of secondary concern to Tony. Vengeance for the dead Negritos was the priority.

Steel asked for the names of the dead, but he didn't recognize them.

"So what's the deal then? We're still on for the hike? Right?" Jo Jo asked.

Tony shot a look at Jo Jo then nodded. "We are going into the mountains with you to carry equipment for you and Captain Steel and his woman, and we will also look for the murderers and kill them." He patted the bolo knife sheathed in leather and hanging from a strap around his waist.

"Tony, this is Anne, and she's nobody's woman." Steel looked at her and she nodded once.

Steel took a deep breath and considered Tony and his rifle, the bolo, and then Anne. He spoke in Tagalog. "Jo Jo, what do you think? Do we really want to get involved with fucking Negrito dramatics?"

Jo Jo glared at Anne. "You can do what you want, William-san, but this is nothing we haven't dealt with before. I'm going with Tony back to the cave. I want to leave some more things and try to make contact with the Japanese straggler. You know I've spoken with some Japanese newspapers, and they said they would pay money for his story. Big money."

Anne stood, gaping. Steel tugged on her sleeve. "There could be some unexpected trouble. The Negritos don't usually carry so many weapons for our trips. But you heard, there were some Negritos killed by bandits or somebody. Shouldn't be a problem. You still game?"

She winced at the crack of a fired M1 round. "Oh yeah, I'm game," she said, staring off to where a group of Negritos were firing at brown-husked coconuts sitting on a rotting horizontal log. Steel could see the village chief, Tony's uncle June, directing the shooters, egged on by a dozen children and women, yelling and singing and adding to the excitement of the warriors' impeding departure.

Several children approached Anne, pointing and laughing. They held two smaller children who struggled and kicked. Anne got down on one knee and smiled at the kids.

"What are they saying?" said Anne.

Steel slung a small pack on his shoulders." The older ones are scaring the young ones, threatening to feed them to the evil white witch."

Anne stood up, frowned, and picked up her pack. Steel reached over and grabbed a strap. "Hey, that's heavy. Let's get one of boys to carry it."

She pushed his hand aside. "I got it. I carry my own load, thanks."

"Suit yourself." He watched her flip her pack on her back. Beads of sweat sprayed into the air. She puffed at the strands of escaped red hair that danced around her forehead and sunglasses.

Steel called over to Tony, "Are we ready now? I want to get going. I think you all have established that you are proficient at killing coconuts."

Tony ignored him.

"How many porters we have?" Steel asked.

Tony, eyes on June, answered, "Maybe ten or fifteen."

"Jesus, that's too many," said Steel. Nothing like a Negrito war to bring in the troops. He looked at Jo Jo, "Let's take eight paid. Whoever else tags along, it comes out of Tony's pocket. Make sure he knows that."

"Okay, boss-san." Jo Jo was passing gear down from the back of the truck to Pongpet and Ganchee, who were stacking it on the ground.

Steel switched to Tagalog. "Have one of the boys go without a pack. The white witch here insists she's carrying her own. I'm not sure how long she'll last."

Jo Jo glanced at Anne, who was adjusting her waist strap. "She shouldn't do that. She's already a liability," he said.

Jo Jo walked up to Steel and held out a cloth sack. Steel fumbled around inside and pulled out a shoulder holster with a Colt model 1911 .45 pistol. He held up the holster and angled the straps so he could slide his arms in. The gun was bulky and dug into his skin, but he knew he didn't want to be the only one unarmed. He watched Anne eye his weapon.

"Don't worry, just a precaution." He tapped on the holster, "Tony loves drama."

"Who would want to shoot at us? Is it about the treasure? Have you ever been shot at?" she asked.

"It's always about the treasure. People are greedy."

"So have you been shot at?" She repeated her question.

"Yeah. I'll tell you about it on the hike. No worries. We won't get involved with their Negrito feud. We're just looking at a new cave, and Jo Jo has his mission."

"The Japanese straggler?" she asked.

"We'll see if he's real. I'm skeptical. But someone took the Japanese things and pinned a note on a tree to say thanks."

"How about treasure. Have you found any?" She lowered her sunglasses.

He met her gaze. "Like I told you, only trinkets, but I'm hopeful. Anyway, it gets me out in the great outdoors." He waved a hand at the mountains.

"I get the feeling you'd be out here even if you had found it. You clearly have an Indiana Jones complex."

"Maybe," said Steel.

"It's all about the adrenalin rush. The dream that haunts all desk jockeys right? Except you're living the dream?"

"That's me."

"I want it too," she said.

Jo Jo called out, "Boss-san, Tony has picked out the eight men." Jo Jo squinted into the sun. A group gathered around Tony. They were loaded down with gear, some theirs and some Steel's.

"Let's move'em out," Steel yelled, then turned to Anne. "Last chance. Let me have someone get your pack. Look I'm carrying a light load."

"I saw your girl pack." She patted it.

Steel smiled. "All right Tony, let's get the fuck out of here,"

He called out over the din of the Negritos milling around the truck.

Steel paused and wiped his brow with his sweat rag and turned his head waiting for Anne to join him. It was two p.m., and the sun was raging high in the sky. They'd been on the trail a good five hours. Behind her he saw Pongpet and Ganchee pacing in circles probably annoyed they had been assigned rear duty behind the slow Americanos. It had been a steep uphill climb and a difficult slog through the scrubby eight-foot-tall tangles of jungle.

Overall, except for some twinges in his ribs he was feeling great, but Anne was visibly sagging under the weight of her pack. She pushed up next to him and bent over at the waist, puffing. Her T-shirt was soaked, and her damp red braid dangled at her side, sprouting clumps of escaped hair.

Steel let her catch her breath before he spoke. "Not much farther now. Tony will have the camp ready for us when we get there. There's a nice stream to wash up in."

"Great. Sorry, I thought I was in better shape than this." She coughed and spit.

"No worries. The humidity is brutal. You weren't acclimated enough. My fault. Here drink some water." He handed her his canteen, and she slurped at it, dribbling some down her chin and onto her shirt.

"Okay, I'm ready." She stood up and grasped tightly the walking stick Steel had made for her.

He nodded and started back on the trail, letting her keep up with the bravado for the moment. He'd take the damn pack off her when they stopped again. He indulged in a momentary fantasy of ripping the equipment and her shirt off her sweaty back but was pulled back to the jungle by the sounds of gunfire. The rounds ricocheted overhead and off tree limbs, mincing the vegetation. He pulled Anne down, smashing her into the dirt.

"Fucking Tony," Steel grunted. "I knew I should have cancelled." Anne looked at him with wide eyes, her face streaked with earth and sweat.

He raised his head and saw Ganchee and Pongpet, squatting, jabbering, and pointing with their hands and rifle barrels. "No, you stay with us and keep a look out," Steel barked in Aeta, pointing a finger at them. He heard more firing in the distance, and rounds whizzing high up in the trees. Remembering his pistol, he rolled on his side, pulled off his pack, removed the .45, and with a two-handed motion, chambered a round. He made sure the safety was on. He rolled over next to Anne. She lay on her belly and with her round, fat pack, she resembled a turtle. More gunfire rattled, and more rounds ripped through the air.

"You can hear them." She yelled, her eyes darting to Steel and then into the sky. "I've only been on the shooting end at a range. Never the target end."

"The sounds are terrifying." Steel laid his pistol on the ground and tugged at Anne's pack straps. "Get the pack off. We might have to move fast." She started to sit up, and Steel pushed her back. "Keep down. Get on your back and I'll help. She complied, and he rolled on top of her and fiddled with the straps. She arched her back to pull her arms out. He felt her taut stomach push against his pelvis. She managed a grin. "It didn't take much to get me on my back."

"Just gunfire."

She bucked her hips and raised him in the air; he flipped to his hands and knees. He scanned the horizon and focused on Ganchee and Pongpet, still at their post, squatting and pointing their weapons. He was amazed. He figured they would have gone to see where the gunfire was coming from.

The bush and the air became thick and disturbingly quiet. The shooting had stopped.

"Ganchee," Steel called out. "Go and see what the hell's going on." The Negrito leapt up and disappeared into the jungle. "Pongpet you stay here. Keep alert. Make sure no one comes up on us from behind." With less enthusiasm, Pongpet nodded.

"Let's scoot to that patch of bamboo over there. It'll provide cover until the cavalry arrives," Steel said.

He and Anne low-crawled over to the thicket and hid in the massive tubes of tall green-and-yellow bamboo. Steel said, "Fucking Tony. I told him to keep us in sight and—"

Anne's scream stopped Steel mid-gripe. She thrashed, kicked her feet, and hugged her arm. "Fuck . . . fuck . . . fuck that burns."

"Jesus, what happened?" Steel said.

"Something fucking stung my arm. A big fucking bug." She clenched her eyes and pain shriveled her face.

Steel ran over twenty-five feet, retrieved his pack, pulled out a first-aid kit, and examined the huge welt and puncture hole in Anne's arm. A single hole. Not double, like those made by poisonous snake fangs.

"You're sure it was an insect and not a spider?"

"Yes," she gasped.

"How big?"

"Fucking big."

"Sounds like a wasp. The spider bites will really mess you up and the cobras will kill you. The centipedes are no fun either. Had one bite me and my foot blew up to the size of a watermelon." Steel pulled out a pack of cigarettes, flipped some out, ripped off the filters, and peeled the paper. He piled the shredded tobacco on a banana leaf, poured a few drops of water on it, and mushed it with his fingers. "Tobacco is a great poultice. It will help draw out the poison."

"Jesus, this hurts," she said. She flopped on her back, scrunched her eyes, and grabbed her arm. Tears streamed down her cheeks.

"Yeah, it's no fun." He put the wad of tobacco on the sting, covered it with a gauze pad, and applied pressure. Anne screamed and lashed out with her free fist, landing several solid hits on his head. Steel grabbed her flailing hand, bore down with his body, and continued his lecture. He grunted out the words. "Because of the intense instantaneous pain, I suspect it was the tarantula hawk, or spider wasp, in the family Pompilidae. An amazing insect. It hunts huge tarantulas and other arachnids and uses them as hosts for its larvae."

"Ow, fucking ow," she moaned.

In a few minutes, she stopped struggling, and Steel loosened his grip. "Here keep the pressure on it." He guided her hand to the pad then turned his attention to the other cuts and scrapes on her arms. As he worked, he scanned the jungle around them and listened for noise.

"Damn, the pain was so intense. It's letting up some," she said.

"The trademark for the spider wasp's sting is the intense but short duration of the pain. On the Schmidt Sting Pain Index, these wasps are rated number two, second only to the bullet ant," he said, holding her hand.

"You know way too much about wasps," she said.

A bird's shriek rang out. Steel grabbed for the pistol. The call was answered by another animal. Pongpet to their rear. A few seconds later, Steel heard Jo Jo bellow, "Steeelllleee-san."

Steel stood. "We're over here. Don't shoot. We're over here.

Jo Jo and two Negritos, fully armed, raced into the clearing. Jo Jo was bleeding from a large wound on his arm.

"Jesus, Jo Jo, you hit?" Steel yelled out.

Jo Jo saw Steel and moved toward him. Jo Jo threw a look

at Anne, who was sitting on the ground still holding her arm, then spoke between gasps for breath. "Is she okay? I got a cut when I dove down after the shooting started. What the hell is it lately with all the gunfire? Jesus Maria Joseph, I'm thinking of retiring soon." He dropped to his haunches, sat back hard on his ass, then lay out flat on his back.

"C'mon, big guy, take some deep breaths." Steel used his pack to elevate Jo Jo's legs. "Here, drink some water." He pushed the neck of a green canteen to Jo Jo's lips.

He took a few slurps then slumped back down. "We ran right into the bandits. They fired shots at us then fled. The Negritos returned fire, and Tony and June are chasing them down."

"Were they bandits or NPA or maybe the mystery guy with the Japanese machine gun?" asked Steel.

"Jesus, that's a long list of suspects," said Anne.

"Didn't see anything but shadows and muzzle flashes," Jo Jo said from his horizontal position. "But I'm sure it wasn't the Japanese machine-gun fire we experienced before."

Jo Jo tried to sit up, but Steel pushed him back. "Let's take a break so I can clean those wounds. We'll rest until Tony comes back."

In less than an hour, Pongpet announced Tony and the other Negritos' arrival with high-pitched yelps. Steel was pleased to see they were carrying their packs, and none appeared wounded.

"Did you kill any of the bastards who shot at you?" Steel asked.

Tony shook his head. "They ran too fast, like scared women. June and others are chasing them down. But I returned here to make sure you are okay."

Steel softened his tone. "Thanks, I know you wanted to get those guys."

"June will find them and kill them."

"I have no doubt."

Jo Jo stood unsteadily, found the packs with water and food, and passed some to Anne and Steel. Anne took a peanut butter sandwich. Her eyes flicked from one person to another before she spoke, her mouth full of bread.

"What's next?"

Steel stared at the swelling the size of an orange on her arm. "I guess we'll press on to the Japanese cave. I can't imagine Jo Jo will want to bail out."

A smile lit Jo Jo's face. "Yes. We've come this far and . . ." Jo Jo cocked his head. Pippip blasted on the scene and began talking to Tony, who gestured with an unsheathed bolo in reply.

"Jo Jo, what's going on?" Steel said, chomping on a blueberry frosted Pop-Tart.

Jo Jo shrugged and took a big drink from his canteen.

Tony marched over to where Steel and Anne sat. "Pippip arrived with a message from June. He has captured some people, but they aren't the bandits. Two of the peoples he thinks are Americans, and one is a giant Negrito." Tony laughed and added, "I think Pippip means an Americano Negro."

"Americans? Where?" Jo Jo said, trying to swallow a mouthful of peanuts.

Tony pointed at a dark dry patch of scrubby ridgeline to their rear. "Pippip says they are there. They were following our trail."

"Following us? Christ. June must have doubled back." Steel stared at the ridge wishing he had binocular eyes. "What fucking Americans would be following us?"

Anne shrugged, touched her wound lightly, and said, "Some real dumb-ass Americans."

Jo Jo chuckled. Good, Steel thought, maybe Anne's grit and positive attitude was winning Jo Jo over. It certainly was working on Steel. He wanted to fuck her more than ever.

Hobbs and Whale sat on the jungle floor, tied back-to-back by the wrists. A loop of braided vine roped around both their necks, ensuring if one moved the other would strangle. Hobbs breathed deeply through his nose, unable to use his mouth because of the rag jammed inside. He tested the rope securing his hands. Stiff vine covered with small thorns. Whale grunted and wiggled his hands in reply. After a few painful minutes, Hobbs stopped moving. There was no escape. He glanced over to the two Phil ex-army guides who had brought him and Whale this far. They were hung like piñatas from an acacia tree. Alive, but the amateur fuckers deserved to be dead. They had been worthless when the Negritos ambushed them. Hobbs stared at one old Negrito, shirtless, barefoot, and wearing a brightly embroidered loincloth. He squatted on his haunches and cradled an ancient carbine in his lap. He reminded Hobbs of the Hmong tribesmen he had worked with in Nam. They made eye contact, and the dude cracked a sly smile. Hobbs looked away. He could kick himself. He and Whale should have hired those little Negrito brothers, like Steel did. But they went with the local boys, and see where they ended up. Captured and in the middle of a jungle, who knows where. If this were Nam, he would of been fine. He knew that terrain. But here he felt like an amateur, a bozo. What the fuck were they going to do?

Pippip led them into the clearing less than a kilometer away. Steel smiled when he saw June, posing with his M1 carbine. He had carried it in World War II. The tough old bastard had scouted for U.S. forces and, despite his age, could outmarch Steel on any given day. June waved. Other Negritos were lounging or digging through piles of equipment—including two M16—littered on the ground. They seemed oblivious to the two Filipino men hung upside down from a large acacia tree. Their hands were tied behind their backs and rags were shoved in their mouths. Steel thought they were dead until one looked at him with bulging eyes. They were dressed in a mixture of civilian and military clothing and appeared to be Phil army types.

"Hanging like fucking hams," Steel muttered.

"And two Americans over there," Anne said, pointing to two prisoners tied up back-to-back on the ground. "At least they look like Americans."

"I'll be damned," Jo Jo said.

"Who the fuck are they?" Steel grabbed Tony by the arm.

Tony shrugged and scratched his head and pointed to June who stood at attention. "June was chasing the bandits but found these instead. They aren't the devils who shot at us. June smelled the barrels of their weapons. They haven't been fired."

Both Americanos glowered at Steel. The black one looked like a body builder. He wore Vietnam-issue tiger-striped fatigue pants and a tight green military-issue T-shirt. He had an empty pistol holster under his arm. Even soaked in sweat and covered in jungle debris, he looked ripped. Steel imagined the Negritos couldn't have had an easy time subduing him.

Steel's eyes flashed to the hulking white one, also in a green military-issue T-shirt smeared with dirt, sweat, and a spattering of jungle debris. Steel was taken back by the man's white flabby skin and bulk. His hair was shaped in a tight crew cut, and a tattoo marked his upper arm; a map of the Republic of Vietnam. Likely a Nam vet. Steel sighed. He was angry that they were tailing him.

Jo Jo searched the Americans and found no identification other than international drivers' licenses that identified them as James Arnold and Warren Fields, U.S. citizens. Steel was almost certain those were fake names. The documents looked counterfeit. Steel cocked his head to get a better view of the captives, squirming against their bindings. He reached out with both hands and removed the cloth rags in both mouths. They grunted in unison.

"So who do we have here? Want to give us some real names gentleman, and tell us why you're following us?" said Steel.

"Fuck you," said the black one.

"Is that any sort of language to use in front of a lady?" Steel said.

"Why are you following us?" Jo Jo yelled.

"We were just out hiking and were attacked by these crazy-assed little dudes." Again the black one.

"You're lucky they didn't kill you. I find the odds of you just happening to be at our rear astronomical. Why are you following us?" Steel said.

"Fuck you."

Steel pulled a combat knife from his boot sheath. "Had the shit kicked out of me. Been shot at. My patience is in short supply." He tested the edge of the blade with his thumb.

Jo Jo squatted down next to Steel and got in the white one's face. "William-san is crazy. Just do yourself a favor and give him the information he asks for, and we'll send you on your way." Jo Jo patted the sneering captive on the cheek, wobbling his jowls.

Steel traced a random tailor pattern on the guy's shirt with the knife blade, but his eyes remained passive. The milling crowd of Negritos buzzed. Steel switched the angle of the blade and popped the sharp point into flesh.

"William, don't," Anne called out.

"Why not? It's a big jungle. No one will find their bodies," said Steel.

"Especially after the Negritos roast and eat them," said Jo Jo.

"I imagine the fat guy here would be especially tasty." Steel poked again with the knife.

"I thought you said we couldn't eat people anymore?" Tony said.

Steel glanced at Tony and fought smirking at his creativity.

"Look, guys. I'm only going to be rational about this for a short time, then I'm letting them serve you for dinner. Why are you following us?" Steel pushed deeper with the knife tip and drew blood.

Anne grabbed Steel's arm. "These guys are clearly Americans. Let's just take them to the police."

"We're on a nature hike," the white captive said, and earned a crack in the forehead with a thick bamboo walking stick from Jo Jo.

The man grunted and fought against the ropes tying his hands. His tantrum tightened the rope loop around both prisoners' necks.

Anne pressed the back of her hand against her mouth.

June waved two huge six-inch-wide spiders that looked like tarantulas in the faces of the bound men. He pinched the arachnids on their hairy backs while their inch-long razor sharp mandibles snapped open and closed. Steel wondered if the Americanos knew they were really huntsman or wolf spiders and harmless. June spoke in Aeta to Steel. Raucous laughter erupted from the Negritos. Steel nodded and grinned at June. He placed one spider on the black guy's stained shirt, and the beast crept forward. Beads of sweat trickled down his face.

"Oh, the banana-death spider's bite is painful. You are right to remain still," Jo Jo said.

"Ya brother," Steel grimaced. "I remember seeing one poor farmer die convulsing and vomiting. Thirty minutes of pure agony. On the up side, the Negritos won't be able to eat you because of the spider toxin in your system."

June held the other spider in one hand and lifted the white prisoner's shirt to expose his fat belly. Pitpit fell to the ground with riotous laughter. He posited that maybe the white man had a baby in there. Like a text book movie villain, June dangled the spider over his victim, allowing the tips of the hairy long legs to brush the skin.

"All right—all right! Call him off!" the man blubbered.

"Shut up," the other grunted, between clenched teeth, watching the spider inch towards his neck.

"We were assigned to follow you," the first yelled. "I'm sorry, man. I just can't handle spiders."

"Well, for simple nature lovers out for a walk, you guys don't have much of a tolerance for God's creatures."

"Do you work for the CIA?" Jo Jo asked.

"You son of a bitch. Singlaub," White guy cracked again. "Singlaub, we're working for him. He wanted you followed to see if you found treasure."

"Singlaub? Who's Singlaub?" Jo Jo said.

"General Singlaub?" Steel said and glanced at Anne, whose eyes shifted to the speaker.

"Yeah, yeah. General Singlaub," he said, still fixed on the undulating spider legs flicking at his belly.

"Okay June, take away the spiders." Steel said and looked at the Filipinos hanging from the tree. "Tony cut those guys down. Get everyone organized. Load up the equipment, especially those M16's. We gotta get back on the trail. Steel pulled Jo Jo aside. Anne pushed in to listen. Steel explained how he had read several newspaper articles about how Singlaub had been in Manila with a company called Nippon Star looking for Japanese treasure.

"Fucking poaching bastards," Steel grunted. "We do all the

work then they swoop in. I'm so sick of these parasitic fucks stealing our shit and kicking my ass."

"So what now, boss?" Jo Jo asked.

"Have June assign some armed guys to escort these bastards all the way back to Sampung Bato. Tell June he can have their equipment as pay for his troubles. I want the M16s."

Jo Jo walked over to talk to June and Tony.

Steel grabbed Anne by the arm. "Sorry. I didn't know this was going to turn into a goat fuck."

"You sure know how to show a gal a good time," she said, staring at the Americans.

"Look, we can turn back and—"

"No," she said. "Believe it or not, I'm still game."

Anne stared intently into Steel's eyes and tried to steady her wobbly, exhausted body against his arm. Steel smile warmly, released her arm, and walked over to confer with Jo Jo. She stiffened her spine, gritted her teeth, and switched her focus to the jungle and the expedition ahead. The gunfire, bugs, and searing heat weren't exactly what she bargained for. But what did she expect? Did she think surviving the CIA's case officer training was going to be any easier? She exhaled deeply and thought about the mission at hand. She had to get closer to Steel, get him to open up, otherwise Diamond would be disappointed. He made it clear: No intel on Steel, no chance to train to be a case officer. She needed more than an adventure movie script for her after-action report. Steel did seem to get off on crawling on top of her. And maybe she enjoyed it too, a little, but more likely that was just the adrenaline from all the shit going down, not sex, not attraction. There was still time during the long night to probe him more. Shit. She didn't mean it that way, or maybe she did. But all in the interest of getting the job done. She knew she needed a home-run to impress management. And if that meant fucking Steel, compromising her integrity, because it was in the best interest of her career and the country, then, yep. Maybe just this one time.

It wasn't long before darkness fell, erasing the rich colors from the lush jungle. Grey light washed over objects like the flickering of an old black-and-white movie. Stars began to emerge. The tree frogs, nocturnal insects, and other creatures came to life. Steel watched Anne rise from the gurgling narrow stream. Her white skin was luminous and her musculature, well-defined, sculpted by years in the gym. She flipped her hair, and it shot skyward then cascaded onto her back. Her naked breasts bounced. She grabbed a towel off a rock and dried herself, then scanned the area until she locked eyes with him. He was wearing only a towel, and only around his neck. She wrapped her towel around her body, navigated a stone obstacle course, and sat next to him. For a few minutes they did not speak, heads turned to the flickering heavens.

Anne broke the silence. "The water was beautiful, better than a four-star hotel shower."

"Always is."

"Quite a day. Not what I imagined."

"Yeah. Hikes lately have been filled with way too much craziness. They used to be fun."

Anne shuddered. "Wow, hard to believe I'm cold after roasting my ass off all day," she said.

"It's the combination of the drop in humidity and an increase in the Pacific trade winds."

"Are you always Mr. Nature Professor?"

He laughed and pushed up close, pressing naked thigh to naked thigh. He put an arm around her. Her wet hair draped on him.

"I've been accused of being a nerd on more than one occasion," Steel said.

"You certainly dress like one. Seriously? A lime green Izod shirt?" She gave a deep, hoarse laugh. "But I see you out here surrounded by the Negritos and the crazy random violence, and I see a different man."

They chatted until dark when the mosquitos interrupted them. "We'd better stumble back to camp. In my excitement at the prospect of bathing with you, I forgot my flashlight."

"Not me." She blinded Steel with her flashlight. "And for the record, you didn't exactly bathe with me."

He blinked his eyes and pulled her up by the hand. "You can use the light to watch for cobras and pit vipers. They like the water too."

"Oh great, here, you lead the way." She handed him the torch.

As they approached the camp Steel, could see the outlines of the two tents. One glowed red. Jo Jo was inside, likely reading. The other, neon blue, was Anne's. It was dark and inviting. Around a campfire, a dozen Negritos milled around the dancing flames. A small wild pig roasted on a skewer over a bed of red-hot coals casting off a devilish glow. Pongpet sat cross-legged, slowly cranking the spit. Steel thought the scene subdued, far from other rowdy Negrito campfires he'd witnessed.

Wow the campfire looks surreal," Anne said.

"Yeah. Usually their wine gets them fired up."

"That pig smells yummy."

"You want some?"

"No. The meal Jo Jo cooked was great. I'm full."

They continued to stand in the awkward neutral zone between the two tents. Steel glanced at Jo Jo's red, fart-filled, compartment, then at Anne's. He snuck a peek at her wrapped in the bath towel. It had slipped enough for him to see a valley between her tits that rose and fell with her breath. The choice was easy. He grabbed her arm and slid her towards him. He buried his face in her neck and smelled her wet hair.

"Can I invite you in for a nightcap, Captain Steel?" she whispered.

"Oh yeah."

She pulled him to her tent, zipped open the door, and crawled in. The flashlight illuminated her white ass, and he marveled at it for a second, then followed. She had her sleeping bag open; it covered the floor. She flopped down on her side, and Steel re-zipped the tent flap and crawled next to her. He flipped off the light, and she pushed in tight to him. Steel ripped off her towel, then his, and kissed her hard. They embraced and wrestled, shaking the walls as they thrashed, fighting for dominance and leverage. She flipped on top of him, and he slid in easy. She ground against him, rocking her hips, exhaling loudly. Steel gripped her and pulled her down, wanting to kiss her, but she fought him to keep riding. Steel didn't care and let her ride, and ride, and ride, oblivious to the world around them.

Tony stood and stared into the burning coals at the pig, hoping it would be ready to eat soon. He was starving. The spiders, the small birds, and the snake they had already roasted and consumed were only snacks. A bulbous metal pot hissed on the coals and bubbled up spouts of cooking rice. It was close to done. The sounds of animals grunting distracted him from his hunger pangs. His eyes fell upon the source. The sides of the white woman's tent thrashed. He looked down at Ganchee, who lay propped on his elbows, his chin resting on his chest, half-asleep. Tony tapped him on the top of the head.

Ganchee looked up and frowned.

"The tent, "Tony pointed. "Steel denied she was his woman. I knew that was a lie."

Ganchee sat up, craned his neck. "If she's not his woman, then she's putting up a good fight."

Norgot, who was listening, stared at the rocking tent. "The cloth hut is shaking like an earthquake. Yet she's silent, like a Negrita woman, not disturbing anyone. A good woman."

Dunpit, who sat cross-legged next to them on the communal woven mat, sharpening his bolo, spoke. "She is so white. I thought Steel was white until I saw her skin. I think they will have really white babies."

Ganchee nodded. "But what happened to Steel's other woman, the queen that lived in the big, big village?"

"No. Jo Jo said she slept with another man," said Tony.

"Oh no. Did Steel kill the man?" Dunpit asked, testing the bolo edge with his thumb.

"No, he was just sad for too long," Tony said.

"Ah that is bad. Killing is better than too much sadness," Ganchee said.

Pongpet announced that the pig was finished, knives were drawn, and the group converged on the main course.

22

Zambales Mountains
Sunday, 29 December 1985

J APANESE IMPERIAL ARMY LT. NAGANO Nada paced slowly back and forth in a shaded jungle clearing and scanned the sky. He found the sun and estimated it was still early afternoon. He was wearing a clean uniform. It had been carefully protected in a metal artillery shell crate lined with a tropical wood whose fragrance fought rot. Sweat trickled down his chest and back. For the last two decades he had gone naked most of the time, so the uniform felt stiff, rough, and tight on his body. His head and face were freshly shaven. He rubbed his hand on his skull, and it felt slippery, smooth, and wet. Around his forehead, he wore a white headband decorated with a rising red sun and a poem he hand penned, a favorite of his from happier days. His type-96 light machine gun rested on his back in a leather sling, and his beloved sword was sheathed at his side. He felt like a professional officer—a warrior—something he hadn't felt in a long time.

"Oh Nada-san, you cut a dashing profile in your uniform," Sergeant Kami said, disturbing Nada from his thoughts.

Nada stood rigid and straightened his collar with two hands. "Yes my friend. You did a marvelous job getting my last uniform ready. He bowed briefly to Kami, who sat on the stump of a big dead tree. "Maybe we should just have one last banzai charge down onto the American's camp." With one motion, Nada grabbed the handle of his sword and slid it from its scabbard, the only sound, a melodic metallic ring. "We can go in a blaze of glory for the Emperor." He slashed the air with a quick motion.

Nada continued pacing, anxious, tasting bile in his throat. The source of his distress was the Yankee and the little black men. They had returned to the command post. He knew they were there because he made morning visits to the cave hoping to find more cans of food, packages of dried squid, rice noodles, and newspapers. He pored over the papers, reading every article and scrap of information about the world he had hidden from for so many years.

He had seen the Yankees, and now here he was dressed in his best clothes, watching and fretting. He was torn about whether to make contact, to ask whether the war was truly over. Nada continued pacing. Maybe they were devils cloaked to look like Americans. They wanted to break him, tempt him with earthy pleasures. Demons were terrifying, but in Nada's mind these men were worse. They were harbingers of hope. Hope planted seeds of doubt and crushed the will to fight on. He smacked his forehead with clenched fists until Kami called out to him to stop.

Nada sank to the ground, shrugging back his sword and machine gun, and crossed his legs in repose. He placed his hands in a prayer position and took deep breaths.

"Good. The Lord Buddha can fill you with calm." Nada heard Kami's words, and they soothed. At Kami's insistence, they had built a shrine to the Buddha and burned candles. Nada kept breathing with intention until serenity floated in like puffs of morning mist.

He slowly bowed his head and rested his chin on his chest.

He stayed like that until high up in a tree, a monkey screeched. Nada opened his eyes and smiled at the monkey's antics. He never ate them. They were too close to human.

Nada glared at Kami until he spoke: "I can read your thoughts. You don't want to quit. You only know this insane hatred and fear and—"

"But your plan is to hang our heads in shame, to negotiate with the Americans," Nada said.

"It is time to leave this jungle prison. Have you not read the papers and seen that the world has changed. Have you not eaten the food and tasted home?" Kami said.

Nada scratched the top of his head. "Yes, I know how you feel. I know you're sure. But maybe . . . I'm not. Maybe, I'm scared of what the people will say about us." Nada looked around and spoke in hushed whispers. "We should have killed ourselves like our comrades. Why did we choose to live? We are cowards, afraid of death and—"

"I'm so tired of this endless discussion," Kami interrupted. "It's time. You know it's time."

Nada turned his head, refusing to look at Kami.

"Go and call out to them and issue our demands. We will surrender but only to Major Otsuji, our commanding officer. If he gives us permission, then we will formally surrender," said Kami.

"How will they find him after all these years?" said Nada.

"Now you have doubts? You were firm with this plan. If Otsuji can't be found, our destiny is written. We will die in this wilderness," Kami said.

Nada slumped forward, rocked on his hands and knees, then stood and stretched his limbs, startling the monkey. Nada carefully brushed himself off, and then he and Kami headed out to confront the interlopers.

So, Jo Jo, are we ready to head out." Steel said, looking at the plastic-wrapped pile of Japanese food and canned goods.

"How do you know it's really a Japanese soldier? Anyone could have taken the food and left the note," Anne said.

"Maybe, but the odds of some jungle hermit knowing how to speak and write Japanese are slim," said Steel.

"Well, Cato here can speak it," Anne said.

Steel exhaled. "Good point. I'm sure—"

A voice boomed out Japanese from the jungle. Steel struggled to pinpoint where it was coming from. "What's he saying, Jo Jo?"

"He's asking for me to come and talk to him."

"Fuck. He's really here," said Steel.

June touched Steel lightly on the arm and spoke: "I kept feeling his presence here today, but he is not like you white men or even the lowlanders. His spirit and his earth smells are like the Negrito, and he can live here without detection. I see him now. He is the Haponese. He is a great warrior, I think, because he refused to finish his war against the Americans."

"You've seen him before, haven't you?" Steel whispered to June.

June nodded. "Many times, but I leave him in peace. His house is there, and he has many demons he fights."

Tony furrowed his eyebrows and said, "I've never seen him before. Shall we go and get him now?"

"No. Let's not scare him off." Steel looked around at the Negritos who bristled with weapons. "Everyone put down their weapons. Lay them on the ground." Steel removed his pistol and made a show of laying it on the ground. They looked back at Steel without budging until he glared at Tony. "Tony order them to put the weapons downs." Tony shrugged and called out in Aeta and the rest of the Negritos complied. One-by-one, Garand's thumped to the ground.

Anne's head whipped around, to Steel, to Jo Jo, to Tony, to the disarmed Negrito warriors.

The voice again, and Jo Jo translated. "I want the Filipino who speaks Japanese to come forward alone. I will not harm him. I want to meet him face-to-face under the peace of a white flag."

"Shit I don't know. What do you think, Jo Jo? Are you okay with it? Not sure how risky it is to go alone. I don't like it," said Steel.

Jo Jo shrugged. "I'll be fine." Before Steel could game it some more, Jo Jo called out something in Japanese. "I told him I'm coming without weapons, alone and in peace." He put his arms into the air.

Steel grabbed Jo Jo's shirt. "Be careful."

Jo Jo nodded and started walking towards the hillside toward the voice.

"He will be safe, Captain Steel. I think the Haponese is an honorable warrior," June said.

"Let's hope so," Anne said, biting a thumbnail.

They watched Jo Jo walk into the brush, both his hands raised awkwardly over his head, stumbling on the roots and rocks blocking his path.

"I see him. The Haponese is unarmed." Tony whispered.

Steel groped in his pack for his binoculars, lifted them to his eyes, and adjusted the focus. He watched Jo Jo move in and out of sight, then stop. He was visible only from the waist up. Jo Jo dropped his hands and bowed at the jungle, talking rapidly and gesturing. He disappeared from view for a second then stepped back holding a piece of paper.

"Holy shit," Steel muttered aloud. "The straggler has given him a note." He watched Jo Jo bow again and turn and walk back to them.

"What's going on?" Anne whispered pulling on Steel's shirt.

"Unbelievable, just unfucking unbelievable that's all."

Nada watched the Filipino Jo Jo head back to his companions, then turned, and walked over to the rotted stump where Kami sat.

"I hope we have made the right decision, my dear Kami." Nada said.

He stared at his old, loyal friend and, with tears streaming, bowed deeply towards him. From the top of the stump, Nada gently scooped up the gleaming white skull and marveled at the straight white teeth, forever frozen in a grin. He gently brushed off a piece of bark from the jawbone and carefully placed Kami into a hand stitched silk bag, slid it over his shoulder, and disappeared into the jungle.

23

Manila
U.S. Embassy
Monday, 30 December 1985

ANNE BENTON LIMPED INTO THE station chief's office, favoring her right knee and left ankle. The secretary, Mrs. Davis, was away from her desk, and the door to Diamond's private office was shut. Anne glanced at her wristwatch then confirmed the time with Mrs. Davis's digital clock radio. Her meeting with Diamond was at 10:00 a.m. She had ten minutes. She sank into the waiting room's bamboo-patterned white and green couch. Her legs and back throbbed, and the spot on her arm where the wasp had stung her burned. She had made it back to Manila late last night; the return hike from the mountains to Angeles had taken most of Sunday, and she had had to wait hours for the company car to come to get her.

She arrived at the vault early this morning to type her trip report. She was pleased with the write-up and had a copy sheathed in a red and white classified coversheet that read: SECRET/NOFORN/OCON. Another was waiting on Diamond's desk.

She stared into space, recalling the last thirty-six-plus hours. The expedition to the mountains had been exhilarating and, at moments, terrifying. Not what she had expected. Hollywood movies had in no way prepared her for the auditory shock of machine-gun rounds whizzing overhead. And one thing was for sure, she had underestimated USAF Capt. William Steel. What the hell was his deal? More than ever, she doubted the intelligence reporting on him. How could he be a regular military officer and be involved with all the crazy shit that surrounded him? Diamond had been adamant that Steel wasn't a black-program operator. But who the fuck were the two Americans tailing him? Christ, the look of terror on those guys' faces when Steel interrogated them. God, she hoped they weren't company guys. And what the hell had gotten into her? "Well, his cock for one thing," she muttered. It had been crazy good sex, and she needed it. Could hardly remember the last time. But to fuck a source. Her first source. She banged her forehead with the palm of her hand. Damn, what an idiot. She stared at a shelf of books, blamed her abandon on her over eagerness to get in his head. But she felt cheap. She stared at the folder. It wouldn't happen again. That's how she justified keeping it all out of her report.

The sound of Diamond's door opening drew her out of her thoughts. Mrs. Davis, a tiny energetic woman with short grey hair, silver-framed glasses, and a deep tan flitted in. She had been at the embassy for two decades, and Anne surmised that Mrs. Davis, like many civil servants, provided a seamless continuity between the station chiefs who came and went, abruptly at times. She shot Anne a friendly smile, "Ms. Benton, Mr. Diamond will see you now."

Anne nodded, stood, straightened out her long shirt, and marched into Diamond's office with file in hand. Diamond sat behind his desk reading.

"Good morning, sir," she sang out.

He glanced up. "Have a seat. I'll be with you in a sec." He resumed reading.

She thought his voice sounded terse, and her heart sank. God, he must know she fucked Steel. The silence was punctuated occasionally with "hmms" and the slap of pages turning. Anne's stomach gurgled loudly. She wished she had made a breakfast of protein and starch rather than just coffee.

"Looks like you had yourself quite an adventure," Diamond said, nodding at the red welt and smattering of cuts and bruises on her bare arms.

"Yes it was. I do feel I won Captain Steel's confidence," Anne said.

"So who the hell were these guys Steel and the Nee-gree-toes were pursuing?"

"Steel said they were tracking bandits who had murdered Negrito tribesmen. They ruled out the Americans who were captured and interrogated. Their weapons hadn't been discharged."

"Out of curiosity, how did they determine that?"

Anne hesitated. "One of the Negritos reported that the weapons didn't smell like they had been fired."

"I see."

"Sounds strange, I know, but the Negritos have incredibly well-developed senses."

"So did you find any of this so-called Japanese treasure that our young captain seems to want us to believe is the real reason he's out gallivanting in the jungle?"

"No, but we did investigate two small caves. Steel has been developing a new theory, investigating World War II transport routes. He wants to see if the Japanese army used these forgotten old roads and riverbeds to move treasure from the airfield at Clark to the mountains."

Diamond seemed to perk up now they were talking treasure. "So, no treasure?"

"No."

"Do you think he ever found any?" Diamond asked.

"I think he might've. As I get to know him better, he might choose to confide in me."

"Did you see any evidence he lives beyond his means, fancy cars or an opulent house?"

"Nothing stands out. I saw his truck and his home; both are reasonable and consistent with his paygrade."

"Were you and he intimate?

"Sir?

"Did you sleep with him?"

"No," she said trying to sound definitive. "We had separate tents." Her heart raced, sweat tickled down her back. She was pleased she wasn't wired to a detector.

"That's unfortunate. Pillow talk is an effective tool that I would expect you to have in your arsenal."

Anne was stunned.

Diamond did not seem to notice. "Quite incredible that you encountered a Japanese citizen who claims to be a World War II soldier. I find that hard to believe. What do you think?"

"I think in all probability he's legit. It's happened before." Anne took a deep breath and hoped she wasn't blushing.

"Amazing," Diamond said.

"What do you think about the Americans tailing us?" Anne asked. "Do you have any guesses about who they might be?" She thought it strange the Americans hadn't been the first question out of Diamond's mouth.

Diamond peered over the top of glasses. "No, not really. But clearly they're no friends of Steel. He's got plenty of enemies out there."

"They must have been carefully watching Steel to know he

was heading out into the mountains. Maybe phone taps. Pretty sophisticated logistics at their disposal to be able to follow us. We left in a hurry and through some rough terrain."

Diamond shrugged.

"You undoubtedly read that the Americans said they were working for Singlaub. He's an agency guy, right?"

"Was. He's a private citizen now. A war hero. An American hero. These slugs you captured probably were just looking for someone to blame." Diamond frowned.

"Seems like an odd choice to blame someone specific like him. Maybe we should check out their stories and—"

"Not necessary. Singlaub is off-limits. He's here for meetings with the Philippine government about state matters."

"I thought he was here looking for treasure. Steel said the Phil papers reported Singlaub has a company based in Manila looking for—"

"Rubbish. Those papers are rags at best."

"Have we checked with Philippine intelligence?" Anne asked.

"Mr. Morris is on it. We have those bases covered. I'd like you to continue to run Steel. I hope you can ratchet up the pressure. You need to win over his confidence by whatever means."

"Yes sir, I think I have his confidence."

"Yes, yes, of course you did well, thus far, considering the extraordinary circumstances of this operation in the mountains. And, of course, without adequate training on your part."

His patronizing tone rankled her. "I worked hard getting an invite to tag along on the trip. His, er . . . partner wasn't all too happy I was along. I kept up with them."

"Well, I'm sure you can get closer to him. Really close."

She nodded, and he stared into space.

A knock on the door broke the silence. Mrs. Davis poked

her head in. "Mr. Diamond you have a call, Non-secure line. "Do you want to take it?"

"Yes. Anne, I think we're done for the day. I'll look at your report again. In the meantime, keep cracking on Steel. I'm sure you have plenty to offer him." A sleazy smile slid across his face.

Mrs. Davis put a hand on Anne's shoulder, ushered her out, and shut the door, leaving Diamond staring at his phone. He had been waiting for the call. More accurately, dreading the call.

He picked up the receiver and held the phone like it was red hot. "General Singlaub, thanks for returning my call. Yes, I was briefed on the bad news about the surveillance. I'm not quite sure what happened. No, no it . . ."

Anne walked out of Diamond's office angry. She had gone in thinking her report would be well-received. "That was mistake." She should have gone with her gut feeling—that Diamond, with zero overseas case officer experience, was a creepy male chauvinist pig, a Company dickhead who would nit-pick her work to death. She took a deep breath and headed back to the secure vault. She had heard her friend Greg would be there. He was a nerdy engineer and communications specialist, and they had been on several assignments together. He had been assigned to Manila station for over a year now.

Anne punched the four numbers in the cypher lock of the thick secure steel door leading into the vault. Greg was at a blinking computer terminal, typing on a keyboard. His back was to her. He was wearing black stereo headphones the size of muffins, likely engrossed in some British punk rock. She walked up behind him and lifted both fat headphones off his ears. He swiveled in the chair and his face lit up. He stood, and they hugged. She squeezed him longer and tighter than their status as just friend warranted, and the blissful smile that erupted on his face said it all.

She pushed him off, and he readjusted his black glasses. "Wow, great to see you- Gree— . . . er Benton. I missed you." He smiled goofily.

"I missed you too. It's been a mixed bag here," she said.

"Holy shit. Look at your arms," he said. He reached out and touched the welt.

"Ow, shit that burns." She pushed his hand away.

"Damn, sorry," he said.

"Oh here, I brought these." She reached into the handbag that hung over her shoulder and pulled out two cassette tapes. He had pleaded with her to bring some new Clash. His had disappeared during his move.

"Cool. Thanks, Benton. I've been buying these cheap-ass knock-offs on the local market. Sound quality is real bad. Shit. Have a seat."

"Thanks. So how's life been here in Manila?"

"Great. So good to be out of Langley. The economy is super cheap here. I have a fantastic apartment. Maid service and a driver if I need one."

"How are the clubs?"

"Mostly bad. But there's a few hard-rock places I go to. No punk scene."

"The ladies treating you well?"

He looked past her. "You'll have to check out my pad. I got this incredible Nakamichi sound system when I was in Japan. Top of the fucking line. We can hit a club, or two, if you like. It would be fun to show you around."

"Sure, great."

Greg kicked back in his chair, and the springs clanked. He folded his hands across his chest. "How does it feel being a honey pot?"

"Honey pot? What the fuck is that supposed to mean?"

Greg dropped his head and his glasses slid down his nose. "Oh. Nothing. I thought you knew."

She glared at him then leaned forward and smacked him hard in the chest, rolling his chair backwards.

"Shit, that hurt," Greg gasped, grabbing his chest and readjusting his thick glasses.

"It's not nothing. What did you mean by 'honey pot'?" She waited a few seconds then slid forward again and drew back her arm, ready to let fly another fist.

Greg rolled back a few feet in his chair and held up his arms. "Whoa there."

"I'm not anyone's honey pot."

"No, I don't in anyway think of you as one. I was an idiot. I just repeated what someone said about you, as a joke," Greg said.

"Look I'm not involved with anyone right now. I'm nobody's honey pot. Who said it?"

"I can't tell you that."

"She grabbed both of his chair's arm rests and pushed her face into his. "Oh yes you can. You can if you don't want me to punch your lights out."

Greg looked at her heaving tits and back at her. "I think you're misinterpreting the meaning of 'honey pot'?" He bit his lip fighting staring again at her breasts. "A honey pot, or honey trap, is the term for a— " He paused. "It's a compliment. They think you're attractive enough to lure a target and—"

"They're using me as sexual bait." Damn. At least that explained Diamond, she thought.

"Jesus, Benton, I thought you'd find it funny. Sorry. Look you're a hot babe. Who wouldn't be attracted to you?" Greg held up his arms as if preparing for another beating.

"So you heard someone—Diamond or Morris maybe—saying they recruited a honey pot for the Steel case."

Greg stared blankly at his shoes.

"Damn." She exhaled, sat back in her chair, and closed her eyes. "Sorry I didn't mean to take it out on you. I'm just a little sensitive right now." She opened her eyes, dug around in her purse, and pulled out the file. "Here, take a minute and read this."

Greg raised his hands, "Already read it."

"I thought it was in private channels."

He lowered his hands. "Yeah, but I saw you logged in early this morning. You didn't secure it properly."

"You fucking liar. I did too."

"Well maybe you secured it from a person of normal intelligence and average computer skills but not from me."

"Nosy bastard. What did you think? Diamond hated it."

"Well," Greg leaned forward and whispered. "He has reason to."

"What do you mean?"

Greg looked around the small room. "You mentioned Singlaub. He knows the guy. They talk on the phone all the time."

"How do you know that?"

He shrugged.

"Jesus, you're monitoring his calls."

"Shhh. I'm not listening to all of them. Just anything to do with you. I use a word recognition program that trolls for key words. If they're spoken, it records."

"That's some heavy shit."

"Diamond's a bad apple. Tech dude I know—a Company guy—says Singlaub's got some powerful friends who pull strings inside. Diamond's their boy. You know conspiracy, anti-Commie shit."

"What's the treasure angle?"

"Moolah. Cash. Gold. All provide power. The powerful want more of it. Singlaub's a right-wing boy who needs cash to fund his kill Commie projects."

"My God."

"Yeah, watch your back," Greg said.

"Goddamn it. I thought this whole thing seemed screwy, even by Agency standards. But you know what really pisses me off? They used me as bait. A honey trap." The words stuck to her tongue like sour milk. "Those bastards knew I wanted a case officer spot, and they used me."

"Don't feel bad. I thought you did an amazing job on the trip. Indiana Jones shit. James Bond shit. You got the instincts, talent, and smarts to get to the farm. It'll happen. Just wait and see."

She leaned forward quickly, and he flinched. She planted a kiss on his cheek. "Sorry for slapping you around. You've always been a pal."

He nodded. "Got your back, and your front. So you really took some fire. Must have been terrifying. I'd shit my pants."

"You have no idea . . ."

24

S TEEL ROLLED THE DATSUN UP the narrow dirt-packed road in front of Jo Jo's compact concrete block and wood house and tapped lightly on the horn. In the fading light, Jo Jo's barangay was sleepy and smoky. Some neighbors framed in kitchen windows cleaned dishes from the evening meal. Others lazed in the slight evening breeze on airy front porches. A skinny dog walked over to the truck and pushed its nose up to a tire. Entranced by the cornucopia of scents it found there, the remnants of mountain treks embedded in the treads, it lifted a leg and marked the Goodyear radials.

Steel was still in his uniform. He had missed dinner and his stomach growled, but Junior had left word that their monster truck was ready for inspection. Jo Jo deserved to come along for the unveiling. Steel hadn't seen Jo Jo since the encounter with Lt. Nada, the Japanese straggler. Jo Jo had been in hyperdrive ever since, recontacting newspapers and ramping up his Japanese language lessons.

Jo Jo jumped in the truck and checked his watch. "Eight p.m. You're working late tonight."

"Yeah, sorry, had to catch up on a bunch of stuff. Mostly trying to keep Thimble off my ass. He and Kuncker are heading to Jakarta for a conference, and I'm putting together a brief for them. Whatever gets them out of my hair." Steel shifted into reverse, backed up, and turned the truck around. Jo Jo pushed his head out the window and called a warning to two tiny toddlers rolling in the dirt. "I made contact with Mr. Yonada at the Japanese Embassy, "he said. "And he has their military attaché checking out Nada's story. He said the likelihood that Nada's boss is still alive is remote. But they are trying to find him. And get this. The Haponese newspapers are in a bidding war with me on who gets to cover the story. I'm up to 5,000 U.S. dollars."

"Shit, that's great, but don't sell yourself short. It could be the story of the decade."

"I'll play them off each other. Your cut will be significant." Jo Jo waved to a group of men playing cards at a rickety wooden table.

"Yeah that's great and with all this cash you're gathering, you still trying to get to Canada for a visit with your girls?

"Yes, but unfortunately the Canadian officials at their embassy aren't being too helpful. Apparently, I'm not the only Pinoy with dreams of visiting the frozen tundra."

"Too bad. I wish I knew someone."

"I'll keep trying, but I have offered to fly the girls here for a visit on their spring break."

"That's good," Steel said speeding up out of the barangay, clipping a rooster and sending it over the berm in an explosion of squawks and feathers.

Steel sat in front of Junior's massive and elaborately welded double gates and made several hits on the truck horn. They waited a minute, then Jo Jo shrugged, exited the Datsun, walked over to the gate, and peered through a crack in the metal. In another minute, a young boy opened the gates and waved them in. Junior approached, shirtless and in a pair of saggy pants. His large brown belly cascaded over his belt. He lived in an expansive compound adjoining the shop. His extensive family comprised most of his workforce. Steel gave him a double take. He'd never seen Junior so clean. Normally, his skin was coated in blackened grease. The only bodily marks of his profession tonight were the permanent tan lines on his forehead from his welder's goggles.

"Captain Steel? Would you like a beer?" Junior held up a brown bottle of San Miguel.

"No, but I'll take a Coke if you have one."

"Jo Jo, beer?

"No, Coke is good. Thanks."

Junior shrugged and called out to his eldest son—a skinny version of himself. "Boy, bring two Cokes. Come, let's look at this truck. I'm proud of the progress we've made. I've dropped all my other projects and put my best men on it."

Junior was laying it on thick Steel thought and winced, probably preparing him for the bad news on the final price tag. He'd heard some of the figures and estimates from Curtis. Steel hoped he wasn't being too overly ambitious with the project. Deep down he knew he needed a vehicle capable of hauling tons of treasure out of the mountains. He'd be damned if he was going to be screwed out of it again because he couldn't carry what he found. He'd just have to postpone that additional check for the orphanage. He felt bad about gambling with the kids, and Father Rudy's money, but like they say: You have to spend money to make money.

They walked into one of the back vehicle bays, and there stood the behemoth. It was four-door 1981 Ford F-350, dually rear tires, 4 x4, with crew cab and extended bed—pearl white with only slight traces of rust. A double gun rack hung in the rear window; the bumper sported a "Don't Mess with Texas" sticker. Junior banged on the hood with a flat palm.

"I've never had the privilege to work on such a big American truck. It is truly a well-made and solid vehicle, and, with the modifications we are making, it will be like an army tank, only the best of everything."

Steel grabbed his gut. Junior had to hear it churn. "The best, sure, if absolutely necessary. We haven't found the treasure yet, you know."

The truck was surrounded by scores of wood boxes, tool-littered tables, rolling dollies, two tall metal tanks, and a dangling web of rubber hosing attached to a welding torch. Dr. Frankenstein's motor lab.

Junior and Boy pushed aside equipment, Junior pulled a lever, a prehistoric lift groaned and strained, and the beast rose skyward.

Junior grabbed a flashlight and pointed out various modifications. "Sergeant Washington has been a demanding boss. He insisted that it carry a max two-ton load capacity off-road. I am happy to say, I think we are close to that." He whipped the flashlight around like a disco light show.

Steel nodded, his brain flashing to the flood of checks he had written to Curtis for parts.

"Provided the road isn't too bad, it should perform well in rough conditions, and on a real road, you will have smooth sailing with good speed and acceleration," Junior said.

"Excellent," said Steel.

They looked at the modifications to the truck bed and the special compartments hidden in the side panels. Steel leaned in and whispered to Jo Jo. "Those will come in handy for hiding weapons."

Junior stood on the bed and pointed. "It will have the heavy removable canvas top and side mounted fold down benches for extra seating, here and here. We will have a thick sheet of plywood on the floor, easy for moving objects in and out, and it will protect the metal bed."

Steel looked at the layout, figured it could hold ten Negritos per side; many more piled in on the floor between equipment, if necessary, and all safe from weather under the canvas top and sides.

They did an engine inspection next. Junior then discussed the truck cab's interior modifications, and in less than twenty minutes they were finished with the tour. It was coming along nicely Steel thought. Junior was sure they could finish in the next couple of weeks. Perfect timing. Steel was anxious to get it out into the Zambales and down old an old Japanese road he had found on a map. If he found gold again he had the vehicle to get it out. He was sure, almost sure, the monster truck would turn out to be worth its weight in gold.

25

Manila
Intramuros District
Friday, 3 January 1986

A COMPACT TOYOTA SEDAN WITH TINTED windows jetted up and bumped the curb parallel to the Cathedral Basilica of the Immaculate Conception, less formally known as Manila Cathedral. The sedan's windshield was foggy, and its wipers swished madly. It waited its turn behind the other vehicles queued to unload passengers. Tourists and pilgrims disgorged from a rainbow assortment of mini-buses and jeepnies, dodged huge puddles, and raced to shelter under the cathedral's stone entryway.

A figure wearing a raincoat and holding a newspaper over her head darted from the Toyota to the cathedral entryway but did not push through the crowd there. Maria Corazon Sumulong Cojuango Aquino, known as "Cory," didn't want people to think she was cutting in line. She glanced over her shoulder, checking one last time, ensuring she had lost Marcos's henchmen. They were her constant shadow—her constant dark, evil shadow.

Satisfied her driver had eluded them, her eyes darted to the wall of people in front of her. She had an important appointment to keep, an appointment that could change everything for her country. She put her head down and pushed between the wet, slippery, and stunned pilgrims standing and staring in awe at the majesty of the church entrance. One, a short, middle-aged Filipina woman, did a double take. She recognized Cory and pulled on the sodden shirt of her companion, but before he looked up, Aquino disappeared through the doorway.

The cathedral afforded anonymity; but even if she were recognized, Cory had a reputation as a pious Catholic, and her presence here would not be seen as unusual. Once inside, Cory kept her head down and eyes lowered. She walked carefully to the front of the church, listening to the squish, squish her soaked sensible brown-leather shoes made. She performed a curt genuflection in front of a life-sized ceramic Jesus, its bloody form gazing woefully back at her.

She plopped down on a wooden pew, removed her yellow raincoat and her glasses, and wiped them on the corner of her white blouse. She ran her hands through her short black hair and smoothed her plain, long skirt. She had followed instructions: Sit in the right front pews and wait for someone to make contact. It was all very secret. But with all the evil the Marcos's had perpetrated on her family, she was comfortable taking extra security precautions.

She lowered her head and stared at the water pooling on the concrete floor, dripping from her shoes and raincoat. She thought of her husband Benigno. How proud he would have been of her decision to run for president in his stead.

To be sure, no one thought "the simple housewife," as the press had dubbed her, had the smarts or the backbone to win a national race. But they were wrong, she told herself. She was from a long line of prominent Filipino politicians. She was educated. She had graduated from college in the U.S. with a degree in mathematics and French. She had been enrolled in law school in Manila when she met Benigno. She had given it up to raise their five children.

She had been at her husband's side throughout his political career, quietly advising and guiding him through the Philippines' treacherous political waters. She remained staunchly loyal to him. And when he was wrongfully imprisoned, and U.S. President Jimmy Carter pressured Marcos into releasing him, she followed her husband to exile in Boston. She had had a premonition of his death; she had begged him not to return to the Philippines.

But he returned, and was killed, and she returned two days later. She led millions of Filipinos in his funeral procession and, on that sad day, became the unofficial face of the anti-Marcos movement. But she lacked title or bureaucratic power. And now, with her children grown and a presidential election coming up, she could devote herself to carrying on her beloved Benigno's work. She wanted to deliver Marcos and his cronies a political defeat and provide justice and revenge for her husband's death. To do so, she knew she needed courage and maybe divine intervention.

She picked up a Bible from the shelf in front of her and opened the cover. She sought comfort but also wanted an excuse to keep her head lowered. She read for a few minutes before she noticed an individual standing in the shadows. He was dressed in a neat white robe. He made eye contact, glanced around the church, lifted his hand waist high, and gestured for her to come over.

Aquino nodded and slid out of the pew. She followed the man through a secluded side door, which he locked behind her with a heavy, black skeleton key. They walked down a dark corridor. The clunk of their shoes echoed off the stone walls and the ancient brick. It smelled like burning candles and centuries' old dust. Without speaking, he waved her through another door topped with a white sign that in simple black letters read: "Rectory."

Cory walked into the spacious, sparsely furnished room. She gazed at a painting of the cathedral in brooding dark colors and set in a garish gold frame. Cardinal Jaime Sin whisked in from an anterior room and over to her. He was in a flowing white alb that did little to hide his round paunch of a belly. They stood eye-to-eye for a moment. Cory had forgotten how short he was. He looked taller on television.

"Cory, my dear, it's been too long," Sin smiled.

Aquino bowed slightly and kissed Sin's ring.

"Please, let us sit. May I get us some tea and snacks?" Sin asked and motioned to an eight-foot-long Spanish colonial-era couch.

"Yes, that would be wonderful," she said, and sat perched on the edge while Sin lounged, his arm comfortably propped on a red velvet cushion. She continued, "I apologize for how I must look. I was nearly drowned running in from the car." She fluffed her skirt.

Sin waved off her comment. "You are most presentable. Teddy, bring that tea, will you, please."

Teddy nodded and left the room, shutting the door behind him. "No, it is I who must apologize for all the secrecy surrounding our visit. I'm already in hot water with my superiors. Well, my earthbound superiors," he chortled, "for my interest in politics."

"I know better than anyone how dangerous politics can be," she said.

"Yes, it's been over two years since Benigno's funeral. How are the children coping?"

"They miss their father greatly, but they know he is in heaven watching over them. They believe he didn't die in vain."

She kept steady eye contact. "He was a righteous and honorable man wanting to help the people as I want to help the people."

Sin nodded. "For too many years, our flock has been only a second thought to the present government."

"Yes, the needs and rights of Filipinos have been violated and trampled. We are an industrious people, unjustly held back by corruption. Filipinos deserve better."

"They deserve much better," Sin acknowledged. "But, as history has shown, the present government will stop at nothing to stay in power. They will kill innocents. That is where I am torn. I don't want Filipino blood spilled again." He looked at her with kindness, and she stared at her lap.

She took a moment to compose herself. "I too believe there has been too much killing. I want to make legal changes from within the system. That is why I have chosen to run for the presidency." She paused, letting her words hang in the air. "I want an honest and fair campaign, and I was hoping, Your Eminence, that the church would give its support and blessing."

The door opened, and Teddy slid in, carrying a tray. He closed the door behind him with his hip. He placed the refreshments on a low coffee table in front of the couch.

Sin sat up, reached for the china teapot, and poured deep orange-brown liquid into two cups. Then he leaned back, balanced his cup and saucer, and took a sip of tea. "Have a biscuit. They are from my last trip to the Vatican, such delicate sweet wonders." He smiled and took one.

She sipped her tea.

"You know that, officially, the church cannot take sides in any political contest. The government wouldn't hesitate to crack down on priests who did so. But there are subtle ways we can help. The people can most certainly be an army of God's will but only a peaceful army. I am a believer in Mahatma Gandhi's teachings of non-violence."

"I'm not advocating armed confrontation. I just want people to be free enough to vote against Marcos," said Aquino.

The Marcos name hung in the air. The first time it had been mentioned.

"I'm not sure Marcos will allow a fair election. He controls the system that monitors the votes," Sin said.

"That is mostly true. But I have contacts in the Commission on Elections who say there are good people within the organization who are tired of the hypocrisy."

"That would be blessing, if they could push back."

"Your Eminence, my supporters and I were hoping that the church could help by providing people to guard the voting stations."

Sin sighed and closed his eyes. "I'm not sure we can get that overtly involved." He raised both palms into the air. "I think we can make sure our flock gets out and votes their hearts."

Cory put her cup down and faced Sin. "Your Eminence, if there are the slightest signs of illegality or vote rigging, we are going to organize a massive protest. We won't stand for it. We will send millions and millions of Filipinos marching peacefully in the streets if the system fails us again."

"We should try to get some international attention for the election. Maybe some poll watchers," Sin said.

"Yes some friends are investigating that as we speak."

"Well, let's hope for a miracle, that there is a fair election and the right candidate—you Mrs. Aquino—is elected." He pointed a finger at her.

Cory slid over and pulled his hand to her face and kissed it. He put the hand on her shoulder and said, "I will pray now for you and your family."

Sin bowed his head and closed his eyes and mumbled a prayer. When he was finished, he slumped deeply on the couch, folded his hands under his chin, and met her eyes. He liked what he saw. She had a tough and determined edge. He knew that now. Not like at the funeral. There, she had appeared a distraught widow in a polite mask. There was no mask now. Her strength was genuine and her own. Sin smiled. Marcos and cronies had better not underestimate this "simple housewife." If they did, it could cost them more than the election.

26

Angeles
Saturday, 4 January 1986

J O JO BEEPED THE HORN several times but no Joseph. The gate remained closed. Jo Jo shrugged his shoulders. Steel jumped out of the truck and opened the gates himself. He was in a great mood after an afternoon of playing pool with Jo Jo. Afterwards, they went to Tony's house and rolled out a big map of the Zambales, tracing old road and riverbeds and picking Tony's brain on potential caves to explore. A dive bar, treasure talk, good friends. Life didn't get much better.

Steel entered the house and froze in the threshold. The place was an unholy mess. The living room looked as if a whirlwind had ripped through it. VHS tapes and books lay scattered over bunched and twisted oriental runners. His coffee table was upended on top of three months of *National Geographic* and *Life* Magazines. His TV and stereo system were gone. Jo Jo pushed around Steel, bags of vegetables and fruits dangling in his hands, stopped and gasped.

"What the hell? Where's Rosa?" Steel said. "Rosa," he yelled out.

"Someone's robbed us?" Jo Jo said and dropped the bags with two percussive thumps. A small watermelon rolled slowly across the floor.

Steel yelled out for Rosa again and walked quickly to the kitchen. This had to be a joke. Curtis having one off on him for throwing around the truck money like a big shot. Well, he'd gone too far this time.

"Rosa," Steel shouted as he crossed into the kitchen. "This isn't funny." She had to be at the stove this time of day trying to hold back her giggles and stirring something savory for dinner.

She wasn't at the stove. She was tied to a chair, hands lashed behind her, a bandanna wrapped around her eyes, and a rag shoved in her mouth. Her head slumped and her chin rested on her chest. Blood and mucus splattered her white uniform. Steel slid to his knees, slipped the bandanna off her eyes, and removed the rag from her mouth. More blood and saliva dribbled down her neck.

"Jo Jo, untie her hands," Steel barked, then whispered. "Oh Jesus. No, no. Please be alive, please." He gently cradled her head and a red tinged bubble formed in one nostril and then the other. "She's breathing," he said. "Jo Jo, she's breathing."

Jo Jo fell to the floor beside Rosa and fumbled at the rope securing her hands. "Goddamn it," he said and grabbed a knife from the kitchen counter.

"Jesus Christ, William!" Jo Jo shrieked, dropping the knife and pointing over to a dark corner of the backdoor's foyer. Joseph was face down in a pool of his own blood, his short broken yard bolo in one outstretched hand. Jo Jo stumbled over to Joseph. Steel started to rise, and Rosa moaned. He lifted her gingerly from the chair and lowered her onto the floor. He cradled her head, elevating it slightly, straining to recall any of the first aid courses he had taken.

"Joseph is dead." Jo Jo screamed. "He is not breathing. I can't feel a pulse."

Steel watched Jo Jo grope at the yard boy's shoulders, fixated on the ruby red lake that was pooled around Joseph's body. Joseph's father's face and words cut into Steel's thoughts. *Joseph is a good boy and we're trying so hard to keep him from the evil beings that hide amongst the lambs.* The smell of metallic blood hung in the air like the aftermath of a Saturday village cockfight, and Steel choked down sour vomit.

"There's a big wound in his back, maybe a bullet or knife," Jo Jo said, pulling up Joseph's ragged and stained T-shirt.

"Motherfuckers," Steel said, rocking Rosa.

Jo Jo straightened Joseph's shirt, stood up and stared at the blood on his own hands and pants. "Not Joseph. He's just a boy. Who would kill him?"

The Datsun screeched in front of the security checkpoint at Clark's Friendship gate. Steel had decided not to wait for an ambulance from the base and to drive Rosa to the ER himself. Too late to do anything for Joseph, but he couldn't think about that now. He thrust his military ID at the wide-eyed USAF security policeman, told the guy they were heading to the emergency room, and to call ahead to alert them.

The airman squinted at Steel's ID then leaned in and looked at Rosa's slumped body, a pile of gory maid's attire.

"C'mon," muttered Jo Jo from where he sat supporting her head.

"Yes, sir. Proceed. I'll make the call." He saluted quickly and turned back to the guard shack.

Steel blasted through traffic lights and stop signs, drawing honks and expletives at every corner. He fishtailed to a stop in front of the ER and waved at two hospital personnel in white uniforms standing next to a gurney. A nurse with silver lieutenant's bars on the lapels approached the passenger-side door. Steel ran around the truck to join her.

"She was attacked in my home. They killed Joseph, my yard boy." Steel pinched his temples and tried not to scream at her.

The lieutenant grimaced when she saw Rosa and called out for the gurney. Steel watched the hospital folks load Rosa on the wheeled bed and push her inside. "Go park the truck and find us," he called out to Jo Jo.

A doctor met the gurney and snapped, "Let's get her to an exam room." He walked quickly ahead of them. Steel stayed at Rosa's side, holding her hand. He was intercepted by another nurse, one with captain's bars on her blue blouse. She took her eyes off his bloodied shirt, offered a weak smile, and spoke. "Hold on there. You won't be able to follow. We'll take good care of her. Come with me to the admissions. I need some information."

Steel nodded and let her grab his arm. She guided him back to the entrance.

"Are you Steel?" Steel felt the tug on his sleeve and looked up to a man with a stethoscope around his neck. Steel glanced at the nametag. Dr. Blunt.

"I'm Steel. How is she?"

"Are you related to the woman who was just brought in?"

"How is she?" Steel said, his voice an octave higher than normal. He stared into the thick lenses of Blunt's glasses.

"I'm Captain Blunt. I'm the OIC of the emergency room. We are contemplating moving the female Filipino national into intensive care for further treatment. Her injuries are extensive. We're listing her as critical." He stared at a brown clipboard in his hands. "It says here that she sustained these injuries during a robbery. She's your maid. So she isn't your dependent?"

Steel squeezed his eyes shut. What was the doctor trying to say?

The doctor tapped the clipboard with finger. "Does she have a dependent ID? If she's a local national, we can't treat her. I suggest we get an ambulance and get her moved to a hospital in Angeles."

"You have erroneous information. She's my mother," Steel said flatly.

"I'll need you to sign some paperwork and provide her ID so we can continue to treat." The doctor stared briefly at the streaks of blood on Steel's face, then at Jo Jo who had pushed tight into Steel, maybe to steady him, or hold him back.

"I don't have her ID. Look, Doc. Just treat her."

"I'll have to have official documentation," Blunt insisted.

"If you need more I'll give my friend General Smith a call and ask him to straighten this out. Trust me he will." Steel felt Jo Jo's grip tighten.

The doctor tapped on the clipboard.

"Please, doctor. Treat her. She's my mother," Steel said.

Blunt sighed and continued tapping.

Steel pushed in tight to Blunt's face and hissed. "Fucking admit her or you'll see me in your nightmares, like the mist of death." He'd heard Tony use the phrase.

Capt. Theodore "Teddy" Blunt maneuvered the mangled Filipina's medical chart to make some space between him and the clearly deranged airman in front of him. His mother, fat chance. The guy was as white as the driven snow But Blunt had done his residency in a Washington, DC, inner city hospital and was streetwise enough to recognize that the guy's cold, crazed eyes were not an act. Not worth fighting over a couple of regs. He called out to the nurse to move the patient to intensive care.

Steel marched over to the nurses' station, picked up a black phone sitting on a desk, and called Smith. He was taking no chances.

"Inay, mother . . . Inay . . .What have I done to you?" Steel whispered, holding her hand. She gave him a sideways glance then stared straight ahead. Out of the bandaged and swollen face emerged a scowl. Rosa was still in there, underneath all the gauze and medical tape. Steel tried to smile, for her, or maybe for himself.

He had spent the best part of the last two days and nights in the waiting area and in Rosa's private room. Gen. Smith and his wife Becky had stopped by, as had Lt. Col. Kuncker. Two OSI agents and several local Angeles policemen had turned Steel's house into a crime scene. They interrogated Jo Jo, who had at some point been the one who had to deal with Joseph's body. It now lay in the police morgue in Angeles. The OSI agents grilled Steel at the hospital. Do you have any idea who could have done this? Was robbery a motive? What items were missing? Steel had no answers. Rosa gave no answers.

Jo Jo had surveyed the house. He said it looked like robbery. Why would they beat Rosa? She would have been easily overpowered. Joseph probably got killed trying to help her. They had ransacked the bedrooms and took the four .45-caliber pistols, boxes of ammo, and couple of grenades that Steel kept secured in a big wood footlocker in his bedroom. They had pried up a lockbox he had screwed to the floor. It held hundreds of dollars—maybe even thousands. He bet they had even taken his most prized possession—his father's Rolex watch. It had been in the box. It had broken years ago. He had meant to have it fixed. But the possessions were meaningless. The fuckers had stabbed Joseph in back.

Steel felt a tug on his shirtsleeve. Rosa's hand. She slowly mimed writing with a pencil. He grinned, and his jaw ached with the unfamiliar movement. He dug in his backpack and found a pad of paper and pen and handed it to Rosa. He watched her carefully etch out some words.

"How is Joseph?"

He didn't say anything but squeezed her hand tight. He couldn't form the words. She looked away, staring out towards the bright sunshine bursting in from a bank of windows in the room. Tears rolled down her cheeks. His too.

Steel's nemesis, Ex Scout Ranger Romeo Magos, exited Maloo's sari sari store just off of MacArthur Boulevard on Angeles' west side. The storefront was legit, but the rear was a bustling fence business, where the owners purchased pilfered goods, most stolen from Americano homes off base and from warehouses and buildings on Clark. He was disappointed with the paltry prices he had gotten for the electronics they'd removed from Steel's place. It all just made Magos angrier that he hadn't found Steel's treasure cache. Magos thought for sure Steel would have some hidden it in his home, and maybe he did. That old cow they had tied to the chair wouldn't talk, even after a good beating. She must have known something. And that idiot boy who came in the back. Too bad Magos had to kill before he got a chance to interrogate, but the kid had a knife or something. Oh well, at least we got this. He patted his pants pocket and felt the wad of cash he found in Steel's bedroom—no small sum indeed. His gang seemed elated with their cut, anyway. He was confident that the PC idiots investigating the crime wouldn't link him. He'd keep an eye on the Americano—especially if he headed up in the mountains again. He hailed a trike and jumped in its sidecar. He was headed back to his hideout on the edge of town where his men would be celebrating their good luck with plenty of loose women and beer. He didn't want to miss that.

27

TWO DOZEN MEMBERS OF THE Reform the Armed Forces Movement operated radios, talked into phones, and squinted over Manila street maps. Their movements and words were efficient and clipped, military. They didn't wear uniforms, but most were active duty Philippine Army personnel, and all were seasoned combat veterans. They gathered in an expansive home in an exclusive Makati City neighborhood, minutes away from the heart of Manila's central business district, the house their leader Lt. Col. Devincia had surreptitiously rented with the blessing of his boss, Secretary of National Defense Enrile. Devincia, no doubt worried that the house was under surveillance, had his two intelligence specialists sweep the place for listening devices twice a week. If Marcos got into their hideout, he would have all he needed to arrest them.

Devincia and Enrile sat alone in a compact room off the living room, discussing the upcoming presidential elections and coup plans. Enrile was dressed in a dark-blue suit, white shirt, and red tie with a small Filipino flag pinned to his lapel. The air-conditioning, as per his request, had been turned to high to dilute the cigarette haze wafting in from the adjacent room. His glasses slipped down to the end of his nose as he flipped through a notebook filled with briefing points. He nodded at each page, and when he reached the end, pushed his glasses up, closed the folder, and tossed it back on the coffee table.

He sighed and stared at Devincia. The report was thorough and insightful. Devincia was a professional staff officer, even when the subject was armed revolt. He was dressed more like a mercenary than a decorated AFP officer, though. Blue jeans, black cowboy boots, and a beige safari shirt with a worn brown leather shoulder holster holding a 9 mm Berretta pistol. Enrile watched Devincia brush hair back over his ears and rub his eyes. "Antonio . . . Antonio, I don't know if you're right. We have little to go on but your gut feelings. I've known General Eddie Ramos for many, many years. He didn't get the nickname Fast Eddie for nothing. He is a survivor. Remember." He pointed a finger at Devincia. "He was the enforcer of Marcos's martial law. But we are now to believe he is willing to go against Marcos and side with us if it all goes to hell?" Enrile took a long sip of coffee.

"But, sir, were you not part of Marcos's martial law too? And now here you sit with us." Devincia raised his hands, and his thick moustache bobbed up with the force of his big smile.

Enrile chuckled and nodded. "True. But I'm not sure if Eddie has fallen as far from grace as I have . . . enough so to join our putsch."

"I have it from a good source close to Ramos." Devincia leaned in. "His military aid, that the general is not happy with the Marcos's. Ramos is sick of the hypocrisy, and I think, should the election be full of irregularities and should the people take to the streets, he will support them. And then us."

"But Marcos's henchman, General Ver, controls the Army,

and his generals will follow him. They owe their lives to the Marcos's."

"That is why we must strike a blow against the Marcos's." Devincia stabbed the folder with his finger. "At Malacanang Palace, the seat of imperial power. If we can control it and some TV and radio stations, then I think we destroy their lackey general's will to fight. The only branch that worries me is the Marines. They'll remain loyal to their command. I have the allegiance of many junior and midlevel Marine officers in RAM, but nothing higher than major."

"So after the elections, if the people rise up, then we implement this?" asked Enrile.

"We will strike multiple targets. I'll lead the assault on the palace and will arrest Marcos myself. We'll also take the airport and block key intersections so Marcos can't send in reinforcements."

"I read your plan. It's very ambitious and requires a lot of men and equipment."

"We have the men, and we are stockpiling equipment," said Devincia.

Enrile set his coffee cup down. "It's good we take immediate control of the media. If Marcos is arrested, we need to get the word out quickly. That will push the fence sitters to our side."

"I agree. Most will fold or run," Devincia said.

"If we undertake this craziness, I want to make sure we can mobilize an army of the people. Hundreds of thousands . . . maybe even millions of angry civilian supporters marching in the streets, surrounding the palace and army encampments," said Enrile.

"Yes, a sea of people providing a moat of protection for our boys."

"Cory must be protected at all costs. Marcos will strike against her if he feels threatened," said Enrile.

"We are on that. Our support for Cory is central—we must never be seen as opportunistic military men bent on establishing a dictatorship," said Devincia.

"Right. The people must understand we seek to restore democracy and install a duly elected president. More importantly, we want to curry favor with the Americans. I think they will support us. They are just as sick of Marcos as we are."

"I have two dozen men who will be assigned to Cory's security team. We'll move her to a secure location after the election—with or without her permission," said Devincia.

Enrile nodded. "Good. We'll need to get her on the air right after we take the," he paused before he could speak the word, "president. We can't kill him. We have ensure he and his family remain alive."

"Yes, sir. We'll do our best to take them alive, and we'll get Cory sworn in as president as soon as possible. About that army of civilians, sir, I was hoping you'd schedule an appointment with Cardinal Sin, just to let him know how you feel. Of course, not about our plans, but just to keep him as an ally. The voice of Catholic radio could get the word out to support the coup."

"Good thought. I'll speak with the cardinal in vague terms, of course. Good thought."

"Couldn't hurt to have God on our side too." Devincia put his hand on his heart.

"True enough. Also Antonio—I fail to see anywhere in your report protection for me during the revolution. I'm sure I too will be high on the Marcos hit list."

"Definitely sir. I've . . ."

28

Barangay Sampung Bato
Thursday, 9 January 1986

"THERE HE IS." PONGPET TUGGED on Tony's shirt and nodded in the direction of the lowlander sitting on the wood bench in front of Chan's store, a popular sari sari store in Barangay Sampung Bato. "We saw him when we were buying the things you asked for."

It was 8 p.m., and the sun sat low on the mountains, casting a dull orange glow over the scene. Tony lifted a hand to his forehead and shielded his eyes. He stared at the man but couldn't see his wrist. The man, dressed in a dirty white T-shirt and blue pants, was talking loudly and waving a brown bottle of San Miguel beer. He was clearly drunk. Tony stared for a few more seconds then turned and sighed. He'd never seen the man before. "Are you sure you saw the watch? I'm not sure I could remember such a small detail," Tony said.

Pongpet elbowed Ganchee in the ribs. "Is it not big and shiny with a blue face? You saw it too, right? Tell Tony."

Ganchee nodded. His eyes were wide, and his pig-bone necklace bounced noisily on his chest.

Pongpet continued. "Remember when Steel took it off and showed it to us. He said it was his father's, the one who died in the Great War. It had the glass bubble on it that pointed to the direction so to find the way."

"It is the same thing that I saw Steel wear," confirmed Ganchee.

"Ah the compass on the watch," Tony said, more to himself than to his rural cousins.

"Yes, the compass," Ganchee repeated.

"You said to us that robbers broke into Steel's house and hurt his Rosa and killed his Joseph," Pongpet said.

"That is what I said." Tony glared at the lowlander man, who was gesticulating, and wondered if he really had Steel's watch. How could that be possible?

Pongpet pulled on Tony's shirt again. "I liked Joseph. He was always nice to us when we visited. Remember when he brought us the bottles of drink when we were waiting for Steel when we brought the rusted gun and the—

Tony interrupted, "I liked Joseph too, and Steel is very sad about Rosa. Jo Jo said they stole things. Maybe this lowlander drunk took the watch."

"Maybe so. That is why I told you about the watch," Pongpet said.

"Wait here. I'm going look closer."

Pongpet shrugged.

Tony stood in front of Chan's perusing a wooden bin full of green coconuts. The lowlander gave Tony a quick once over then went back to lecturing two men, both of whom Tony recognized as local drunks. Tony snuck glances at the loudmouth man. Even sitting, he was tall, with a powerful build and enormous hands. His hair was dirty, ragged and longer than most lowlanders'. The man's face sagged on one side and his mouth drooped. He had only a few black teeth. Tony would have remembered these things if he had seen the man before. He smelled like he hadn't bathed in a long time. Campfire smoke hung on him and gunpowder. Tony saw a bulge under the grimy T-shirt, confirming a pistol was tucked into the man's pants. His boots were military, scuffed and covered with dried mud, red the color of dirt found in the mountains. The man angled his arm, enough so that Tony could check out the wrist. There was the big watch with the blue face and silver band with the compass. Pongpet had been right. Tony did remember seeing the watch on Steel's arm, but Steel hadn't worn it in several years. Tony knew why. And he knew how to find out if the watch was genuinely Steel's. He would ask the man.

"Excuse me, friend, do you have the time?" Tony approached the man.

He glared at the Negrito. A sneer stretched his face and his eyes wandered independently, seemingly unable to focus.

"Friend, your watch. Can I see the time?" Tony pointed to the wristwatch.

The man covered it with a hand stained with grime. "It's broken right now. Find someone else, little nog nog."

Tony had to stop his hand from going for his knife. He nodded politely, and went in the store. Chan, the shriveled old Chinese man who owned the place, stood up. "Good evening, Mr. Tony, what can I get you?"

Tony stood on his tiptoes and leaned in across the countertop. "Mr. Chan, the big man, sitting out front, do you know him?"

Chan frowned and whispered. "The loud drunk is buying beers for those two idiots." He pointed to the porch. "He is flashing lots of money around town."

"Lots of money?" said Tony.

"He paid for food earlier with this." Chan fumbled in a drawer behind the counter and shook a U.S. $50 dollar note in the air. "Took all my change. He wanted to know if I could trade him some pesos for more dollars."

"Salamat po, thanks, Mr. Chan." Tony nodded and walked out by the man and back across the street to the shadows.

Pongpet and Ganchee rushed Tony. "It is Steel's?" Pongpet said.

Tony put a hand on Pongpet's shoulder. "Yes. As always, cousin, you have sharp eyes. Steel will be pleased we have found the man who robbed his house."

"Yes, he will be."

Ganchee pinched his nose and spoke, "The man smelled very, very foul. But he smelled like mountains too."

"I thought so as well. Maybe he is part of the gang we have been tracking. The Negrito killers," said Tony

Ganchee's eyes widened. "That would be good for us to have found him here."

"It is also as we thought, that the gang comes and goes to the mountains. That is why we haven't been able to track them there." Tony stared at the man again. "We need to create a plan. This lowlander is a powerful man and armed with a pistol. I want him alive to talk to us about where his den of killers live." Tony felt the smooth handle of his knife and tried to ignore, just for this moment, his blood lust for revenge.

Steel pushed his groin against Anne's naked ass curled against him. The streetlight near his bedroom window illuminated her white skin and cascading red hair. Her body was warm and comforting. The buzzing ceiling fan offered up a steady breeze. Steel welcomed Anne's arrival yesterday. Sexual exhaustion helped him sleep, gave him a chance to shut down his brain. At least Rosa was a little better. She had been moved out of intensive care and, a few days later, discharged, despite having suffered internal bleeding, a concussion, a fractured jaw, and breaks in her nose, three ribs, and her hand. She was a bad patient. Steel had paid for an ambulance to take her to her sister's house in Manila. He had also hired nurses to provide full-time care. He didn't want her to recover in this house and imagined she didn't want to either. The memories had to be too raw.

Joseph's funeral was in the morning. It would be a simple affair, but Steel was sure there would be a crowd. Joseph had been a popular kid in his barrio. Jo Jo and Steel would be pallbearers. Steel dreaded the whole thing. He fought choking up every time he walked through his lush green garden and had to blink hard not to see a pool of blood every time he walked into the kitchen. He got the feeling that everyone was blaming him for Joseph's death.

Most people at work had been kind but in a mechanical manner. He could sense some thought he was taking the attacks on his household help way too hard. The general had been there for him. The OSI and the local police were still in the process of investigating the crime. Rosa had been blindfolded through most of the ordeal. But one fact she relayed haunted Steel. She had reported she thought she recognized the voice of one of the intruders. "Where was the treasure?" she scrawled. Then she wrote, "He kept yelling at me that he wanted gold." It gnawed at Steel. Could it have really been someone they knew? What a nightmare.

Steel glanced over at his clock radio—11:15 p.m. He listened to Anne's rhythmic breathing and felt her heart beating through the palm of the hand he pressed tightly to her chest. Outside the sound of an engine knocking cut through the usual cacophony of tree frogs songs. It sounded like a vehicle had stopped in front of his house. A few seconds later, the clunk of the gate latch. Steel strained his ears, was sure he heard the faint metallic squeak of hinges. He rolled over and reached for the pistol on the bedside table. The wood dimples on the grip of the Colt .45 dug into his skin and molded into his palm. He slid off the bed and cocked the weapon, sliding one round into the chamber, pushing back the hammer. He slid the safety off and moved over to the window. He was ready to kill the motherfuckers if they were back.

Steel saw human shadows fall on the pea-gravel path and heard the slight rustle in the tangle of jasmine vines in front of his window. More rustling and a face pushed tightly against the black screen. Steel jammed the barrel of pistol hard making contact with flesh. The apparition vanished with a crash of foliage. Steel aimed the pistol at two dark figures lying on the ground and tightened his finger on the trigger.

"Don't shoot, Captain Steel. It is I, Tony, and Pongpet. We have found your watch and need you to come with us."

Steel blinked hard, trying to focus on the meaning of Tony's words.

"Tony, what the fuck? I almost shot your ass," Steel said hissing through clenched teeth.

"What's going on?" Anne asked. Steel turned. She sat upright in bed.

"Nothing. It's just Tony."

"Christ," she said, pulling up the sheets to cover her, staring at Steel.

He clicked the pistol's safety on. "I'm going to see what Tony wants." Steel slid on his gym shorts without letting go of his weapon. He strode to the front door, opened it, and peered out. "This better be good." Tony and Pongpet stared back, wide-eyed, focused on the pistol dangling at Steel's side.

"We found your father's watch." Tony dangled it from one hand. "Is it not the one you used to wear before it was broken?"

Steel snatched the watch and held it up to the light. He flipped it over and read the inscription on the back: *Captain*

Raymond Steel: Love you always, Lily. It had been a gift from his mom to his dad.

Steel's mouth gaped open. "Where'd you find it?"

"A lowlander goon was wearing it," Tony said.

Pongpet pushed forward his chest puffed out. "Ganchee and I found him in the village, and I saw he was wearing the watch with the com-passes that shows the directions." He stopped talking and squeaked his bare feet on the red tile on the landing in front of the door.

"Come in. Let's talk inside," Steel said, eyes still on the watch in his hand. He waved the Negritos over to the couch and sat himself in a papasan chair.

Tony perched on the sofa's edge and relayed the story.

"Where's the motherfucker now?" Steel's said, clutching the watch tightly. He knew he sounded like a robot, but couldn't seem to shake his monotone.

The Negritos stared at him, no answer.

"Where is he now?" Steel yelled.

"In my house."

"You kill him?"

"No, he—"

Jo Jo rushed into the living room clutching a M16 in his hands. "Jesus Maria—what the hell is going on here? It's in the middle of the night," he said his face contorted into a grimace.

"I don't know yet. Pull up a chair and join us," Steel asked.

Jo Jo remained standing.

"My watch." Steel held it up.

"What the hell?" Jo Jo said.

"So, back to my question. Did you kill him?" Steel said.

"No, he is tied up in my house. My brother-in-law and two friends are watching him."

"Who's tied up and who watching who?" Jo Jo asked.

"Maybe one of Rosa's attackers," Steel said.

"Jesus," Jo Jo exhaled.

"Good. Do you know the guy? Have you seen him before?" Steel asked.

Tony and Pongpet shook their heads.

"Rosa said she thought she recognized one of the voices of the men who attacked her. So you never saw this guy around?"

"No, he is not known to us or anyone in the barangay."

"He's going to lead us to the rest of them. I know there are more," Steel said, laying the pistol down on a side table sitting next to his chair.

Tony nodded. "Yes, we think he is maybe part of the gang that killed our relatives. Maybe they move from the mountains to their hideout with the lowlanders."

"That is why we haven't found them in the mountains. Because they come and go to there," Pongpet added.

Steel watched both sets of Negrito eyes flick towards his bedroom door and followed their stares. Anne stood in the bedroom doorway. She was wearing one of his T-shirts, fiddling with the hem, trying to hide her naked ass.

Steel turned back to Tony, "I want to talk to this guy, but I can't do it tomorrow. I have Joseph's funeral. Take him to June's village and hold him there. I'll come the day after tomorrow. Saturday. We can make him talk."

"Make who talk?" Anne called out.

"Long story. I'll fill you in," Steel said and stood up. The Negritos stood as well. "Don't let him escape . . . but keep him alive."

Everybody nodded.

29

I T WAS EARLY MORNING, AND Steel and Jo Jo were in the Datsun, banging down a gravel road in route to June's village, where Tony was holding Joseph's killer. Steel stared out the window, watching the dense foliage fly by. He was filled with black bile. Joseph's funeral yesterday kept flashing through his brain: the dead boy lying in the coffin, dressed in a Sunday suit two sizes too big. The poor kid hadn't even had the chance to grow into it. From Joseph's family, stares tinged with hatred and unspoken words of blame. Even Jo Jo at once point burst out, "We have Joseph's blood on our hands." Steel had wanted more than anything to drink himself senseless but fought the urge. Instead, he survived by shutting down, thinking only of bloody revenge and a thousand ways to torture and kill the perpetrator.

They pulled into the assemblage of bamboo and woven-grass huts that comprised June's village. The usual throng of dogs, kids, and teenagers greeted them with whoops, waved hands, and throaty jungle bird calls. A bleary and red-eyed Tony quickly approached the vehicle.

"Captain Steel, it is good you are coming to us today. The big man is too much the trouble. I should have just killed him."

"I'm happy you didn't. It means a lot to Jo Jo and me that you found him," Steel said, following Tony, who was walked at a fast clip towards a small thatched grass and bamboo nipa hut. Outside stood June and two twitching Negritos, both pointing rifles at the doorway. Steel nodded to June.

"Captain Steel, I'm not sure how much longer we can keep this great monkey captive," June said.

"Who the hell is this guy?" Jo Jo said.

"A piece of shit as far as I'm concerned." Steel peered inside, clutching the grip of the pistol in his shoulder holster. He pushed inside, and Jo Jo and the Negritos crowded in behind. The interior was dark and smelled of sewage and puke. A man sat on the hard-packed dirt, naked except for filthy boxer shorts. Even sitting, he was the biggest Filipino Steel had ever seen, at least three inches taller and one hundred pounds heavier than Steel. The man had rolls of fat on his stomach, but Steel guessed that below the blubber was muscle. The man glared at them, his slanted eyes barely slits on his face and his mouth drawn into an evil sneer. Chinese ancestry probably explained his eyes and size, but the face, while deformed, had Filipino features. The man jumped to his feet with surprising agility. Steel pulled the pistol almost out of its holster as he fought fear, but he stood his ground. The steel chain and padlock around the man's wrists seemed puny, and the tree growing through the hut to which he was tethered, flimsy. He looked at Steel and jerked hard against his restraints, growling like a deranged pro wrestler. Steel took a few quick steps backwards, stepping on Jo Jo's feet.

"Sorry for the bad smell, but he threw the bucket we gave him to shit in," June said.

"Yes, poor Pongpet took the bucket in the chest," Tony said, grinning.

Steel gritted his teeth and moved towards the prisoner, just out of reach of his kicking feet. The man stopped straining and yelled that he was going to kill everyone if they didn't let him go. Steel stared at the brute. Did this animal murder Joseph?

"Tony, how the hell did you subdue him?"

"It was like trying to capture a big carabao, water buffalo, alive. But Uncle June's wife solved our problem," Tony said.

"What are you looking at, you fucking nog nogs?" the man screamed, strings of drool hanging from his mouth.

"How?" Steel said, picturing the wispy Mrs. June, who couldn't have weighed eighty pounds.

"She is a medicine woman and told me a long time ago about the plant roots that can cause sleep. They are strong medicines. If you put them on an arrow or knife blade, it attacks the body quick. I used the blowgun."

"Take off the lock, and we'll see who is the man and who is the woman." The man's voice broke hoarsely.

"It took two darts and six men to get him here," Tony said.

"Did he say where he got my watch?"

"No, he just yells and kicks like a crazy monkey."

"You're the fucking nog nog monkeys," he screamed, spitting at them.

Steel pulled the Rolex out of his pocket and held it in front of the man. "Where did you get this?"

He looked at the watch and snarled at Steel with snaggled teeth and blackened gums. "I found it."

"Where'd you find it?" Jo Jo said, pushing past Steel.

The man kicked out at Jo Jo, who grabbed his foot and flipped the man backwards. When he struggled to rise, Jo Jo kicked the man in the shins.

"You can kick well for a woman," he said.

"Where did you get the watch? I'm not going to ask again," said Steel.

The man's narrow eyes opened wide, as if he suddenly realized he might have something to bargain with.

"Did you kill my houseboy and beat my maid?"

"Maybe," the man said with a guttural laugh.

Steel pulled the .45 from his holster, locked and loaded the pistol with a click-clack, and pointed it at the big man's head. The brute's eyes fixed on the barrel of the pistol and his mouth sagged.

"You killed Joseph and beat a defenseless old lady just to get money and this watch." Steel patted his pocket.

The man tilted his head and blinked several times. Steel stared at the man's face, trying to read it like a gambler would. He's betting the skinny Americano doesn't have the balls to kill an unarmed man, Steel thought.

He was probably right. Steel sighed. He relaxed his grip, dropped his aim to the man's bare right foot, and pulled the trigger. The .45 round exploded and reverberated off the walls of the confined hut. The big man stood motionless for a second, then his head drooped and he saw his mangled foot. He was missing the big toe and two others. The remaining digits hung to a bloody stump by stringy sinew. He fell to the ground, his mouth open in a silent scream. He thrashed against the chain like a wounded animal. After a few futile tugs, he settled into a fetal position, moaning. Steel got down on one knee and shoved his face close. "So now that I have your attention." He pressed the pistol barrel against the man's good foot, and he jerked it under his legs and tried scooting backwards on his ass.

"Did you kill my Joseph?" Steel moved after the man trying to jab the foot again.

"You shot my foot. I can't believe you shot my foot." The man coughed out the words and scuttled against the wall.

"Why didn't we try this? He is very cooperative now," Tony said and shrugged.

"I took it from your house along with the money," the man said.

"Did you kill Joseph?" Steel said.

"No. I didn't kill that boy or beat the woman. I don't waste my time with them."

"Who did then?" Steel asked.

The man's silence was met with another deafening shot. The bullet struck the ground two inches from is good foot.

"Romeo Magos did it! He's a coward. I shouldn't have let him do it," said the man.

"Romeo Magos, the former Scout Ranger?" Jo Jo yelled over the reverb from the Colt's blasts.

The name Magos ricocheted in Steel's head like one of the .45 rounds. The former Army renegade Magos was a known thief who had almost gotten Steel killed on a treasure hunting trip a few months back. And Magos knew Steel's house. He had been there trying to sell shit souvenirs he had found in the mountains. Rosa must have remembered the voice.

"That motherfucker! Why did he kill Joseph and beat my maid?"

"He said he wanted to make the old woman tell us where the treasure was hidden. But she didn't know and the Magos killed the boy because he tried to attack us with a bolo," he moaned.

Steel closed his eyes and his chin hit his chest. Treasure. They had killed Joseph trying to get at the treasure they thought he had stashed in his house. He shook his head, his eyes still tightly closed, and whispered. "Joseph didn't have a bolo just a broken fucking garden tool." Steel's eyes flashed open, he fired another round, and the bullet pierced the loose folds of the man's baggy underwear. "Where is Magos?"

"We have a house in Mabalacat where we hide out. We go between that one and the mountains."

Tony pressed his head next to Steel's waist, and he remembered the Negritos. "Did you kill the Negritos a couple weeks ago?" Steel asked.

The man looked over at Tony. "Yes. But . . . but Romeo and the others killed them. I have nothing against nog nogs."

Tony rushed forward and jammed the point of his knife against the throat of the big man. "Where are these hideout places you live?"

The man's eyes dimmed and his breathing became shallow, likely from blood loss. Steel could see a red pool on the ground. "I can take you there," the man whispered.

"Tell me!" Tony's knife drew blood from the man's neck, but there was no answer. He had passed out.

Steel pulled Tony's arm. "Leave him for now. Get someone to treat the foot. We have to keep him alive so he can lead us to Magos."

Tony barked at June to fetch his wife. June nodded and left.

30

Angeles
Monday, 13 January 1986

"WILLIAM-SAN, YOU WANT AN ICE tea?" Jo Jo called out from the kitchen. He had been filling Rosa's role, trying to return some order to the house.

"Yeah, thanks," Steel called back and, still wearing his Air Force blues, flopped on the couch in his living room causing the rattan legs to slide and squeak nosily across the highly polished wood floors. Despite Jo Jo's valiant efforts, the house still seemed empty and violated. Without Rosa and Joseph, it just didn't feel like home anymore.

It had been an exhausting few days. Yesterday, the big man gave them directions to a small ramshackle house in Mabalacat. Jo Jo had hired a retired Philippine Constabulary sergeant, who lived in Jo Jo's Barangay, to investigate before they unleashed a motley crew of heavily armed, pissed-off Negritos. It turned out the bandits weren't at home. The sergeant was to keep the hut under surveillance and call when they returned.

Work today had only added to his pounding headache. He'd put his papers in to resign his active duty Air Force commission. The general's executive officer had helped him accomplish the task and to apply for a reserve commission.

Anne thought his decision rash. She had counseled against making any big moves on the heels of the attack. But he assured her his quitting was long overdue. It was nice to have someone other than Jo Jo to bounce things off, at least by phone. She'd been pushing to visit Steel, but he'd put her off. He needed to keep his focus on trying to find Joseph's killers.

Jo Jo walked in and handed Steel the ice tea. "You quit the U.S. Air Force today?"

"It was for the best. With everything going on, I was doing a bad job lately anyway. It'll give me time to clear up some of this mess. I expect they'll approve the paperwork relatively quickly and, once we deal with these very bad people, we can get back to looking for treasure."

Jo Jo jumped in, "We also need to lead the Japanese embassy folks back to find Lieutenant Nada. They're still trying to find his commanding officer back in Japan and—" A phone ring pealed over his words, but Jo Jo continued. "Maybe it's the sergeant, and he's seen the bandits . . . but probably, it is more likely Rosa's sister calling. I think they are both sick of her living in Manila—"

"Just answer it and find out."

"Oh wait, Cham called earlier today, and he said to remind you he's coming here at the end of the month." The phone continued to ring.

"I remember. Why don't you just answer it and find out who it is."

"Okay, but I think it's Rosa," Jo Jo said heading over to the phone.

"I think Rosa wants to come home," said Steel. "I feel bad she's still in Manila, but I just hate to have her move in back here, so many nightmares. You know, I'm thinking about moving us to a bigger house, maybe to a farm with some acreage."

Jo Jo yelled from the study. "William-san, it is the man who called twice before."

Steel got up and took the call. Ten minutes later he walked into the kitchen and found Jo Jo bent over the sink, washing a big bowl of uncooked rice.

"Who was it?" Jo Jo asked.

"It was Roxas's brother—Edgar—in Baguio."

"Edgar Roxas?" Jo Jo said, swishing the rice like he was panning for gold. "Ah that makes sense now. The voice was so familiar."

"He said he wants us to come to Baguio and see him. He has something important to tell us. I told him I couldn't leave Angeles right now. He said he'll come to us tomorrow. Must be big. I don't see him as the traveling type, especially with his sick little girl."

"Maybe he has a cave for us to check out," Jo Jo said.

"I told him to meet us at the Chili Pot at six."

"Sounds good."

Neither Jo Jo nor Steel picked up the stained plastic menu. They'd been to the Chili Pot so many times, they had memorized it.

"What ya having?" Steel asked.

"The tacos, like always."

"They're great—but so's the chicken."

"What is good is this ice tea." Jo Jo took a big slug.

The banter was familiar, comforting. Steel needed it. Jo Jo checked his watch. "I wonder if Edgar made it to Angeles on time. He's staying with a cousin, right?"

"He said he'd be here." Steel turned his head and checked the door. They had asked for a quiet table in the corner out of the way. Edgar said he wanted privacy.

They chatted for ten more minutes when Jo Jo sat up and strained his neck looking at the doorway.

"I'll be damned, there he is."

Steel stood and waved to Edgar. He was wearing a baseball cap and his black-rimmed glasses. He had the collar of a light blue windbreaker pulled up, and his eyes darted around the restaurant. He acknowledged Steel with a quick wave, walked over to the table, and sat down. He kept the hat and jacket on. The three chit-chatted about his trip, the weather in Angeles, and other mundane topics, and Edgar all the while kept his eyes on the door.

"So you want to order some food?" Steel asked.

"Yes, but could you please wait for a moment," Edgar stood and walked towards the exit.

"He's leaving," Jo Jo said and rose from the table.

Steel whipped his head around. "What the fuck?"

Before they could go after him, Edgar returned with someone else in tow. They both slunk over to the table; Edgar took a seat and offered another to the stranger.

"Captain Steel, Jo Jo, I'd like to introduce you to my brother Rogelio."

Rogelio extended a hand to Steel, then Jo Jo, leaned in, and in a faint voice said, "Nice to meet you both. Edgar has told me good things about you how you gave him money to help my niece. That was kind."

Steel's heart thumped hard—the famous Buddha man in person. This must be important news if the man himself was here delivering it.

Steel stared at Rogelio face. His eyes were sunken black holes set deep in his skull, and his ashen skin was stretched tight over high cheek bones. He looked like a cadaver. The price of living in the shadows, Steel surmised, and maybe also of enduring torture at the Marcos goons' hands.

"You should eat something," Steel said.

Rogelio nodded. "That would be good."

They flagged the waitress, ordered food, and were in the process of eating when the conversation changed from minutiae to the real purpose of the visit.

"I think you know of my unfortunate history with the Marcos government, so I won't go into it now. Instead, let me be direct. I have a map that my friend recently found. His father died, and it was hidden in an old trunk in his house. I believe you know the story of my friend whose father was a soldier in the Japanese Army. This map, I believe, shows the location of a possible site. A site of special interest." He stopped short of saying treasure. He looked around the restaurant, his eyes sweeping over the half dozen tables filled with diners—mostly Americans—before he continued in a whisper. "The site is an old mining tunnel, part of pre-World War II silver mining operations. I need your help to investigate the tunnel. I visited the site in secret and I think it looks promising."

"Why didn't your friend dig it out?" Jo Jo asked.

"He is not well. For many years he has been crippled with sickness and fear He lives secluded with relations in the mountains."

"Why do you need our help? Can't you and your brother just dig it out like last time?" Steel asked.

"No. Never again will I be able to dig. I took a risk just going to the place. I had to go to great lengths to make sure I wasn't followed. Today as well." He paused for a moment, choking. He was clearly unused to speaking, and his voice had become raspy. He took a drink of tea.

Jo Jo leaned in, almost knocking over his drink. "What makes you think this site is good?"

"Rogelio thinks it has a similar layout to the previous one he found," Edgar said.

Rogelio nodded. "I am almost certain. I found what appears to be a false wall. It will take some effort to dig out the entrance to the special rooms, but I think I know where to start. We will need men, equipment, and maybe explosives."

"I have the men. Good, reliable, honest men. I'm interested. But I don't think we'd be able to move on it immediately. We have some pressing business here in Angeles. What kind of financial arrangement are we talking here?" said Steel.

Rogelio and Edgar looked at each other, as if to reconfirm previous discussions, until Edgar spoke. "We were hoping for a sixty percent share."

Steel took a long drink of tea and scrutinized them.

Jo Jo broke the silence. "I don't think we can do that. We'd give you twenty percent. We are taking all the risks."

Steel glared at Jo Jo but kept quiet.

Rogelio and Edgar again made eye contact. Edgar gave his brother one silent nod and Rogelio spoke.

"Okay. We aren't in a position to bargain. That is fair since you will be doing the digging; it is your equipment."

"Let's see what you have," Steel asked.

Rogelio took a pen from his pocket and started to sketch out the details of the map on a napkin.

31

S TEEL PARKED HIS NEW TRUCK. Ten p.m. on a Thursday
night and traffic was light. A handful of jeepneys and
trikes cruised by, paying him little notice. The place he
had set to meet Devincia was readily accessible by vehicle but
provided a degree of privacy. The truck windows were rolled
down, and night air carried in the smells of nocturnal Angeles:
burning trash, open sewers, and tropical flora. Less than one
hundred yards away, the bar district was a black silhouette
punctuated by flickering lights. Faint music from the clubs
drifted toward Steel, but he couldn't make out a particular
song, just the faint jumble of tinny music. Off to the side, Steel
could see the outline of the huge salakot monument, shaped
like a traditional peasant hat, which cars passed under heading
toward Clark's main gate.

Steel had made contact with Devincia through Vida. She
was happy to help. Almost giddy. He had choked down the
bitter words he wanted to spit at her and fought to remain
cordial for as long as it took to get the bitch's help. Devincia
returned the call twenty minutes later. He was curt, nowhere
near as friendly as she had been. Steel, mindful of bugged
phones, spoke around the subject of a potential Japanese

treasure site but offered up a tantalizing enough sales pitch that Devincia agreed to drive to Angeles and meet.

A pair of headlights lit up Steel's truck. He sat up tall in the seat and watched a jeepney cruise by. False alarm. It was empty except for the driver. Compared to his Datsuns, the over-sized crew cab of the Ford F-350 seemed cavernous. The reinforced suspension system, heavy shocks, and comfortable seating made driving the beast on the Perimeter Road a wet dream. Steel reached down, flipped open the hidden compartment between the seats, and checked his two Colt .45 pistols and spare clips. The compartment was one of many he'd had Junior install.

Steel leaned out the driver's side window and peered into the sky. He could see a smattering of stars and a big half-moon. The dashboard lights glowed, casting the only interior illumination. The F-350 idled at a low rumble, and the parking lights were on. Devincia had told him to wait like this. Steel checked the clock on the dash. He hoped the colonel would be on time.

Dealing again with Devincia made Steel's gut churn. Besides taking his girlfriend, the colonel had nearly killed Steel over treasure once before, and now here he was, trying to make Devincia a treasure hunting partner again. On the general's advice, and after those couple of beatings by thugs, Steel had quit drinking. So why couldn't he quit treasure hunting? Was Joseph's life worth this? What would it take? No doubt, Joseph's murder had shaken Steel. But before he could give it up, he had to get rid of the bitterness, spit it out like a bad bite of mango. Bitterness at Devincia for his double-crossing and at the corrupt Phil army for screwing them both. Bitterness at the Singlaub men who tailed him into the jungle. Bitterness at the women who turned up for him more often than gold, fool's gold. Bitterness at Magos and his band who would kill an innocent boy and beat an old lady at just the hint of treasure. They all lusted for Yamashita's fortune, would stop at nothing to get it. They all used him. They used his weakness for gold. Goddamn them. Steel banged on the steering wheel. He needed to outsmart them all. Hone his skills. Use his resources wisely. Be always one step ahead. Then he could quit. Tonight was a test.

A white Honda sedan cruised close to his position and caught his attention. It stopped one hundred feet in front of him and flicked its headlights twice. Steel did the same. He switched off the radio and the truck engine. Only his parking lights remained on. His eyes flicked nervously from the sedan to the terrain around him. Shadowy moonlight highlighted colorless grey bushes, tall grasses, and a ditch that could provide cover for an ambush. A man exited the car. He moved with confidence, scanning the environment. He approached like a man who had hunted, or had been hunted by other men. Steel saw no weapon, but his hands were situated at belt level, ready to draw. The man moved on the driver's side of the truck and peered in. He opened the door, and Steel slid out. He recognized the stocky sergeant from their previous encounter. The sergeant pushed his hands roughly up and down Steel's body, checking for weapons, then grabbed his arm and guided him towards the car.

The sergeant shoved Steel to the passenger side and opened the door. Steel had to bite his lip to keep from laughing out loud. The sergeant surely thought he had the upper hand, but he had no idea what waited behind the sedan's tinted windows. The sergeant's poker face slacked in surprise. Sitting next to Devincia in the back seat was Tony, a .22 Smith and Wesson revolver shoved in Devincia's ribs.

Tony produced a tight smile and a single nod then thrust the barrel of the pistol deeper, eliciting a wince from the colonel. Steel watched the sergeant's head swivel forward toward the front seat, as if to appeal to the driver for help, but the driver sat rigid. His hands gripped the steering wheel, his eyes held wide and front, and Pongpet's knife blade rested on his neck.

The sergeant reversed out the vehicle and reached into his shirt for the black 9 mm Beretta tucked into his belt. Before he could remove it, Jo Jo whacked the sergeant's arm with a three-foot-long rattan arnis stick, and he dropped the pistol.

Steel picked up the Beretta, examined it, then whomped the man on the side of the head. He doubled over and crumpled to the ground.

"That's for the black eyes you gave me," Steel hissed.

He nodded at Jo Jo, who stood with the arnis stick in one hand and an M16 slung on his shoulder, Pitpit and Ganchee at his side. Jo Jo kicked the downed man in the gut.

"That's for hitting my kuya and making him ugly," Jo Jo said.

Steel opened the door to the back seat and pointed the Berretta at Devincia. "Thanks, Tony," Steel said. "The colonel and I need a moment alone to chat."

Tony smiled and slipped out of the car. Steel asked Pongpet to leave too then slid in the back and turned to Devincia. "Sir, would you excuse your driver?" Devincia nodded.

"So, Colonel, thanks for coming." Steel lowered the pistol.

"You are always full of surprises." Devincia said.

"Consider this a training exercise for my men. Besides, I felt I owed you and your boys an ass-kicking."

"Oh, don't worry. I still suffer with the tooth you loosened when you punched me in the face last time we had the pleasure of meeting." Devincia touched the outside of his jaw. "It's very sensitive to hot and cold, a constant reminder of you."

"I'm glad. Well, enough of this charming chitchat. I invited you here to discuss business. I might need your help with another treasure venture."

"You found another site."

"Possibly." Steel stared at Devincia before he spoke again. "But I want to ensure I'm not thwarted again by thugs."

"Marcos's men?"

"You, or any Marcos cronies."

"Marcos is problematic. I'm sure his men are watching you," Devincia said.

"Isn't everyone?"

"Not me. I'm busy with other matters. What assistance can I provide?" said Devincia.

"If I manage to find gold again, I'll need someone watching my back. Can you have your people keep an eye on Marcos's henchmen—specifically Colonel Panglio? And if I get into trouble, I might need a fast rescue."

Devincia sighed.

Steel continued. "We can work out an arrangement. You know, make sure everyone gets a cut, me and the Filipino people. But this time, I want to set the terms."

Devincia shifted in his seat. "I'd like to think I could be of some help. But with the upcoming elections, I'm likely to be booked up."

"I was afraid of that. But just keep me in mind if you hear anything. I'm not going to move until after the election in any case. So maybe, Colonel, you'll be free to help after all."

"Maybe. But, God willing, I will be engaged in things that are more noble by that time."

Steel nodded. "Always good to see you, Colonel. Do you have a number where I can reach you? I'd prefer not going through Ms. Abucayan."

Devincia moved his hand to his pocket, and Steel raised the Berretta.

Devincia removed a wallet. He pulled out a business card and scrawled a phone number on the back. "This person knows how to get hold of me 24 /7." He handed Steel the card and held out his hand.

They locked eyes and shook. Steel leaned in, hung onto Devincia's hand tightly, and whispered. "Remember Tony's face Colonel. If you fuck with me again you'll awake in the middle of the night and see it and feel his blade slitting your throat." He released Devincia's hand and sung out. "Good luck, Colonel. I'll keep in touch. I really hope Cory wins. God help the country if she doesn't." Steel opened the door of the car and got out. He nodded and grinned at the sergeant, who glared at him. He, Jo Jo, and the Negritos headed back to the truck.

32

Angeles
Friday, 17 January 1986

S TEEL WALKED INTO THE LOBBY of the Jet Hotel and tucked his blue Air Force flight cap, same in shape and size as a McDonald's counter worker's hat, into his belt. He was carrying a brown shopping bag. Inside was a new Panasonic clock radio. A school of giant black, orange, and speckled fish swam among fluorescent painted rocks and fake corals in the spotlessly clean aquarium in the hotel foyer. He nodded to the woman at the front desk, and she gave a friendly wave. He'd regularly patronized the restaurant here since his arrival at Clark. Steel checked his watch. It was noon, and he was on time for his lunch with Philippine Army Captain Lenard "Boy" Mitra. Boy, an intelligence officer, routinely passed on updates on the NPA and military personnel gossip. Boy had called last night and said he had some important information that impacted Steel directly, but that they had to meet in person.

Steel strode into the dining room, anxious energy coursing through his system. He couldn't remember Boy ever insisting on a face-to-face before. The restaurant was empty except for an American dependent wife and two squirming kids. The place was decorated in heavy Spanish-style furniture. The tables were covered with cheap red plastic cloths. Reflecting the heritage of the hotel's owners, Chinese paintings of boats, landscapes, and dancing women hung on the walls. Tucked in the far corner, Steel saw Boy, dressed in olive-green army fatigues, sitting at his own table and engrossed in a newspaper.

"Captain Mitra, looking sharp."

Boy stood and extended a hand.

"Captain William Steel. Good to see you, my friend."

Steel shook Boy's hand then leaned in and gave him a hug.

"About time they promoted you," Steel said tapping the black captain's bars on the collar of the green fatigues.

A slow smile spread across Boy's face.

"I do approve of the mustache," said Steel.

Boy touched his lip. "Thanks. It took me two months to grow it. My people just aren't hairy like yours."

"Damn. On the way here, I was trying to remember the last time we met up," Steel said.

"I think it was over a year ago, when I was at headquarters in Manila. Now I'm back at headquarters again."

Steel nodded and scrutinized Boy. He had spent the last nine months assigned to a unit up north in Abra province fighting bloody engagements against the NPA. Steel noted how the field deployment had changed him. Pounds of baby fat had fallen away, and his uniform was snug against a lean muscular frame. But his face was haggard. Counterinsurgency would do that. They sat in silence while Boy folded up his paper.

"So you said you had something for me?"

"You hungry?" Boy asked.

"Yeah. Had a hankering for the fried chicken and rice they serve here."

"Good. Let's eat first, then we can talk," Boy said.

"Okay," Steel said trying to act nonchalant.

Boy raised his hand and beckoned the waitress over, and

they ordered. "I was sorry to hear about the attack on Rosa. She could cook a wonderful pork adobo. She's doing better I hope?" Boy said.

"Yeah. Doing much better. Thanks."

"They killed your yard boy too?"

Steel nodded.

"Such senseless murder. I made some calls to my PC counterpart. The Angeles City boys know HQ is watching them on this one."

"Thanks."

"No problem my friend. At this point it seems like robbery was the motive—but with you, who knows diba, right?"

"I appreciate you keeping tabs on me," Steel said.

"You've helped me out many times my friend," Boy nodded.

Their food arrived and they ate and chatted about politics and world events until Boy checked his watch. "I'm afraid I must cut our visit short. My car and driver are waiting outside. I'll stop in Baguio for the night then head farther north in the morning."

"You're always welcome to bunk at my place. You know I got plenty of room."

"You're are too kind, but I must get going. I have some special orders to deliver." Boy reached down then placed a leather satchel on the table top. "I didn't want to spoil our reunion by giving you this earlier. But I think you should see it. I warn you, it is not going to make you happy." He removed a manila folder from the satchel and slid a folder across the table.

Before Steel could grab it, Boy jabbed it with an index finger. "You are like an American soap opera. You have layers of people following your activities. Marcos people and—"

"Fucking Marcos goons." He thought of Rogelio and Edgar. "Panglio again?"

Boy sneered. "Of course, that rat is always lurking about. His boys are tracking you. But you already know this."

"I haven't seen them." Steel's eyes darted around the room.

"You never said why Panglio is obsessed with you, and I have never asked," Boy said.

"Better you not know."

Boy gave one nod. "There are also two factions of Americans very interested in you. The Singlaub group for one and—"

"Two American factions? There are others?"

"Singlaub is the least of your problems." He leaned in and whispered, "There are much bigger fish."

"Bigger?"

"Your CIA is the biggest."

Steel made a stop motion with his hand. "No worries. They called me in a couple of months ago to read me the riot act, but we worked it out."

"Riot act?"

"They called me to let me know they were displeased with my, er . . . activities."

"Apparently they are keeping a very pretty set of eyes on you." Boy tapped the file folder.

"Pretty eyes?" Steel pictured Tetchi.

"You owe me big time for this." Boy lifted his finger.

Steel exhaled loudly and flipped open the file. What Philippine intelligence lacked in high-tech equipment they made it up in spades with shear manpower. They ran huge networks of inexpensive informants. He shuffled through several black and white photos then slammed the file with a fist making salt and pepper shakers dance a jig on the table.

"I take it you know this woman." Boy raised an eyebrow.

"Yeah."

My sources tell me she's CIA, a case officer newly arrived in country.

Steel couldn't take his eyes off the grainy photo of Anne hurrying through the front gate of the U.S. Embassy.

Boy stood. "Sorry to eat and leave you stewing." He motioned for the waitress to bring the check.

Steel shut the file. That bitch. That lying bitch.

"Thanks. Always good to see you. It's been way too long." He spit out the words through clenched teeth.

"Yes, way too long, and again sorry for your loss and now this." Boy waved a hand at the folder.

When the waitress approached, Steel grabbed the bill from her. "Let me get it."

Boy shrugged. "I'll call if I hear anything more."

"Oh, I almost forgot. This is for you." Steel passed the gift bag to Boy. "Congrats for your promotion."

Boy looked pleased.

Steel dropped some pesos on the table, snatched up the folder, and followed Boy out the restaurant.

Steel decided not to go back to the office. He needed to work out. Needed to soak in hot water. Needed to break something. He opened his gates and pulled in under the carport. Inside, he found Jo Jo sitting on the rough woven mat carpet in the living room. Random piles of camping, treasure hunting, and killing equipment surrounded him.

He stood, holding a disassembled flashlight. "Did you get my message? I left one with Curtis. Jesus called. He said there's activity at the bandit house. He thinks some of the bastards have returned."

"No. I came straight here after lunch."

"I thought I'd organize our equipment. So what's the plan?" Jo Jo said reassembling the flashlight.

"We'll hit the place tonight," Steel said. He was in a killing mood.

Jo Jo nodded.

"Did you call Tony?"

"Yes. He said he would be ready. I said you'd call and confirm."

Steel nodded, walked over to the phone, and dialed. He was glad for the distraction. Fucking bitch.

He hoped Tony would pick up. Steel had only recently given a phone to Tony, and the Negrito was not entirely used to it yet. It rang three times before a voice came on.

"Tony is speaking on the phone."

"Just say hello when you pick up the phone," Steel said.

"Just say hello," Tony said.

Steel took a deep breath. "You heard the bandits are back in town?"

"Jo Jo called me on this telephone and said it is so."

"I'll come over later this afternoon, and we'll make plans. You put on your black uniforms and sharpen your knives."

"When it is darkness, we will go and kill them," Tony said, his voice an octave lower.

"How many Negritos can you round up?"

"I think maybe four or five. Most have gone home to the mountains."

"Good enough."

Steel walked back into the living room and found Jo Jo poking a cleaning rod into the barrel of a .45 pistol.

"What did Tony say?"

"He's going to get the boys ready. It was a good idea, getting him the phone."

"He's almost figured out how to use it. He's great on answering. But I think his wife still dials for him."

"Whatever it takes. Hear from anyone else?"

Jo Jo clanked the .45 down on the glass top of the

coffee table. "The White Witch called. She's coming over this afternoon."

"Anne?"

"She said she was coming to see you today."

"Fuck." He checked his watch. "Probably too late to try and stop her."

"I figured you'd want to invite her along."

"You figured wrong." Steel picked up the pistol, released the ammo clip, and slammed it back in, unsure of how he'd handle this latest betrayal.

It was 3 p.m. by the time they had prepared their gear and hashed over a plan of attack on the house. Revenge burned in Steel and crowded out any thoughts he had of letting the PC deal with the bandits. He heard the front gate open and Anne's voice call out. His hands balled into fists.

"Damn, we almost avoided her completely," Jo Jo said.

Anne came in the front door without knocking, a canvas overnight bag hanging on her shoulder, and walked grinning to Steel. She put a hand out towards him, and he shrank back. Fucking bitch.

"Why the pistols and black pajamas?" she asked.

She leaned in closer, fingered the butt of the .45 in his shoulder holster, and tried to kiss him.

Bitch was one hell of an actress—he'd give her that. He turned his face, pushed her off and headed towards the front door. "Wait here. I'll be back later this evening."

She frowned. "What do you mean?"

"Just that. Hang here until I back. I'm sure you can handle that."

"Why are you being so weird?"

"You shouldn't have come without checking with me first."

"I didn't think it was a problem. It's not like I haven't been staying here."

"My mistake," Steel said.

"Seriously. What the hell's up? Why all of the sudden the attitude? And what's with Ninja outfits and guns?"

"Have some business to take care of. Like I said, just wait here. I'll be back. Jo Jo, let's go get Tony and the boys."

Steel shoved out the door, and Jo Jo chased after him, balancing an armload of equipment. Steel marched over to the Ford truck, opened his new set of gates, and headed out leaving Anne staring at them. Her mouth was set in a deep frown and her face fire red, an even deeper shade than her hair.

They returned to Steel's house at a little after 10 p.m. with a truck full of armed men. Jo Jo angled the Ford in front of the gate. Steel opened the door and jumped out. As he did, he glanced at Tony, Pongpet, and Pitpit sitting in the back seat, dressed in black clothes, jabbering to each other and waving their arms like excited teenagers. Two more men were seated on benches in the covered back bed and interacted with Tony through the sliding window inside the cab.

"Wait here," Steel said.

"Why are you seeing the witch now? You seem angry with her. I don't understand." Jo Jo said aiming a thumb at the house.

"I have my reasons." He lied. He really hadn't thought it through. He was furious at her betrayal.

"Dumbass reasons," Jo Jo shook his head. Steel slammed the door shut.

"Why is Captain Steel bringing the woman with us? I think you are right, it is a bad idea." Tony said, leaning over the seat.

"He's acting strange, even for him. I'd better go after him

and make sure he doesn't do anything stupid," Jo Jo said, opening the truck door.

Pongpet stood up and hung over the seat next to Tony. "I think the tall white woman with the red hair is his good luck amulet. Dumpit said she is a witch. Maybe she has dark powers, and Steel wants to use her magic for the fight?"

"Are you crazy? She has no powers," Tony said.

"That's not what Dumpit said. He said she bewitched him." Pongpet raised his hands and waggled his fingers at Tony's face.

"I think Captain Steel wants to impress her with how good of a warrior he is." Pitpit added.

Tony scratched his head. Pitpit's explanation was as good as any.

Steel slammed open his front door and saw her sitting on the couch, watching TV. She jumped up and their eyes met. Steel's gut churned with a mishmash of anger, some festering from his past, most directly attributable to her. He lurched forward and grabbed a clump of her hair.

"Ow. Ow, let go my fucking hair," Anne shrieked. "Why are you doing this?"

"You fucking lied to me," Steel said.

"You're fucking insane." She struggled, but he didn't loosen his grip.

"You want something to report to your chain of command. Here you go. I am insane. Clearly deranged."

She closed her eyes. "Why are you doing this?"

"You're using me. And I fell for it." The betrayal hit him anew, and his rage deflated like a popped tire. He released her.

"I...I don't know what you're talking about," she said.

"I know who you work for. It all makes sense now. Wow,

what a fucking idiot I was. Meeting you in the embassy. What a dumb ass."

Her eyes were wide, and her upper lip quivered.

"You can't even be honest with me now." Steel stared into her eyes.

She stomped on Steel's foot. Her heel landed squarely on his small toe. Steel leapt in pain. She followed up with a roundhouse punch, thrown with too wide an arc to do much damage, but her fist slammed Steel in the right ear.

Jo Jo, who had been standing dumfounded in the doorway, listening, reacted forcefully and efficiently. His front kick caught her in the chest. Steel thought he heard a chuckle. Jo Jo had probably wanted to do that for a while. Anne flew backwards, landing hard on her ass. Jo Jo surged forward stepped on her stomach, his arm cocked, ready to fire a punch into her face. Steel grabbed his arm.

"Let's get out of here." Steel pulled Jo Jo off Anne.

Anne sat up clutching her chest.

"What about her?" Jo Jo said.

"She's C . . . I . . . A. Sent to spy on us. Get her out of our house," Steel said, walking away.

"The bitch." Jo Jo glared at her, then jerked her up by the arm and quick marched her out the front door.

It was a tense, quick ride to the outskirts of the bandit village. They parked the truck in a rice field a hundred yards from the shack and out of sight. Steel gathered his team and reviewed the plan. They would wait until the bandits went to sleep, then move on the house. The group loitered around the truck, quietly chatting. At 11:30 p.m., they moved out, following the PC sergeant, across the field.

As they approached, the sergeant pointed to the black silhouette of the bandit hut, which sat far removed from the other dozen or so structures that comprised the village. The hut was far enough away that there was little chance of civilian collateral damage or interference from neighbors. Several mongrel dogs began to bark. Steel pulled out a pair of high-dollar binoculars and peered into open windows. The ink-black interior was broken only by a flickering candle. Nothing moved. No confirmation that the scumbag Romeo Magos was there. Steel toyed with the idea of rolling a couple of grenades under the hut, but thought better. First, he wanted to make sure Romeo was there and that he was dead.

"Here have a look," Steel said, and passed the binoculars to Jo Jo then addressed Tony. "I don't think there's a guard outside, but I can't be sure."

Tony pointed in the direction of the hut. "Pongpet said he saw someone sitting in a chair near the front door. The man is now sleeping."

Jo Jo leaned forward eyes shielded behind the binoculars. "I see him."

"Good eyes, Pongpet," Steel whispered. "All right, let's go. Jo Jo, you wait here with the sergeant. If things go to hell, cover our retreat with the M16." Steel touched the rifle hanging from a leather strap over Jo Jo's shoulder.

"Watch your ass," Jo Jo said.

Steel nodded, jerked out his pistol, and led the five Negritos into the darkness.

Pitpit's dark, ghostly form approached the sleeping bandit slumped in the chair. Even if the man had been awake, he wouldn't have seen the Negrito. Pitpit killed him with one quick bolo slash across the throat. The man, still seated, locked his hands around his throat, trying to stem the gushing blood. In silence, he slumped forward in a final convulsion. Steel kept moving forward, followed by four black forms. They stood next to the dead bandit. Steel stared at the blood pumping from the criminal's body and thought of Joseph lying on the kitchen floor in his own pool of blood.

Steel finally pulled his eyes from the body and motioned for the Negritos to climb the ladder up into the hut. He watched Pitpit, the fifth Negrito, slowly climb the wood steps leading up to the front porch, a bolo blade extending from his hand. No point in following them inside. He could never match their stealth. Steel flipped off the safety from the pistol and gripped it tightly, like a security blanket.

Steel searched for any movement, listened for muffled screams but heard only his own labored breathing and his heart surging.

Time dragged on. Steel fought the urge to climb the steps himself. Finally a woman's shriek pierced the air, and then dimmed as if muffled by a pillow. The sounds of breaking wood and fist on flesh and bodies bouncing on the thin floor of the hut burst forth. High-pitched metallic ringing, the sounds, Steel guessed, of bolo blades swinging, sung out then silenced, deadened, he guessed, on flesh. Steel watched the hut's woven walls heave with what seemed like the movement of a dozen men and women battling. Screams of pain and terror pealed out. Then as quickly as the noise erupted, it stopped. The silence returned, punctuated by the continued barking of the dogs.

Steel pointed his pistol at the doorway and swiveled his head around. No curious neighbors appeared. Maybe they had grown accustomed to the bandits' noise. Maybe they just feared the brutes who occupied the place.

Steel let out a sigh when Pongpet appeared in the doorway. He waved, a toothy grin plastered on his face, like a child exiting a ride in an amusement park. He was followed by four other Negritos. Tony paused for a moment in the doorway. Even in the dim light Steel could see Tony's face and chest were splattered with gore. In one hand he held his bolo and in the other he dangled Magos's severed head. Tony held it up by its hair and grinned. The skin on the face hung loosely in folds, and the eyes were fixed in a blank stare; the mouth gaped open, and a red tongue poked out. Spaghetti strands of flesh and esophagus dangled from the ragged cut across the neck. But even through the gore, Steel could recognize Romeo.

They joined Steel and trotted back to where Jo Jo and Jesus were waiting. Steel pushed forward, flicked on his flashlight, and greeted Jo Jo with a thumb's up.

"Romeo was there?" Jo Jo asked, re-slinging his M16 to his shoulder.

"Yeah. He was there with others," Steel replied.

"Yes, and now he is here," Tony said, hoisting the head.

Steel shone his light on Tony and the head.

"We need to leave." Jesus said. His eyes darted toward the village. "Someone probably called the police."

"Come on, Tony, let's go." Steel aimed his light into the distance, where the vehicle was parked.

Tony shrugged and, still holding Romeo's head, walked with the others in the direction of the truck.

33

NINE A.M. STEEL, Jo Jo, and twelve Negritos were packed in the Ford F-350. They had gotten an early start and were now an hour north of Baguio City. On both sides of the road, the rough mountain ridges and deep valleys of the Cordillera Mountain Range flew by. At almost six thousand feet, the air was thin but crisp and cool. Steel shoved his head out the open window and inhaled the mountain air, a stark contrast to the steamy smog of Angeles City. He looked up and marveled at the mountains, a patchwork of scrubby forest, banana groves, and centuries' old stone-terraced rice and vegetable fields. It could be a poster on a travel agency's wall.

Eventually, they turned off the main highway and bumped along an old mining road built by the Benguet Mining Corporation in the 1930's. Steel shifted his boot. His little toe still throbbed, a reminder of Anne's betrayal a week ago. He peered into the truck's side view mirror and smiled. The new box trailer, eight-by-five feet and modified with off-road tires and heavy suspension, was holding up just fine. Jo Jo had hired Junior to make the trailer, and he had surprised Steel with it as a gift. It provided additional storage space for pry bars, picks, shovels, a spare spool of heavy wire-cable for the electric winch on the Ford's front bumper, a red 1981 Kawasaki 125 cc motorcycle, two heavy-duty wheelbarrows, and crates and boxes full of food and ten-gallon plastic jugs of water.

The side mirrors on the truck smashed against vegetation on a road barely wide enough for the ubiquitous carts drawn by water buffalo in which local farmers and illegal miners traversed the road. While Jo Jo struggled behind the wheel negotiating ruts, Steel perused the hand-drawn map Rogelio had given him, outlining the route to an abandoned mine. Steel periodically scanned the side mirror, checking to see if they might be tailed. Jo Jo had said he thought he'd seen men in vehicles surveilling their house. But Steel was calm and felt prepared for any confrontation.

In the backseat, Tony, June, Pongpet, and Pitpit also dangled out the windows, pointing, talking. Unaccustomed to the cold of the Northern provinces, each Negrito wore a navy blue wool hat and an eclectic assortment of sweaters, jackets, and wool gloves. Pongpet complained how wearing the sweater was like being eaten by an enormous python. Steel heard Pitpit say that these big mountains must have powerful gods.

Negrito heads sporadically appeared in the sliding window separating the back seat from the canvas-covered truck bed. Eight Negritos sat there on benches, wedged in among stacks of equipment in plastic tubs, cardboard boxes, a wood crate of dynamite, and a smaller box with fuses and a spool of detonation cord. Steel saw Nanpo's head pop up. He was the gang's explosive expert, but now he was serving as a waiter, passing around a paper cup filled with sliced mangoes. Steel had made several stops along the way for visits to roadside fruit stands, where he had bought the crew green coconuts, mangos, and pineapples. As much as possible, he had kept the Negritos out of sight. The posse of tiny men would have drawn too much attention. Tony passed the mango cup to Steel, who grabbed a piece and took a bite of the sweet firm fruit. Jo Jo took one too, shoved it in his mouth, and juice dripped down his chin.

"Looks like we're not far, provided Rogelio's map is accurate," said Steel.

Steel tried to match the terrain that flicked by with the landmarks and mile markers on the penciled map. He asked Jo Jo for the mileage on the speedometer every few minutes. When he replied "five miles," Steel told him to take it slow, hung his head and shoulders out the window, then called out for a stop. He glanced several times from the map to an enormous pile of round boulders next to a thick grove of bamboo.

"Damn. That's it. Turn here. The tunnel is . . ." He grabbed a compass dangling from the rearview mirror and angled it into the air. . . . "A couple of hundred feet that way." He pointed to the right.

Jo Jo jerked the vehicle sharply off the dirt path, and the powerful Ford engine rumbled and roared. The sturdy tires ground up scrubby brush and plowed through spotty patches of grill-high undergrowth. Branches and leaves littered the hood and windshield. Some flew inside the cab.

"There," Jo Jo said.

Steel could see the dark outline of a tunnel entrance behind a wall of emerald green jade vines that covered the doorway like a giant spider web. "Damn. Glad the map was accurate. We'd of never found it. Get in close, and we'll unhook the trailer. I want to back the truck right up to the entrance."

Steel exited the truck and waved Jo Jo closer to the cave. After several cuts, the truck stopped, doors opened, and Jo Jo and the Negritos spilled out. Steel walked to the entrance and estimated that, behind the thick tangle of vines, the tunnel was at least fifteen-by-fifteen feet in diameter.

"All right. Let's cut away some of this shit. A big enough

hole to back the truck in, if need be." Jo Jo and five Negritos started hacking through the green growth. Steel called over to Tony. He instructed him to take June, one other Negrito, and Norgot to a position fifty yards up the road. If unfriendly forces were sighted, Steel wanted to be able to deploy a quick roadblock. He told June to find a big tree and rig it with explosives.

Steel unloaded the weapons he had stashed in the hidden compartments in the truck. He stationed two men armed with M1's and grenades along the trail in front of the cave. The rest of the men remained with Steel and carried their own M1's, M16's, or carbines. Jo Jo sported an M16 slung his over his shoulder. Negritos and their machetes made short work of the vines. An entranceway, big enough to accommodate the truck, appeared through the hacked greenery.

Steel pulled out new metal miner's helmets with headlights for everyone who was going into the tunnel. They trooped behind Jo Jo into the shadowy opening. Fifty feet in, they lost light from the outside. The clank of metal and the thud of boots on the gravel and dirt floor echoed off the walls. The air was dank, thick with mildew and mold, and stuck in Steel's throat. It was at least ten degrees cooler than outside.

Several hundred feet into the tunnel, Steel saw decayed wooden railroad ties on the floor. Ore carts must have once run here, transporting minerals. No metal rails, probably looted and sold as scrap years ago. The floor was littered with bits of paper and plastic trash as well. Steel and his crew weren't the only ones who had visited. Looked like locals had found the place too.

"William-san, you think there are bats in here?" Jo Jo said. His flashlight beam bounced across the ceiling and walls.

"Probably."

"Fucking flying rodents." Jo Jo swatted at the air.

They walked another two hundred feet, and the passage branched to the left and right. The group halted and bunched around Steel. Their headlamps shone in a dozen directions and made him dizzy. Maybe the headlights were a bad idea. He pulled out Rogelio's map, flipped it over, and examined it. Rogelio had sketched the tunnel in detail and annotated it.

One note read: "Take the passage to the left for one hundred feet. It leads to a chamber room. The wall there seemed false. Maybe manmade."

Steel took the left tunnel and Jo Jo and the Negritos followed. He silently thanked Rogelio for saving them who knows how many hours of fruitless exploration.

As soon as they made the turn, the solid granite walls, chiseled and smooth to the touch, narrowed to less than eight feet.

Steel read aloud, his voice echoing. "The wall you are now facing looks man-made. The color is right but the texture is wrong."

Steel touched the gray wall. It was smooth, moist and cool. He agreed with Rogelio; something about it felt fake. Steel had read that World War II Japanese engineers employed ceramic and concrete experts to develop composites to fortify and camouflage their treasure crypts. The ceramic mixture made the concrete hard and resilient. Steel banged on the wall with a fist. It felt solid, but he couldn't tell how thick it was.

"Jo Jo, what do you think?"

Jo Jo pounded on the wall and shrugged his shoulders.

Tony reached out and tapped on the wall with the dull slide of his bolo, then leaned in and sniffed. "It smells like old concrete," he said.

Pongpet and Dom Dom did the same and jabbered in agreement.

"All right,"" said Steel. "Let's go get the shovels and find out."

After two hours of banging with picks, heavy pry bars, and sledgehammers, they had barely chipped a four-inch-deep, one-foot-diameter hole in the wall. Space inside the tunnel was tight, and only two people could pound at a time. Steel and Jo Jo had stripped down to their T-shirts and were soaked in sweat from their labors.

"It's not natural rock," Jo Jo said examining a piece of chipped material. He rolled it around in his hand. "It's harder even than rock."

"I think we need Norgot's explosives," Steel said. "Is he back yet?"

"Yes, Captain Steel, he is here," Tony said, leaning on a pick.

Several lights illuminated Norgot, who scrunched his face like a blind mole rat in response.

"What do you think? Can you blow a hole in the wall without bringing down the whole tunnel?"

Norgot shrugged.

"Well, digging just ain't working. Get your explosives."

It took two hours of hauling the dynamite, fuse caps, and detonating cord before they were ready to blow the wall. Jo Jo pulled the truck from the tunnel entrance. They didn't want it damaged by rock debris in the blast. Steel watched Norgot attach the detonating cord to a detonator the size of a shoe box. It looked to Steel just like the one the coyote regularly used in the *Road Runner* cartoons.

"Ready?" Norgot said, looking at Steel.

"Let 'er rip." Steel took a knee and covered his ears. Jo Jo did the same.

Norgot depressed the T-handle. Three seconds later, a

rumble deep within the mountain, then a boom. A geyser of dirt shot out of the entrance, blowing away the remnants of the jade vine hanging down across the entryway.

They waited a few minutes for the dust to settle before they trooped back in, again laden with digging bars, picks, and shovels. Some carried the tools on their backs and shoulders, other pushed them in wheelbarrows. Inside the central chamber, Jo Jo illuminated jumbled piles of rubble with the powerful beam of his hand-held flashlight. The smell of burnt sulfur hung in the air. The tunnel leading to the false wall was littered with fallen and broken stone, and they had to scramble over it to reach the six-foot hole the dynamite had blown.

"I am surprised the hole is not bigger with the amount of dynamite Norgot used. This stuff is tough," Jo Jo said and banged a chunk against the granite.

Tony slid in next to Steel, heaved his shovel into the hole, and started scooping out debris. Dust and loose rocks showered down. One large chunk banged on Steel's metal helmet. He backed up a few feet and let Tony and Jo Jo work side-by-side. With pry bars, they removed loose wall and chiseled. Behind them, Steel, Dom Dom, and Pitpit formed a line and passed out chunks of the wall to the wheelbarrows, which Norgot and Lingot pushed out. After an hour of intense work, Steel and Jo Jo slid their hands and fingers around a blocking boulder and moved it, revealing a space large enough for a body to squeeze in. Steel wedged himself into the hole and wiggled through. He bounced hard on the rock floor in a cavern on the other side. Jo Jo followed.

They stood and Jo Jo flashed his light around. The chamber looked natural. Steel's eyes followed the beam to a tall jagged ceiling. The air was chilly and smelled damp and moldy, like the old springhouse his grandfather had on his farm in Ohio. Below, a pool of water the size of a swimming pool shimmered like black ink and flowed into another space off to the left. He flashed on images of nightmarish aquatic monsters and subterranean whirlpools. Dark bodies of water did that to him.

Tony, Pitpit, and Jo Jo pushed by Steel and walked ahead on a narrow path that led past the pool. He watched their headlamp beams leave terra firma and dance on a pile of neatly stacked, oblong wood crates.

"Jesus Christ," Steel blurted. They looked like heavy-duty ammunition boxes, the type with thick rope handles on the ends. His heart pounded, and he felt lightheaded as he followed the others around the pool. Steel slid past Jo Jo, then squatted next to the boxes and frantically used his knife to pry at the lid on one. Jo Jo joined in with his own knife, and pieces of wood splintered and shot through the flashlight beams. The lid finally creaked, and the nails let loose their decades' old grip. The men used their hands to pull the top off. It banged on the rocks and all eyes focused on the contents—metallic rectangular shapes that reflected light in myriad tiny mirrors. Steel dove for a bar and hoisted it. Only about six inches long, but it must have weighed twenty pounds.

"Holy shit," he yelled, his voice echoing in the tight space.

"Jesus Marie Joseph, is that what I think it is?" Jo Jo whispered. He reached in and struggled to pick up two bars and raised them like two dumbbells in a gym.

"Oh yeah. Gold, my friend. There's a lotus flower stamped into them. The mark of imperial Japanese treasure."

Jo Jo whistled. "There are ten bars in this crate."

"Probably twenty pounds per bar, maybe a total of 300 ounces of gold." Steel used his finger to draw the sums in the air. "At $350 an ounce, that's over $100,000 per bar."

"Ayeeeee." Jo Jo grabbed Steel's arm. "We're rich."

"Hell yes. It's a fortune."

"A fucking big fortune," Jo Jo said, doing arm curls with the bars.

"We're looking at a million dollars per crate," said Steel.

They set the gold down and chiseled at another crate. The wood splintered easier this time.

"Sweet Jesus, it's the same." Jo Jo slapped his forehead.

"Two million," Steel yelled, his words bouncing through the chamber. From a squat, Steel rolled backwards, holding a bar in the air. He lay there for a minute, trying to breathe. He needed to maintain focus and keep to the plan. He'd been here before. And it was at about this point last time that the treasure had been snatched away.

"William-san, I thought this smaller crate was empty because it's so light. But look." Jo Jo said.

Steel sat up and crawled over. Tony was peering over Jo Jo's shoulder. A rainbow of colors filled the box. Uncut gems and a coiled and tangled mess of necklaces, bracelets, and religious icons studded with polished diamonds, rubies, and sapphires. The uncut stones looked like the ones he had found in the Buddha, but the crate held ten times the amount.

"Shit, this is nuts," Steel said, pulling out a twisted golden chain and dangling it in the air.

"Let's check more crates," Jo Jo said, hopping around like a small child. He pulled on the rope handle of another crate. It barely moved two inches before a loud metallic click rang out from beneath the crate and a muffled boom enveloped them. It was deep and rumbling, but lacked intensity. Steel couldn't tell where the explosion came from or what had made it. Ghosts from the past knew its origins.

June, 1943: Japanese Imperial Army Major Hiro Otsuji peered over the shoulder of a burly army engineering sergeant squatting on his haunches. The air was cool, thick, and moist and smelled of the sergeant's unwashed body and the sushi breakfast he had just consumed. Otsuji stared at the man's delicate hands and oddly thin fingers, out of place on such meaty arms. But, Otsuji thought, well-suited for the delicate wiring jobs. The sergeant picked through a web of red and black cloth-coated fusing wires and attached them one at a time to a pressure plate detonator lying in the dirt. He slid forward, his belly pressed to the cavern floor, as he carefully placed the plate under one of the wooden crates filled with gold bars. If the crate was moved, the detonator would blow a charge thirty feet away. Otsuji's eyes flicked from the detonator to the explosive hidden in the fake wall. Behind it thousands of gallons of water from the underground river had been diverted and damned up. He tried not to think about the water enveloping them should the detonator go off accidently. He always had a fear of drowning, the major reason he had chosen the army over the navy. The sergeant stood, and Otsuji scrutinized the man's face. It was streaked with orange-brown dirt, sweat, and mud. Otsuji dropped his eyes and examined his own soiled trousers and boots. He had given up trying to keep a proper military appearance in this underground hell. The sergeant saluted and reported the explosive charge was set.

Otsuji nodded, turned, and marched with a renewed vigor to the entrance of the cavern. It wouldn't be long before he could return to his job in Manila where he had served as a senior counterintelligence officer. Six months ago, he had been transferred to the tunnel to supervise the final stages of this operation. This site was one of dozens. At first, he had been flattered when he had been recruited for the top-secret mission by a Japanese Imperial Navy rear admiral who said he worked for Prince Chichibu, the younger brother of the Emperor. Otsuji wasn't shocked to hear of Chichibu's presence in the Philippines. He'd heard rumors that the imperial family was directly involved in organizing and transporting billions worth of captured treasure and had visited potential treasure sites throughout the country. But, truth be told, he hated leaving

Manila and the perks and privileges his job brought him—
first and foremost the nightlife and its plethora of beautiful
female companions.

Otsuji looked over his shoulder at the sergeant framed in
the flickering light of the kerosene lantern hanging on the
wall. He was staring at the large of pool of water, his thick
arms propped on his hips. Otsuji thought maybe he was
contemplating the long ordeal of building this hiding place.
It had taken the specialized engineering unit that the sergeant
belonged to nearly two years. The unit along with hundreds of
slave laborers had toiled here. Many had died in the tunnels.
Otsuji took one last look at the crates and wondered how long
before the emperor could retrieve his treasure. An aggressive
and large Yankee navy was making shipping by sea risky. Air
travel as well. The Americans had a string of military victories,
and their capitalist industrial war machine had overwhelmed
Japan's armed forces on many fronts. Maybe the treasure would
have to remain hidden for years. Well, most of it would stay
hidden. He chuckled aloud. He had managed to remove a leather
satchel full of uncut gems when no one was looking. He would
have loved to grab some gold bars too, but it wasn't realistic to
think he could move the heavy prize out of the country. He'd
read enough classified intelligence cables to know Japan's end
was near. He'd need money for his postwar life. He wasn't sure
if any of his family's businesses would survive the next few
months. Unlike most of his fellow officers, he had no plans to
die in battle or commit suicide. He walked out into the main
tunnel, listening to his boots squishing with mud and water.
He wondered how long the bobby trap would keep working in
this dank place.

"Sounded like a bomb," Norgot said.
"A bomb?" Jo Jo yelled.
Steel dropped to his knees and examined the crate Jo Jo

had just moved. "Jesus. I hope it wasn't booby-trapped. The explosion seemed to happen just as you moved the crate."

"I think the bomb noise came from behind that wall." Tony said shining his light next to the pool of water.

"Look. Cracks. And water. They weren't there before," Jo Jo said.

"Shit," Steel double-timed over and cupped his hands under the streams of water spurting out. "It's another false wall. If it were a charge, it looks like it didn't go off completely. That's the good news. The bad news is, there could be more."

"What now, boss-san?" Jo Jo said.

Steel grabbed the collars on Jo Jo's camouflaged jungle fatigue jacket and got up in his face. "All right brother, this is where we fucked up last time."

"Never again."

Steel stared at the wall. Water shot through a dozen fissures and streamed into the subterranean pond. His stomach clutched in fear. Fear that this was an ancient booby trap, set by Japanese soldiers long dead. Fear of being swept away in a wall of water. Fear of the evil, bloodthirsty men who right now, maybe right beyond these cave walls, would do anything for gold. Do anything for his gold.

Illuminated by early evening's fading sunlight, Steel and Jo Jo stared at a mound of six crates stacked behind the truck—probably twelve hundred pounds of gold and the crate of gems. There had been no more explosions as they wheeled, grunted and manhandled the treasure to the entrance of the cave. The work was brutal. Steel was filthy, cut, bleeding, bruised, and his back throbbed.

"I hate to send you away, but you know what's next," Steel said.

"Yeah," Jo Jo said.

"You have the number?"

Jo Jo nodded and patted his jacket pocket.

"Tell him to get his ass here quickly if he wants his share. Bring some vehicles and his men. He's supposed to be waiting for the call."

Jo Jo shook a finger at the crates. "Seems a shame to have to share it."

"I made a promise. The Filipino people need their part. And, for better or worse, Devincia is the best representative they've got right now. Besides, we gotta stick to the plan. We might need him."

"Provided he doesn't double-cross us," Jo Jo said.

Steel followed Jo Jo outside and handed Steel his M16, simultaneously tapping the .45 pistol in his shoulder holster under his jacket as if reassuring himself he still had some protection. He slid his arms into a military rucksack, slung it on his back, and jumped on the Kawasaki. The engine shuddered, then kicked on with a high-pitched whine. The noise startled the Negritos, who gathered around the bike. Jo Jo flipped on his goggles gave a thumbs up, and disappeared into the brush. Steel had considered leaving Devincia out of it, just packing up the truck and abandoning the rest of the gold for the next lucky sucker to show up. But his mantra was "stick to the plan." Yep, the plan. Steel turned and headed back to the truck to get some water and some food.

34

S TEEL SWATTED AT A FLY buzzing at his face. The sun had just begun to rise. He was slumped against a tall coconut tree, his wide straw hat pulled over his eyes and an M16 slung across his lap. He hadn't slept much. His mind was reeling. He was sitting on millions worth of treasure.

Jo Jo had been gone nine hours. Not that that surprised Steel. Devincia had a long trip from Manila, not to mention all the political shit he was likely involved with. Jo Jo had to wait for and escort the rescue team back to the tunnel. That was the plan anyway.

An explosion in the distance rocked the jungle. Steel jumped up. His straw hat flew into the air and his hands gripped the M16. Muscles spasmed up his spine, doubling him over. His first thought was another charge in the tunnel had gone off.

"Shit," he yelled. June must have detonated the tree. He better not have blown it on Jo Jo. More likely the Marcos's goons or Singlaub's boys were on their way. Sporadic rifle shots erupted, far enough off that they sounded like kids firecrackers. Or June's M1 carbine.

"Goddamn it." Steel aimed his weapon into the jungle.

What the fuck was going on? He thought he'd been careful. Maybe Jo Jo was right. They had been watching him. Fucking Anne could have ratted them out. Steel swiveled to stare at three Negritos sitting on the edge of the brush, jabbering, their weapons trained on the jungle.

June and Dumpit raced into camp, yelling over each other. They said that two big Philippine army trucks and a jeep approached their position, and they had blown the acacia tree and blocked the road. June said he fired a couple of warning shots when the soldiers exited the vehicles. Steel asked if Jo Jo was there. June said no, just the trucks, and many soldiers with many weapons.

Several loud booms erupted in the distance. Steel assumed the soldiers had used their own explosives to get rid of the obstruction. He ordered June to take four Negritos and their weapons and packs and move into the jungle to observe. They weren't to fire or make contact unless they heard from Steel. June nodded and disappeared, leaving Steel and eight Negritos. He moved everyone back into the cave.

It wasn't long before Steel heard the roar of heavy truck engines. He peeked out the entrance and saw an army deuce-and-a-half stopped twenty yards in front of the tunnel. Philippine Army troops, loaded down with weaponry, including several M60 machine guns, swarmed. They took positions behind trees and rocks and aimed their rifles at Steel's camp. Steel and Tony watched from inside the tunnel, the entrance shielded by their own truck. Steel kept calm. He didn't want any shooting. That wasn't part of the plan.

Finally, the Philippine army broke the silence. "This is Captain Fernandez. Captain Steel, we know you are here. We don't want any bloodshed. Just come out, and we can talk."

Steel waited. Tony pulled at Steel's sleeve. "I can't believe this has happened again. We have no luck."

"We have luck. Bad luck, when we find treasure. But don't worry, the plan will work. Jo Jo will be here soon. You'll have enough money to take care of your family for life. Build a new house. We'll be okay." He smiled at Tony. "You remember what you're supposed to do? Norgot ready?"

Tony nodded.

"Good. I'm going to go and talk with these guys. If it goes badly, hide in the tunnels then head to the forest and link up with June. Wait for Jo Jo. He'll come back for you."

Tony grabbed Steel's wrist. "This amulet you wear. You remember when I gave it to you?"

Steel fingered the woven bracelet.

"It will protect you. You won't die today. The spirits say you will have long life."

"Good to know." Steel handed his M16 and .45 to Tony and headed out of the tunnel. Before he rounded the truck, he shouted, "I'm coming out. Don't shoot. You hear me?"

"Yes, we hear you. We won't shoot," Fernandez said.

Steel held his arms up and walked towards the soldiers, bracing for gunfire. Three approached him cautiously, scanning the terrain as they moved. One reached inside Steel's jacket and patted him down for weapons. Once finished, he prodded Steel with tip of his rifle. A dozen other heavily armed men glared as Steel was marched to where the army truck and jeeps were parked.

Two men stood next to the lead jeep. Steel's blood pressure rocketed. He recognized the army officer behind gold-rimmed Ray-Ban aviator sunglasses.

"Fucking Panglio," Steel muttered.

And the bastard had been promoted to general. Steel glowered at the black star embroidered on the chunky man's cap. Panglio's fatigues were starched and pressed and looked like they had never seen a day in combat. His fat stomach rolled over the green web belt that held his holstered 9 mm pistol. The soldier standing next to Panglio was young, tall, and lean, with a hard and cruel face and an Uzi slung over his shoulder. The nametag on the captain's olive-green jacket read: Fernandez.

Panglio waddled forward. "Captain Steel, I see you have been up to your old tricks again. I'm surprised that your chain of command has kept you at Clark after your last incident. I have heard General Smith is transferring back to the US. You'll undoubtedly miss him. It is good to have friends in high places, diba?"

Steel stared unblinking at the general. He would know, the fuckhead. Marcos must have rewarded Panglio with the star on his cap for swiping Steel's treasure last time around.

Panglio pushed in close to Steel and scowled up at his face. "So Captain Steel, what are you up to today at this old mine? You know you're trespassing on private property."

Steel stared at his reflection in the green lenses of the Ray-Bans. "Spelunking," he said.

"Spelunking? What is this term?" Panglio asked.

Steel sighed and shook his head. "Idiot," he muttered. He didn't see Fernandez's fist in time to duck. It caught Steel on his right ear. He staggered backwards.

"You will show respect to the general and address with him as 'sir,'" Fernandez said.

Steel rubbed his head. "Of course," he said. "As you know, sir, I love caves."

"Captain Steel, let's not banter. You are looking for more treasure. You have a knack for finding it. And I have a knack for taking it from you," Panglio said.

"You mean stealing don't—"This time Steel was ready. He blocked Fernandez's fist and punched him in the chest, knocking the man over. Two soldiers rushed to Panglio's side, rifle butts raised. Panglio held up a hand and they froze in mid-strike. Fernandez jumped to his feet and hoisted his Uzi.

"Captain Steel, this is not necessary. Let us proceed to the tunnel. You have your Negritos drop their weapons, and no one gets hurt." Panglio pointed to the cave.

"Sure...sir," Steel said with clenched teeth. "Let's take a look at the tunnel. But my boys will keep their weapons."

"Where are they?" Fernandez demanded.

"Around."

Fernandez eyes darted to the jungle. "Men fan out. Find the Negritos."

"Oh, I wouldn't do that," Steel said.

Panglio grabbed Fernandez's arm. "Leave them. We have the captain here. They won't cause problems. Right?"

Steel nodded.

"Show us the cave, Captain," Panglio said.

Fernandez prodded the short barrel of the Uzi into Steel's chest. Steel thought the man had dead eyes. He wouldn't hesitate to pull the trigger.

Steel stopped in mid-stride and turned to face Panglio. "So Col—I mean General, how'd you find me?"

"Your new friend Rogelio isn't as careful as he thinks. One of my sources followed him here to the tunnel then back to you, and, of course, you are always of interest to us." A smug smile bisected his fat face. "But my men found nothing at this mine. My guess is your trip is for nothing."

Motherfuck, Steel thought.

He turned and strode towards the tunnel. As he passed the back end of the green army truck, he glanced in, and then stopped dead and stared. The two Singlaub men, the Americans they had captured and released on the hike to the Japanese straggler's cave. They sat on benches with their hands tied behind their backs. A fresh-faced Phil soldier, barely out of his teens, sat nervous guard over the giants. Steel glared at the black guy. The veins and muscles in his neck bulged, and his bulky forearms strained against the rope. He stiffened, nodded, smiled weakly, and rolled his eyes.

"What's up here?" Steel said.

"These men were following you. We found them sitting in their vehicle up the road. I believe they are American operatives," Panglio said.

"You know who these men are?" Fernandez said.

Steel stared at the white guy, a massive lump of flesh with impassive eyes.

"Maybe your CIA?" Panglio said.

Steel slapped the truck's tailgate with hand and addressed the Americans. "I suggest you find a different line of work. You're just not good at this one." Steel pivoted and walked towards the tunnel.

Fernandez pointed to the truck. "We should bring these men along." His eyes darted around the jungle surrounding them. "The Americans can be our shields on the way to the cave."

Panglio thought for moment. "Bring them."

Steel led the parade. He was followed by a squad of soldiers and Panglio and Fernandez with the two Americans poked along in front of them, ready but probably not willing to take the first bullet. They stopped and Fernandez peered into the back of the trailer which sat disconnected from the truck. He sneered and called out that it was empty. Steel double-timed it to the entrance to the cave, he ducked around his truck and grabbed Jo Jo's heavy flashlight. Tony and Pitpit stood a little to the left in the shadows. Steel whispered in Aeta, "Be ready, wait for a signal." The Negritos stepped back into the darkness.

Fernandez pushed the two Americans forward, alternating poking them with a stiff arm and the tip of his Uzi. He scanned the tunnel and a grimace contorted his face. The soldiers took up positions around the truck.

Fernandez thrust aside the canvas canopy flap that hung loosely above the tailgate. Steel's gut tightened.

"Captain, what have you found?" Panglio said.

"Digging equipment, sir."

Steel saw Panglio's face deflate. "I'm disappointed, Captain Steel. I thought maybe you had better luck than my men."

Steel shrugged. "Can't win 'em all. So I guess you'll be heading back to Manila now."

Panglio grabbed Steel's arm. "Nonetheless, I'd like to proceed into the cave and see what else there is."

"Suit yourself." Steel flicked on the flashlight and trotted down the main passage.

Fernandez barked out a command, and two soldiers sat the Americans next to the truck and thrust weapons in their faces. Panglio and the rest of his men fell in behind Steel.

In the ghostly blackness, Steel saw Tony, or at least his shadow. Steel whispered in Aeta that the Negritos should take up positions in the cave with the remaining gold boxes and wait. The shadow vanished.

Steel paused in front of the fake wall they had blasted and tunneled through. He was making the plan up as he went. He needed to stall to give Jo Jo time to arrive with the cavalry.

Well, General, this is where it gets tight. You might have to get your uniform dirty," Steel said.

Panglio leaned over, peered into the passage, and frowned.

"General, maybe I should take Steel inside first and check it out. I don't remember this part of the tunnel." Fernandez said. Steel caught the apprehension on Fernandez's face. The man knew he would be vulnerable crawling into the tight space.

"No, Captain, I'm not above this." Panglio waved his hand. Steel smiled. Greed had stiffened the sleazebag's spine.

Steel dropped to his hands and knees and crawled into the tight passageway into the room with the remaining crates. Fernandez followed closely and then the soldiers. Panglio brought up the rear. Steel had no idea what to do next. He hadn't counted on having to entertain guests before Jo Jo showed up.

Fernandez pushed in on Steel's heels, struggling to get his Uzi into position. Steel stood and he spotted Norgot's shadowy form standing three feet from Fernandez. Apparently the Negritos had their own plan. The dull side of Norgot's bolo slashed out from the darkness and cracked bone in Fernandez's hand. The Uzi clattered to the ground. Pitpit materialized behind Norgot and pressed the blade of a knife against the captain's neck. As the soldiers popped one by one out of the passage, the same scenario played out, with other Negritos lining up patiently to claim their hostages. Steel watched the hole, waiting for Panglio. He was afraid the general had heard the commotion and backed out. But eventually Panglio burst through the narrow entrance and plopped to the rock floor, followed closely by Tony, poking at the quaking general with the tip of an M16. Fernandez croaked something at Panglio then leapt at Steel. The butt of PitPit's Garand met Fernandez's jaw with a dull thud. Fernandez hit the rock floor hard.

Flashlight beams lit Panglio where he lay in the dirt, as if he were a summer stock Hamlet overplaying his death scene. The general's cap was cocked to the side, and dirt streaked his uniform. His face dripped with sweat. Steel jerked Panglio up and removed the pistol from his holster. He clutched it tight enough to cut off circulation in his fingers and thought about how easy it would be to squeeze the trigger. He jammed the barrel to Panglio's forehead; metal cracked on skull. Panglio's eyes crossed at the barrel, and Steel imagined the general's brains blowing out the back of his head, He lowered the weapon. Panglio slumped forward, and Steel let him hit the ground again.

It didn't take long to get Panglio and the soldiers organized into a forced labor gang and transferring the wood crates from the cavern into the main tunnel. Maybe he wouldn't need Devincia's help after all, Steel thought. He hovered next to the subterranean pond and observed, pleased he wasn't having to do the dirty work anymore. Panglio and his men had moved about a third of the haul through the narrow chiseled hole when a low rumbling boom thundered out and a wave of sound and wind engulfed Steel, knocking him to the ground. Soldiers and Negritos disappeared under a wall of water. Steel grabbed his flashlight and struggled to his feet, thankful for the outcropping of rock that had shielded him. Water blasted from the far side of the room in a deafening gush. They must have tripped another booby-trap.

Tony emerged from the passage back to the main tunnel. His eyes were as big as half dollars. He grabbed Steel, shook him, and said, "What happened?"

"The wall blew. How many Negritos are outside with you?" Steel said. He fought the urge to run away.

Tony thought for a second. "I think everyone but Pitpit and Dumpit."

"Yeah, I remember now. They were over there." Steel pointed the light to where the water flooded out the wall. He scanned the area where the remaining stacked crates had been. He was gut punched with the thought that they might be lost forever to the rising flood.

"Over there. Pitpit. He's hanging onto rocks." Tony's flashlight illuminated Pitpit struggling against a heavy current.

"Dumpit's with him," Steel yelled. "Shit, the water's rising fast."

An injured soldier crawled through water, already inches deep, to Steel's boots, and he grabbed the whimpering man.

"Let's get out of here. I need to get some rope to rescue them," Steel shouted to Tony.

They exited into the main tunnel and dumped the wounded man next to where Panglio, Fernandez, and the rest of the troops huddled under the guard of Norgot and four Negritos.

"Norgot, if any of the fuckers move, kill em." Steel pulled Panglio to his feet and, with Tony and Pongpet, headed out of the cave. As soon as Steel spotted the truck, he pushed Panglio in front and shoved a pistol into the back of his head.

"Tell your men to put down their weapons," Steel growled. Panglio yelled out an order, and the three soldiers dropped their guns.

As Steel brushed past them, the two Americans struggled to their feet, their hands still tied behind their backs. Steel retrieved a coil of climbing rope and pack full of batteries from the back of the truck.

The black guy leaned in close to Steel. "Hey, man, what's going on?"

Steel ignored him, focusing on his equipment.

"We heard some screaming. What happened?" The guy wouldn't shut up.

"A tunnel wall collapsed. The cave is flooding. I have men trapped," Steel said.

"Untie us. We can help." This time it was the white guy.

The black guy continued. "I'm Captain Hobbs and this Petty Officer 2nd Class White. We're former SOF guys. We quit Singlaub. We're on our own now. We want to work with you."

Steel fixed intently on Hobbs.

"I'm strong as hell. Whale—I mean White here—he's a Navy SEAL and can swim like a dolphin."

Steel glared at White. Swim like a dolphin would be good. Steel couldn't swim a stroke. He'd never learned. The Negritos couldn't swim either.

Steel whipped out the K-bar knife from his boot sheath and poked the tip of the blade against Hobbs's dirty green T-shirt. He held it there for a second, locking eyes with the sweating giant, then twisted Hobbs around and sliced through the rope binding his arms. Steel released White in the same way.

"All right. You work for me now. But if you fuck with me." He waved the K-bar. "I won't be as generous a second time."

Hobbs nodded, rubbing his wrists. "What's the plan, boss?" Hobbs said.

"Get back to the cave and rescue some friends." Steel handed the coil of rope to White and motioned at Panglio and his men.

"Pongpet, watch them," Steel said, then to Hobbs and Whale, "Let's go." Hobbs nodded and headed for the cave entrance. Whale looked at Steel, and then slammed down his boot on Panglio's foot. The general squealed, and Steel smirked. Again, not part of the plan, but maybe these guys would work out.

Steel double-timed them back into the cavern. The pool had doubled in size. In the beam from his heavy-duty flashlight, he could see Pitpit and Dumpit clinging to a rocky ledge. Pitpit was barely able to lift an arm to wave.

"We gotta get a rope to over to them," Steel yelled over the sound of rushing water.

White gave Steel a tight smile and stripped down to a pair of grimy underwear. The six-foot-three sailor was as white and round as a snowman. Hobbs uncoiled the hemp rope, tied a bowline knot, and slid the loop over White's neck and shoulder. White stared at the current for a moment, then, following Steel's spotlight, walked twenty feet upstream and waded into the water. As Hobbs fed lengths of rope, White made his way on the diagonal towards the Negritos. When the water reached his hips, he dove and swam and scissor-kicked his way the forty feet across the pool, crashing against the opposite wall. He pulled himself along it like a floundering polar bear until he reached Pitpit, grabbed him, and stuffed him under an arm like a rag doll. Hobbs tightened his grip on the rope and, hand-over-hand, dragged White and the Negrito. Steel kept the light on White, marveling at how he could fight the current with one arm. When the water was shallow enough, he stood and walked ashore carrying Pitpit like a small child. Steel waded in to meet them. The water instantly froze his legs. How the hell was White able to stand the cold? Whale was an apt nickname. The blubber was probably saving him from hypothermia.

The current ripped Steel as Whale handed him Pitpit and headed back for Dumpit. Steel rushed the half-frozen Negrito to the small sliver of dry land and wrapped him in a jacket. Steel watched Hobbs feed more rope and Whale swim then glanced again over to where the remaining crates had been stacked. Had the first booby-trap functioned properly, he'd have lost the whole lot to the raging waters. The dampness had likely fouled the explosives. Steel thought as hugged Pitpit in the jacket and watched Whale grab Dumpit and swim back. A lucky break indeed. About time.

35

Angeles / Manila
Saturday, 25 January 1986

ANNE WAS DRESSED ALL IN black—knit hat, tennis shoes, tight pants, and long-sleeve T-shirt. Beads of sweat covered her face. She held the small flashlight in her hand and headed to Steel's bedroom. She knew the way. She had no fear of being discovered. The surveillance team had lost track of Steel. He appeared to have been headed to the mountains in his specialized truck. Diamond was pissed and had ordered a new a new surveillance team transferred in to deal with the rogue American captain.

She slipped into Steel's bedroom. It was dark and filled with shadowy silhouettes of furniture. She glanced at the clock radio, its dim green numerals showing 2:12 a.m. She fixated momentarily on the bed and tried to blanket over any thoughts of their shared nights. She was a mix of emotions. Pleased to be leading the mission but sad that she had let herself get pulled into an affair with Steel, a source. She'd fallen in bed with him way too quickly. She felt like such an idiot, but the hurt and hatred in his eyes had cut her deep, too. Yep, she'd fucked him over for sure. Now here she was skulking around his house with three CIA contractor thugs. It was what she wanted, what she dreamed of. Yet she felt dirty. She moved to a bedside table, slid open a drawer, and directed the light beam in. She slowly shook her head. A black 9 mm pistol and a box of condoms. She poked at several opened and empty condom packets. The fucker hadn't wasted time moving on. She slammed the drawer shut and moved around the room, rooting in his dresser and digging in his closet. Nothing but clothes. Nothing at all to give any insights into his personality or background. No doubt an indication he was a psychotic loner. Not like her own bedroom back in Virginia filled with college sports equipment, work mementos, and family photos. She kicked closed a dresser drawer. There certainly were no bags of jewels or bars of gold. What was Diamond expecting to find? She snorted. Steel was no dumb ass.

Anne took one last look at the dark bed and headed back to the living room. The contractors were working other rooms. Diamond had told her to find anything tying Steel to the rebels trying to overthrow the Philippine government and, he had offhandedly added, any information on Steel's treasure-hunting activities. She felt Diamond was less interested in Philippine politics than he was in the loot. The contractors had brought along some new experimental listening devises and remote video cameras. Diamond was sparing no expenses. She glanced over at Steel's study and saw a light bouncing around the room. She headed over to join the search there.

Anne hopped into the elevator of her pal Greg's apartment building in Makati, Manila. She was exhausted. It had been a brutal twelve hours since the break-in at Steel's. Greg had insisted she come over. He said he'd heard some crazy shit she'd want to know about. His tone convinced her to get over to his apartment building rather than crawling home to her own bed. She watched the panel in the elevator as lighted numbers flipped on and off. Greg lived on the 8th floor. He had insisted that she come there if she wanted to talk—not the office.

She rang the buzzer on apartment 801, and Greg opened the door quickly. He was dressed in blue jeans and a faded and worn, Simple Minds T-shirt, appropriate wear for a weekend. He stuck his head out and scanned the hall. "You weren't tailed, right?"

She nodded.

He pulled her inside and shut the door. Anne looked around the living room. From the bland furnishing, she assumed he had rented the place furnished with everything except the wall of blinking electronic stereo components and speakers. The Dead Kennedys played in the background. The apartment was tidier than she expected. Greg ushered her over to a rattan sofa with fat tropical-patterned cushions. "You want a beer, coke or something?" he asked.

"No, I'm good thanks."

He slammed himself into a papasan chair opposite her, and the rattan legs squeaked across the wood parquet floor. "Look, sorry to drag you here, but my place is clean. I sweep for bugs weekly and not the creepy crawly kind. Diamond has had some new listening devices installed in the office."

She nodded, laid her head back against the cushions, and closed her eyes.

He lowered his head, peeked over the top of his glasses, and stared at her, his eyes blinking spastically. "Jesus, you all right? This the quietest I've ever seen you."

"Been a bitch of a couple of weeks."

"Yeah. You can say that. What the fuck have you gotten yourself into?" He leaned forward and spoke in a whisper as if he were afraid his sweeps had missed an electronic bug. "These Special Activities Division personnel Diamond has brought in through back channels are bad news. These dudes are hardcore. The Division has been used to round up Libyan terrorists . . . hijacker suspects. They are doing renditions of suspected terrorists. They are discussing renditioning your boy Steel."

Benton sat up quickly. "Rendition? What the fuck is that."

"Well, strictly legalistically speaking, it's transferring a person from one legal jurisdiction to another . . . but the kicker here is that our government has recently started up a dangerous game they're calling extraordinary renditions. Means moving captured terrorists or hijackers to cooperative allied nations where, let's just say, Miranda rights aren't provided.

"You mean torture?"

"Yep. Interrogation and torture for intelligence." Greg mimicked his hands tied in front of him.

"But Steel's an American citizen. Christ, he's a US military officer."

"Was. Apparently, they know he's put his papers in. You'd noted it one of your reports."

Anne lowered her eyes and stared at the floor, trying to remember what else she'd reported.

"Which ally of ours would condone this?" she said.

"Thailand apparently is an option. They're setting up a series of black interrogation sites as we speak."

"This isn't right. You can't hold American citizens without due process. Hell, I'm not sure I'm for secret interrogation centers for anyone, but especially an American."

"Yeah. Tell me about it. What's to stop them from slamming our asses in one if they suspect us of crossing them?"

"Fuck. That's why they wanted dirt on Steel about supporting the anti-Marcos crowd. They want to label him a terrorist."

"Christ . . . that would provide them cover. They could slap a terrorist cap on your boy. Brilliant." Greg nodded, satisfied with his analysis.

She flopped back again the couch. "This isn't right. I didn't sign up for Diamond's CIA. It's not what we stand for as Americans . . . just . . . not . . . right." She closed her eyes. The soft couch pillows were sucking her in. The enormity of the fight and her exhaustion had taken its toll.

36

Benguet Province North of Baguio City
Saturday, 26 January 1986

STEEL LOUNGED IN THE SHADE of a banana tree outside the old mine—the late afternoon sun was fading behind the mountains in the background. Next to him, Hobbs, Whale, and Steel's warriors littered the ground in various states of rest. Dumpit and Pitpit were wrapped in a colorful assortment of warm clothes, their hair still damp. It hadn't been long since Whale had fished the Negritos out of the water. Panglio, Fernandez, and their two dozen men, all hogtied, sat guarded by June, wearing Panglio's Ray-Bans.

Hobbs slid his boot over and tapped Steel on the leg. "So what's the plan now? We gonna move those crates outta here? They're full of gold, right? They're heavy as shit. Damn near busted a nut dragging those boxes."

Steel didn't answer, stared into space.

Whale rolled over. "What we waiting for? Let's load up that truck of yours and beat feet out of here." Whale aimed a thick thumb at the road.

A rifle shot rang out in the distance. Hobbs and White jumped to their feet like the military men they were. Steel glanced at the soldiers, who stirred nervously. June leveled his carbine at them.

Steel motioned in the direction of the rifle shot with an arm. "That was a warning shot from our scout. Let's hope it's Jo Jo and not more of Panglio's boys. Tony, move yourself and three men in that direction. Be ready if there's trouble. Hobbs, you and Whale hang with me."

"You want me to take one of the 60s." Hobbs pointed to a pile of captured weapons.

"Nah. The Negritos have our backs." Steel grabbed the web strap of his M16, slung it over his shoulder, and ushered his fellow Americans into the brush just out of sight.

In a few minutes, the rumble of vehicles filled the air. Steel thought they sounded like jeeps, not big trucks. Jo Jo and Ganchee, followed by two men in AFP uniforms, entered the clearing. Steel took a deep breath and released the M16's plastic handgrip, allowing the weapon to dangle from the shoulder strap.

"Jo Jo, over here," Steel called out.

Jo Jo and several uniformed Phil army soldiers moved toward Steel. They paused when they reached Panglio and the rest of the detained herd. Steel stepped out of the brush and stopped short. He had not seen Devincia in uniform before. He cut a swaggering figure in the green fatigues and Uzi. He stretched out a hand and strode toward Steel.

"Colonel. Good to see you," Steel said and grasped Devincia's hand.

Devincia nodded, but his eyes were on the group of captured soldiers. "Panglio?" he whispered.

"Yeah," Steel said.

"Jesus." Devincia shook his head.

Steel leaned forward and hugged Jo Jo. "Good to see you."

"What the hell happened?"

"Long story," Steel said. He motioned to Hobbs and

Whale, still standing half in the jungle. "Some Americano friends of ours."

"Those bastards." Jo Jo pointed a finger.

"They're our bastards now," Steel said. "Colonel, let's adjourn to the tunnel and figure this out. I have something else to show you."

When they got into the tunnel, four armed Negritos were waiting. Devincia and his sergeant skirted delicately around them and followed Steel to one of the stacks of gold crates. Steel pulled out his knife and pried open the lid of the top one. Devincia whistled loudly. He struggled to remove one of the bars. "It's heavy," he grunted.

"About twenty pounds each," Steel said.

"God, how much is each one worth?" Devincia stared at the bar.

"A lot of pesos," Jo Jo said.

"Maybe one hundred thousand dollars each," Steel said.

"They all full?" Devincia pointed to the other crates.

Steel nodded. "See the lotus engraving on the bar. Jap loot for sure."

Devincia smiled. "I'll be damned. I thought for sure this was a wasted trip." Devincia's eyes migrated toward the entrance to the cave. "How'd Panglio know about this?"

"Another long story," Steel said. "More importantly, what the hell are we going to do with him and his men? They aren't too happy and will be less so when we leave with the gold."

"So Panglio stopped you from taking all of it?" Devincia shot him a sideways glance.

"I'm keeping to my side of the bargain. I want half."

"Not half." Devincia shook his head. "Is there more inside?" he gestured with his chin.

"Might be problematic to find more," Steel said.

Devincia nodded.

Steel's eyes narrowed. "I want half."

"No," Devincia said.

Jo Jo pushed forward, his hand reaching under his jacket. Pongpet swung his weapon toward Devincia and his sergeant.

"Looks like we're at a standoff then," Steel said.

Devincia dropped the gold bar into the crate. The metallic clank echoed through the chamber. "My men have the cave surrounded. I'll be reasonable. You can have one crate. That will make you rich. I want the other crates for the Filipino people."

Steel kicked the crate with the tip of his boot knocking the lid completely off. "Seems we're in no position to bargain."

Jo Jo turned to Steel. "No, we need our half."

"I know, brother. But we have little choice," Steel said.

Devincia sighed and his face softened. He extended a hand. Steel let it hang before he shook it.

"How are you going to handle Panglio?" Steel said.

"I have a secret weapon waiting for him." Devincia didn't elaborate. He turned and exited the tunnel followed by his sergeant.

"I can't believe we're getting screwed again. Let's shoot it out," Jo Jo yelled.

"What secret weapon?" Steel mumbled. Then he spoke rapidly in Aeta and men followed him out of the tunnel.

Devincia paused briefly behind the trailer. He smiled and his trademark moustache rolled skyward. "May I look in your vehicles? Not that I distrust you. But you know."

Steel's eyes shot to the dirt. He spoke to his men in Aeta, then addressed Devincia. "Be my guest." Devincia opened the back of the trailer, and the sergeant climbed inside and dug around for a few second. "Nothing but equipment, sir," the sergeant said.

They walked to the back of the truck. The canvas back was rolled down. The Negritos crowded in close behind Devincia, who tightened the grip on his Uzi and flipped up the short barrel. The sergeant pushed aside the canvas, uncovered the nose of an M1 in Dumpit's hands, and reared back. Steel lowered the truck's tailgate and jumped up on it. He finished pulling off the canvas flap and, with a theatrical flourish, revealed Ganchee aiming the Garand at Devincia's head. Devincia without as much as a flicker of concern, pushed the gun away and looked into the truck bed. "What's in the crates and boxes? Sergeant, open them." The sergeant leapt up onto the tailgate and brushed by Ganchee. The sergeant opened the big wood and cardboard boxes and shook his head. "Nothing."

Devincia lowered the Uzi. "No problem, William. You understand."

Steel gritted his teeth and exhaled silently through his nostrils, suppressing his relief. Junior had charged him a fortune for the secret floor compartments in the bed of Ford, but they were literally worth more than their weight in gold. Steel chuckled to himself. He walked around the cab and called out to Hobbs. He had the burly Americans push the wheelbarrow with their gold crate from the tunnel, and Steel and Jo Jo helped them pack it in the back. Steel called out in Aeta, and June left his guard post in front of Panglio. More Negritos emerged from the jungle and joined their compatriots in the vehicle. Steel counted twelve to make sure everyone was accounted for. Jo Jo jumped into the driver's seat and cranked the engine, and Hobbs and Whale loaded themselves into the back seat. Steel walked over to Devincia.

"Colonel. I need a man to ride with us, an officer preferably. I don't want any problems with PC checkpoints on the way back to Angeles."

Devincia shrugged and called out a name. A young man with captain's bars on his lapel stepped forward and followed Steel back into the truck.

As the Ford exited the camp, Devincia shot a quick salute. Steel reciprocated. He watched Devincia walk over to Panglio. That was going to be an interesting conversation. He almost wished he could stay and listen. They drove through the brush and a dozen heavily-armed soldiers waved him by. Beyond them was a white Toyota sedan and leaning on it were a gray-haired man with a camera around his neck and a cool Filipina goddess in Ray-Bans and a beige safari pantsuit. Steel's gut tightened and the damaged muscle in his back seized. Vida. So *Malaya*'s star reporter showed up, with a photographer. Damn, Devincia may be an asshole, but he was a smart asshole. The press was Devincia's secret weapon. If there were an article in tomorrow morning's paper reporting that Japanese treasure was discovered in the mountains, neither Panglio nor Marcos would be able to deny the find. Makes it a lot harder for Marcos and Panglio to spend it all on caviar and fine champagne if the people know about the gold. Vida gave Steel a tight smile as they drove by but no wave. The cameraman pointed the camera at the truck, and his flash fired three times. Steel barked at Jo Jo, who slammed on the brakes and jumped out. He snatched the camera from the old man's hands, flipped it open, and ripped out the film. Jo Jo got back in and accelerated away.

Four hours later, they reached the outskirts of Angeles and pulled into a deserted dirt parking lot in front of a construction supply store. Steel reached to the back seat and handed Devincia's captain a wad of pesos.

"This is your stop. Take the bus back to Manila. Thanks for the help."

The captain started to protest, but Hobbs placed a massive black paw on the young man's shoulder, reached over, opened the door, and pushed him from the back seat.

They drove close to Clark's main gate, and Jo Jo pulled the truck into an empty lot. The sun had set, and the evening sky glowed red-orange. Music from the nightclubs floated over from Perimeter Road. Steel exited and called out to Hobbs and Whale to do the same.

At the back of the truck, Steel pulled down the tailgate and jumped up on it. He lifted the canvas and went inside. Twelve sets of eyes followed to him as he gently moved Tony and Pongpet and lifted up a bench lid. Steel reached inside and grunted as he pulled out a gold bar, then three more. He thrust them inside a military backpack, along with a 9 mm pistol. He drug the pack and it scrapped over the plywood floor back outside where the Americans waited.

"Well, gentlemen, this is where we part company. I owe you for saving my friends. Consider this compensation from the company." He jumped down and pointed to the backpack sitting on the tailgate.

Hobb's grabbed a strap and started to lift it until his arm muscles strained at the weight. He stopped and peered inside then waved Whale over.

"Thanks, man," Hobbs said as he pulled out the pistol and shoved into his waistband. "You take care. Let us know when you're ready to find some more gold." A big smile bisected his face and he extended a hand.

Steel grabbed the hand. "Definitely," Steel nodded, thinking that these two could come in handy when he headed over to Southeast Asia to find his father. "How can I reach you guys in Bangkok? I see a mutually beneficial future for us."

Whale stared at Steel a moment then blurted, "The White Whale. Look me up there. Gonna be my place. You drink for free."

"A lady pal of mine named Boonsri. She works in the reference section of National Library of Thailand in Bangkok. She'll always know where to find me."

Steel nodded. "Boonsri ref section of National Library . . .

got it." He headed back to the cab. Before Steel jumped in Hobbs called out.

"Steel. When we were hogtied in the jungle your Negrito had those spiders fucking with us. Were they really poisonous?"

"Deadly." Steel smiled.

"I knew it." Whale nodded.

Steel waved and jumped in the truck. Tony, June, Pongpet, and Pitpit had claimed the backseat. Steel returned to the front. Jo Jo started the truck, and the Ford jetted forward. They drove in silence for a few minutes until Jo Jo squealed. "You bastard! Where'd you hide the rest of the gold?"

Steel slumped back and closed his eyes. He was exhausted.

"What makes you think we have more than the one crate," he said without lifting his head.

Jo Jo slammed a hand on Steel's leg, and he shot up.

"You my friend are not angry enough to have given away a fortune. Besides, even with all its heavy shocks and big engine, this beast is straining, and not just on the hills."

Steel burst out laughing and whispered. "Very perceptive my old friend . . . six crates worth of gold and gems are stacked under the floorboards in the secret compartment of the truck.

Jo Jo laughed and the guys in the backseat joined in, though Steel was fairly sure they had no idea what they were laughing at. Good to be celebrating for once, Steel thought, and rolled down the window, humming a tuneless victory march to the humid night air.

It was after midnight when Jo Jo pulled in to Barangay Sampung Bato to drop off all the Negritos except for Tony and the three others who were staying with Steel to help him protect the gold. They still had to get the treasure to Manila and on board Cham's ship. It was docking in a week. Steel hoped they were still laughing then.

37

Angeles
Friday, 31 January 1986

STEEL SAT AT HIS DESK in his home study surrounded by cardboard boxes and packing material. He picked up a white ceramic mug with a 13th Air Force Intelligence Division logo, his name and rank emblazon on the side, examined it for a moment, then wrapped it in brown paper and put it a box. Storing the mementos from his four-year tour at Clark had somewhat dampened his otherwise euphoric mood. It had been a nerve-wracking five days sitting on a thousand pounds of treasure. It was safely hidden in a camouflaged concrete vault in his backyard. One of Joseph's projects he had completed before he . . . Steel choked down a sob.

They had five days until they were due to deliver it to Cham on his chartered freighter docked at the Port of Manila's North Harbor. Steel still couldn't absorb just how fucking rich he was, potentially anyway. With that much money at stake, any whiff of it, the vultures, scumbags, and parasites would be prowling about. As a precaution, he had had Jo Jo laying low. He was vulnerable. Steel, as an officer in the US military, had the protection of the government, at least for a few weeks more, then he would officially be Mr. Steel.

So much could go wrong. They had to get the treasure to

Manila. Cham had to sail it on to Thailand then transfer it to his thug network of black marketers. Panglio would be snaking around Manila, angry as a skewered bull and gunning for Steel. If they got by him, Cham would have to negotiate pirates and customs officials. Steel wasn't sure which was worse.

He wasn't envious of Cham's job. It was just as dangerous as finding the treasure. Steel was torn about whether or not to send the entire load of gold bars and gems, risking it all. He had a few more days to decide. He snatched up the copy of the *Manila Bulletin* sitting on the desk. Featured on the front page was a black-and-white photo of Devincia and Panglio, smiling, squatting next to a stack of open crates. Another photo showed in close-up the neatly stacked gold bars. The headline read: "Gold Looted by World War II Japanese and Worth Millions Found North of Baguio City." Steel scanned the lead paragraph and slammed the paper down. He knew he should be glad his name wasn't mentioned. But those two smiling goons! It was his find. They didn't do anything but try to take it from him, unsuccessfully. At least Vida, the bitch, knew the truth. Or most of it.

Steel stared at a cardboard box of pens and scraps of paper. Some notes for a briefing on Thai air force deployments to Clark that he never got to give. A menu from a restaurant at the Orchid Farm where he had taken Vida one weekend about a million years ago. A shopping list for a long-abandoned garden project he and Joseph were going to work on when the weather cooled down. Goddamn it. He tossed the whole box into a trash bag. Once they got the treasure safely to sea he could concentrate on the move. He had bought a half-finished, cinderblock farmhouse sitting on five hundred acres of mixed agricultural land backing up to the Zambales Mountains on the outskirts of Angeles. The place was in Jo Jo's name. Steel intended to build an enormous home with a wing for Jo Jo, a spacious room for Rosa, and a room for Renaldo and Bong Bong, the orphan boys he'd parked at Father Rudy's orphanage. He was going to adopt them outright—no more weekend Uncle Great White Hope. Becoming a father was his next step in growing up. He wanted to build houses on the property for Tony and the rest of the Negritos who had helped him too. Safety in numbers, he hoped. And he would have his own opulent master bedroom suite with a single bed. No room for Tetchi …Actually, no need to rule out the occasional visit from Tetchi or some other friendly bar girl once in a while, when he needed a break in being a dad or the king of the Negritos. Anything was possible if Cham could sell the treasure.

In fact, Tetchi was Steel's date to an art show in Manila next week. Romy, Cham's partner, was putting it on, a project a long time in the making and, coincidentally and fortunately, wonderful cover for Cham's presence in town. Steel had asked Tetchi out without paying a bar fine. She'd said yes. Maybe a king bed would be the prudent investment.

Steel picked up a framed photograph of him and the general taken months ago in Hawaii at an awards ceremony. The general had presented Steel the Air Force Cross for bravery, second only to the Medal of Honor. Smith was leaving next week, headed to DC. Steel would miss him. He put the frame in a cardboard box marked "KEEP."

Jo Jo entered the room, padding on bare feet and fiddling with the .45 strapped to his shoulder and outside his T-shirt.

"Boss—you won't believe who's at the gate."

Steel threw out the first name that came to mind. "Devincia."

Jo Jo sneered. "The white woman—the CIA spy. Shall I ask her to leave?" He pulled the gun out and waved bye-bye with it.

"Is she alone?"

Jo Jo nodded.

"I'll go see her."

Steel walked out of the study and through the living room. The coffee table was littered with half-eaten plates of food, empty soda bottles, and an assortment of weapons. The air reeked of body odor, unwashed Negrito to be exact. Tony, Pongpet, Dumpit, and Ganchee lounged on chairs and the floor watching a Filipino soap opera. He had hired them for security, but also, except for the smell, he didn't mind the company.

Anne bit her lower lip and stood staring at her sandals thinking about the dirty look that fuckhead Jo Jo had given her when he opened the gate. She wanted to turn tail and run. But no. She needed some closure. She tugged at her bra and white linen blouse and felt beads of sweat trickle down her back. She felt stupid for fussing over what clothes to wear. She pulled up her loose-fitting pants. They didn't fit as snugly as they had done two weeks ago. She had lost weight over-exercising, not eating. Her huge oval sunglasses hid dark rings under her eyes; she couldn't remember when she last slept through the night. She had rehearsed what she was going to say him numerous times, unhappy with each iteration. She was ashamed and angry for letting Diamond use her. She felt as cheap as her wide-brimmed straw hat.

Steel opened the gate, just enough to see her. He stared at her for a second, his eyes removed the layers of baggy clothing she wore and flashed back to their steamy nights together in his small tent. But anger trumped lust, and he looked past her to the street beyond. An unfamiliar Toyota idled there, a shadow hunched at the wheel.

"Well, if it ain't Anne the spook."

"Can I come in?"

"No."

"I just wanted—"

Steel cut her off, "No need to explain. I know what you are."

She stared at her sandals.

"Well, nothing to say," he said.

"If you'd just shut the fuck up for a minute, I came here to tell you I'm sorry. I'm not happy with the way things turned out. I'm not going to go into everything, but just to let you know I'm leaving the P.I. I regret it all. I'm going back to headquarters. I've contacted the I.G. I'm exposing all the Station shit going on here. I'll find another way up the ladder."

"Yeah. Shoving people to their deaths as you climb."

"Fuck you. I'd of been goo in the treads of your Ford truck if I'd stood in the way of your goddamn gold. Don't lecture me."

Steel glared at her.

"Like your yard boy and Rosa. Your beloved family. They paid a pretty high price for your treasure," she said, her eyes meeting his.

Steel's chest deflated and his shoulders dropped. He closed his eyes. Joseph would be alive if it weren't—

"I'm sorry I said that," Ann said and took a step toward Steel. "I know you care about them, cared. Look I didn't come here to fight with you. Just watch yourself. The man who assigned me to your case is a fucking backstabbing, sniveling bastard."

He opened his eyes. "Diamond?"

She nodded.

Steel's tone softened, "Yeah, life can take twists and turns. What the fuck does Diamond want with me?"

"He wants what you want."

"Happiness?" Steel said.

"Treasure. He has friend's scary-high up in the government. They'd kill—have killed—for the gold. I want no part of it."

"I'm still trying to figure out if it's worth it. Sure as hell wasn't worth Joseph's life. But there's nothing I can do about that now. I'm going to take care of the living." He gazed beyond her ridiculous hat to the Toyota across the street. "Now if you'll excuse me, I have some packing to do."

"You're leaving?" she asked.

"I've found a new place to live. This house has too many bad memories."

"You're leaving the Philippines?" she asked.

"Nah, this country's my home. You take care of yourself. I hope you find what you're looking for." Steel nodded and turned back to the house.

"You too, William," Anne whispered to the closed gate, resting her head a moment on the warm metal. She gave her forehead one light bang, winced a moment at the pain of it all, then pivoted and headed back to her waiting car. Time to go home.

38

Manila
Makati Business District
Saturday, 1 February 1986

JO JO PULLED UP IN front of the five-star Peninsula Hotel in Makati's business district in his new black Mitsubishi Montero, a luxury four-door, four-by-four with dark windows and 2.5-liter turbo diesel engine. Steel exited first. He winced, the pain attributable to one of the myriad of injuries he'd sustained over the last several months. The night air was thick with carbon monoxide and heavy with humidity. He ran a hand through his hair, smoothing back imaginary waves. He had had it buzzed to a brush crew-cut. He was wearing a black Nehru style jacket, black pants, and a white silk shirt. The clothes had arrived in the mail from Bangkok. Cham had an eye for fashion. Steel opened the back door, offered a hand, and Tetchi stepped out, fully inhabiting a short black halter dress, her full breasts untethered and swinging freely. A heavy silver necklace, a gift from Steel, bounced off her chest. She completed the punk rocker ensemble with ankle-high boots and a haircut almost as short as Steel's. Their arrival drew stares from the dozens of people gathered under the hotel's marquee. He watched several photographers' fire off quick shots. Tetchi definitely looked hot enough to be someone famous—or be with someone famous. The art show was a major social event, and Manila's elite were in full attendance. The event's patroness, Imelda Marcos, was sure to make a grand entrance soon. Steel remained at the car door and offered his hand again. Rosa took it and stepped out, less dramatic, but infinitely classier in her knee-length black dress. She glanced nervously at the throng of people staring and gripped Steel's hand tightly.

"I'll find a place to park and join you," Jo Jo called out and roared off.

"We'll wait for you inside." Steel said as he escorted the ladies toward the foyer.

Steel waved at Jo Jo as he navigated the cavernous lobby's Italian marble flooring, swerving around enormous potted palm trees and groups chattering in clumps of couches and chairs. The place was swarming with foreign hotel guests and people headed to the gala. Jo Jo drew a few admiring looks as he darted through the crowd in his jet blue barong Tagalog shirt and black pants, hair and beard neatly trimmed. Steel reached inside his jacket and felt for the envelope with the invitations. He ushered his group down a side hall into a huge ballroom. Steel approached the gala's reception desk with Tetchi on one arm and Rosa on the other. He passed the invitations to a woman seated at a desk.

"My mother, brother, and girlfriend," Steel said, sneaking a look at Tetchi to see if she flinched. She did not. They were given name tags, and two security men patted Steel and Jo Jo down and examined Rosa's large purse. They skipped over Tetchi's tiny clutch purse. Whether that was because it was too small to hold a weapon of any significance or because they couldn't take their eyes off her breasts, Steel wasn't sure.

Cascading chandeliers with sparkling crystals of light hung from the ceiling. Jo Jo, his eyes glued to the crystals, banged into Steel, who had paused to look around for Cham and Romy. Dozens of artists milled around their works set up throughout the room. Steel glanced at Rosa. A tight smile dissected her face, and she swung her head from this grouping of paintings to that collection of sculptures. Tetchi ooh-ed and ah-ed loudly backed by a six-piece orchestra playing classical music in the center of the room. Steel wandered to a table covered in white linen with multiple layers of silver plates and platters of tiny triangle-shaped sandwiches, imported cheeses, fruits, and vegetable assortments arranged around an ice sculpture of President Marcos's head. Across the street from the hotel, they had seen masses of people sleeping on cardboard and picking through the trash for scraps of food. What would they make of this, and of their president, melting away at its center?

"Zeus na lang," Rosa gasped between clenched teeth, when she saw the table.

"So much food," Tetchi said.

"I hope we can eat. I'm starving," Jo Jo said.

"Why don't you take Rosa with you and get a plate," Steel said, and watched Jo Jo escort Rosa.

"Rosa is lovely. Is she always this quiet?" Tetchi said.

"Nope, her jaw is still sore, I think."

A waiter dressed in a neat black-and-white suit approached them with a tray of glasses. "Champagne, sir?"

Steel looked over at Tetchi. She shook her head no. He held up a hand and thanked the man. As he did, he spotted Cham and Romy across the room. Steel could see Romy's work, mostly done on large canvases, some hanging on the wall, others propped up on easels. His paintings were distinctive because of their bold use of orange, abstract Bangkok street scenes alive with people, markets, and vehicles.

"William." Cham rushed forward and hugged Steel. Cham wore a miniature version of Steel's outfit. "So good to see you.

The clothes look marvelous on you, and your hair, I love it." He nodded and smiled at Tetchi. "This is Tetchi, right?" He tucked a fist under his chin, cocked his head back, and gave her the once over. "My, my, you are fabulous looking. The boots and dress are incredible." He extended a hand. "So nice to meet you."

"Will has told me so much about you."

"All lies. Come, let's go over and say hi to Romy. He's so nervous and excited. He's already sold two paintings."

Romy glanced toward them. He was trying to extract himself from the bear hug of a heavyset woman who was clearly enamored with one of his paintings, and perhaps with Romy, whose exotic movie-star looks drew many women admirers to his exhibits. He shook her manicured paw off him, as if it were a black widow spider crawling up his arm.

Steel's attention was drawn from Romy's polite tussle to a four-foot-tall oil painting hanging nearby. Romy had depicted, in uncharacteristic dark hues and realistic representations, a white man from behind. He leaned toward a looming and luminous glass window, behind which Asian women dressed in long evening gowns with shimmering jewelry perched on tall chairs. Steel smiled as he read a small white name card sitting on the edge of the easel: "The Fishbowl and the Farang." He had to have it.

Across the ballroom, Panglio checked his watch. His fat gut filled his barong Tagalog shirt. Fernandez fingered the pistol inside his loose black jacket. Panglio hated babysitting duties, but he'd been tasked directly by Armed Forces Chief General Ver to take charge of the Marcos's security detail. Panglio's eyes darted towards the elaborate banquet table, and he started to move in that direction but halted in his tracks when he spied Steel across the room. What on earth was he doing here?

Could he be a patron of the arts? His glare intensified, and he gritted his teeth. Deep in his belly, he wanted revenge for the humiliation he had suffered in front of Devincia. He'd love to have his men drag the Americano into a back alley. For now, he'd have to be satisfied that he had bested the arrogant captain again, having given his crates of gold to the government. In fact, Panglio's troops were still at the tunnel with new equipment. His men had told him they had seen more treasure in there before the flooding. The Marcos's were pleased by that news. Yes, he'd keep an eye on Steel, and good that the Americano enjoyed the finer things in life. He'd need more money to finance it. And when he went to find it in the jungle caves, Panglio would be there to steal it away. He just might get that second star. And next time, he'd make sure he ferreted away a cut for himself. Panglio tugged on Fernandez's jacket and whispered in his ear. The captain grabbed with his right hand for his .45 Colt pistol and spun towards Steel. His left arm was still in a sling. One of those little black men had shattered his wrist during their adventure at the cave.

Panglio grabbed Fernandez's good arm firmly. "Captain. This is not the time nor the place. We have more important duties."

Fernandez nodded, shoved the pistol back into its holster, and shot daggers with his eyes at Steel, who was milling about the banquet table oblivious.

Panglio's gaze zeroed in on Tetchi, who approached Steel and slid an arm through his. A slow, sleazy smile spread across Panglio's face.

Clutching small white china plates, they used toothpicks to skewer prawns, pieces of mango, cheese, pork, and tiny rice balls with fish and bamboo shoots. They chatted for another hour before Steel heard a commotion in the exhibit adjacent to

Romy's. Steel swiveled his head and saw Imelda and a posse of assistants and photographers make their entrance.

Cham whispered excitedly, "Oh, she looks marvelous, such grace and savoir fare. Oh look at that evening dress. Of course, a stylized traditional Filipina dress. Those pointed puffy shoulders, a round neckline, and long pleated skirt, probably silk and chiffon."

Steel nodded. He was trying to tamp down his disdain for the emperor's wife. But he couldn't take his eyes off her. It wasn't the clothes but her imperial arrogance. Wow, he thought, only six days until the presidential election, and she was confident enough in its outcome to leave the campaign trail to host this event.

She held court at each display of artwork and, like a queen, was surrounded by fawning courtiers. The procession stopped at Romy's exhibit. Steel moved a polite distance back away from the paintings with Cham, Jo Jo, and the ladies at his side. Cham was beaming with pride as Romy bowed his head to Imelda. She pointed and commented on each painting.

Steel glanced over at Rosa, who stood motionless, tears streaming down her cheeks, her mouth agape. Steel knew she was bowled over in the presence of the living embodiment of the perfect Filipina. Even Tetchi was caught up in the royal moment, and Steel felt her hand shaking in his. Steel stared at Imelda's cascading diamond earrings and green emerald necklace, almost out-shimmering the chandeliers, and thought of his own crate of jewels. Maybe hers were stolen war loot, too.

Imelda stopped at the painting of the fishbowl. She removed her Christian Dior eyeglasses and pushed her face closer, then took two steps backward. She screwed up her face and whispered to a young Filipina woman next to her, who put a hand to her face to suppress a giggle. Imelda nodded at Romy and walked on. Steel wished he could read lips. Cham, however, caught Imelda's slight. He tugged on Steel's jacket and whispered, "Oh, but you know, I don't like her hair. It's badly dyed to its original color and way too sculptured and hair-sprayed into that odd layered dome."

"Yeah, you gotta wonder if there are bugs nesting in it," Steel whispered.

Cham turned his head and tightened his lips to stifle a laugh.

Steel watched Imelda move on to the next display and his thoughts drifted to the next day. He planned to head back to Angeles this evening and, early tomorrow morning, grab the gold and meet Cham's docked ship. Steel fingered the woven Negrito amulet on his wrist.

"It will be fine, my friend. Everything is ready on our end. All you have to do is get yourself and your gold to the dock," said Cham.

Steel smiled at him. His confidence was infectious. "You'd better go help pack up," he said and nodded in the direction of where Romy was standing among wooden packing crates and stacked paintings.

"See you tomorrow then at 8 a.m.," said Cham, touched Steel lightly on the arm, and scooted across the room to his partner.

Steel scanned the thinning crowd in the hotel's massive lobby looking for Tetchi, who had excused herself for the comfort room. She'd been gone a while. He whispered to Jo Jo that he needed to use the head. Jo Jo said he'd join him.

As they rounded the corner to the restrooms, Steel finally spotted Tetchi. She was backed up to one of the smooth marble walls adjacent to the women's restroom, her arms folded defensively on her chest. Standing in front of her, and a head shorter, was Gen. Panglio. What was the bastard doing to her?

Steel would never forgive himself if Tetchi became another victim of his treasure hunting–and the enemies he had made along the way. He felt as if he had been sliced in the gut with a fish filet knife. He balled his hands into tight fists and jerked mechanically forward, as if on a moving walkway.

Steel paid little attention to the phalanx of four security men around the general. Steel lowered his head and barged into them like a NFL player. As Steel hit the wall of flesh, the men grabbed his head, arms, and the material of his Nehru jacket. Jo Jo, close on his heels, was absorbed by the scrum. Steel, fought, thrashed, and lashed out at Panglio. Tetchi crumbled against the wall, her hands plastered to the sides of her distraught face, the tears and black mascara streaming down her cheeks. Even a shiny .45 Colt pistol jammed against the side of his head failed to slow him. Jo Jo saw the brandished weapon and screamed out, "Everyone calm down."

But, it was too late for calm. Fernandez reared his good arm back and whipped the heavy Colt barrel against the side of Steel's head. The last thing Steel saw was Panglio's self-satisfied grin.

Steel's eyes fluttered as he struggled to regain lucidity. Flashes of light, sounds of soft voices, and outlines of faces flashed before him. Slowly, Tetchi's face appeared, and in an odd twist, Steel thought, so had Vida's. Must be a dream. He blinked his eyes and fought to sit. It was Vida. She had a hand on his shoulder and her brow and mouth furled into a frown. On the left, Jo Jo and Rosa.

Jo Jo pulled Steel to his feet and navigated him to a chair. Steel put a hand to the side of his head and felt liquid and a painful cut on his scalp. He checked his fingers and saw blood. Suddenly he remember Panglio. Steel swiveled his head around trying to find him.

Jo Jo filled Steel in. Vida's intervention, with her photographer and three of Devincia's men, had likely kept Panglio from dragging Steel out the back exit. Panglio not wanting a confrontation or any bad publicity, left quietly. Vida had been at the event to do an unflattering article on Imelda.

Steel briefly spoke with Vida, thanking her. He couldn't help being touched by her concern. She and Tetchi exchanged catty stares before Vida and her entourage departed. Jo Jo grabbed Steel by the arm, forcefully ushering him and the women, towards the lobby's front doors. They still had a long night ahead of them. Steel glanced at Tetchi. She had his ripped jacket around her shoulders. Her faced was still streaked with mascara and her puffy red eyes locked onto the shiny marble floors as she walked.

"You okay?" he asked her softly, but she didn't answer. He had more questions, like why was Panglio after her in the first place, but he would save them for the long ride home.

Twenty minutes out of Manila, Rosa slept in the front seat. Jo Jo twisted his head to the back, where Tetchi and Steel rode in stony silence, each staring out their passenger windows at the black rice fields whizzing by.

Jo Jo shot a thumb at the snoring Rosa, "Should I turn the radio down?"

"Actually," said Steel, "do you mind cranking it up a bit? Nothing wakes up Rosa when she's out like that. And Tetchi and I need to talk. In private."

Tetchi swung around and scowled at Steel. Jo Jo turned back to the road, nodded once, and rotated the volume knob to high. Foreigner sang out about ice-cold women.

"So talk," Tetchi hissed.

Her tone surprised Steel. He was feeling guilty that he had

put her in the path of Panglio. But she didn't sound scared. She sounded matter of fact.

"What did Panglio want with you? What did he say?" He put his hand on her thigh.

She paused a moment before she spoke in a flat monotone, "He's a client. Just a nice, quiet man, or so I thought, who gave me lots of cash. I found out too late who he was. He wanted me to spy on you. After the party when he had me pinned against the wall, he threatened to retaliate against my brother if I didn't cooperate." A single tear rolled down her cheek.

"Panglio was a customer? You fucked him?" He grabbed her arm.

She pulled away. "What did you expect? It's not like we are married or anything? You know what my job is."

Steel turned his head and banged it hard against the passenger window and winced. The cut he had sustained from Fernandez's pistol-whipping stung and started to bleed anew. Steel reached up and felt the big lump on the side of his head. But if he was honest with himself, he would have to admit it didn't hurt nearly as much as what Tetchi just told him. Jesus, the thought of Panglio grinding on top of her almost made Steel retch. But like Tetchi said, it was her job. Steel made himself recall the moment he had seen Panglio pin Tetchi to the hotel wall. Steel had locked eyes with him, and the smile on Panglio's slimy face said it all. Steel moaned. When would he learn?

39

Manila
Port of Manila
Sunday, February 2 1986

THE FORD 350 BOUNCED HEAVILY into a Manila pothole deep enough to swallow a bicycle. Steel's body slammed against the passenger-side door, and he woke with a start. He stretched his arms, and his hands hit the cloth ceiling. They were in Manila already. He checked his watch. Seven a.m. Apparently, they had made good time from Angeles. Sunday morning traffic was scarce.

Steel was tired, angry, and his head throbbed from his run-in with Fernandez last night and his break-up, if that's what it was, with Tetchi. Steel wallowed a few moments in his physical and emotional funk until the heavy breathing from the backseat distracted him. He cocked his head and glanced there, where Tony, Pongpet, Dom Dom, and Dumpit were jammed in a row, dressed in matching black clothes: Steel's tiny commandos. They stared intently out the windows. Steel was sure nothing could have prepared them for the sprawling urban mess of Manila—even viewed from behind the truck's tinted windows, sealed tight in an air-conditioned cab.

The streets had only partly begun to fill with churchgoers, shoppers, and workers on their day off. Jo Jo passed a red-and-white trike loaded down with four people. A triangle shaped "Cory for President" banner on the radio antenna flapped in the wind. Steel watched a shrunken old woman in a long skirt sit sidesaddle on the back of the bike, smoking a misshapen, hand-rolled, chocolate-brown cigarette. She considered the big truck with sleepy eyes.

It took only fifteen minutes from the edge of town before the Ford pulled into the Port of Manila, a sprawling, one-hundred-and-thirty-seven-hectare tangled mess of narrow muddy streets, crushed coral parking lots the size of football fields, warehouses, docks and office buildings. They passed piles of industrial equipment, stacks of metal shipping containers filled with everything from refrigerators to plastic kids' toys, and rows and rows of used cars, castoffs from Japan. Other mounds held Philippine exports: enormous mahogany logs, many taken illegally from rain forests, neat stacks of milled lumber, and twisted mounds of scrap metal. After that, row upon row of tin buildings, humming with giant electric refrigeration compressors. Steel wrinkled his nose as the pungent smell of less than fresh fish penetrated the truck's cab.

Per Cham's instructions, they headed to a section of the North Harbor. The 20,000-ton freighter *Apisara Tritan* was moored at Pier 7 and registered to a Thai company owned by a relative of Cham. Steel cracked his window and let in the humid air, redolent of rotting garbage, diesel fuel, and unwashed humanity. Jo Jo slowed the truck to a crawl. In the distance, Steel could see several ships docked. One was enormous, with stacks of metal shipping containers piled on the deck. Another, about half the size, looked most likely to be the *Apisara Tritan*.

As they moved closer to the vessels, Steel pointed to a white sign. Pier 7. They rolled to a stop, and Jo Jo kept the truck idling. Someone would make contact, Cham had said.

Steel opened the glove compartment and pulled out a pair of binoculars. Early morning sunshine illuminated a patchwork of rusted reds and oranges, like one of Romy's paintings, around the hull of the ship. A crew member, his hat over his eyes, slumped among the wood boxes and tangled cargo nets scattered over the deck.

"There she is." Steel handed the binoculars to Jo Jo.

"Jesus . . . that is one rust bucket of a ship. I hope it makes it back to Thailand." Jo Jo said.

"Yeah," Steel said and then asked Tony to pass forward two bulletproof vests. This morning's activity presented an opportunity to use them. A retired Army Special Forces friend of Steel's had purchased the vests on the black market stateside and mailed them a few weeks ago. They were battle-tested in Grenada in 1983. He hoped they weren't needed. Steel and Jo Jo squirmed around in their seats, donning the protection. Steel adjusted the straps on his. The vest was bulky and hot, but it gave him peace of mind. He slid into a light windbreaker to hide the thing, which did not do anything for his skyrocketing internal mercury. He opened the door to a hidden compartment between the seats and removed two pistols. He handed the .45 to Jo Jo, who removed the clip, checked it, and tucked the weapon between his legs. Steel took a 9mm Beretta, the one that he had confiscated from Panglio, and slid it into his waistband. He reached in deeper to the compartment for a grenade. It was smooth and cool to the touch. He slid it into his jacket pocket. He ordered Dumpit and Dom Dom to move into the back of the truck and arm up. One-by-one, they crawled through the sliding window of the rear cab and into the canvas-covered truck bed. Tony and Pongpet remained. After a couple of seconds, Dumpit passed Tony a carbine. The sounds of weapons being locked and loaded echoed through the cab.

They waited and watched for twenty long minutes. Steel prayed the big American truck wouldn't draw the attention of the dock security guards. A white Mitsubishi van with heavily tinted windows slunk into view. It rolled towards them. The driver flicked his headlights.

"Looks like show time," Steel said.

Jo Jo flicked his headlights back then glanced into the rearview mirror and slid the gearshift on the steering column into reverse. He put one foot on the brake, the other on the accelerator, equally ready to advance or retreat. Good man, thought Steel.

Steel called out in Aeta to his men. They all watched as the van pulled to a stop about fifty feet from them. Its sliding door opened. Steel's gut tightened when he saw the distinctive outline of an AK-47 rifle in the hands of one of the backseat passengers. Four men exited. They looked like Yakuza gangsters: black sunglasses, tight blue jeans, muscle T's under baggy silk short-sleeved shirts. Madam Chong's goons. The tall man of the group, with the longest stride, marched forward first. As he did, his shirt blew open, and a silver pistol tucked into his belt reflected sunlight. They split up and approached both sides of the truck. Steel pulled the 9mm out, cocked it, and tucked it under his arm.

One of the men rapped on Steel's window. His jet black hair dripped from under his red bandanna to his shoulders. He had a jagged scar running diagonally across his face. Steel rolled down the window.

He gave a quick look at Steel then grunted in broken English. "Captain Steel, you have equipment for shipment?"

"Where's Cham?" Steel said, gripping the pistol under his arm.

"You have equipment?"

Steel nodded.

"I get in with you, and you follow the van." Scarface reached for the front door and tugged at the locked handle.

"Negative," said Steel and rested his pistol on the open window. "Where's Cham?"

The thug glared at the black barrel. A tight smile dimpled his wrecked visage. "He's around the corner."

"Go back to your van. We'll follow," Steel said.

Scarface turned and called out an order in what Steel thought was Thai. The other men walked backward a few steps, then swiveled and returned to the van.

Steel muttered, "Fuck, fuck" under his breath as Jo Jo drove. The van made a right turn and stopped next to a box truck. The van door slid open again, and the men got out. One walked to the box truck and hopped up on the step next to the passenger window. In a few seconds the door opened, and Steel exhaled deeply. Cham took the man's hand and jumped out the cab. He waved at the Ford. Steel gripped the pistol handle tight. He could see a bloody bandage on Cham's head.

"Wait here. If it goes to shit, back the fuck out of here," Steel said, opened the truck door, and stepped outside. "Tony, you and Pongpet cover me." The two Negritos slid out the rear cab door. They slunk along the side of the truck out of view of the thugs. Steel tucked his left arm behind his back, the Beretta in hand; his other hand stayed inside his windbreaker, clutching the grenade.

"Be ready to fire," Steel whispered to Tony. "Don't hit Cham. He's the short one dressed in the white long-sleeve shirt." Tony repeated the instructions to Pongpet.

Steel took three steps away from the Ford. He called out, "What the fuck's up Cham?" Steel remembered their safety question. "Was the show a success?"

There was only one right answer. Steel slid the grenade,

slick with sweat, around in his hand. Cham stepped forward. Scarface had a handful of Cham's shirt.

"Was the show a success?" Steel said, forcefully enunciating each word.

A smile erupted on Cham's face. "Yes, yes, it was most successful."

Steel let out a gush of air and sagged, relaxing his death grip on the grenade and the Beretta. Cham approached, dragging Scarface with him.

"William, so glad you're safely arrived. Sorry for all the drama, but my cousin Chaow, here, insisted on it."

Steel nodded at Chaow and said to Cham, "What's up with the bandage?"

"Oh this. I fell out of the van. The step was too high. I get very clumsy when I'm excited," Cham said and touched the bandage.

"Jesus you freaked me out. What's the plan?"

"Come on show me what you have." Cham grabbed Steel's arm.

The group rounded the truck and met Tony and Pongpet, their weapons still held high. "Cham, you remember Tony."

Cham shot off some staccato Thai commands to his men, which Steel suspected were to explain who the Negritos were. "Of course, Tony, nice to see you again."

Tony nodded.

"That's Pongpet." Steel put a hand on the Negrito's shoulder. Pongpet extended his arm, and like a politician at a state fair, shook several surprised gangsters' hands. Steel ordered Tony and Pongpet to keep a watch out for anyone coming and added, "Jo Jo, stay in the cab and keep the engine running, just in case."

Steel opened the tailgate and jumped up on it. Cham whispered to his cousin, who waved some of his men to positions around Ford. Steel lifted the canvas hanging flap and offered a hand and pulled Cham up on the truck. They went inside. Chaow joined them, eyeing Dumpit and Dom Dom, standing guard with their baby AmaLites.

Steel reached down and opened a panel in the top of one of bench seats and removed a two-foot-long wooden box, set it on the bench, flipped open two small latches, and lifted the lid. The rainbow assortment of gems, some raw, some cut and polished, winked in Cham's bright eyes. He whistled long.

"Shit. They are incredible. This is so much more than the Buddha held. A fortune," he whispered.

Steel thought for moment. Should he tell him now that he'd decided to send only half the gems? Nah, later.

Cham shut, and then opened the lid, practically swooning in the glitter. "We are rich, but, hardly enough treasure that we needed a ship. I thought you said there were gold bars." His eyes darted around the truck.

Steel laughed, bent over, and fished out a small crowbar from a tool bag. He dropped to his knees, and ran his finger across the wood floor of the truck until he found a small indentation. With his index finger, he levered up the thick plywood enough to jam the crowbar in the crack.

"Chaow, would you mind backing up a few steps? And help me lift the plywood."

The two-foot-wide panel popped open.

"Oh, very tricky. Very clever." From his perch on top of the bench, Cham waved his hands over at the rows of gold bars lined up like soldiers.

Steel opened a second compartment. "There are a total of sixty-eight bars; probably, a thousand pounds or so.

"That's a ship worthy amount of treasure, to be sure." Cham jumped down from the bench, and Steel grabbed the slight man's arm to keep him from falling face first into the gold.

"This is a fortune. A king's fortune," Cham said, dancing away from Steel's grip.

"Make us stinking fucking rich," Steel said.

"Oh, this is not a problem. Our forty percent is going to make us very happy. We're going to buy ourselves a new house and . . . "

Steel held up his index finger. "Remember, we have to pay the Roxas brother's twenty percent right off the top. But the balance I want to split with you fifty, fifty. We are brothers in crime, are we not?"

"We are indeed brothers. In something" Cham said, still hopping leg to leg, like a circus clown.

"All right brothers. We'd better get outta here. This much gold sitting in this alley is making me nervous," Jo Jo said, his face framed in the sliding window from the front cab.

"Yeah, let's get this gold moved. You have crates?" Steel said.

"Yes, I've taken care of the shipping crates. I'm glad I had them made extra strong with secret compartments, which are almost as nice as your clever little hiding place," Cham said.

He bent down and struggled to pick up a bar. "This is absolutely amazing. I've never held a piece of gold so big. Chaow, have the truck back up. It will make loading easier."

Steel looked over at the sliding window. "Jo Jo, maneuver the truck so our tail gates are damn near touching." Jo Jo saluted, and his head disappeared from the window.

Steel watched Cham as he rubbed a finger on the lotus flower seal engraved on the top of the gold bar. "A lotus flower, but maybe too beautiful a symbol for all the death and destruction the Japanese subjected the world to to acquire so much gold. I feel the bar is heavy with the spirits of the dead."

Steel stared at the bar. He'd never thought of it in those terms. Only in terms of the death and destruction it had leveled on his family in Angeles. The truck rolled forward, and he reached out and steadied Cham.

Steel stared at the gold. "Be careful, Cham."

"Don't be worried, my friend. You did all the hard work getting it here. I have a well thought out plan and . . ."

Cham went on but his words faded. Steel stared at the bars lined up like golden oblong tiles. He saw reflected on their shining tops destroyed temples strewn with dead bodies. His mind flickered through scenes from old World War II newsreels he had seen in history class. The destruction the Imperial Japanese soldiers wrought as they marched through Asia. Maybe Cham was right, the gold was cursed. So much blood. So much blood.

40

The Zambales Mountains
Monday, 10 February1986

JUNGLE VEGETATION TOWERED OVER HIM, around him, like a thick privacy fence. Lt. Nada stood erect, took a deep breath, and gently patted the cloth sack dangling at his side. Kami's presence was reassuring. Insects punctuated the air with their steady calls. A bird shriek broke their monopoly, and Nada glanced quickly in its direction. He was dressed in his best army uniform. It was only the second time he had worn it in four decades. It felt stiff and smothered his body. He stared at his hand as it gripped the eel skin handle of his sword sheathed in a shiny brown leather scabbard clipped on his belt. The hand, permanently stained with decades of grime and campfire grease, shook uncontrollably. He glared at it intently and squeezed, trying to will the trembling to stop.

He had found food and a new letter written by the Filipino Jo Jo at the cave command post, and his distress over the letter's contents had manifested itself through the last days in a crescendo of nervous ticks, fitful sleep, and dark frightening dreams. Yesterday Nada had discovered there were many people camped at the cave. He had spied on them but couldn't confirm their identities, except for Jo Jo and the annoying small warriors. Now, here he was, dressed in this military costume, hiding safely out of range of the little black men's abnormal senses.

The Filipino Jo Jo had written that he was returning with Japanese officials from the embassy in Manila. The words "Japanese officials" left him horror-struck. Why were they coming? To try and talk him into surrendering? To arrest him and put him on trial for cowardice? He'd never submit to the public humiliation of a trial—this he swore to Kami. And he had been clear with the Filipino Jo Jo; Nada would only stand down at the order of his former commander.

He stroked Kami's bag and smoothing words came forth urging Nada to meet with the officials. Kami was right. Not to hear them out when they had traveled so far would be rude. Nada's nostrils twitched as a slight breeze brought faint smells of the interlopers' campfire. As his brain separated out smoke and food odors, a loud crackling Japanese voice shattered the silence. Nada ducked and covered his ears with his hands. The shrill speech on the loudspeaker was in native Japanese, not the Filipino Jo Jo's halting pidgin. Nada did not want to listen. Kami urged him, in gentle tones, "Go, my dear comrade. Let us end this." Nada gritted his teeth, balled his hands into fists, and marched blindly into a thick grove of banana plants. He slammed into a massive spider web, and it engulfed his face. He thrashed about in the sticky threads.

He stopped, winded, and tried to compose himself. He'd move close enough to the cave so he could peer at them with the telescopic sight he had removed from Kami's rifle. After twenty-five yards, he dropped to his knees. His dangling sword banged the ground, and he crawled the last thirty feet to an overlook. He rose up on his elbows and aimed the sight. He put the black crosshairs on a group of men seated around a small campfire fifty yards away. The Filipino Jo Jo, came into view, then five tiny black men, all seated on the ground eating breakfast. He flipped the lens around the campsite, and a dozen other individuals sitting near the tunnel entrance came into view. Nada's stomach seized. They were young Japanese men dressed in civilian clothes, probably in their twenties or thirties. One had the bullhorn in his lap. Several had cameras with long black lenses dangling around their necks. Two other men cradled weapons in their arms. These two were lean and muscular, and Nada thought they looked like fellow military men. He focused last on an older man with a shock of white hair. He was bent, his face wizened. Nada wondered how the old man could have made the trip. He spied a wooden litter laid out on the ground nearby. That was how. Nada peered again at the man's face. Something about him seemed familiar. And then it hit Nada, and his jaw dropped. He knew the man's face. It was if someone was playing a cruel trick, as if someone had aged Maj. Otsuji with theatrical makeup. How was it possible that he had survived the war? The scope slid from his eye, his forehead hit the dirt, and his body heaved with shuddering sobs.

Former Imperial Army Major Hiro Otsuji leaned back, closed his eyes, and rested his head on a rolled-up sleeping bag. He couldn't believe that after all these years he was back in the jungle. He had survived the war and a perilous escape from the Philippines on a merchant ship. Thanks to his Chinese language abilities, he had been able to pass himself off as a refugee from Hong Kong. He made his way to French Indochina and eventually returned home to Tokyo. Or what was left of Tokyo. His parents were dead, and the family home and businesses destroyed. Over a hundred thousand Tokyo residents had been killed and million rendered homeless by the Yankee's indiscriminate incendiary B-29 bombings. He slammed his hand on the plastic mat he sat on. They put his compatriots on trial for war crimes. Where was the justice for his elderly parents who were burned alive?

In Tokyo he reunited with a younger brother, the only other family member who had survived the war. They used the money Otsuji had made from selling the stolen gems to buy cheap land. It turned out that the brothers had a knack for real estate speculation. They amassed a large fortune.

Otsuji raised a thin, bony arm and slapped at the insects incessantly attacking his ear. The buzzing sound encapsulated all the horrors he had endured during his months of living in the jungle and supervising the tunnel construction. The death, the filth, the dysentery, the tuberculosis and the malaria had tortured his mind and body for four decades. Otsuji jerked upright then his body spasmed, wracked with a fit of coughing. One of the young Japanese men from the embassy rushed to Otsuji's side and laid a supportive hand on his back. When the hacking subsided, he offered Otsuji a metal canteen of water. He waved it off.

Over the years he had toyed with the idea of returning to the Philippines to clandestinely excavate the treasure tomb. Had it been a financial necessity, he might have pursued those thoughts, but he had enough money to live comfortably, and he had no heirs. Otsuji glanced at a six-inch centipede marching along the jungle floor on a thousand undulating legs. Recalling that species' painful bite, he slid his leg further onto his plastic ground cloth. The insect was another reminder of why he hadn't wanted to return to this hellish place.

But, three weeks ago, senior officials from the Japan Self-Defense Forces had showed up at his door. They had informed him that his former subordinate Lt. Nada had been found hiding out in the Philippine jungle. Otsuji was stunned by the news. This man had to be an imposter a scam artist. But if anyone could have survived the war, it was Nada. He had been tough and fanatical. But to have hidden in the jungle for all these years? He must have gone mad.

Otsuji knew the JASDF officials had serious concerns about involving him because of his health, but they were also worried that Nada wouldn't surrender to anyone else. The thought of returning to the Philippines as a celebrity appealed to Otsuji's vanity, though, and he convinced them he could make the trip. Besides, Otsuji had been toying with the idea that maybe he could find a way to visit the treasure tunnel. Maybe this trip to the Philippines was more than coincidental. Maybe it was his fate to unearth the treasure again.

A fracas coming from the Negritos around the campfire to his right caught his attention. They were pointing to the jungle. Otsuji's eyes zeroed in on the source of the commotion. Twenty yards away, like an apparition, stood Lt. Nada, older, dirtier, shakier, but Nada, there was no doubt. In his imperial army uniform, he looked frozen in time. How could this be? Otsuji tried to stand too quickly and collapsed onto his knees. He rose again and stared. He could see Nada's eyes darting, like a cornered animal. Otsuji had seen that look before, in shell-shocked and dying soldiers. He made eye contact and felt his heart surge and his body quake. His lip quivered uncontrollably. He thought it must be a malarial attack. A deep guttural surge of raw fear overcame him. His face contorted and he clasped the sides of his face with both hands. He struggled to breathe and his vision blurred. Was it Nada the soldier, or a ghost from the past, the kind of monsters that haunted Otsuji's night terrors? He felt a hand on his arm as one of the embassy flunkies steadied him. Cameras lens clacked, and the pool of reporters buzzed. Otsuji wanted to turn and run, but the embassy man had a firm grip. Nada, or the fiend of his nightmares—who knew which—stopped four feet in front of them. Otsuji gaped at a face that slowly morphed back into his old comrade and breathed a sigh of relief that the demon had gone.

Tears streamed down Nada's dirt-streaked face. He snapped to attention, his sword swaying on his belt, executed a perfect salute, and held it. Otsuji unfolded his crooked spine and stood at attention too. After a long pause, he returned the salute, gazing into his soldier's eyes until all went black.

41

Clark Air Base
13ᵗʰ Air Force Command Post
Wednesday, 26 February 1986

S TEEL STUMBLED INTO THE 13ᵀᴴ Air Force conference room carrying two large empty cardboard boxes and dropped them on the floor. He paused for a moment and looked around the room. He loved visiting this place. He'd given hundreds of briefings in it, many in front of Gen. Smith. The room had been built prior to World War II and furnished with heavy mahogany tables and chairs. The walls were covered with floor to ceiling burnt-wood paneling that smelled of the linseed oil that Joe, the janitor, used to keep them polished. Fading black-and-white photographs hung in groups on the walls, some of previous commanders, others of US aircraft. But even with all the familiar trappings, the room seemed empty today. The air was stale, and remnants of cigarette and cigar smoke lingered. It had been a hell of a couple of weeks. The place had been a beehive of activity. Steel had been part of it, part of the intelligence team monitoring the events surrounding the presidential elections and the "people-powered revolution," as the press had dubbed the political and military upheaval that had shaken the Philippines. Steel turned his attention to a sprawling table loaded down with piles of documents, half-filled ashtrays, and paper cups of stagnant coffee. He'd been tasked with cleaning up the mess—Major Thimbles' last jab. Steel had only a few days left on active duty before he became Mr. Steel. He still hadn't heard from the reserves about his transfer.

He picked up a stained yellow note pad, one he had used to record a timeline for the revolution. He flipped through page after page and glanced at the scribbled notes. Might make a great book someday, he thought. He was going to keep the pad, but he had to scrub it of all the classified information. He didn't want to give Thimble any reason to fuck him over one last time. He plopped down in a swivel chair, feeling like Captain Kirk on the USS Enterprise. Steel leaned back and flipped pages. When he reached the last one, a summary he had recorded late yesterday, he paused and read aloud.

"Presidential elections were held on 7 February1986, and the Commission on Elections (COMELEC) declared Marcos the winner. The National Movement for Free Elections (NAMFREL), an accredited poll watcher, declared Aquino the winner, citing widespread reports of voter fraud and violence on behalf of Marcos. In support of NAMFREL's findings, twenty-nine COMELEC workers resigned protesting Marcos's election rigging and took refuge in a Catholic church. On the 11th of February, the Catholic Bishops' Conference of the Philippines issued a statement condemning the election. On the 22nd, Cory Aquino evacuated Manila for sanctuary 350 miles away on the island of Cebu. Also on the 22nd, according to sensitive intelligence sources, Minister of Defense Enrile and Lt. Col. Devincia finalized RAM plans to attack Marcos and his cronies, who were ensconced in Malacanang palace."

Steel picked up a yellow highlighter and marked the last sentence for redaction. He continued reading. "After several arrests of senior RAM officers, large numbers of Marines loyal to the government surrounded the palace, and the RAM attack on Marcos was put on hold. Also on the 22nd, US Ambassador to the Philippines Stephen Bosworth along with US President Reagan's Special Envoy Philip Habib met with Marcos and reportedly told him that Reagan believed that Cory won the election, that Marcos is finished, and that asylum in the US is offered." Unsure of its classification, Steel put a big question mark in yellow next to the last sentence.

"On 22 Feb 1986, Enrile, Ramos, and their RAM supporters retreated to Camp Aguinaldo, where they renounced their support for the Marcos government." Steel stopped reading and smiled. He recalled that after Enrile and Ramos defected, the new 13th Air Force Commander USAF Gen. Richardson lamented how he wished he had information on what was going on there. Two hours later, an administrative sergeant called out that Gen. Ramos was on the line and wanted to speak to Capt. Steel. Steel remembered how the room silenced, and all eyes turned to him. In the cold light of Thimble's jealous glare, Steel had calmly handed the phone to Gen. Richardson and told him he should take it. Steel had called Devincia, and Devincia had made the Ramos call happen. It was nice to have a source that owes you a few million pesos worth of favors. After a twenty-minute conversation, Richardson hung up the phone and gave a thumbs up to Steel. In your face, Thimble.

Steel continued reading his notes. "At nine p.m. on the 22nd of February, Cardinal Sin, on Radio Veritas, appealed to his flock to aid the beleaguered rebels. Hundreds of thousands of Filipino civilians, including priests and nuns, marched peacefully to Camp Aquinaldo to form a human shield. On the 24th of February, Aquino returned to Manila and the Armed Forces of the Philippines continued its fracture into troops supporting the rebels and those still loyal to Marcos. Some gunfire had been exchanged but overall no huge outbursts of violence.

"Also on the 24th, Aquino and the rebels contacted the US government and requested military support to overthrow Marcos. US military aid came in the form of F-4 Phantom fighter jets from Clark overflying Manila at Mach speed and hitting afterburners at low-level, creating an ear-splitting shockwave. Though neither side knew for whom the display was intended, intelligence indicated that Marcos took note and felt it was directed at him.

"Shortly thereafter, Marcos contacted the US government and requested safe passage from Manila to his hometown in Northern Luzon. HH-3 helicopters from Clark Air Base's 31st Aerospace Rescue and Recovery Squadron removed the President, his immediate family members, and Armed Forces Chief General Ver to Clark." Steel remembered thinking when he wrote this about a story a USAF cop had told him. Apparently when Marcos's family were boarding the helicopters to the Clark, they were loaded down with suitcases and cardboard boxes. The cop said one box broke open, and US dollars and jewelry spilled out. Imelda and her aide scrambled on their hands and knees, scooping up the bills blowing all over the ground. Steel would have loved to have seen that. He jotted down the anecdote in the margin and kept reading. "The Marcos family spent the night at Clark and were moved in a C-9 Nightingale and C-141 cargo aircraft, not northward to Marcos territory in Ilocos Norte, as he wanted, but into permanent exile in Hawaii." Steel added an exclamation point to the last line and slammed the yellow notepad on the table. Shit, you just can't write fiction like this, he muttered to himself. He picked up a gooey ashtray and dumped it into a trashcan. Better get this cleanup over with.

The job should have been the responsibility of one of the

admin sergeants, but Steel took Thimble's pettiness in stride. Cham had come through on the sale of all the gold and some of the biggest gems. Steel, well Mr. Smith anyway, was a man with $4 million in a Bangkok bank account. Steel still hadn't told Cham there were more gems to sell, so even more money was due to come Steel's way. He was set for life. Well, an ordinary life. But he had plans for extraordinary. He would start making trips to Thailand and the Laotian border. With Cham's help, he'd cultivate sources inside that insular Communist country who could hunt down information on his MIA father. The gold bars he had given Hobbs and Whale had secured their local expertise and loyalty. He planned on contacting Hobbs this week. Maybe when he got done emptying fucking ashtrays.

Steel picked up several coffee cups, consolidated their congealing contents, and brushed what he thought were donut crumbs into the cup. He thought of his farm and the renovations that would have to wait a couple of months. Jo Jo was preoccupied. One of his daughter's had implied that his wife had a boyfriend, a doctor at the hospital where she worked. Jo Jo had made several more trips to the Canadian Embassy in Manila to try to secure a tourist visa to go see his kids. He'd even hired a high-powered immigration attorney. Thanks to the gold, he was a man of means. He'd sent his wife, Baby, photos of his new car and the farm.

Steel picked one of the cardboard boxes off the floor and began filling it with binders, reference books, and papers. The half-built farmhouse was becoming shipshape thanks to Rosa and her two nieces. They and the orphan boys were living there full-time. Tony, Pongpet and Dom Dom and Dumpit and Ganchee and their families camped nearby in temporary nipa huts and provided security. Steel gave Tony his old Datsun and purchased two new jeepnies for him and the rest of the families. Yesterday, after work, as Steel pulled next to his farmhouse, he saw sprawling piles of concrete block, iron reinforcing rods, neatly stacked fresh cut lumber, and two thick bundles of roofing tin. A small hand-painted wood sign in bold black block letters read: "Barangay Negrito." In larger letters: "Tony Bato, Barangay Captain." Tony had been busy.

Steel worked on box number two and his thoughts turned to Tetchi. She was out of his life. He wished her the best. He thought of Anne more than he liked. He'd gotten a postcard in the mail, a picture of the Washington monument with a a Virginia PO Box return address. It read: *Thinking of you. Hope all is well. The tae hit the fan at work. (I found a Tagalog language book in the library.) My official IG complaint touched off a firestorm. Making those tough, painful, life changes. I'll make a point of staying in touch. Please send me your new address. Keep safe. Mabuhay Grace Green. (Aka Anne).*

This Saturday, he, Jo Jo, and Tony were heading to the mountains. Tony was thrilled to be relieved for a few days from his construction burdens and the stresses of serving as Mayor of Negritoville. Steel had to admit that he, too, was looking forward to hiking and camping—no crazy treasure hunts. Just time to think and relax. And if they came on a promising cave, well, what would it hurt to take a quick look?

ABOUT THE AUTHOR

Nick Auclair has over twenty years' experience as an U.S. intelligence officer, five of those in the Philippines where he spent his free time chasing after the Tiger of Malaya's treasure. He currently lives with his wife on a small farm in Virginia and teaches counterinsurgency at the Virginia Military Institute.